THE CONTINENT
OF LIES

James Morrow

THE CONTINENT OF LIES

HOLT, RINEHART AND WINSTON / NEW YORK

Library of Congress Cataloging in Publication Data
Morrow, James.
The continent of lies.
I. Title.
PS3563.0876C6 1984   813'.54   83-18359
ISBN 0-03-062861-X

First Edition

Designer: *Kate Nichols*
Printed in the United States of America
1 3 5 7 9 10 8 6 4 2

Grateful acknowledgment is given for permission to reprint from "The
Upas Tree" by Aleksander Pushkin, translated by Babette Deutsch
in *A Treasury of Russian Verse*, copyright 1949 by Avrahm
Yarmolinsky. Reprinted by permission from Adam Yarmolinsky.

ISBN 0-03-062861-X

To my father,
William Morrow

Sleep, baby, sleep
Thy father guards the sheep;
Thy mother shakes the dreamland tree
And from it fall sweet dreams for thee,
Sleep, baby, sleep
—MOTHER GOOSE

We are not so evil as the interpretation
of our dreams would lead us to suppose.
—SIGMUND FREUD

Contents

CONTENTS

PART THREE

Acknowledgments

For editorial acuity, I would like to thank Judy Karasik and Donald Hutter. For moral support, I would like to thank Patricia Berens of the Sterling Lord Agency. For typing much of the manuscript, I would like to thank my mother. For braving the early drafts and offering advice, I would like to thank Joe Adamson, Linda Barnes, Scott Cinsavich, Denali Delmar, Daniel Dubner, Joan Dunfey, Justin Fielding, Jean Morrow, Robert Stewart, and Bonnie Sunstein.

PART ONE

1

A Dreambean Deciphered

When I was ten years old, my father called me into his private
study and said, with a solemnity not typical of him, "Son, don't
ever let anybody tell you there's no such thing as reality." He
rapped on his desk, as if to show me what he meant by reality.
"Reality is all we have, Quinjin, and believe me, it's more than
enough."

"All right," I replied.

I had no idea what he was talking about.

In time, however, I came to appreciate my father's advice.
It served me particularly well in my chosen career as a critic
of dreams.

The noostrees have been extinct for more than two decades
now, and I suspect that most of you are too young to have
eaten their fruits and experienced the programmed halluci-
nations, the preplotted mirages, stored inside. So let me now
assure you that everything you have heard about cephalic apples is true. Compared with a good cephapple dream, gourmet

food was about as satisfying as a sore throat, sex about as involving as a blink. For the dreamweavers, you see—those gifted, solitary souls who made the seeds from which the noos-trees sprouted—were not mere technicians. The dreamweavers were not mere conduits of the story line. The dreamweavers were artists. Great artists, failed artists, pure artists, corrupt artists. But artists.

Now, I won't pretend that all the cephapples I reviewed could be properly termed works of art. Most of them, in fact, could be properly termed garbage. *Other* critics got to analyze realistic psychological dreams about love, hate, marriage, divorce, friendship, parenthood, death, and angst. *I* got to review dreams in which homicidal maniacs stalked through back alleys, sucking out streetwalkers' brains with weaselpumps; in which martial-arts experts felled entire police forces with their feet; in which Antaresian plasmidleopards escaped from circuses and set about terrorizing the nearest elementary schools; in which starship captains brought law and order to hinterland planets, using nothing but their nitrogen-cooled laser rifles and chiseled chins.

I'll tell you something, though. I did not hate the lurid dreams. The best of them had an emotional reality, a core of honest sensation, that brought me nearer to aesthetic truth than did the stuff that the *literati* were always fussing over. Art, I believe, is where you find it.

The story of why and how I helped destroy the art I loved is really a kind of fairy tale, and it happens to begin with a fairy tale. The fairy tale was called *The Toad of Night*. I had this dream on the twelfth of Inanna, Anno Galactica 791. That atypical day began typically, the horalbell summoning me from sleep, my consciousness thawing in usual sequence: damn noise . . . have to finish that piece on *Altars of the Heart* . . . I hope there's an egg on hand . . . are there any really *good* reasons not to stay in bed all day? I reached out and managed to silence the screaming clock after some graceless slapstick comedy involving not only the device itself but also my over-

4

weight cat and a tumbler of water, yet my apartment did not grow quiet. The second layer of noise, as it turned out, came from the vidiphone, which I answered, "Hello," without switching on the camera. Whoever it was, I did not wish to confront him or her in the transmitted flesh.

"Hello, Quinjin." It was Francie, glorious Francie Lem, guiding light behind *Dreambeans Deciphered* and one of the few electrozine editors in Terransector with backbone enough to print my stuff. Dreambeans was what people who took their cephapples seriously called cephapples; people who didn't take their cephapples seriously called them brainballs. "Turn on your camera," Francie continued, smirking down from the vidiphone screen. "I dislike talking to my mental image of you."

Francie's mental image of me was probably fairly positive that particular morning—in those days, before my adventures with the Tree of Death, I was not unpretty—and I wanted nothing to tarnish it. By keeping my camera off, I prevented her from seeing my rumpled pajamas and whisker-infested chin—not to mention the uncovered floors, the bare-ass light bulbs, the fractured plaster, the furniture intended for beaches, and other signs of poverty overtaking my apartment. As a point of pride, I preferred for Francie to believe that my *Dreambeans Deciphered* income was subsidiary to my lecturing fees and book royalties, when in fact it paid the rent and put food on the card table.

I told Francie my camera was broken.

"My left ovary," she replied smoothly, leaning toward her own camera, giving herself a closeup. "You don't want me to see the ash heap you call home."

I think I loved Francie Lem, loved her with the sort of oblique, semiconscious love you enjoy experiencing because it entails no obligations. Two decades my senior, she made being fifty-six seem like a good idea. Our face-to-face communication was confined entirely to the vidiphone, so that I had no notion of what the nape of her neck looked like, though I assumed it was as stately and handsome as the rest of her.

5

"Tomorrow I'm sending you an unsolicited piece on that love dream I was telling you about," I said. "*Altars of the Heart.* A minor effort, sure, and I could do without the title, but it made me fight tears, and we should all rally behind it." This last sentence probably trailed off as I lurched away from the screen in a successful effort to keep Basil the Cat from singeing his whiskers on yesterday's coffee, which my computer had just now decided to reheat.

"Never mind that," said Francie. "Your task for the moment is to get your mouth over to the Cathexis and swallow the first available fruit. The box office knows you're coming."

"What's the show?"

"*The Toad of Night.*"

"Let me guess—a horror bean."

"Not exactly. You haven't heard the news? Doesn't *anything* interest you scribblers besides coffee and words?"

My screen showed that, behind Francie, the *Dreambeans Deciphered* offices bustled with staff members plugging in their thoughtwriters and groping for their coffee mugs.

"What's the matter with *The Toad of Night?*"

"The press release calls it a modern fairy tale—an allegory on that old Brothers Grimm thing about the Frog Prince."

"Allegories give me hives."

"Anyway, near the end there's evidently a scene where you bury somebody alive."

"Hell, Francie, can't I cover some subtle stuff for once? I wish—"

"So yesterday this poor crazy ten-year-old, Suzie Freed, drops by the parlor, eats the apple, goes home, tosses Baby Brother Phillip into a shipping crate, and sinks the crate in quicksand. Death by asphyxiation."

I was sorry but hardly shocked. Art, I knew—real art—is no prissy pastime, and the dreambean medium, with its unprecedented credibility, had a particularly notorious record of inspiring lunatic acts. Indeed, this Suzie Freed Tragedy was following hard on the heels of the previous month's Wendy

Cromboc Tragedy, in which a young woman of psychotic persuasion had thrown herself in front of a maglev train after
eating Reinwort's adaptation of *Anna Karenina*. And before
that, the Paxton Wolfe Tragedy. And before that, the Martin
Mergeron Tragedy. "Why do you always give me such *weird* dreams, Francie?
Don't tell me the offbeat is my beat—I've heard it. What about
Altars of the Heart? What about—?"

"Quinjin, I need *help.*"

"Let me guess. SUPEREGO wants to shut down the show."

"*SUPEREGO* wants to shut down the whole goddamned
dream industry. The situation demands more than a simple
review, of course. It demands a counterblast, and you're the
man to write it."

SUPEREGO. Bad news. Very bad news. To wit: the Society
for Unconditionally Purging Entertainment by Restoring Ethics and Godly Order. The SUPEREGOists' numbers were
growing every day, and my boss was not being paranoid when
she suggested they had the power to make cephapple-eating
illegal. The SUPEREGOists talked a great deal about God.
They knew where God stood on every issue.

Furtively I kissed Francie on her glass lips. "You don't suppose this incident heralds another Vorka Massacre, do you?"

Her habitual breeziness died. "Vorka is an ancient crime,"
she snapped. "It did not, does not, and never will have anything
to do with cases like this. It was completely . . . *other*. Put
Vorka in your article, and you'll see what editorial tampering
looks like."

Perfect word: *other*. The next five years would gradually
disclose just how *other* events at the Vorka Psychoparlor had
been. But that morning all I knew of Vorka were the grim
statistics. I knew that four hundred and six people had bought
tickets to a matinee . . . that four hundred and six people had
eaten cephapples . . . that four hundred and six people had
assumed they were ingesting an innocuous romantic comedy . . . that four hundred and six people had apparently been

slipped something else . . . that four hundred and six people had gone insane. "Massacre," of course, was an exaggeration. None of the Vorka victims died. But they had all needed shutting up in the bughouse, double locks and steel strictusuits, and not one had ever come within hailing distance of reason. The perpetrator remained unidentified, the motive unfathomed, the crime unsolved. And ever since Vorka, the world lived in fear that the plague would visit again.

The chatter of thoughtwriters began pouring from my vidiphone speaker, but Francie's agitated tones easily beat it down. "I'm expecting a masterpiece, Quinjin. An epic. We'll spread it over the next three issues. Get the Suzie Freed business out of the way, then give us a whole smelly story of Dream Censorship—start with the book burners and work forward. I'll pay on manuscript receipt."

"You pay on manuscript receipt and you'll receive no manuscripts."

Francie showed me a brittle smile and shut off her camera. "Your check is in the mail."

The basement floor of my apartment building was conveniently contiguous with a troglobus station, so that every parlor in Shadu City stood less than five minutes from my thoughtwriter. Of course, many cephapples of note never played Shadu City. Some never even played my home planet, Zahrim, sole captive of my home star, Alpheratz; I was a seasoned faster-than-light traveler.

As I milled around the subterranean platform, shin-deep in gum and eager for the bus to come whooshing down the tunnel, I realized just how annoyed I was at my editor. She hadn't come out and said so, but she clearly had no intention of purchasing my *Altars of the Heart* insights. True, it was a conventional dream, it did nothing new with the medium, but it still deserved space in *Dreambeans Deciphered* beyond the usual capsule review.

My annoyance had evaporated by the time the bus arrived.

Staying mad at Francie Lem was no easy undertaking, for, among bean critics, to know her was not only to love her but also to have been helped out of at least one hopeless jam by her. In my case, the hopeless jam was the notoriety I had achieved upon publishing—in an electrozine called *Family Hour*—a review of that grindingly inspirational bean, *By the Wind Grieved.*

> *By the Wind Grieved* (A.G. 788). 84 minutes. Weaver: Emory Crostik. A biographical dream that turns you into the self-made bastard Edgar Whittlecrop, who started out with seven veneers in his pocket and, upon discovering the jungjelly used in FTL transportation systems, wound up a billionaire. The viciousness, greed, and spiritual squalor that most historians agree were the hallmarks of Whittlecrop's character are underplayed to the point of whitewash, and the focus becomes how you assembled the first jungjelly derricks and enlisted God in selecting their locations and exploiting the unimaginable wealth they generated. This is the sort of apple we're all expected to adore because it embodies something called "decency in dreaming," but the decency of *By the Wind Grieved* is a selfish, irresponsible decency, a decency predicated on the belief that the ruthless should inherit the earth, a decency I trust about as far as I can pee mercury. . . .

From there I went on to attack SUPEREGO, creeping theocracy, the profit motive, and the ethics of the pangalactic bourgeoisie.

After reading the first wave of hate mail, my editor at *Family Hour* took about five nanoseconds to decide I needed firing, a sentiment destined to sweep through nearly every electrozine office in Terransector. Get labeled "controversial" in this life,

and you wind up either fabulously rich or permanently un-
employable—more likely the latter, unless, of course, it is your
felicitous fortune to run into Francie Lem. Fast as the heroic
dogthing in Crostik's *Woggle Comes Through*, Francie galloped
to my rescue, giving me moral support, a cover story in *Dreambeans Deciphered*, and regular work thereafter.

Troglobus rides are meant to be uneventful, that's their
point, so after the expected nonexperience of traveling uptown
I left my seat, crossed the platform, climbed to street level,
and walked one block to the Cathexis Psychoparlor. It was a
warm morning in Shadu City, blessed occupant of a latitude
where just about every day managed to be spring. As Alpheratz
crept toward noon, giant shadows flowed down the marble
façades of the banks and offices hemming Nindukagga Square.
Shadu has always been a regal city in my book: clean, rational,
a true urban Arcadia, suffused with a smell like noostree syrup.

Above my head a looming, sunstruck billboard exhorted the
people of Shadu to go see *The Toad of Night*. The billboard
showed a fairy-tale castle, all buttresses and spires, superimposed over a young girl whose face consisted primarily of teeth.
The name of the dreamweaver was also provided: Roger
Conchfiller, who, my cephapple-addict's memory informed me,
had been responsible for *Gratuitous Violence*, an underrated
comedy of two years ago.

The Cathexis would be open till midnight, but already the
line coiled twice around it, with a new clump of customers
arriving every few seconds. Yesterday's holovision coverage of
Phillip Freed's murder was clearly turning to gold at the box
office. Even if SUPEREGO managed to yank it out of the parlor
by sundown, the bean would probably turn a profit.

Marching up to the ticket window, I gave my name to a
middle-aged woman whose life was clearly not going as she
would wish, whereupon a liveried usher, female and pretty,
appeared and led me past the front of the line and into the
place where dreams came true.

Typical of parlors built in the first half of the century, the

Cathexis was high-domed and mosquelike, its rubber chairs
filled with amniotic fluid, its voluptuous walls padded for the
protection of those occasional customers who wriggled out of
their seatbelts and ran amok. Parlors of more recent vintage
were nothing but rectilinear warehouses strewn with aquacots,
an arrangement more suited to fornicating than to hallucinating. I always suspected that couples who mixed the two
media experienced neither to its fullest. (The exception, of
course, was the kind of dream explicitly intended to be consumed under the influence of lust. If you played your cards
right, you could be party to a kind of quadruple orgasm: yours,
your character's, your partner's, your partner's character's. I
had known such synchronicity only once, but the memory will
always linger.)

The usher pointed to the one vacant seat, and I saw that it
held a scrap of paper containing my name, misspelled. Before
slumping down, I took the opportunity to observe the other
customers, for often such mental notes worked their way into
my reviews. ("The audience seemed composed mainly of pimps
and kidnip addicts, as would befit this latest assault on civilization from the weaver of *Hydraulic Nights.*") They were a
diverse bunch, all ages and shades, but unified by the zombie
impassivity that haunts the face of the bean-eater. Over here
bloomed a momentary smile, there a fleeting chuckle, behind
me a truncated gasp; no one's dream was completely in step
with anyone else's.

By buckling myself into my seat, I caused a mechanical arm
to emerge from the floor like a mesmerized cobra. The arm
culminated in a gloved hand. *The Toad of Night* lay in the
palm. Like all dreambeans, it was a simple object: no core, no
pit, no seeds, nothing but bland meat enveloped in glittery red
skin. Reaching forward, plucking my cephapple, I experienced
a twinge of nostalgia. In the good old days, the usher brought
you your dream on a platter.

Three bites, and *The Toad of Night* was in my stomach. My
senses began shutting down, my incredulity trickling away.

11

I am not a scientist. Don't ask me to explain what a ceph-apple actually did after its enterprising little molecules had started soaking into your cerebrum. A microbiologist once told me that, when you examined a cephapple sliver under a pho-tonscope, you did not see orthodox vegetable tissue but a hon-eycomb of throbbing hexagons, each preset to activate a particular population of brain cells at a particular nanosecond, like a blasting cap in a carefully orchestrated explosion. Nat-urally this technology and its innumerable antecedents, both dubious (LSD-49, for example) and legitimate (Rossiter magic mushrooms, for example), could have evolved only in the last century, when neurocartography crystallized into a science of impeccable empiricism, and the inducing of narrative hallu-cinations became a mere matter of blazing the right enzymatic trails. But I'll tell you something. This same microbiologist confessed to me that one facet of the cephapple phenomenon was always a total mystery. No one really knew how, during his creative trance, the dreamweaver could author a drama so biochemically cohesive that, precipitated as a plasmid, planted as a seed, nourished as a tree, and consumed as a fruit, it transformed its eventual audience into one of its characters. So you see, apples were an art.

My blindness was soon supplanted by a vision that was all form and no content. I did not see objects; I saw seeing. Nor in my deafness did I feel deprived. Those appendages called ears had simply never existed.

You can understand why it was both unlawful and unwise to dream outside the parlors.

Heat now, wave after wave. I had officially left the air-conditioned Cathexis, had irrevocably entered the story. The heat rolled across my skin like a scalding dew. My eyes un-clogged, and the cause of the heat became clear: *The Toad of Night* began in a sweltering jungle.

I stood beside the hull of a spaceship, a golden sphere glint-ing amid creepers and ferns. "*The Toad of Night*," intruded a resonant voice upon my earless hearing. "Written by Fauver

Yost. Weaved by Roger Conchfiller. Planted by Pamela Bosque."

The cephapple gave me knowledge. I was a willowy girl, about to explode into adolescence. I was a princess, and beautiful, and smart to boot. Exploring the Regulus system, I had run afoul of a meteor shower, landed my shattered ship on the first available planet. It was now incumbent upon me to master this unknown world, living by my wits until I had collected the raw materials needed to repair the damage.

Oh, for heaven's sake, my Quinjin self began moaning, it's a goddamned space opera.

I trekked through the jungle, performing the usual heroics: slaying serpents, smashing scorpions, outwitting cannibals, ho-hum. All these clichés were partially redeemed by the conviction with which dreamweaver Conchfiller had transformed me into a twelve-year-old. I *felt* twelve, I *experienced* adolescent stirrings—extraordinary illusions that were certain to earn excited adjectives in Quinjin's review.

But Conchfiller's greatest gimmick came when the swamp appeared. He gave it an amazing smell. Decayed but not disgusting, alluring but not perfumed. Moss and vines bobbed on the blind, dark waters. Before long I noticed a string of air bubbles rise to the surface, as if the swamp were aboil. The bubbles foretold life. Amphibious life—what else?—a repellent humanoid toad that suddenly hopped out of the water and landed at my feet.

The toad's popping eyes were the first two things I noticed about it. The third was its skin: brown, crinkled, a terrain of silt-creeks and warty hills. Sealed by slime, its mouth ran ear to ear.

The mouth opened. The creature talked.

He said that he was king of this planet. He had power, treasure, slaves. For him, restoring my ship was a favor he could grant with a mere snap of his webbed fingers.

But I had to promise him something. On an unnamed future date, I would have to let him come live with me as my husband.

Assuming that this was the toad's idea of a joke, I consented.

Quinjin gasped at my naïveté.

Back home, I grew to womanhood. My sixteenth birthday occasioned a lavish feast at my father's palace. In the middle of dessert, the banquet hall trembled with the thunks of the door knocker. The court jester froze in the middle of a punchline. When a servant opened the door, the light of three moons gushed into the palace.

One hop, and the Toad of Night was over the threshold. A second hop, and he was inside the banquet hall. A third, and he was on the table, smoothly relating to my father the details of our agreement.

The toad said that he had come to foreclose.

A bargain is a bargain, was my father's reaction. Characterization has never been the strong suit of the fairy tale.

And so I began living with a monster. With each passing day, and especially with each passing night, my revulsion doubled. Eventually I could stand it no longer.

Dawnlight probed the palace. The toad slept beside me. I gathered up the sheets, secured the bundle with rope, deposited the beshrouded creature in an airtight coffin, and hurled the whole arrangement into a bog not unlike the toad's natural habitat.

Within hours, however, I began experiencing severe pangs, as if I were in labor—absolutely the best simulation of pain my Quinjin self had ever experienced during a cephapple dream. It was the princess's conscience, struggling to be born. Shaking with remorse, I ran back to the bog, dived in, retrieved the coffin, lifted the lid.

As soon as the Toad of Night opened his gooey eyes, joy overcame me. I began kissing his bumps, every one of them—whereupon, of course, he turned into a handsome prince.

The wedding cost my father several small fortunes.

A voice said, "The End."

And I was Quinjin again.

Back on the troglobus, I tried composing a grabby line or two for my series on Suzie Freed and Dream Censorship. "Our culture is crumbling for sure when we decide to regard ceph-apples as the captains of our fates and the masters of our souls." That sounds pretty good, I thought. "If *The Toad of Night* 'caused' Suzie Freed to kill her brother, then why didn't it 'cause' the same behavior in the child sitting next to her? Why has there been no epidemic of fratricides?" Not bad.

The bus moaned to a halt, and I shuffled onto the platform. Flanked by an animadvertisement for deodorant pills and by a poster for *Altars of the Heart*, a newsscreen showed me its dormant glassy face. With no conscious intent I lobbed in a few coins and called up last week's issue of *Dreambeans Deciphered*. Allowing the device a few seconds in the rapid-scan mode, I instructed it to loiter near my review of a recent Wexel McPoon retrospective. Wexel McPoon was a perpetrator of my least favorite genre of dreambean, the avant-garde. "There's a quip circulating among beanbuffs this month," I said aloud, reading my words with growing unease. " 'How do you bore a hole in a diamond?' And the answer is, 'Take the hole to a Wexel McPoon retrospective.' "

Now you probably think that a dream reviewer's job was a real plum, but as far as I'm concerned it was a no-win situation. If you didn't give a weaver like McPoon a hard time, you risked cultivating in your readers wishy-washy standards and general narcosis. But if you went too far, you could plummet a promising talent into an unproductive despair. When I initially wrote my Wexel McPoon piece, I thought it instructive and clever, but now it just seemed cruel.

Starting down the hall toward my apartment, I realized that it simply wouldn't do to assail SUPEREGO with sarcasm and flip dismissals. No, I would have to concentrate on the *meaning* of *The Toad of Night*—the deftly dramatized transition from sex perceived as mysterious and repulsive to sex perceived as natural and miraculous. Thus I would demonstrate how, in attacking the dream's violence and its supposed effect on Suzie Freed, SUPEREGO was completely missing the point. By the time I reached my apartment door, I was prepared to rush whole paragraphs of polemic into my thoughtwriter.

At which point the universe went awry.

This same door, emphatically locked when I had left for the Cathexis, was now angling into my dark, windowless living room. Thieves!

Thieves? Then why were the lights off?

"Hello?" The voice had nothing of the organic about it.

"Good afternoon." Two cautious words, followed by two cautious steps forward.

A light came on, and there in my favorite beach chair sat an object that I immediately recognized as a robot of the genus *Pseudocortex*, just about the wisest breed of machine ever bolted together by man or woman. Basil the Cat, atop the bookcase, was spitting on it.

When I say "robot," you probably picture the sort we have today, athletic-looking manikins stuffed with circuits. But in the year A.G. 791, people did not want their servomechanisms to look like themselves. Doppelgängers gave them the willies. The problem was solved by retaining the highly efficient humanoid design and then plastering the flesh with pointless capacitors, meaningless resistors, absurd diodes, and existential wires.

"My common name is Iggi," the machine said, "though I prefer the unabridged version, Intelligence Gathering and Grouping Interface. In other words, I'm a spy"—the vanity in his voice was both irritating and poignant—"at least, that's how my program goes, which is why I had no trouble picking your lock." By "spy" I assumed Iggi meant an industrial spy. His pride in this heritage was understandable, for robots who did such work led glamorous and risky lives—stealing secret formulas, smuggling prototypes out of factories, trading unorthodox sexual favors for blueprints. I once gave a rave review to an industrial-espionage bean called *The Meaning of Fear*.

16

"Unfortunately," Iggi continued morosely, "Clee Selig prefers to use me as a slave and messenger boy—you can't imagine how humiliating that is. Do you recognize my master's name?" In those days, not recognizing Clee Selig's name was like not recognizing yourself in a mirror. Iggi was apparently retained by the cephalic apple's renowned inventor. What protocol was proper to such a rare visit? Should I offer to play the robot a quick game of chess?

"He has something to tell *me*?"

"The message is this." There followed an android equivalent of throat-clearing, after which Iggi launched into what I took to be a flawless impersonation of Selig.

MR. QUINJIN: YOU ARE A TALENTED CRITIC. I SHALL PAY YOU THE SUM OF TEN THOUSAND VENEERS, CASH, FOR A REVIEW OF AN UNTITLED CEPHAPPLE PRESENTLY IN MY PRIVATE COLLECTION. IF YOUR ANSWER IS YES, PLEASE BE IN MY LIBRARY BEFORE HOUR 18 TOMORROW NIGHT, SOUTHERN QUADRISPHERIC TIME. IGGI HAS YOUR DECONSTRUCTION TICKET. SINCERELY, CLEE SELIG, PH.D.

At this point, the robot was again assaulted by feline saliva. Ten thousand veneers! In A.G. 791, ten thousand veneers was not a sum to draw sneezes. With ten thousand veneers I could appease the landlord for a year, place my rump on something softer than beach furniture, treat Basil to an occasional can of tuna, and in general haul myself out of shabby poverty and into genteel poverty.

Iggi looked ready to spit acid on my cat. "I shall deliver your reply as soon as I receive it."

"Ten thousand veneers?"

"Cash."

"For one crummy review?"

"Correct."

"Where do I sign?"

2

The Lotos Factor

Even at the height of its celebrity, Wendcraft University was not on the map. It was on *maps*, naturally—deceptively frivolous-looking scratchings mailed each autumn to the incoming class—but it was not on *the* map, not on the official government-issue map that most people had been brainwashed into believing charted every part of Terransector worth a visit. Wendcraft's proprietors preferred it this way, of course, possessed as they were by the conventional wisdom that science flowers most fully away from the prying eyes and meddling morals of the general public. My fateful meeting with Clee Selig might never have happened had Iggi not told me exactly what roads I should follow after being funneled halfway around the planet to the seacoast town called Utuk.

Utuk was on the map. Its humble teleport, incapable of handling more than a dozen travelers at a time, evidently boasted crackerjack maintenance, for after my deconstruction in Shadu, I was shipped and reassembled without a scratch. I rented a waftcar, then pursued the knotty route to the University, urged on by the screaming wind and driving rain that were among this region's permanent realities. Wendcraft was at this time a legend on the rot. Gone and also forgotten were the hefty grants and prestigious professors of the University's halcyon days, that period when the Faustina vaccine, the temporal trifurcation theory, and the *Pseudocortex* android had been for the faculty all in a day's work. Just one department, Selig's private school for dreamweavers, continued to attract top students, and then only because the man who had cooked up the phreneseed was still the man who could best relay the recipe to apprentices.

Reaching the campus shortly after dusk, I made a prescribed right-hand turn at an abstractectonic sculpture by the celebrated neodecadent Lucaizai and found myself sharing the lane with a tall, bearded, umbrella-armored pedestrian. When I stopped the car, both of us immediately pushed buttons, he one that caused his umbrella to vanish into its handle, I one that prompted the rear half of the viewbubble to slide away. A kilometer ahead, the lambent disks and rectangles of Selig's many-windowed mansion gleamed through the downpour.

"Mr. Quinjin?" Selig asked in a brass voice familiar to me from Iggi's mimicry. He settled into the back seat, smelling of weather.

"Just Quinjin," I replied, making the bubble whole again. "A critic's affectation."

My passenger is perhaps best evoked via one of those Darwinist charts that show the phyla vacating the sea in a single-file ascension from amphibians to reptiles to mammals to anthropoid apes and so on. With his momentous forehead, wise beard, and ramrod posture, Selig belonged somewhere between *Homo sapiens sapiens* and the minor-league angels. He explained that stormwalking, as he called it, was his second favorite hobby, the first being Lucaizai sculptures, and that, given the tortuous character of my journey, he had not really expected me until later that evening. He explained these things and more, much more, with a raconteur's talent so hypnotic that I absorbed almost none of the procedures by which we ended up in his library on the mansion's second floor.

Iggi, who had beaten me to Wendcraft by several hours, served us cognac. "I'm *supposed* to be a spy," he said, huffing away.

Civilized furniture, savage fire, dozens of original Lucaizais, hundreds of rare books, mood of moldering intellect: all these amenities permitted the room to win me over immediately and completely. Within minutes I had disclosed a fair amount about myself—my chagrin at being divorced, my pride in being a father—but Selig's real interest seemed to be my experiences in the psychoparlors.

"You cover a lot of apples in the horror genre," he asserted, draping himself across the full length of his couch, then immediately popping up like a corpse undergoing rigor mortis. Beneath his majestic exterior, Selig was, I could tell, a torn and troubled man.

"Horror beans are hardly my forte," I protested, snuggling my rump into a portly lounging chair. "The best piece I ever did was on Pandriac's adaptation of—"

Selig parried by pulling some electrozine printouts from his pocket. The thick silk of his robe seemed spun by worms fed on ambrosia. "But I see your by-line on this review of *One Million Lunatics*." He rattled the pages accusingly. "It appears here again on *Bestial*. And again on *Sermons by Satan*."

"I wrote them," I said in a confessional tone.

"Don't be ashamed. I love every noostree, the vulgar and backward as well as the beautiful. They all have their place, they all help people shake the dreariness from life. My trees are my children. They can think and feel—did you know that? I put brains in their taproots. And now that somebody's trying to ruin them, now that—" A sudden sadness jammed his throat. He swallowed audibly. "You want to know why you're here," he continued, voice restored. "What dream I want you to review. But first I must tell you about Simon Kusk."

"Simon Kusk?"

"The worst person I ever met. If you had known him, Quinjin, you would lower your opinion of unmitigated evil. For it was Simon Kusk, you see, who committed the Vorka Massacre."

"Flowering Judas! Do the police know?"

Again Selig attempted to stretch out, again he performed a sudden, jackrabbit sit-up. "Travel with me to A.G. 758. I was forty years old then. He was eighteen. Simon Kusk achieved depravity at an early age."

And then my jittery host told me a story that, whether it was true or not, would have made one hell of a dreambean.

There was no honeymoon in the Selig-Kusk relationship, no time when they assumed the roles that naïve observers expected: brilliant professor and star pupil, kindly mentor and grateful prodigy. As Selig told it, Kusk was obnoxious from day one, exuding the attitude that no part of the Wendcraft curriculum would be news to him and that, in fact, he could teach the faculty itself a thing or two about hallucinating. He let it be known that he had enrolled mainly to get his hands on the equipment: the neuroactivity amplifiers and gene synthesizers by which dreamweavers turned potent imagination into palpable seed. Classes became for Selig a nightmare of challenge and humiliation, with Kusk repeatedly seizing the floor to lecture his fellow students on how the "true potential," the "primal purpose," of cephapples was still unguessed and how the University was afraid to try cracking the mystery. But only in the privacy of Selig's office would Kusk say exactly what he was seeking: a dream so vivid, so intense, that its eaters would forget they were hallucinating; a hyper-reality in which the audience would completely lose its way. "Unwilling suspension of disbelief—that's your invention's destiny," Kusk kept telling his professor. "It's the logical climax to noostree evolution." He even had a name all ready for this new dimension of the medium. He called it the Lotos Factor, after the amnesia-inducing fruit posited by Homer in *The Odyssey*.

Were Kusk simply a conventional egomaniac, then the situation would have been, if not more tolerable, at least less ambiguous. But the boy had a gift. The portfolio that had gotten him into Wendcraft was a dazzler: love beans that could make a lumberjack weep, horror beans that could rattle the scythe right out of Death's hand. When it came to fulfilling the studio assignments, however, Kusk's dreams invariably emerged looking hasty and uncaring. He was too busy tracking down his Lotos Factor to be a mere student. And so, when his shoddy projects (not one of them turned in on time) stood stacked against a shoddier attendance record and a midterm-exam score of 43 out of 100, his department head made a momentous decision.

For an apprentice weaver to be booted out of Wendcraft University by Clee Selig himself was no trifling event. You didn't just check into the next school down the block. *Excommunication* would be a more accurate term than *expulsion*. From that moment, your chances of finding a planter to bankroll your dreams hovered between the implausible and the inconceivable.

"And so it was that I destroyed my best student," mused Selig, whirlpooling his cognac, "and made myself a target for retaliation. The viper must have started sneaking into the studios at night—secret experiments, a fanatical war on disbelief—and before the academic year was out, he had indeed found his Lotos Factor." Selig lifted his glass in a mock toast. "So Kusk plants the seed, the sapling yields its first full crop, and he smuggles the dreams into the Vorka parlor."

"What could it have been? Some sort of ultimate horror bean?"

Talons of lightning reached across the sky. Rain clattered against the windows as if a thousand delinquent children were pelting Selig's mansion with pebbles.

"Probably it defied the categories you critics like to use. As soon as the massacre hit the newsscreens, I suspected that a lotosbean tree was the cause, and that Kusk was out to destroy me. He wanted to give my children such a terrible reputation that I would become a pariah. I must admit, I don't quite understand why I wasn't lynched. If Kusk had gone on to commit more massacres, we wouldn't be having this conversation now, I assure you. I'd be . . . I'd be—"

"But he *didn't* commit more massacres."

"Yes. That's because he died. I killed him."

My heart did something that it is not normal for hearts to do. But I decided to let Selig explain himself.

"It was not premeditated," the inventor claimed. "I'm no monster. My plea—should these events ever come to trial—my plea would be that I prevented a far greater crime. It happened not long after Vorka. The moons were cloudy, the rain was thick, and I was stormwalking home from Acheron Hall, puzzling out the tragedy, wondering whether to inform the police of my theory. And suddenly somebody rushed up and struck me from behind."

"Kusk?"

"Kusk. I awoke in the most abominable hovel I have ever seen—a small, murky place, filth on everything, a sputtering incandescent bulb the only light. Kusk showed me his vile seedling, all infested with lotosbeans. It grew right out of the dirt floor. He had a spade in his hand, and when I asked about it, he said that he was going to dig up the tree and ship it to a hydrasteroid belt. 'A hydrasteroid belt,' he insisted, over and over, taunting me. 'A hydrasteroid belt.' "

A hydrasteroid belt. There was a time when more than a third of all inhabited star systems boasted a belt of moist, terraformed, nutrient-laden asteroids around their primaries. Hydrasteroids. Whenever a fallow hydrasteroid received a baby noostree, a professional planter would oversee a force of farm laborers in caring for the thing—fertilizing it, fussing over it, swaddling it in carbon dioxide, until it grew up and brought forth millions, literally millions, of psychoactive fruit in its season. The word *noostree*, of course, is misleading, for the adult of the species was certainly more forest than tree, and more vegetable-continent than forest. A noostree enveloped its mother hydrasteroid like moss enveloping a rock.

"So he was setting his sights on genocide," I said. "Enough lotosbeans to turn an entire planet into a lunatic asylum. But why the abduction?"

"He wanted to torture me—my emotions. He wanted me to know that my trees would be forevermore defamed, that there would be Vorka upon Vorka until my own mother would spit on me. He insisted that he had covered his tracks well, and that if I put the police on the scent I would merely get to see how incompetent police can be."

"Did he threaten your life?"

"No, my reasons for killing him were more interesting than that. If you had ever seen the face of a Vorka victim, Quinjin— I visited the madhouses often—if you had ever seen Madeline Gosi or Reginald Boryk or Marta Rem, you would understand why I pulled that spade out of Kusk's hands and broke his head. He staggered around for a minute . . . moaning, but not loudly . . . then he grabbed his tree. He died holding the trunk, watering the roots with his blood. So I dug it up, put his body in the hole, and threw back the dirt. There remained the need to extinguish the seedling. I severed every limb, smashed every lotosbean. I'm ashamed to admit how well I slept that night."

"And you never told anyone?"

"A few trusted friends—and now you. I'm doing so because, if we're going to work together, the air must be free of mysteries. Hell, Quinjin, stop looking at me that way." I was indeed looking at him as a canary might look at a cat. "Haven't you ever eaten a spy thriller bean? Can't you see that if I go to the police, even now, they'll call my story fantastic and arrest me for Kusk's murder at the least and probably for the Vorka Massacre as well?"

Having eaten a fair number of spy thriller beans in my time, I understood Selig's paranoia, and, while the situation did not lack ethical ambiguities, I tried to be sympathetic.

"It's good to know there won't be another Vorka," I said.

"If only we could be sure of that."

Once again, my heart turned inside out.

Rising from the couch, pacing across a carpet so thick he left footprints, Selig went to a wall of particularly primeval-looking books. Caught by the fireplace glow, their gilt titles were spelled in flame. He scanned the shelves, selected a foilbound copy of Homer's *Odyssey*, which, when opened, proved counterfeit, nothing more than a box, its velvet lining depressed by a sphere the size of a cow's eye.

"Two days ago this appeared on my doorstep," he said, approaching, depositing the book in my lap. The color of the husk—pink—testified that the bean's parent was still only a seedling.

"The trick volume, too," I asked, "or just the dream?"

"Both. I find the meaning explicit. We are expected to think that the Lotos Factor has been rediscovered. We are supposed to conclude that some disciple of Kusk's has learned how the viper made his garden grow."

This time, when Selig threw himself on the couch, he remained supine, glued by lassitude and despair. "God, God," he moaned, "I thought this foul business ended when I butchered that seedling. I'd rather be dealing with the viper's *ghost* than with another of his perverted dreams."

When I stared at the apple's burnished surface, it showed me my eyes. They were hot with frustration and anger. "So *this* is the fruit you want me to eat? *This? This?* A lotosbean? You called me all the way out here so I could drive myself crazy? Forget it, Professor!"

"The apple's true nature must be known." Selig spoke in the steadiest voice he had used all evening. "If it's really a lotosbean, there could be another Vorka coming. Somebody will have to find the tree and kill it. Now, we're not talking about a *pleasant* dream, of course, but a person with your background is peculiarly prepared to handle it. Over the years, you've eaten every horror imaginable."

"Yes, but the Lotos Factor would overwhelm all that," I replied, sneering. "I'm a veteran of deranged murderers, monsters from hell—I even got through Verdewort's *Cacodaemon*. That dream was never distributed, you know; I had to contact the bean-eating underground to find it, the thing is so grisly. Vorka apples? Hyper-reality? Obviously a different art entirely! Pay me in sacks of gold, pay me in galactic empires—you won't get me to eat!"

The professor twisted his beard into a barb. "Very well. But before you leave campus, before you make me search out another critic, do me a favor. Drop by Acheron Hall, Studio A, and talk to our psychobiologist. She has a few interesting ideas about arming a person for a lotosbean fight. You'll like Dr. Aub. She's something of a witch."

"Urilla Aub?"

"Yes," Selig replied, closing *The Odyssey*. "Have you met her before?"

So great was my self-absorption as I strolled across campus the following afternoon that the architectural strangeness of Wendcraft impressed only the remotest parts of my mind. Towers jutted toward storm-gray skies; spires twisted around each other; crooked belfries harbored uneasy alliances of bats and doves; gingerbread dormitories flew anarchist banners, drying laundry, and other signs of the students who occupied them; yet none of these sights could compete with the gushing pressure of my thoughts.

Yes, I had met Urilla Aub before. Our intellects had met, our spirits had met, the bottoms of our bellies had met. The affair had begun and ended in college—Arquebus University, to be exact—and throughout its brief history the subject of marriage never came up, nor did the word *love*. But we certainly *talked* as if we'd be spending the future together. We pictured ourselves as a famous dreamweaving team, both of us writing the scripts, Urilla making the phreneseeds. A typical date was spent sketching out plots for apples, the best of which was probably *Redemption of Things Past.*

In *Redemption of Things Past,* a woman named Sallie Sequenzia builds a time machine and sets out to rectify all the embarrassments and bad decisions that haunt her memories. She plans to tell a certain young man she loves him, just to see what will happen; she plans to avoid reading Ob Vargo's muckraking classic, *Crime in the Suites,* thus sparing herself six wasted years of trying to spread economic utopia throughout the Milky Way. The central irony is that, having discovered how to turn her life into a work of art, Sallie becomes a perfectionist, seeking to erase every minor flaw—the snappy comeback she should have made at some cocktail party but didn't—and soon growing more frustrated than she was the first time around. Urilla and I passed many a long hour smoothing over the paradoxes and mollifying the contradictions that time-travel stories inevitably raise.

Then, one day, Urilla told me—I shall never forget her annoying word choices—that she had "managed to fall in love with Toland Barnes." Toland Barnes was a would-be dream critic with a lewd smile and too many muscles. I retaliated by falling in love with Talas Pru, by staying in love with Talas for as long as one can stay in love with a conceited actress, and by becoming a more honest reviewer than Barnes would ever be.

Acheron Hall was a cylindrical building that in a different age would have been called a castle. As I stepped inside, a female undergraduate hurried by, clutching a compendium of dreambean reviews—though unfortunately not *Oneiromances,* the compendium authored by me. I smiled at her. She smiled back. I hoped she somehow realized that I smiled not to be polite, not to express cheer, but simply because she was so painfully pretty.

In typical Wendcraft style, the way to Studio A was convoluted and ambiguously labeled, and I found it primarily by accident. Cautiously I opened the door, trying for and achieving silence, and the tactic paid off. I got to notice Urilla before she got to notice me.

The place was a hexagon, curiously barren for something called a studio. Glowing transplastic tiles formed the floor and ceiling. The walls, likewise glowing and transplastic, supported holovision monitors on which a wraparound surreal landscape—reindeer with fires in their antlers, women giving birth to snakes, the usual sort of thing—was currently taking form and void from Urilla's fertile brain. She sat on the floor, legs crossed, palms up, showing me her profile and wearing an electroderby. The gleaming metallic helmet spanned her head from ear to ear, eyebrow to nape. A red robe spilled from her neck like a lava flow.

Selig was right about one thing. There was clearly a witch or two up Urilla's family tree. Not fairy-tale witches, not hags with warty noses, but raven-haired enchantresses of the sort who got burned at the stake in those grade-B horror beans where you played the magistrate and by this office accrued a curse on yourself and all your descendants. High-cheeked, sharp-nosed, thin-lipped, diamond-eyed, her face was of a type that looked sinister one minute, sensual the next. Whatever the intervening years had stolen from Urilla, her sibylline beauty remained largely uneroded.

On the screens, the flaming deer, newborn snakes, and other psychic detritus faded into visual noise. Standing up, Urilla removed her electroderby and turned in my direction.

"I've been thinking about Scene Six," I called out, anxious to have the first line of our reunion. "Wouldn't Sallie try learning how Mack's life turned out *before* she went back and proposed marriage?"

In a matter of seconds Urilla had her seizure of surprise, wiped the symptoms from her face, and picked up the beat. "No, no—how many times must we go over it? Sallie's too *irresponsible* for that. Now Quinjin, on the other hand, he's responsible as hell, so responsible he's going to authenticate that lotosbean of Dr. Selig's." She flashed a delicious witch's smile. "Good God, I knew we had a critic coming, but I never guessed it was *you.*"

"It's me," I replied. "Only I haven't agreed to *authenticate* anything."

We approached, ran through a gamut of greetings—handshakes, arm-wavings, two hugs, a quick, suctionless kiss. Chattering, we condensed the past 144 months into 3 minutes. To her credit, Urilla had never married Toland Barnes. To her chagrin, she had never become a dreamweaver. Instead she had joined Selig's staff: each morning she lectured apprentice weavers in the neuropsychology of bean-eating; afternoons found her classifying the non-narrative hallucinatory idioms on a grant from the Verthandi Foundation. Like me, she orbited the art but she did not *make* the art, though she claimed that she was going to change careers as soon as her research was concluded. "I'll get *Redemption* into a parlor yet, you'll see!" she insisted, polishing her derby with a tress of her hair.

"Should I eat Selig's apple?" I asked suddenly. Critics are blunt.

"Let me put it this way. If I were talking to Toland Barnes now, I'd be saying, 'Look, Toland, eventually somebody will have to try the thing. To stop a plague, one must first identify the disease. But it shouldn't be you, Toland. Don't be tempted. You're not strong enough.' After all, Barnes is just a journalist, isn't he? He treats cephapples as mere news. But you're different, Quinny. You're a critic. You keep analyzing even as you dream. You've made a *career* of detaching yourself from experience. Beyond that, there are certain weapons we can give you, certain pieces of psychic armor the Vorka victims never had. I'll be honest, though. We cannot guarantee—double your sanity back—that the dream won't hurt you. If you bite the bean, it won't be because I've made you feel completely safe. Your real reasons will lie elsewhere—and I don't mean the ten thousand veneers."

29

"Tell me about this psychic armor," I said hastily.

"I want to turn you into a weaver—not a real one, mind you, not a good one. But somebody who can get his fantasies fruiting. We must strip the medium of all mystique for you. We must cut the worm of mystery from the cephalic apple."

Leaning forward, she crowned me with the derby. The wired nodes lining its interior pressed against my scalp like little sucking mouths.

"I'm not one to refuse a free lesson," I said, "but don't assume that this bowl on my head means I'm going to test the—"

She seized my left hand, trapped it between her erotic palms. "Dreamweaving, Quinny, is the art of unalterable attention. If your thoughts stray from the story, the illusion is wrecked." My arm became a tether, leading me to the floor. "First we need a setting. We won't try any pure fiction today—that's not for beginners. Put yourself in a familiar place."

I decided on the flea-bitten amusement park where I had taken my daughter during our last visit—an impossibly protracted four years ago—and without difficulty I hauled it before my inner gaze. All about the studio, the screens began to quicken, their static gradually resolving into a merry battleground awhirl with Ferris wheels and carousels, bellowing mountebanks and fire-snorting calliopes, lurid animals and disquieting clowns. In the farthest distance, a roller coaster arched its spine and delivered its passengers to their reversible exterminations.

"What's that?" Urilla asked, crushing my concentration and blinding the screens.

"It *was* an amusement park," I explained testily.

"You'll get it back." She was right; the park materialized in half the time its initial creation had required. "Give yourself someone to meet."

After some neurological strain, I managed to place Lilit-as-I-remembered-her, Lilit age eight—a damned good replica, I felt—on the nearest screen, satisfactorily capturing her lithe frame, her bubbly cheeks, her lemon-puckered mouth, her bronze hair, the excellent sensuality that is the lull before adolescence.

Lilit and I used to come here often. A lifelong aficionado of whimsy and wasted time, I suspect that I enjoyed such outings even more than she did. From the moment of her birth—*whoooosh*—and it was off to the dog show, to the toy store, to the wigglewort races, to the chocolate factory, to the circus, to the psychoparlor. In this regard I have always been particularly well suited to parenthood. In other regards . . . well, perhaps Talas *did* deserve custody. A cephapple critic was certainly away from home a great deal, tracking down promising-sounding dreams in grubby little towns and attending conventions on backwater planets. Of course, Talas, with her acting career, was not exactly a homebody, and I could never forgive the judge's draconian decision to restrict my visits with Lilit to times selected by her mother. "Mothers should control these things," the judge had said, right to my face. "In hunter-gatherer societies, the women always determined when the men were with the children." And I had replied, right to his face, "Were you there? You look like you were, you cross-eyed mastodon."

Because Lilit's friend Risha had usually joined our amusement-park jaunts, I decided to paint her into the scene. A pleasant task—little Risha was even cuter than Lilit.

The three of us reached unspoken consensus, marched arm-in-arm to the carousel. There was no line; such are the advantages of illusion. Hopping aboard, we inspected the possibilities. Lilit soon decided on a dragon. Risha selected a large pig who looked fully capable of unseating anyone who tried to make a pig joke. I mounted a unicorn who had a licorice coat.

Our feet entered their respective stirrups, and I set the world spinning.

On the holovision screens, bright dappled blurs rushed by. My dizziness told me that, for an amateur, I was weaving well.

"Remember, Quinny," Urilla intruded, "you're in training

31

to fight an apostle of Simon Kusk. Think of a maddening climax. Do something terrible to yourself."

And, indeed, the situation suggested any number of "terrible" outcomes. I could, for example, have increased the carousel's speed, flaying myself with friction. I could have turned the brass ring into a noose, lynching myself on the spot. I could have transformed my unicorn into an Antaresian plasmidleopard.

These semi-thoughts—these notions that I did not dare mold into visible fantasies—unnerved and depressed me. When I spoke, my voice seemed to be in the next room.

"No," I said. "The lesson is over."

"As you wish."

I began dismantling the dream. On the screens, the animals stopped revolving. Lilit and her friend dismounted, skipped out of view. The roller coaster collapsed. The Ferris wheel rolled away. The carousel began to evaporate, until nothing remained but my black unicorn standing in a white haze.

Urilla approached, blotted my brow with her handkerchief. "I'm pleased with your progress," she said. "Firm images on the whole. Crisp contours. I think Kusk's disciple has met his equal."

She pulled the derby from my heated brain.

Ambling out of the studio, we entered an elevator and in ten seconds plunged as many decameters below street level.

We exited into a phreneseed nursery—a sprawling grotto abuzz with neuroactivity amplifiers, guanine vats, adenine flasks, cytosine vials, thymine tubs, reaction chambers, highly patented computers, and milling technicians. It was to this place, I knew, that the derby had relayed my maiden attempt at dreamweaving. In processing such a broadcast, the machines regulated the introduction of several hundred artificially synthesized neurotransmitter genes into plasmids appropriated from an ordinary plant spore; inserted back into the spore, the plasmids replicated like mad, turning it into a phreneseed.

Urilla took us to an alcove labeled OUTPUT: STUDIO A, and

I found myself staring at a petri dish, its lip a mass of rubber tubes that ran every which way like the arms of a brain-damaged squid, each eventually disappearing into one of the reaction chambers. Inside the dish, our seeds incubated, two gelatinous gray lumps: my hypothetical holiday with Lilit, Urilla's venture into non-narrative idioms.

When Urilla drew up next to me, all she did was lay a hand on my shoulder, yet I experienced a superlative sexual satisfaction, so great was her power to redistrict my erogenous zones. "The greenhouse is overcrowded," she said. "Posterity will forgive us if we don't allow these to become crops."

Pulling a small knife from her robe, she plunged it into the seeds. Sap spurted out, liquid tissues oozed to the edges of the dish, and then it was over—two noostree abortions.

The following afternoon I went back to Studio A and continued my apprenticeship.

In Lesson Two, I again visited the amusement park, sans Lilit, and garroted myself on the brass ring.

In Lesson Three, I became a harlot running afoul of Jack the Ripper in the Terran nineteenth century.

In Lesson Four, I hurled myself into a snake pit.

Lesson Five. A nest of spiders, each the size of my cat.

Lesson Six. An inquisitional dungeon where heretics learned that nothing is more painful than fire.

Urilla, smart Urilla, had been right. "Your real reasons will lie elsewhere," she had said, and when it dawned on me that I was indeed committed to battling the dream, I understood what she meant. Yes, I felt that, as a critic specializing in the uncanny, I stood a good chance of winning. Yes, I believed that my six practice seeds had toughened my psyche. But ultimately I would eat the apple because I had to find out what was down there—in the dream, in me. I would eat the apple because the unknown is a temptation as well as a threat, a desire as well as a fear.

I would eat the apple because I wanted to eat it.

3

Figure and Ground

Selig decided to test the lotosbean in his private laboratory, a conglomeration of bottled brains, antique computers, and huge murals of neurons pressing their dendrites forward in hopes of communication. It was here that, fifty years earlier, Selig had braved the sneers of his fellow microbiologists and brought forth the only art form ever derived from recombinant DNA. Someday, I figured, the whole place would be sprayed with fixwrap and carted to a museum, every speck of dust a matter of permanent historical record.

Spiraled around the dissection table, leather straps paralyzed my head and body, and for a few moments I knew what terrors a quadriplegic must endure. Wires clung like vines to my naked chest, trailing away to a machine whose shrill beep-beep-beeps assured me that my heart was still beating.

"I would like you to sign something," said Selig. He sat behind his desk, peered at me across a cortical hemisphere that floated in formaldehyde like an aquatic pet. "A release form. The fine print, bluntly translated, says that I and the Dream Department and the University itself are not responsible for anything the apple might do to you. And, of course, it guarantees that after you've had the dream, ten thousand veneers will go to you or"—his tone became sheepish—"your heirs."

Like an usher from the psychoparlors' golden age, a nurse moved toward me with a platter bearing the fruit. In her other hand she clutched a pen and a piece of paper. I signed the paper without reading it. I could hear my heirs applauding.

The nurse's face was old and skull-like, with a wide smile made permanent by an absence of lips. She inserted the dream in my mouth, began taking my pulse. My jaw was the one joint I could still operate, and I chewed effortlessly if not eagerly.

"It's only a cephapple," I rasped sotto voce, the tribal chant of the bean-eater who finds his aesthetic distance narrowing precariously. "It's only a cephapple, it's only a cephapple."

"Are you losing vision?" asked the nurse. "Do your ears feel numb?"

That was the strange part. A regular bean would have been bricking over my senses already, but I experienced nothing of the sort. "No," I said. "I haven't left the station."

My heart kept beeping in my ear.

Selig turned on his vocalith machine and began to clock the seconds by making a pendulum of his beard, ticking it back and forth.

"Even if it's a dud," I informed him, "I still get the ten thousand ven—"

And then, in less time than it took me to blink, the lotosbean blasted me out of the lab.

It deposited me on a lawn.

I had started to earn my fee.

The grass beneath my feet was an inconceivable green. If green were the color of fire, I would have thought the lawn was burning. I advanced across the glowing green coals.

Everything in the dream was keyed to the intensity of that lawn. Fingers of wind tore at my hair. The air, rapier-cold, went for the nerves beneath my teeth. Gray, roily clouds moved across a sun-bright sky, staining the lawn with black-on-green shadows. The smell of the place, a piercing mix of ozone and diseased vegetation, was so strong I feared my nose would bleed; bile rose in my mouth. I heard music, a six-note melody played over and over on an invisible instrument that I pictured as a she-dragon's udder.

A mounted figure approached. Plump and ungainly, he rode on an enormous goat. Its backbone swayed like a hammock. The goat-rider wore a black cloak. His head was roofed by a black cowl that made his face an abyss.

The goat-rider dismounted.

Fetid breath spewed from the gloom that was his mouth. He pointed to his animal. "A goat," he said, as if he and I spoke two different languages. "In this place we also have a well. And, furthermore, a hedge."

The goat-rider told the truth. Not far from where I stood, a ring of stone, four meters across, went round and round. The outside surface rose modestly from the grass, reaching a height of perhaps ten centimeters. The inside surface dropped into shadows. Twenty meters beyond the well, a hedge stretched across the horizon—a motley rampart of leaves, limbs, blossoms, and thorns, broken near the middle by an arched gateway.

A lawn, a goat, a rider, a well, a hedge. I had girded myself for hell on a bad day, but so far the dream was merely vivid. If I were reviewing the dream for Francie Lem, I would have called it pretentious; I might have said, as I had said in my review of *Sermons by Satan*, that it was about as upsetting as spilt milk.

A burst of swamp gas told me that the goat-rider was about to speak again.

"This is all a dream, of course," he said. "Shall we give the dream a title? Let me forgo modesty and call it *The Lier-in-Wait*—my name. And for whom am I lying in wait? For you, gentle sleeper. Walk with me to the well."

The Lier-in-Wait started off. The goat and I followed. The organic music continued.

Just remember—you weren't there.

You didn't peer into the terrible buried tower that was the well. But I did.

You didn't hear the Lier-in-Wait say, "Behold the one you love best!" But I did.

You didn't see the enormous rock sitting at the well's arid bottom, nor did you see the quivering figure hunched on the rock, nor did you see that the figure was imprisoned by chains embedded in the rock and threaded through iron manacles, nor did you see that the ends of the chains were spliced together by a padlock. But I saw those things.

You weren't there.

You weren't there when a red, pungent, organic liquid began swirling around the rock, as if the well were being fed by an aquifer of blood.

You weren't there when the sun stabbed through the clouds and illuminated the face of "the one you love best."

You weren't there, so it's easy for you to say, "Quinjin's daughter wasn't *really* in the well. She wasn't *really* about to drown. Quinjin was simply succumbing to suggestion, was simply in thrall to a kind of hypnosis."

Easy to say.

The links of Lilit's chains clanked against each other, making a song such as a vulture might sing. Breakers of blood splashed the rock. The whimpers that floated up from the well were the saddest sounds I had ever heard.

Everything was so real, so realer-than-real, as if my life had thus far been lived under anesthesia, as if I were just now waking up. In retrospect I would compare the Lotos Factor with that famous optical illusion in which the contours of a goblet suddenly snap into two vis-à-vis profiles. Figure becomes ground, ground becomes figure. So it was that *The Lier-in-Wait* became for me an absolute truth, while my actual past became nothing more than the memory of a dream.

Is the goblet more gobletlike than the profiles are profilelike? When the shadow attains every last property of the substance—its weight, texture, smell, soul—then which is casting which?

At length the clouds showed me mercy, once again covering the sun and obscuring Lilit.

More words made their way through the Lier-in-Wait's miasmic breath. "You require a key, sleeper. I know where it is."

"Tell me!"

He pointed to his goat, which was cropping the fiery grass.

"The key is in the goat, sleeper. You need only to take it out."

Rummaging inside his cloak, the Lier-in-Wait produced a dagger, its blade a serrated smile, its grip a setting for jewels that looked like eyes.

"You might find this useful," he said, handing me the dagger.

Over the six-note melody, I could hear the blood rising in the well.

My quavering legs carried me to the goat. The eyes in the dagger grip winked at me. Sunlight was sucked to the blade.

Realer than real. Hyper-reality.

The goat stopped grazing, looked up. Its eyes were dark, wet, inexpressive. Its mouth, curled in an unfelt smile, capped a stringy beard. I was pleased to observe that neither of its horns, not the clockwise twist, not the counterclockwise twist, seemed a match for my weapon.

And the blood kept rising.

The goat danced, bleated, rushed to the hedge, bolted through the gateway. I followed, hot on its cloven hooves.

Beyond the gateway, more hedge. Not a single course this time, but a series of vegetable walls set at confounding angles to each other, with gaps leading to cul-de-sacs and other gaps leading to more passageways.

A maze.

A hedge-maze.

A hedge-maze whose constituent branches bulged and snaked like muscles breaking through flayed skin. A hedge-maze whose thorns were a million hypodermic needles poised to shoot nameless botanical poisons into my blood. A hedge-maze into whose stratagems the vital goat had evidently disappeared. Running madly—not running but being run, by my fear, by my rage—oblivious to all but Lilit's predicament, I refused to feel the rips in my skin when the briars hooked me, refused to watch my warm blood sluicing down my arms—running, running—now left now right no no cul-de-sac reverse try again turn cul-de-sac no no now left no no cul-de-sac stop don't drop the dagger go back cul-de-sac try this way now right no no cul-de-sac go back keep the dagger shit help God turn no no try again reverse cul-de-sac turn go run run yes yes good the center the center good the center good center—

In the central courtyard of the maze was the goat. It chomped on the green-times-green grass.

Hedge-walls rose on all four sides, and in each of the four corners stood a marble nude of the type we associate with the Terran Greeks. Two of the statues were male, two were female, and each had a skull instead of a head. Sunlight filtered down, washing the marble, giving it the limp whiteness of a drowned pig.

The goat ripped up a wad of grass, stared ahead stupidly. The thorns turned toward me.

Exhausted, crazed, tear-soaked, tormented past all articulation, I pounced. The goat kicked, unwittingly depositing a rear hoof in my grasp. My other hand dropped the dagger, seized a horn, yanked. To the music of the dragon's udder, I wrestled the goat onto the grass, retrieved my weapon. A front hoof split my chin. My blood plopped onto the scraggly swirls of hair that ran like a stitch along the goat's belly.

The dagger entered easily. Steam rushed into my face as the viscera met the cold air. I removed the stomach and opened it.

Blood, acid, half-digested grass, a stench like a public squat-rocker. But no key.

I opened the heart. No key. I opened the lungs. No key. The kidneys. No key. The cranium. No key. Methodically, diligently, my dagger searched every one of the goat's stinking chambers.

I screamed my frustration. "No key! No key!"

I turned this same frustration into violence, smashing the goat's horns with my fists.

A dozen keys spilled out of the goat's left horn, tinkling against each other, then lying silently on the grass.

A dozen more keys spilled out of the goat's right horn.

Lilit's deliverance was now assured, yes? Yes? Yes?! Yes?!?!

But this was a nightmare. The fountainhead of nightmares. The nightmare that a character in a nightmare might have.

My ordeal rushed to its climax.

A transmutation.

The keys were alive.

Each had become a black beetle, carapace smirking in the sun.

It was a climax of ancestral insidiousness, but in my particular case it failed to achieve its manifest purpose of driving me mad. Quite the opposite: the climax shocked me into sorting fact from phantasm. I became detached. Alienated. Distanced. For the first time since the nightmare began, I was not simply Quinjin the Dreamer; I was Quinjin the Critic contemplating Quinjin the Dreamer. And then, through a Promethean employment of spirit and will, the critic intervened.

See how the keys have grown feelers and legs! I instructed myself. Beware, dreamer—this joke is intended to unhinge your brain! Now notice how disturbingly, how asynchronously their legs row as the beetles scurry across the grass in twenty-four different directions—don't be fooled, dreamer! And, finally, observe how the tiny demons sprout wings and, ascending, remove your only hope of saving your daughter! A mere *trompe l'oeil*, dreamer! Remember who you are! Quinjin the Critic! Your father was right, there *is* such a thing as reality—and this is not it!

As I slumped down beside the dead goat, the airborne beetles collected themselves into a small, black, ever-rising tornado. Hoarding my sanity with every cell of my intellect, fighting the dream with every tendon of my soul, countering the Lotos Factor with every gene of my critical instincts, I watched the last of the keys rush away like a sorrow from Pandora's box. And the next thing I knew I was . . .

. . . hearing the muffled chatter of Wendcraft students. They were discussing a sport of some kind. An aquacot sloshed beneath me. My heart beep-beeped. The air was clotty with steam heat. Looking about, noting the unrelenting blandness of my surroundings—rectilinear furniture, oval windows, kitschy holograms of children on the walls, everything so unlike the thralldom where I had just been—I guessed that I was in a back room of the campus infirmary.

"Don't greet me," Selig demanded as I cracked into consciousness. "Just free-associate." Hunched at the foot of the cot, he resembled Lucaizai's one and only representational sculpture, *The Deity Crouches.*

My eyes felt like two dry stones lodged in my skull. My tongue was fat and gluey, an overweight toad. Gauze lined my throat. I began testing myself for sanity. Who is the President of the Pangalactic Senate? Elliot Frowze, I answered (correctly). What is your favorite dreambean? *Known Quantities.* How old is your daughter? Twelve.

A mechanical hiccup: Selig's vocalith machine was on. Outside the room, the students' conversation shifted from sports to politics. Freely I associated.

41

I told of the hooded figure . . . Lilit in the well . . . running through the maze . . . sacrificing the goat . . . the climactic surprise of the keys turning into winged insects.

"Give me your judgment," Selig demanded. "Was it a lotosbean?"

"If not a lotosbean, then something just as potent. While I was in there, it was . . . everything." Critics are accustomed to passing off their opinions as facts, but it was no mere opinion when I added, slowly, "Without the precautions I took, you'd be packing me into a strictusuit right now, Dr. Selig. You'd be enrolling me in the laughing academy."

Selig took this verdict as I expected he would. He looked as if he had seen a ghost, and the ghost had brought bad news. "Well, that's one mystery solved," he stammered. "But why was the thing created? Who did the weaving?" His fingers ascended the upper reaches of his vast cranium. "I'd give the smart half of my brain to answer either of those questions."

"The dream contained no clues—none that I can remember." As I sat up, a dreadful pounding arose in my head, as if a thought were trying to escape the prison of my skull. "Could the weaver be another ex-student of yours? Have you expelled anybody lately?"

"No, Kusk was the only enemy I ever made. And while I might find a kind of flattery in knowing that a lotosbean crop was being cultivated for a new anti-Selig vendetta—well, no, there's obviously something *else* going on this time."

Urilla came in, and I believe it was at that moment that I fell—refell—realized that I had never unfallen—in love with her. She had her sensual face on. Her blouse was white and lacy; she seemed to be dressed in cirrus clouds. After confirming that I had indeed won the fight, she kissed me in a manner suggestive of foreplay.

"I was worried about you, friend," she said. "What was it like? A deep-sea dive toward pressures not meant for human minds?"

"Hyper-reality is . . . a pussycat." My headache had subsided. I was feeling quite good now.

"Selig says you gasped and shrieked."

"No doubt."

"You should be proud, Quinny. A lesser critic—Toland Barnes or somebody—would have misinterpreted the dream. A weaker intellect might have taken it for truth."

Walking up to Selig, she playfully inserted her fingers in his beard. "So now your quest is cut out for you, eh, Professor? Deathtree at large."

Selig kneaded my aquacot, working it into a mountain range. "Needle in a haystack," he mumbled wearily. "No, worse than that. I could *find* a needle in a haystack. Burn the haystack, that's all. Sift the ashes with a magnet."

"Teardrop in an ocean," said Urilla. "Soap flake in a snowstorm."

Selig flattened his mountains.

"The odds," he said, "are with the Lier-in-Wait."

I slept in the infirmary that night, still suckled by the heart monitor. A nightmare came. I was back in the hedge-maze, venturing into a cul-de-sac. The Lier-in-Wait appeared, his body wrapped in fog, breath spewing from beneath his hood.

"You believe that my dream is out of you, sleeper," he said. "You believe a lie. There is more to the Lotos Factor than you will ever fathom, sleeper, more than you will ever dare to imagine."

I awoke shivering, the heart monitor screaming like a wet cat.

The skull-faced nurse came in and asked me what was the matter. I told her that I wanted to go home.

Even in this pornographic age of ours, where sex has become so familiar that it breeds more contempt than it does children, certain transactions between mutually lusting adults still manage to attain intimacy and wonder. The position called Finders Keepers is one. Sharing an umbrella is another. As Urilla and I headed out of the Mandala Psychoparlor in downtown Utuk and began splashing toward her apartment, her umbrella huddled us into a superbly erotic union. For the first hundred paces we were content merely to breathe the textured, salt-sea air and to mull over the dream we had just consumed, a surprisingly absorbing pirate adventure called *Uncharted Parsecs*. But eventually I mentioned how saddened I was by the thought of my imminent departure.

"I'll be gone soon, too," Urilla replied. "Selig is giving me a sabbatical. It is my ambition to become a great hero." It was as if she had said, "It is my ambition to become a real-estate agent," so casual was her tone.

"A hero?"

"Yes—like Captain Hornlaster in that dream back there."

"How does one become a hero in this day and age?"

"One finds the Tree of Death," she said. "One kills the mother of the Lier-in-Wait before there's another Vorka Massacre."

"A foredoomed task."

"Not if you've got accomplices. Come on, Quinny. Are you with me? Selig thinks we can do it. He stands ready to support such an expedition in every way. He'll even give us his robot—that Iggi machine."

"I'm a critic," I said, taking the umbrella away from her. "I like to earn my living on my buttocks."

Raindrops sparkled in the facets of her diamond eyes. "There's more to you than you think, friend. You conquered the lotos-bean. Aren't you anxious to hunt some bigger game?"

Stocked with reflections of Utuk apartments, puddles lay everywhere. By concentrating slightly, I was able to see the puddles as holes in a wafer-thin street, holes through which an underground city could be glimpsed. Instead of overstepping the puddles, I began to slosh right through them. Thought possessed me. Did I want my life, with its uncertain paychecks and ubiquitous deadlines, to stay just the way it was? Of course not. Did I want, instead, travel, thrills, adventure, and the honors that would inevitably befall anyone who helped prevent another Vorka? No, I didn't want those things either.

But Urilla would be going.

"All right," I said. "Let's give it a tumble."

"Selig has a theory. He believes that *The Lier-in-Wait* will resurface amid some morbid cult he calls—I think this is right—incubibers."

"Incubibers," I confirmed. "The bean-eating underground."

"Well, I'd never *heard* of them, but I wanted that sabbatical, so I pretended otherwise. I told Selig you know lots of incubibers. Do you?"

Incubibers. The word had its own odor, at once repugnant and compelling. Incubibers. Drinkers of nightmares. So named because they rarely consumed a cephapple unless it was first crushed into juice and mixed with animal or, better still, human blood. They plied this perversion outside the parlors and, hence, outside the law, wanting their fruit to be forbidden in all senses of the word. Only the most *outré* and outrageous dreams could satiate them. They were epicures of repulsion, tasters of tastelessness, connoisseurs of the avant-avant-garde—any bean that by accident or design turned out so bizarre that no reputable distributor would touch it. Whenever a planter found one of his charges bearing such fruit, he knew how to avoid counting the investment a total loss. Before burning the seedling, he would harvest the first crop and smuggle it to the Nightcrawlers, the Sunkillers, the Weird Sisters, the Brotherhood of the Abyss—whichever sect offered the prettiest penny.

The sleazy truth was that I counted a full-fledged Nightcrawler among my friends. In the article I wrote about him, he was called Ben Braxis. His real name was Jonnie Rondo. Jonnie was sixteen, spoiled, and as rich as God, but as incubibers go, he was only moderately depraved. The relationship had its compensations. By knowing young Jonnie, I got to experience a kind of art that never played the parlors. At Jonnie's last party, for example, I had eaten the legendary *Cacodaemon* and was consequently attacked by a monster so horrible as to make the combined works of E. A. Poe, H. P. Lovecraft, and W. W. Vardularg read like birth announcements.

I confessed to Urilla that I sometimes consorted with a Nightcrawler.

"Is he on this planet?"

"He's orbiting it. Owns an eighty-meter space yacht."

"Here's Selig's logic. Assume for a moment that the dreamweaver in question plans to go beyond dropping lotosbeans on doorsteps—that he plans to transplant his seedling to a hydrasteroid. He'll be needing professional help, right? He'll have to collaborate with a planter. Now, at some point this planter is going to peg the dream as something out of the ordinary. And, like all planters, he would never miss a chance to squeeze a few extra veneers out of his situation. So, is the man going to take his small, early harvests and flush them down the squatrocker? Ha! It doesn't matter *how* much he's being paid to keep the garden under wraps. He'll be sneaking those crops to the cephapple conventions and selling them to the highest-bidding incubibers. We start the hunt by making sure that one of those highest-bidding incubibers is your Mr. Rondo."

There was no more incubiber talk during our walk, no more braggadocio about slaying deathtrees. The distance remaining between us and Urilla's place was filled with the more comforting and familiar topic of *Redemption of Things Past*. It was during this conversation that Urilla gave not one, not two, but three hints that she hoped our "relationship" would resume, that if she could "patch up the past like our friend Sallie Sequenzia," she would never have tossed me over for Toland Barnes.

The human body is a paradoxical medium, at once public and private, never fully relinquishing the imprints of those who pleasure in it. Seeing Urilla undressed—her breasts, older now, were striated by veins that seemed like deposits of a wondrous blue gem—I understood myself to be in a club whose other members I would probably never meet. Her past lovers did not arouse my jealousy, not even Toland. I felt a strange, ghostly brotherhood with them.

People are probably more alike in moments of lust than at any other times.

I spent the night—on a mattress stuffed with Urilla's unfinished cephapple scripts. Once again my sleep was haunted by the Lier-in-Wait. Once again the cloaked figure claimed that I was not truly free of the dream, that there was more to his lotosbeans than I would ever dare to imagine.

As it happened, these suspicions of my subconscious were soon to be confirmed.

My stay at Wendcraft ended as it had begun, with Selig and me getting drunk in his library while rain assailed the windows and lightning cleaved the heavens. The meeting was his idea, the location mine; I liked that library better than any other spot on planet Zahrim.

Selig pulled his beard into two goatish horns, threw a log on the fire, and spoke. "Four days ago, when you awoke in the infirmary and told me about *The Lier-in-Wait*, you described how the keys became beetles and disappeared. You seemed to believe this was the apple's last scene."

"Yes. I can still feel the frustration."

"It's time for me to come clean with you, Quinjin, all secrets banished like phantoms at cockcrow, even if it means you decide to let Urilla catch the tree by herself. To be brief, there is reason to assume that the apple had another climax."

"Oh?" I replied, downing cognac to defeat a sudden chill.

"You might recall that we made a recording while you dreamt. Near the end, we've got the 'No key!' line, followed by six minutes of moaning."

"Moaning—my reaction to the beetles taking flight."

"And *then* we've got you talking again."

The cognac ended up in my nose.

Selig's vocalith machine lay on the same table as a reading lamp, a small Lucaizai, and the bogus edition of *The Odyssey*. Approaching, he impaled a coin-sized disk on the spindle. The machine talked.

"My only god is Goth," I heard myself say. "My only god is Goth . . . My only god is Goth . . . My only god—"

Selig pinched the disk. "You said it a hundred times. I counted."

"Goth?"

"Goth."

"What does it mean?"

"Don't ask *me*, Mr. Critic. *I* wasn't in the dream."

I ransacked my memory of *The Lier-in-Wait*. I could recall no Goths.

"The name evokes no awe, no epiphanies?"

"Not a one."

"It would appear that you are concealing part of the experience from yourself. A common phenomenon, actually. Freud called it repression." Selig returned to his fireplace, twisting his hands as if to mold something from the flames. "Try to remember. If we could find out who Goth is, a lot of the pieces would jump into place. I think we'd know the purpose of the dream."

Again I riffled through my neurons.

"Nothing," I said.

A lightning bolt zagged across the sky.

"Does this news disturb you?" Selig asked.

"Possibly . . . probably . . . yes."

"Are you still on the hunt?"

"Yes," I said, wishing my conscience had permitted me to say otherwise.

The voice of the lightning boomed into the room.

My only god was Goth?

4

The Soothsayer

Portholes ablaze, Jonnie Rondo's private pleasure yacht rode the arid sea of space like a garish, overpriced toy. As our shuttle drew near and we could read the yacht's name, *Fleshpot*, Urilla said, "Someday I'm going to make a political dream, very seditious. I don't have a plot, but I've got a theme—the pornography of wealth."

I was tempted to remark that she would put the audience to sleep, but I didn't want to cause a quarrel. Urilla and I had been quarreling a great deal lately, ever since she'd started noticing I had faults. She was particularly eager to clarify which of these faults explained my divorce. "I'll bet it was your snobbery," she would say. "Or your habit of reviewing people as if they were dreambeans. Wait, no—let me guess—it was the way you snivel and whine when you catch a cold." As a matter of fact, I really didn't know why things had gone rancid between Talas and me. I knew only that we'd lost the knack of tolerating each other, that every one of Talas's foibles and neuroses had started arousing in me a wholly incommensurate reaction whose only name was disgust, and that she had become equally allergic to me.

The two spaceships matched speeds, mated airlocks, and soon it was safe to cross over.

Gilded and posh, *Fleshpot* could get awe from a stone. Even the airlock was swank, with a ceiling decorated by a gold-and-jade mosaic depicting an interspecies orgy. Leaving the lock, Urilla, Iggi, and I allowed the pedbelt to take us to a lounge where mirrored pillars anchored a ceiling of mountainous chandeliers to a floor of carpeted craters. *Fleshpot* guests lolled in about half the craters, sipping cocktails and chatting up a storm. The walls displayed more gold-and-jade orgies, beautifully rendered. Jonnie's operation was enough to give hedonism a good name.

I could not tell whether the cheery young woman who greeted us was a guest or a servant. Her manner suggested a guest, but her promise to go and announce our presence suggested a servant. I later learned that she was a robot, part of Jonnie's trollop collection.

"Take any seat that looks tempting," she said. "Order any drink that sounds incorrigible."

Plunging into a vacant crater, Urilla and I threw some self-explanatory switches that soon prompted a pair of tiny hot-air balloons to glide toward us. The gondola of my balloon held something called a Satan's Mouthwash. Urilla had ordered a Sweet-and-Sour Synapse-Kicker.

We were on round two when our host arrived, scooting across the lounge via a pair of antigravity boots. His incendiary red hair billowed behind him, and his shoulders flew a jewel-encrusted cape that could probably have put my entire high-school graduating class through college. He had an honest-to-God sword buckled around his waist. Urilla gawked at his princely good looks.

For me, Jonnie Rondo's very name has always conjured up

the sort of person he was, a rakehell *manqué*, too silly, cautious, and diffident to reach any real dissolution, a Dorian Gray whose portrait would never look a day over thirty. Most incubibers frightened me, but young Jonnie, for all his attempts at sin, would always be something of a clown.

"You're staying for dinner," the blood-drinker said. It was more a command than a question. "The entrée will be stuffed oysterhog, and for dessert we've got a double feature of erotobeans. Do you appreciate prurience? Tonight it's *Money Where Your Mouth Is*, followed by *The Million-Year Foreplay*. Classics!"

So, I thought, Jonnie doesn't get *all* his laughs from incubibing. Ordinary hard-core pornography also tempts his palate. Although I generally disliked erotobeans, I knew it would be polite to seem impressed.

"With desserts like that," I said, "you won't get rid of us for a week."

Introducing my companions, I sensed that they aroused in Jonnie two different kinds of longing. Urilla he appreciated for her beauty, the robot for its costliness. It is commonly supposed that aristocrats have a cavalier attitude toward money, that it doesn't excite them, but I find they are as obsessed with the veneer as are the rest of us.

"So, what brings you to my den of iniquity?" he asked as he shut off his boots, descended, and sat down between Urilla and Iggi.

I suggested to Jonnie that a little privacy would be in order. He threw a switch. On all sides, glass triangles grew out of the floor and, in a kind of reverse-time explosion, welded themselves into a bubble above our heads.

"A strange apple is loose in the world," I said. "We think it's going to turn up on the black market, and we want you to be our broker."

"What sort of apple? What's the title?"

"*The Lier-in-Wait*."

"Never heard of it."

"There's reason to believe the weaver knows the technique behind the Vorka Massacre."

Jonnie looked like a baby learning that its mother lactates ice cream. "Legend of legends! Another Vorka dream! When my Nightcrawlers find out, they'll shit lizards!"

"Now hold on, Jonnie," I said. "We expect discretion here."

"The tree in question is still quite young, still yielding small crops," Urilla explained. "We hope to take an entire harvest out of circulation—nine or ten beans."

Jonnie drew his sword, pretended to pluck a hair from his head and bisect it. "Let me lay your cards on the table, friends. You don't just want me to find a few wormy apples. You want to know who planted them. More than that: you want to know who made their seed. More than that: you want to know where the tree is. Well, *those* kinds of questions can get a fellow's throat slit."

I took a pull at my Satan's Mouthwash. "I'm appealing to your conscience, Jonnie. There's a second massacre in the offing here."

"Conscience I never discuss in my cocktail lounge. Conscience I discuss in my swimming pool. Yesterday we stocked it with peltbass. Have you tried that, Quinjin? It's a whole new art form!"

For my money, swimming with a peltbass will always be too unstructured a sensation to merit the label "art form," but I must acknowledge its premier sensuality. As the three of us treaded water and the hair-laden fish came nuzzling up, I realized that human flesh harbors a latent hunger for animal fur. Jonnie may not have been doing anybody in the galaxy any good, but he sure as hell lived his pointless existence in style.

For a full hour we glutted our nerve endings, and then Urilla got us down to business.

"Look at it this way, Mr. Rondo. If the beans aren't found,

if SUPEREGO learns that the Lotos Factor has been rediscovered, the whole dream industry might topple. Your incubibing days could be over."

The nerve this struck in Jonnie was considerably thicker
and deeper than those being massaged by the peltbass.

"Very well," he said, looking at Urilla but not seeing much.
Saturated with green dye, the water was prudently opaque.
"I'll poke around the planet for you. I'll go to some cephapple
conventions. I'll keep an eye peeled for your *Lier-in-Wait*. But
we're talking a goodly sum—I hope you realize that. I'm happy
to sacrifice any broker's fee you were planning to pay me—
you're my friend, Quinjin—but the planter will want a lot of
veneers."

"Our backer is Clee Selig," said Urilla. "I figure he's good
for fifty thousand."

"A pauper's ransom. The bidding will start at twice that
much."

A peltbass slid down my left buttock. "Just remember, Jonnie, if you don't invest in us, you may never dream of tentacled
horrors again. No more unspeakable rites. No more quadri-
lateral sex."

"All right, all right, I'll make up the difference. You must
promise me something, though. When the beans are in hand,
I get to keep one."

"What for?" I asked.

"I need a paperweight—what do you mean, 'What for?' I
want to eat it."

"No, you don't," I said. "I've been there. The ending is so
painful I repressed it."

"You were *always* repressed," said Urilla.

That night, for the first time in a week, the Lier-in-Wait again
visited my dreams.

Not until we were back in my beloved city of Shadu did I fully
appreciate how fearfully committed Urilla was to becoming a

professional dreamweaver. In her unhumble opinion she had mastered all the basic techniques of the medium, and now was the time to start writing scripts, contacting planters, wooing distributors, and thinking big. Her determination intimidated me, so accustomed was I to viewing the future as an onrushing horde of unpleasant surprises—crash goes the job!—pop goes the marriage!—and to concentrating on keeping as little of it from happening to me as possible. But for Urilla, fate was something to be arranged, like a party; you engineered it, like a bridge. And so it was that my apartment became an author's haven, with a rough draft in every nook and a half-finished cup of coffee in every cranny.

Urilla was the really prolific one, averaging a script a week, though she never dared submit any of them to my acidic scrutiny. She seemed embarrassed by this omission. "They're milk runs," she would say. "Warmups for *Redemption of Things Past.*" Then, as a more candid afterthought: "If you hated them, I might hate you back." As for me, I was now grappling with the second article in the Dream Censorship series, the first having been single-handedly responsible for the most profitable issue of *Dreambeans Deciphered* ever broadcast. I persistently suggested to Francie Lem that anyone who could produce such gems probably deserved a position on her staff, and she persistently replied that if I had a position on her staff, I would no longer be inspired to produce such gems. (True, true.) So I still had money worries, even with Urilla paying half the rent. The ten thousand veneers I got for eating the lotosbean had all found new homes in a matter of weeks. A third of them went into a waftcar. I loved that car. I wanted a fleet of them. Once tasted, money, like blood, whets the appetite.

At night, Urilla and I would lie in bed together, thinking up plots for erotobeans and putting the best of them into rehearsal. Our masterpiece was entitled *Flesh Before Breakfast.*

Were I found guilty of some cosmic crime and subsequently condemned by God to repeat a particular portion of my life over and over, an existential Chinese water torture, then the one interval I could tolerate indefinitely would be these days of creative writing, creative talking, and creative lovemaking that followed our return from *Fleshpot*. Even Jonnie's dispatches failed to dilute our bliss. True, the news that *The Lier-in-Wait* had not turned up at any of the cephapple conventions got us studying the holovision newscasts each night, nervously watching for signs that the dream had surfaced elsewhere. Had the police been trying to account for the sudden, unexplained madness of a phreneseed planter? Had a psychoparlor audience gone crackers in a chilling replay of the Vorka Massacre? But no such horror stories appeared, and, apart from these edgy vigils, Urilla and I both sensed that our days in Shadu were among the best we would ever know.

The bubble was burst from an unexpected direction. One muggy evening my ex-wife showed up, one arm dragging Lilit's footlocker, the other dragging Lilit.

Lilit!

She seemed different, of course. Four years different. Four years of slogging around with her mother while the Zahrim Shakespeare Company made its first transgalactic tour. Puberty was pushing out. I saw at once that I had not been idealizing Lilit during our long separation. She was grand: pretty but also modest, delicate but also confident, a tracery of flesh and bone. There was a sketchpad wedged under her arm. It contained a horse. Had another girl drawn that horse, I would have said—Quinjin the Critic speaking—that it was uncertain in its contours and overwrought in its details. But this was a Lilit horse; it could have looked like an ape's scribble and I still would have wanted it on my wall. I have learned over the years that people do not take kindly to parents who act as press agents for their children, so I shall merely add that Lilit had always been an unusually sensitive and introspective child. When Lilit was three, and all her friends had imaginary friends, she went them one better and decided that *she* was the imaginary friend of a lonely elf named Willownose.

Lilit's childhood was a golden era in my life.

Introductions. Talas, this is Urilla. Urilla, this is Lilit. Lilit, this is me, your father—remember?—heh-heh. My little jest did not get the chuckle from Lilit that I expected. It got a mechanical smile and a downward glance. Oh, hell, I thought. She doesn't want to be here.

"I'm taking a sea voyage," Talas announced broadly. "You're taking the kid. Okay?" Her voice had always been her most effective asset; it sounded like an expensive bell that Jonnie would buy without knowing why. Her face, by contrast, had always been a shade too shy of pretty to earn her much business as an ingenue. But now an incipient middle age was bringing her a succession of stateswoman parts: Talas Pru as Jocasta, as Lady Macbeth, as Guinevere. "It's an *escorted* voyage, if you follow my meaning."

"Yes," I said. "Your meaning is that some producer has started screwing you." I regretted this remark as soon as it came out. Hardly fit language for a twelve-year-old to hear. But Lilit did not seem scandalized, and no looks of horror came from Urilla or Talas.

What sort of mother was Talas? A bit cold, I'd say, a bit aloof. The love was there, but Lilit had to go looking for it. What Lilit got from Talas was more the representation of love— a generous and unencumbered mother-to-daughter cash flow, for example—than love itself. There wasn't much hugging. Were Talas a dreambean, I would have given her a rating of two stars. I felt that, in her place, I would be doing better.

Sensing a storm, Urilla approached my daughter in a sisterly sort of way and said, "Would you like to see our robot?"

"Robot!" was the extent of Lilit's reply, but it came in a big, enthused voice that meant, Lead the way, whoever the hell you are.

When the two of them were gone, Talas began tolling at full volume. "My companion is not a producer! He breeds racehorses!"

"On an ocean liner?"

"I won't try to maintain any dignities with you, Mr. Ex. I love this man, only he doesn't love me yet, and I simply *can't* bring Lilit on such a trip. We'll circumnavigate Nereus, the whole soaking planet, living on wine and docking at all the most expensive islands. An entire summer of—"

"You sound like a travel folder."

"And you sound like one of your goddamned wisepecker reviews." As Talas sank into her beach chair, Basil launched a friendly attack, pouncing into her lap and going for her palms with his tongue. "I see you still have your dirty cat."

"That cat is not dirty. You could *eat* off that cat."

"Stop stalling. I want your answer now, and I want it to be *yes*. My next recourse is guilt. After that—my lawyer."

"Try guilt."

"You're her father."

"A fact that wowed no crowds at the custody hearing." Would I *always* be bitter about this? "Look, Talas, you know how much I want her here—hell, I want it *more* than you know— but Lilit's not going to like being dumped this way, she's going to resent both of us for it, and I'm not exactly *prepared*."

"You mean the thoughtwriter repairwoman who stayed for breakfast? I hate to disillusion you, Quinjin, but there's no sin in *your* repertoire that she hasn't already seen at my place. Not that I *push* it on her."

"It's something else. I seem to be running with a crowd of incubibers and crazy dreamweavers and—"

I silenced myself. Hold on, Quinjin. Easy, Quinjin. You're in a good bargaining position. You can emerge from this as something more than a camp counselor in Lilit's life, some- thing besides a court-appointed baby-sitter, somebody really crucial. "Don't worry," I continued, slowly, slickly. "You'll get to Nereus—though on my terms. The powers that be have me hunting a noostree in some far-flung hydrasteroid belt. That means you won't get Lilit back for two whole years—*three* whole years."

57

"What about those incubibers?"

"The robot can handle them. He used to be a bodyguard."
(Look at it this way, Iggi—it's not espionage, but it beats serving drinks and delivering messages.)

Talas stammered out a long, unparsable sentence from which
I inferred that she was willing to grant me a "three-year lease"
on Lilit (a *lease!*), whereupon the latter wandered back into
the room, Urilla loping behind.

"I like your robot, Father."

Well, well—the kid had decided to stop calling me Daddy
and start calling me Father. I found this endearing.

Lilit tossed her sketchpad on a beach chair. Fatalistic res-
ignation. "I have to stay with you, don't I?"

"Yes," I replied, bleeding inside, "but we won't be in Shadu
for long. Soon we'll be off on an adventure. Soon we'll be having
fun. You and me."

"Fun," she said skeptically. "Does that mean I don't have
to go to school anymore?"

"School? No, we probably won't be near any *schools*. Iggi
will tutor you."

"Great!"

Talas now inflicted on me the kind of stare a horror-bean
sorcerer might have used in turning an annoying person to
quartz. But she kept quiet.

"What about *her*?" asked Lilit, picking up the pad and
thrusting it toward Urilla.

"Oh, she's part of the adventure, too," I replied. "She'll be
your stepmother."

"A stepmother!" Urilla gushed, glad for an entrée into Lilit's
life. "I *never* thought I'd get the part! I'm not even *wicked*!"

Stepmothers have it easy.

What to do? Later that night, after Lilit was asleep, I went to
the one and only educational parlor in Shadu—the Piaget—
and bolted down Dr. Morris Hexclouter's self-help bean, *Coping with Your Adolescent*. Give your teenage daughter dignity,

that was Hexclouter's advice. Balance firmness with respect. And don't be protective—she's not a child anymore. This seemed to me a feeble prescription. Of *course* one should protect one's offspring. Hadn't Hexclouter been out of his house lately? The Milky Way was a pretty corrupting place—quite misnamed, a galaxy more of blood and crap than of milk, full of liers-in-wait lying in wait. The "respectful firmness" part made sense, though. I gave *Coping with Your Adolescent* two and a half stars.

Morning: off to a good start. After eating a nutritionally responsible (to my thinking) breakfast of fruit-filled doughnuts and prehardboiled eggs, Lilit actually climbed into my lap. "Tell me a story, Daddy."

"I thought I was Father."

"You used to tell me stories."

"Aren't you a little old?"

"I don't mean children's stuff, not fairy tales. Tell me a story like the brainballs you write about. Something with monsters and mass murderers and big kids pumping in the bunk."

"I'll have you know, sapling, that monsters and mass murderers figure in only half of what I criticize."

"If you won't tell me a story, then take me to a psychoparlor."

"Have you eaten *The Chrononauts*?" I asked. "It's the snazziest science fiction since *The Peace Machine*. Then there's *Altars of the Heart*—you like love stories, don't you?"

"No, I like monsters and mass murderers and big kids—"

My index finger cut her off. Why this sudden hunger for horror beans? A phase, I figured. Respectful firmness, that was what I should try, just as Dr. Hexclouter had ordered. "Here's the deal. We'll go to a parlor tonight, and I promise you at least three monsters and two mass murderers." I moved the finger metronome fashion. "But no big kids pumping in the bunk. Not until you're thirteen."

Her face grew warmly bright, like wax in a candle's high, soft crater. "Let's see *The Necrophilia Waltz*!"

"No!" I shouted with firm respectfulness. A few days earlier I had received some advance publicity on *The Necrophilia*

Waltz, and I knew it to be a supremely offensive story in which you spent most of your time prying open coffins. To patronize *The Necrophilia Waltz* would be only a few degrees removed from incubibing.

"*Zero Gravity Werewolves!*" cried Lilit, undaunted.

"That's more like it. Know what? We won't even have to pay."

"Big gappy deal."

I wondered whether perhaps it was the moral issues raised by horror beans—what does evil look like?—how bad does evil have to get before people do anything about it?—that attracted Lilit to the genre. Moral philosophy had always been an interest of Lilit's. When she was a preschooler and the two of us would watch bad Terran movies together on our holovision set, she always tried fitting the characters into an ethical framework. "Is he a good man?" she would ask. "Is that a bad woman?"

There were two psychoparlor visits that night, for after *Zero Gravity Werewolves* (three stars, a diverting if predictable horror-satire) Lilit talked me into *My Mail Comes to My Crypt* (one and a half stars, vile and bloody, don't take anyone under, um, twelve), and many more visits in the nights to come, but Lilit's keenness on me did not sustain itself, and eventually I seemed to be living with a beaten dog, so crushed did she look as she sulked and skulked around the apartment. I knew from Hexclouter that adolescents could be like this, but I didn't like to see it in the flesh, in *my* flesh.

"Is it this neighborhood, Lilit? Are you bored? You aren't making friends?"

"Who'd want to bring friends over *here*?"

"My furniture embarrasses you, right? Should we get other furniture?"

She said nothing. She just sat in a beach chair, sketching horses.

"Would you like other furniture?"

Nothing.

"*Talk* to me!"

She got up and walked away.

As I recall, this particular mood did not subside until the day the mad came.

"Father! The mad are coming!"

Unfortunately, I knew what she meant. The mad to whom she referred were not dreambean characters; they were real, live lunatics.

"We're not interested," I replied. "We have better ways to disgrace ourselves."

She grimaced. The grimace was a bright luminescent blue. My daughter had painted her teeth.

"What have you done to your mouth?"

"Dentgloss, dummy. High fashion."

"It's ghoulish."

"*Urilla* will take me to the Barge," Lilit said vengefully. "I'll go tell *Urilla* about it." The matter settled, she broke free of the holovision's seductive stare and left the room in search of the Wonder Stepmother.

I shook my head—Urilla had been spoiling Lilit to putrefaction lately, taking her to every damn horror bean she wanted to eat, even *The Necrophilia Waltz*—and glanced at the screen. The commercial for the Barge of the Mad was still pounding away. *"This attraction has been officially condemned by SU-PEREGO and may soon be banned throughout Terransector!"* A shot of a garishly painted spacecraft touching down on a fairgrounds melted into a closeup of a tight-toothed schizophrenic, a young woman who looked as if she hadn't emptied her bladder in a week.

The announcer's left-handed boast that the Barge of the Mad might be banned did, of course, eventually prove substantial. It's one of the few Pangalactic Court rulings I can endorse, for the whole thing was, from its inception, a deplorable spectacle, more worthy of a civilization that liked to see gladiators dismember each other than of a civilization that had fostered the dreamweaver's art. The Barge was a traveling insane asylum. You bought your ticket, boarded the ship, and gawked. Each exhibit consisted of a lavishly appointed room where at least one authentic nut-case presided, segregated from his visitors by a glass wall that permitted communication but not contact, so that the room was not really a room but a three-dimensional euphemism for a cage. These were not your garden-variety crazies. The Barge imprisoned no self-appointed Napoleons or slobbering catatonics. Its stars were the famous mad, the romantic mad: men and women who had achieved their insanity, not simply had it thrust upon them. A typical headliner was Welbie Lorcantor, who had lost his mind trying to write an autobiographical novel in which nothing that befell the main character during the twenty-first year of his life, not one flight of fancy or movement of bowel, was left out. In those few cases where the mania could not be credited to the person it possessed, you knew it would be of a highly entertaining stripe. Just now, for example, the holovision commercial was telling us about Kennie Fruxmatter, whose brain lesions compelled him to swallow swords and eat fire.

Hot for a quarrel, the Wonder Stepmother charged into the room. "On Lilit's birthday we're going to the Barge. Want to join us?"

"She's not *your* daughter."

"You think I overindulge her."

"No, I say it's *wonderful* she has a big sister. And the following night, you can rent her out to Madame Blorski's cathouse. Even better, I hear that our local incubibers are sponsoring a corpse-eating contest over at—"

"She wants it," Urilla retorted. "Would you prefer she go sulky on us again?"

At that moment the commercial climaxed with the news that this year's lineup included Marta Rem, a victim of the "notorious Vorka Massacre," and suddenly Urilla's proposal no longer seemed so outrageous. I needed to talk with this woman, much as a war veteran might need to talk with his army buddies, fellow survivors of an ambush where intestines had shot out like party streamers and years later the world had forgotten.

And that is why, on a sunny afternoon that I had originally planned to spend shining up the third and final part of the Dream Censorship series, I found myself in intimate conversation with a caged madwoman.

Intimate is right. Because Marta Rem was thoughtful and articulate and did not screech profundities or gargle bile or mime intercourse with the Devil, she had drawn no other visitors. Lilit was off hearing a lunatic comedian tell dirty jokes— this firm but respectful privilege was my principal thirteenth-birthday present to her—while Urilla favored a physicist driven crazy by his recurrent realization that there has never been a point in history when a majority of humanity did not believe in nonsense.

I had expected Marta's cage to be done up like the Vorka Psychoparlor, but her keepers were more creative than that. She dwelled among books: books stacked on shelves, books stuffed in crates, books rising in wobbly towers from chairs and tables and even from the lid of her squatrocker. The explanatory text nailed to the far wall revealed that, since running short of marbles at Vorka, Marta had embarked on a bibliographic quest, hoping to discover a cure for cephapple-induced madness in some forgotten volume of ancient wisdom. This is, in fact, what she appeared to be doing. Saying nothing, she leafed through Freud's *The Interpretation of Dreams* while, saying nothing, I watched.

(There, but for the grace of God . . .)

"I had a dream once," I said.

Marta Rem fixed me with the glacial stare a trapped badger uses while gnawing off its foot. I could not begin to guess her true age, so totally was it masked by the death-white hair and corrugated skin that were the legacy of her lotosbean ordeal. I noticed that her left eye was lower than her right, as if her face were spread across two misaligned pages in an electrozine printout.

"You didn't bring any microbes in here, did you?" she asked. A chill, brittle voice. A voice made of ice.

"No."

"They're getting larger, you know. The microbes. Last week she saw one the size of a flea. It tried to give her plague. This morning they got as big as hornets. Soon they'll be in bird-cages." She slammed Freud's masterwork shut, as if catching a hornet-sized microbe inside it. "Talk about your dream," she insisted.

"My daughter was going to drown. I had to run through a hedge-maze. I slaughtered a goat. Then, a part I don't remember. It involved a deity. Goth."

"The plot of your dream is not familiar, but the pain of it is. She has your pain, dreamer. She got it at Vorka."

A sudden queasiness accompanied my realization that when Marta said "she," the referent was herself. "I am a professional cephapple critic. I was able to detach myself. Otherwise, I would be in there, too."

"No!" she shrieked, squeezing the book as if to strangle Dr. Freud. "To enter is forbidden! The microbes!" She plunked Freud on the squatrocker with the same rancor Carl Jung might have shown. Her eyes grew as big as a tarsier's. "Listen, dreamer," she wailed. "She sees the things that are to be." Retrieving the book, she began to rip pages out, one by one. "Marta does not know why you ate such a terrible apple"—rip—"or where it came from"—rip—"or who made it"—rip—"or how it was made"—rip—"or what it means"—rip—"but she does know this. Before your journey is done, you will meet the tree that spawned the dream, and you will fight the tree, and you will bear a wondrous treasure away from the tree's lair."

Marta closed her split-level eyes. She vibrated like an un-bolted motor. Sweat coursed down from her white hair. Her voice became one not commonly heard on the bright side of the grave; it echoed inside her, as if everything beneath her skin had dissolved.

"Now Marta looks into your brain," she said. "Now Marta sees a great work growing there."

"A great work? You mean—a bean review?"

The madwoman spat into her palms, flung them wide apart, pushed them against the wall; she was a pinned bug. "And when the ripe moment comes, you will give the great work form. Analysis may be your calling, dreamer, but art is your destiny."

At which point Marta Rem fell fast asleep, still glued to the glass.

Driving my family home from the Barge of the Mad, I repeated to Urilla all I could remember of Marta Rem's rantings. I told of deathtree treasures and great works growing in my brain.

"It doesn't make much sense," I said.

"Of course it doesn't make much sense," Urilla replied. "She's insane."

The remainder of the ride was consumed by Lilit repeating all the dirty jokes she had heard that afternoon from the lunatic comedian. I was too preoccupied to exhibit embarrassment, annoyance, shock, or any of the other reactions she was hoping to get from me.

A treasure, a great work: these were all I could think about.

The minute we entered the apartment, Iggi zipped over with the news that he had just memorized a vidiphone message.

GREETINGS FROM THE CITY OF GANZIR. Iggi's impression of Jonnie Rondo was spookily accurate.

THIS CEPHAPPLE CONVENTION IS AS DULL AS SOAP, BUT I MAY HAVE FOUND YOUR CROP, FRESH FROM THE SABIK HY-DRASTEROID BELT, WHEREVER THE HELL THAT IS.

PROBLEM. SOMEBODY ALREADY BOUGHT IT. HAVE YOU EVER HEARD OF AN INCUBIBER NAMED BAPTIZER BROWN? THE BROTH-ERHOOD OF THE ABYSS—THAT'S HIS SECT. A BAD BUNCH. HE USED TO BE A PIRATE, BROWN THE TERROR OF THE SPACELANES,

BUT THEN HE REFORMED AND WENT INTO SMUGGLING BRAIN-BALLS. YOU'RE GOING TO HAVE TO COME OUT HERE, QUINJIN. THIS FELLOW ISN'T ANY FUN TO DEAL WITH.

BY THE WAY, TODAY I ATTENDED A PANEL DISCUSSION ON THE STATE OF DREAM CRITICISM. YOUR NAME CAME UP TWICE. DID YOU KNOW YOU ARE CONSIDERED CAPRICIOUS?

5

Secrets of the Sixth Stomach

I had not been to a cephapple convention in more than three years, but as our odd little company left the teleport and entered the Hotel Anshar, it became clear that nothing essential about these gatherings, none of the labored frivolity, the grinning despair, had changed.

A pirate ran across the crowded lobby. Black eye patch. Red bandanna. Redder-still shirt. Vest made of lizard scales. A cybersword at his side. I wondered: Was this Baptizer Brown? But then I recalled how cephapple conventioneers liked to dress and disport themselves as the heroes of their favorite dreams, and I realized we were seeing an *Uncharted Parsecs* buccaneer. I surveyed the circus. Near the elevator, the dog-thing from *Woggle Comes Through* wagged both its tails. Midway up the main staircase, the whore who got religion in *Hydraulic Nights* was propositioning the pathetic prizefighter named *Dandy Firemelter*. At the front desk, Prince Bizbac from *Castle Brimstone* leaned on his dragon-proof shield. A few of these characters, I knew, were incubibers in disguise; one could not mistake the haunted eyes, the furtive glances, the civetlike intensity. But most were mere buffs, their collapsed postures and hangdog expressions telling of lives wracked by a vapidity requiring almost continual counteraction in the psychoparlors.

Fiberfoil suits and fourteen-carat cigar holders marked the next largest contingent, the business side of the art, a hierarchy rising upward from the parlor owners to the marketing strategists to the distribution caliphs to the planters themselves, those profit-minded patrons who paid for the dreamweavers' studio time and asked for nothing in return except the right to cultivate the resulting seedlings and keep ninety percent of whatever their crops were worth. And then, finally, arrayed in sweaters so fashionable they were a uniform, and eyes so uniformly sensitive they were a mask, came what I would call the medium's soul: the dreamweavers, of course, and the scriptwriters, but also, I would submit (though they did not wear sweaters or moist eyes), the advertisers who kept the public hungry for beans and, yes, the reviewers who ineffectually urged this same public to boycott the rotten crops and subsidize the good ones.

Dressed in my best fiberfoil suit and accompanied by an expensive robot, a manifestly highborn woman, and a girl who looked as if she would wither unto death in anything but a costly private school, I'm sure I seemed hopelessly allied with the business contingent, and I doubted seriously that anyone would recognize me as Quinjin the Critic. I was quite delighted, then, to be set upon by three buffs seeking autographs, by a college professor who wanted me to know that I had completely missed the point of Niko Surkforder's *Jokes for a Jihad*, and by a distributor who said he would value my participation in one of tomorrow afternoon's panel discussions, "Dreambeans: Do They Destroy Free Will?" Having spent my entire life arriving at some opinions on this subject, I told him to expect me.

I was hoping that Lilit would be impressed by these various encounters with my fans. Instead she hung as far back as possible, pretending to be enthralled by the ferns decorating the lobby. She hated my fiberfoil suit. She said it was horribly out of date, that it was something you'd expect to see on a circus bear or a teacher.

I made a quick vidiphone call to Jonnie's suite, and within seconds he was with us—cape, sword, red hair, and all. He looked unhappy.

"How was your trip?" he asked dully. "Any problems at the teleport?"

"No problems," said Urilla. "Tell us about this Brown of yours, this Brother of the Abyss."

Jonnie perked up considerably upon realizing that our party now included a young girl whose blue-toothed beauty would, in a year or two, be fully capable of driving him out of his mind.

"Hello," he sang. "I don't know you."

"I'm Lilit. I'm an orphan. I'm being raised by this robot here."

"Stop it," I said succinctly.

Tearing himself away from my daughter's silky eyes, Jonnie turned to me and said, "Tonight we're buying Baptizer a drink in the Spiritual Nostalgia Room. He wants to meet my clients in person."

"The Spiritual Nostalgia Room!" The fervor in Lilit's voice, the string of tacit *wow*s, was quite understandable, the Spiritual Nostalgia Room being at that time the most famous restaurant on planet Zahrim.

I gave her a cold, slit-eyed, respectfully firm stare that left no margin for misinterpretation. "Your baby-sitter tonight is Iggi. Do anything you like—have cephapple dreams, play psychic billiards, eat ice cream, anything—but the Spiritual Nostalgia Room is *out of bounds*."

Sensing the futility of committing her best strategies and manipulation ploys to an unwinnable argument, Lilit merely grimaced and said "Your point" in a low voice, after which it became Iggi's turn to grumble.

"Need a baby-sitter? A majordomo? A chief eunuch? A coatrack? Just say my name!"

Urilla stared wistfully at Jonnie's hair. "I assume Baptizer didn't tell you much about his purchase."

"No," said Jonnie. "Except for one thing. It was harvested from a tree named Hamadryad."

"An odd name," I said.

"An odd name," Jonnie agreed.

"Ah, the Hamadryad," said Iggi. "The mythic tree in which the Serpent lived! The tree from whose lumber the Ark was built! From whose planks the Cross was made!"

Everyone turned to the robot with slightly annoyed expressions.

"*I'd* know that, too," Jonnie said, "if *I* had an encyclopedia grafted onto my brain."

Locate a gorilla. Now train yourself in neurocartography, pop off the animal's cranium, and start fooling around—planting electrodes, cutting old connections, stitching new ones, and generally tidying things up. Give the gorilla an improved intellect, an unprincipled cunning, a talent for ruthlessness, an appreciation for art, but do not tamper with its primal bestiality, its essential apeness. If you follow this recipe, you will have a perfect replica of the man we now confronted in the nethermost sacristy of the Spiritual Nostalgia Room.

Right off, I was struck by Baptizer Brown's audacity, for in trying to pass as a mere beanbuff he had costumed himself as one of the *Uncharted Parsecs* pirates—eye patch, bandanna, the whole bit—a camouflage carried to the point of conspicuousness. Nailed to the walls, the bas-relief faces of a half-dozen obsolete, abandoned, or otherwise unproductive gods formed a heavenly choir above the pirate's head. Thor . . . Kali . . . Ymir . . . Dharma . . . Dionysus . . . Tung Wang Kung.

No Goth. The Spiritual Nostalgia Room was dark and smoky. It vibrated with heartfelt conversation. Somewhere a wirelyre player plucked his instrument and sang a threnody for Phoebus Apollo.

As Urilla and I fumbled into our seats, Jonnie made the introductions, found out what we were drinking, and attempted to get things rolling with "I see that Vasco Stormer is presenting his new dream later tonight. Didn't he do that thing you like so much, Quinjin?"

"*Known Quantities,*" I replied shyly, feeling inadequate to any exegesis that might be expected of me. *Known Quantities* had indeed been the brightest spot of my reviewing career and, beyond that, a reason I was glad to be living in the eighth century. Its exquisite premise: a race of amnesiac robots sets out to learn its origins, and must reinvent such concepts as Nature, God, and Knowledge.

"*Known Quantities,*" said Baptizer grandly, "had more loose ends than a diarrhea clinic."

"You missed your calling, sir," said Jonnie. "You're a born critic."

"Quiet, you sniveling little piss siphon. Quinjin and I are *talking.*"

Oh boy, I thought as Jonnie slinked off to pick up our drinks, what a delightful evening *this* is going to be. Urilla rotated her eyes brainward.

"Go ahead," the pirate continued, studying me as he might a suspected mutineer. "Defend the apple."

And what if I fail? Do I get keelhauled on your space frigate? "*Known Quantities,*" I began shakily, "was dreamt on a low budget. Stormer's planter bought him just four hours in the studio, rehearsals included. Hence the lumpy transitions, the uncertainty of tone. But, hell, when did a bean last grapple with such a grandiose theme without falling into grandiosity? I mean, where did Stormer get the *courage*?"

"I think I like you, critic." As Baptizer shifted his bulk toward

Urilla, invisible counterweights traveled up and down his body. "And what about you, Dr. Aub?" His wink was lascivious. "Do I like *you*?"

"I'm here to learn about your dreams, sir, not your fantasies."

"Yes," said Baptizer, "I *do* like you. The piss siphon says you've got quite a few veneers to trade for this crop I just acquired—this so-called *Lier-in-Wait* from so-called Hamadryad."

Before Urilla could respond, Jonnie returned with our drinks, each named for a déclassé deity of the sort whose memory our surroundings were consecrated to preserving. Urilla and I each had Odin Stingers; Jonnie's curiosity had been piqued by the Krishna Fizz; Baptizer was drinking a Wrath of Jehovah, an effervescent preparation sipped through a plastic replica of the Tree of Knowledge.

"There's reason to believe the planter is working with a madman," said Urilla.

"There's reason to believe the apples are dangerous," I added, probing my Odin with my tongue. Strong stuff. "Not just 'unusual' or 'frightening' or however the planter described them to you. Dangerous. The tree may have to be destroyed. And, of course, if SUPEREGO gets wind of this, we could all be out of work."

Urilla tore fearlessly into her drink. "I don't suppose the planter told you which of the Sabikian farms is Hamadryad's?"

Baptizer sucked on his Tree of Knowledge. "That's not the sort of fact a planter normally blabs, now is it, Dr. Aub?"

"Perhaps if you gave us his name, sir . . ." She was trying to sound seductive, but she quickly lapsed into the unrelenting obviousness of a grade-B erotobean. "Perhaps if you told us how to find him . . . perhaps if you took us there, we could—"

The twitchings around Baptizer's mouth seemed to indicate annoyance, and I cut her off. "Of course, our first job is to make sure you were really given *The Lier-in-Wait*, and not just a crop you're supposed to *think* is *The Lier-in-Wait*. Sell us the beans, and we'll have Jonnie test one."

72

"Good plan," said Jonnie, bubbles of Krishna Fizz dancing on his lips.

The pirate grunted. "Let me tell you about my nature, critic. My nature is this. Once I've bought a crop—especially a crop as unusual—as *dangerous*—as this one is supposed to be, I don't ever let it go, not one bean, not for any price. But there's another way you can unmask this dream. Just thirty minutes ago I learned that a dead grorg washed up near Cicada Cove, a short whirlybus ride from the hotel."

At the mention of the word *grorg*, a central totem of my childhood flashed into my mind. A book, *Hunting the Grorg*. In full color, complete detail, I could see the cover illustration— a burly mariner planting a harpoon in the neck of a magnificent aquatic reptile whose only crime was to heat its body with a fluid useful in making waftcar paint. But what could the unexpected appearance of a dead grorg have to do with testing the crop?

Baptizer patted his black beard as a kinder person might pat a dog. "The belly of a grorg is an absolute sort of place— wouldn't you agree?—a real leap beyond the mundane, and certainly the ideal spot for a party. The fun begins in twenty-four hours. Why don't you come along, join the Brotherhood of the Abyss in a little friendly incubibing, and then—if you dare—drink your fill of my alleged *Lier-in-Wait*?"

Not only could I recall the cover of *Hunting the Grorg*, I could also recall the first line of Chapter One. "In the grorg, Nature has fused the body of a plesiosaur to the Buddhist outlook of a dolphin and the voraciousness of a shark." The belly of a grorg would not immediately strike you as "the ideal spot for a party," but then, you are not a Brother of the Abyss.

"Let's do it, Quinjin," said Jonnie.

Drops of Jehovah's Wrath fell from the plastic tree as Baptizer waved it in Jonnie's face. "*You're* not invited, piss siphon! Nightcrawlers *never* come to Brotherhood parties!"

Jonnie's face was a dumb show of humiliation vying with anger.

"We'll accept your invitation," I said, "but we won't drink *The Lier-in-Wait.* It's supposed to be a real mindsnapper, Mr. Brown, nothing less than a sequel to the Vorka crop."

The pirate's eyes swelled. The flab of his face solidified. "Vorka, did you say?"

"Vorka."

Embarrassed by this temporary loss of persona, Baptizer redoubled his bravado. "You are wise to fear such a dream," he sneered, tweaking Dionysus's nose, "and I doubt that your piss-siphon friend could come through it intact either. As for me and my Brotherhood—real mindsnappers are mother's milk to us! Name any drug, any swill, any poison, and there's a scar on my brain where I've tried it out!"

An unnerving man, this Brown. And very likely insane. More and more, our deathtree hunt was looking like a bad idea.

The following afternoon I kept a promise, showing up for the panel discussion called "Dreambeans: Do They Destroy Free Will?" It was really just my body that showed up; my mind dwelled elsewhere, locked on the probability that chasing after Hamadryad would be more ordeal than adventure, that with characters like Brown involved, I was really in over my head. Luckily the discussion was shapeless and never strayed far from the superficial, so despite my inattention it was almost impossible for me to make a certifiably idiotic remark. I remember insisting that, by their endless efforts to ban bean-eating, SUPEREGO and its allies distracted us from the things that *really* cramped a person's "free will" in this galaxy, poverty being a particularly famous example.

This drew applause.

The discussion ended and I went up to our suite, where room service supplied Urilla and Lilit and me with an over-priced plasmidduck dinner.

When my daughter learned that she would not be allowed to attend the upcoming cephapple party, she launched into a thirteen-year-old's version of a temper tantrum. She pouted and sneered and willed thunderclouds over her head. She called me "a repressed fossil" who didn't know how to dress himself. But I stood my ground. I was certain that a dead grorg had nothing to contribute to her education. And the Brotherhood of the Abyss would, I knew, have even less to contribute. I didn't mind her being around Jonnie the Nightcrawler, but I drew the line at the Brotherhood of the Abyss. In my view the two sects occupied two distinct echelons of degradation; if a Nightcrawler would tattoo his skin, a Brother of the Abyss would tattoo his internal organs.

"It's a bruising world out there," I said to Urilla, after Lilit had left for the hotel's psychic billiards parlor. "Nightcrawlers. Brothers of the Abyss. Erotobeans. Necrophilia Waltzes. Vorka Massacres. Deathtrees. Sometimes I wonder how *anybody* survives these days."

"I hate to be the one who breaks this to you," said Urilla, "but the world isn't going to get any better because you *keep* it from her. Stop trying to deliver her from evil."

"I *have* to protect her. If she thinks I don't care, she won't love me."

"Good God, Quinny, the last thing Lilit needs is you brooding over whether she loves you. Of *course* she does—but she's not going to keep *saying* it, like a little child would. She's got enough on her mind without your expecting her to be some sort of pubescent four-year-old."

"You think she should go to the party, is that it?"

"Do you *always* miss the point?"

In addition to Urilla, Baptizer, and myself, the guest list for the party included three Brothers of the Abyss and three Sisters of the Abyss. Baptizer's whirlybus, by contrast, was intended to seat four, so that our trip to the grorg was vividly reminiscent of Mewlmawker's adaptation of *The Premature Burial*. Our arms and legs dangled out of the windows, making the bus look like a badly packed suitcase. By the time we reached Cicada Cove, Urilla and I knew things about our fellow passengers that nobody should have to know.

There was Sprick, a ventriloquist, whose mind belonged to drugs and whose idea of a laugh was to pull a dead toad out of his pocket and make it sing. There was Vultzie, a mere girl, probably even younger than Lilit, but already looking used up, like a piece of arable land whose owner had neglected to practice crop rotation. There was Guig, whose caved-in eyes and loosely wired frame made him appear recently exhumed. There were the twins, Bandar and his sister Tiamet, who dressed in chain mail and who claimed to be collaborating on a book called *Incest in the Womb*. And finally there was Nullissa, a homely middle-aged woman with a glass eye. The eye was transparent and filled with water. A live guppy swam round and round inside it.

The whirlybus landed on an open beach. Nightwinds buffeted feral grasses and whistled around driftwood. In the gloom-soaked sky, two large crescent moons urged in the tide. The Urulu Ocean roared. Waves exploded against jagged rocks. Gulls moaned. The beach was a forlorn and frigid place. We advanced by the light of Baptizer's photorb, which floated before us, balloonlike, on a string attached to his wrist. Our boots squick-squicked across the sand.

And suddenly it was before us, the grorg's vast, Mesozoic carcass pushing against the darkness. It was as big as a space yacht. The head, neck, and front flippers were out of the water; the rest was buried by surf.

There is nothing quite so dead as a dead grorg.

We scrambled into the mouth, climbed over two palisades of teeth. Rooting himself in the soft tongue, Guig issued nostril plugs as we passed. None too soon: as we followed the photorb down the boggy floor of the beast's gullet, we were greeted by odors that would have offended the nose of a roach.

The grorg is a creature of undiscriminating appetites. This became obvious as soon as we entered the first of the half-dozen chambers constituting its digestive organ. In one corner lay a partially dissolved pygmy shark. Over there, a shredded canoe. Beyond, the hood of a waftcar, a section of a wooden dock, an outboard motor of the obsolete internal-combustion type, a colony of ailing octopi, and a lobster trap with a dead lobster inside. Stomach One was about the size of Clee Selig's library. Its walls were wet, pink, and wrinkled. The floor was flooded with a clear liquid that sizzled against our boots.

We seated ourselves on the lobster traps, the canoe thwarts, the waftcar hood: anything would do. Barred by our nostril plugs, the odors tried other entrances, pounding at our mouths, ears, irises. The odors clung to every molecule of air in the place.

"Baptizer," said Guig, stuttering with excitement, "you've outdone yourself."

"It's really quite extraordinary," Sprick chimed in. "My hat goes off to you," he made the pygmy shark say.

Baptizer chuckled.

"Tell me again what we're doing here," Urilla said to me.

Ever since I had first laid eyes on Nullissa, she had been carrying a silken satchel. Now she opened it, taking out a transplastic flask filled with a red liquid that I knew must be the incubibers' *vinum sanguinis*, blood and cephapple juice mixed in addicting proportions. Nullissa uncapped the flask, took a substantial swallow, then passed it to little Vultzie, cautioning her to consume no more than a mouthful. And so it was that the blood-juice circled Stomach One. We looked like skid-row vampires.

When the flask got to me, I asked whether it held Hamadryad's crop, for I had no intention of submitting myself to the Lier-in-Wait's caprices again.

"No," Baptizer replied. "Merely an apéritif. Its title, as you'll learn, is *Worm on a Razorblade*. Before the main course we'll . . . explore. If *The Lier-in-Wait* is half the bean it's supposed to be, critic, only Stomach Six is worthy of it."

Tossing an addled smile toward Urilla, I pressed the flask to my lips and drank. Gore and illusion: the tart combination never failed to curl my tongue.

The party had begun.

Worm on a Razorblade turned out to be a prison-break story in which you escaped from your dank cell only to find yourself on an endless metallic veldt. You were still a prisoner, infinity's captive. For the next hour you ran across the veldt, unseen guards at your back, their footfalls crashing in your ears, their breath blistering your neck. At the climax, you eluded your pursuers by locking yourself in a dungeon exactly like the one from which you had come.

When we awoke, I gave Urilla my analysis of the dream. I told her that the weaver of *Worm on a Razorblade* had achieved an "apex of circularity," and she said, "Is that good or bad?"

Without delay we proceeded to Stomach Two. More of the same: half-absorbed junk, flushed pulsing walls, hot digestive juices.

Once again Nullissa pulled a flask from her satchel, and the red nectar was passed around. This time the dream was *Carnage Pastorale*, which placed you in a waftcar and took you on a moonlight drive past scenes of singular morbidity. A weeping hitchhiker buried up to the waist. Zoom. A headless deer bolting out from behind a sign reading HEADLESS DEER CROSSING. Zoom. A detached human leg inching its way forward through flexion and extension. Zoom . . .

Stomach Three, Stomach Four, Stomach Five: I can't tell you how many dreams we had in these particular chambers, or what happened in them. The dreams' settings, their plots, their props, their personae all began melting and running together into an irreducible soup of chases, demons, howls, storms, teeth, falls, wounds, laughs, snakes, eyes, fights, insects, hands, crypts, flames, skeletons, shadows, blood, and discordant background music. I do know one thing, though. Grotesque as these dreams were, not one of them had the sheer maddening intensity, the hyper-reality, of *The Lier-in-Wait.* Not one of them was a lotosbean.

Stomach Six.

It was a place of bones—human bones, animal bones—as clean and sterile as ingots. The photorb's beams played across a variegated heap of skulls, vertebrae, ribs, clavicles, scapulae, humeri, ulnae, radii, femurs, tibiae, fibulae. Cascades of white erosion rolled down the slopes and spread across the wet floor.

Rummaging among the foothills, Bandar and Tiamet drew out what appeared to be two human pelvic girdles. As the twins were quick to demonstrate, pelvic girdles make excellent stools. The rest of us mimicked their ingenuity, so that our entire party was soon occupying the posteriors of nine hapless grorg hunters. We arranged our stools in a circle.

Silence enshrouded the ossuary.

It was time for the pièce de résistance.

Nullissa pulled the necessary ingredients from her satchel. A brand-new juicer, photorb light crackling off its funnel-shaped mouth and cylindrical housing; a set of gold chalices, festooned with filigree and engraved oak leaves; a gleaming cybersword, which at first I naïvely assumed would be used to slice the lotosbeans, but then the russet stains on the blade informed me of its real purpose.

Finally, of course, the crop itself, ten pink spheres torn from a secret seedling.

Guig grasped the juicer, holding it erect while Nullissa rolled all ten dreams into the mouth. Each encountered the inner workings with a crisp glushing sound, and as Guig carried the device to the center of the circle, the slosh of fresh apple-juice echoed outward.

Baptizer presented Urilla with the same lascivious wink he had used in the Spiritual Nostalgia Room. "You're certain you won't drink? Can't I tempt you?"

"We won't drink—but to prove our good intentions, we *shall* contribute our blood."

79

If I had my faults, Urilla had hers, a prime one being her cavalier attitude toward other people's blood. I fired off a glare that said, "Oh, we *shall*, shall we?" She retaliated with one that said, "We've got to play along."

Someone activated the cybersword, and with a low insectile hum it took to the air, hovering like Macbeth's famous hallucination, then racing to Baptizer's outstretched forearm. The blade sensed flesh, shot forward, sliced delicately. Baptizer withdrew his wounded arm, and the sword moved on, circling the grorg's stomach, bloodying each incubiber. When it reached Urilla, I was impressed not only by the nerviness with which she offered up her limb, but also by the impassivity with which she studied her mutilation. I did not attempt to match her, but instead submitted myself to the ordeal with sharp puppy-whines.

Now each incubiber in turn stumbled across the bony floor, leaned over the juicer, and let it claim thirty drops of blood. Urilla and I topped off the concoction. An entirely odd experience, combining as it did aspects of religious offering and of public urination.

While Guig drained the juicer into the chalices, filling them to their brims, Urilla and I slunk off. Exhausted from a night of dreams without sleep, I followed Urilla up the bone mountain. Pain screwed through muscles I didn't even know I owned. After reaching the summit, I sat down on a clump of backbones. My wound throbbed like an external heart. I studied the communion unfolding below.

Baptizer proposed a toast.

"To madness," he said.

"To madness," the Brotherhood chorused back.

"To sights never before seen," said Baptizer, tearing the patch from his eye.

"To sights never before seen," said the Brotherhood.

"To sounds never before heard."

"To sounds never before heard."

I expected Baptizer to solicit "smells never before smelled," but then I realized that the grorg had already provided the revelers with that particular staple.

Chalices sought each other out, met in pairs. Clank, clank, clank. Beads of blood shot from the incubibers' arms. The photorb flamed in the engraved leaves.

"Now drink, my friends!" Baptizer shouted. "Taste the descendant of the Vorka bean!"

Whereupon Nullissa blurted out, "The Vorka bean? The hell with that, Baptizer! You think I'm *insane?*" Before tossing her chalice aside, she inverted it. *Vinum sanguinis* splashed into the grorg's digestive juices with a burbling chemical commotion.

It was Vultzie who backed out next. Then Sprick. Guig. Tiamet and Bandar in perfect synchronization. Six chalices sat like ulcers in the stomach tissues. Only Baptizer's cup remained full and in hand.

"Cowards!" he screamed. "Slugs! You aren't Brothers of the Abyss, none of you! You're rabbits! Let me show you what the true sensualist does at the edge of the pit!"

Baptizer quit the brink.

The *vinum* flowed down his esophagus, into his stomach. His heart sent it into his brain. Dreamblind, he stared into space.

I found myself picturing the lotosbean's deceptively innocuous opening. The wind. The lawn. The goat-rider. The well. The hedge.

Urilla's diamond eyes pressed on my neck, and I turned.

"I love you," she said.

"I love you," I replied.

"It took us a long while to say that."

"I guess we needed the right setting," I said, gesturing toward an amorphous strand of protoplasm that dribbled from the top of the maw like a stalactite. "We needed the moonbeams."

"We needed the violins," said Urilla. "The lilacs."

We stretched out on the backbones and snuggled.

The habits of the incubibers, the horrors of *Carnage Pastorale*, the stench of the grorg—all the indignities of this long night, this ridiculous "party," evaporated the moment we realized that we had indeed picked up the trail of the deathtree, realized that Hamadryad was indeed the mother of *The Lier-in-Wait*. The evidence was incontestable. Tumbling off his pelvic girdle, Baptizer cried, "No key! No key! No key!"—frustration incarnate, voice ringing off the hard white slopes. Apparently even an incubiber has one he "loves best"; apparently even a Brother of the Abyss could project a person into the Well of Blood. Himself, perhaps?

Ten minutes later the final scene hit—the scene that my subconscious had never seen fit to release. Of the scene's actual content I gained no new knowledge, for what could I learn from Baptizer's behavior—his throes, his moans, his inevitable cries of "My only god is Goth, my only god is Goth!"—except the already established fact that *The Lier-in-Wait* had a denouement as fat with gooseflesh as it was thick with mystery?

Goth? Goth? Goth? Goth? Again I tried to remember, again I failed.

Baptizer had hoisted himself erect by the time Urilla and I were down the bone mountain. The dream, we saw, had left its mark.

Baptizer's eyes were sad, their fires banked. His gorilla face was green. Sweat bubbled up from his forehead and neck. His words had to squeeze past labored breathing and a tight throat.

"It would . . . appear that . . . this is the . . . apple . . . you seek."

"We warned you," said Urilla.

"It goes beyond the pale, doesn't it?" I asked.

"Several . . . pales." Gradually the pirate recovered his powers. "Your Hamadryad . . . offends me, critic. She . . . tasks me. True: I am of the Abyss, I have eluded Vorkan madness. But *humiliation* was committed here tonight, and such a sin must not go unpunished!"

Baptizer extracted a skull from the mountain, began gouging air out of the eye sockets. "The planter's name is Atropos," he growled. "Big, flinty bastard—what my mother used to call a bombproof codpiece." The idea of Baptizer Brown having a mother was something I could accommodate only in light of the information that she talked a lot about bombs and codpieces. "Tomorrow," he continued, "we have the big Closing Night Event, Zorcyst's *The Assemblage of Kristin*. Dream it, enjoy it, and then comes our visit to Hamadryad's keeper. Your job will be to listen. My job, to talk. To talk, scream, intimidate, threaten, scare. And when we go to leave, there will be something new in my sea chest, and it will either be Hamadryad's coordinates or Atropos's head!"

He kicked a stray chalice, turned to his clan, and called them vegetables.

After *Worm on a Razorblade* and *Carnage Pastorale* and the other outpourings of Nullissa's satchel, *The Assemblage of Kristin* was a total joy, start to finish.

> *The Assemblage of Kristin* (A.G. 792). 74 minutes. Weaver: Corbin Zorcyst. Sentimental fantasy about a group of strangers whose mutual memories trace to each one's owning an organ transplanted from Kristin, an adolescent cut down in the prime of life by a waftcar accident. During its transgalactic premiere at the Ganzir Cephapple Convention, *The Assemblage of Kristin* jerked over two kiloliters of tears. Not deep, not existential, but so touching it makes you say, "Yes, of course, *this* is what dreams are all about."

While Baptizer and his fellow blood-drinkers had chosen to flaunt their scandalous presence at the convention, moving right into the Hotel Anshar under their own names, our Mr. Atropos was evidently a more circumspect sort. "He's at the Moloch House," was the first thing Baptizer said to Urilla and me after we located him in the Spiritual Nostalgia Room, a feat we accomplished by looking for the table with the largest number of empty Wrath of Jehovah tumblers. "Follow me."

The pirate led us out of the Anshar and into a nocturnal plaza populated by wounded dogs and pregnant rats. The air was serrated. A broken fountain released water like a bronchitis victim coughing up sputum. Crossing the plaza, we went down a succession of streets that, if you worked it out, probably accommodated more saloons, bordellos, back alleys, crimes in progress, crimes in planning, and pornography emporiums than the laws of geometry allowed.

It seemed a first-rate opportunity to talk with Baptizer about the one thing in the galaxy we had in common, *The Lier-in-Wait*. Coming alongside him, I said, "So what are we to make of this Goth character?"

Baptizer's expression was an inkblot test; you could project anything you wanted into it: recognition, nonrecognition, paranoia, indifference.

"Goth?" He said the name slowly—but was his slowness born of caution or confusion?

"Near the end of the nightmare," I persisted, "you kept swearing that your only god was—"

"Goth?"

"Yes."

"What I know about Goth—-assuming I know anything at all—is not to be shared with *you*, critic."

Cryptic, cryptic. All right, brigand. I'll do my own remembering.

We came at last to a brick building, its sooty façade lit by the pathologically random blinking of a sign that said MOLOCH HOUSE. We entered against my better judgment.

Strewn across split-open sofas, kidnip addicts ruled the lobby. The desk clerk sat on a wooden stool, eyes glossy, breath thick with gin. He was somewhere between sleep and coma. As we stepped forward, tiny things with redundant legs disappeared under the mismatched rugs and warped wallpaper. "Hold your next entomology expedition at the Moloch House," Urilla whispered. "Ask about our group rates."

"Shut up," Baptizer whispered back, urging us toward a stairwell. "Room 314." Apparently no mental energy was to be wasted on the possibility of our using the ramshackle elevator car. It was clearly good only for executing defaulting boarders.

The stairs creaked. They smelled like Stomach One. But they got us there alive. Baptizer marched up to Room 314 and pounded on the door, lancing blisters made of paint and air. We waited. Nothing.

"I don't like this," Baptizer said. "We talked by vidiphone three hours ago."

Nothing.

The pirate took out a tractorgun, sucked up the lock. Seconds later the door swung into the room, a place of disconcerting darkness and the same odor I had smelled rising from the well in *The Lier-in-Wait*.

In all its media manifestations, the genre of horror has used one particular line to singularly chilling effect. I have so far found it in a play, a short story, a Terran movie, a Rossiter magic mushroom, and three cephapples. The line is "And then some idiot turned on the lights."

And then some idiot turned on the lights.

In the middle of the room lay a corpse. Not a conventional corpse, but a corpse with its throat slit open, a blood-sheathed corpse of the sort that SUPEREGO would have tried to censor.

The corpse was male and hulking, a "bombproof codpiece," in the words of Baptizer's mother. It was as naked as a peeled egg. Tearing a blanket from the bed, I covered the deceased planter as I had seen coroners do in several dozen police-procedural beans.

"Atropos?" I said.

"Atropos," Baptizer replied.

85

It was the first and last time I would see the pirate visibly perturbed by something other than *The Lier-in-Wait*.

The three of us now conducted a brisk, impromptu search of the room, putting on our gloves and randomly touching objects as if to confirm that they were not cephapple-generated mirages. Our modus operandi was as redundant as it was mindless. Baptizer would open a bureau drawer and close it, and then Urilla would open the same drawer and close it. Urilla would inspect a closet shelf, and then I would do likewise. A few minutes of this folderol convinced us that no clues to the deathtree's whereabouts would be found here; the murderer had stripped the room as completely as he or she had stripped Atropos.

"And so," I said, "once upon a time, in a crumbling room in a dirtbag hotel on the wrong side of town, the quest for the Unholy Grail came to an end." I turned to Baptizer, looking for some corroboration of my feeling that—thank God—we could finally stop trying to outwit Hamadryad.

"It takes more than one cul-de-sac to thwart a Brother of the Abyss," said the pirate. "If you really want to find this tree, it can still be done—with my help."

Urilla asked, "And exactly what price does your help fetch these days, sir?"

"Merely this—*I* get to run the battle. *I* direct the firebombing. Hamadryad dies by *my* hand, agreed?"

Urilla and I perused each other's eyes, finding nothing beyond confusion mixed with fear and suspicion.

Baptizer saw it, too.

"What do you know about noostrees, critic?" he asked. "Have you ever killed one? Have you ever *seen* one—a full-grown one, I mean?"

"No."

"They're just trees, of course—and then again they're something else. They're a spiteful species—they hate us. They never asked to be born, never wanted their ever-rooted, paralyzed existence. Their hearts pump acid. Their brains feed on sulfur.

Yes, Hamadryad is just a child now, but she'll be an adolescent by the time we reach Sabik—she'll cover a hydrasteroid eighty kilometers across, and God help the bastard who flies within reach of her limbs. To attack her successfully will require certain . . . skills."

Urilla made one more pointless search of the closet, returned to the corpse, spoke.

"There's a zeal in your eyes, Mr. Brown. You want revenge on Hamadryad more than you've ever wanted anything, am I right? You won't rest until she's run to earth and drained of sap. Very well—fine—we'll accept your help. Together we'll cleanse the galaxy of lotosbeans."

Baptizer smiled, showing teeth as black as ebony. "We'll need a ship. And somebody to fly it."

"Jonnie has a yacht," I said. *"Fleshpot."*

"Jonnie the piss siphon?"

"He's a harmless fellow," I said defensively. "I like being around him; he makes me glad I don't have him for a son."

"And besides," said Urilla, "we'd do well to keep this expedition in the family, so to speak." She pointed to the bundle on the floor. Blood had begun seeping through the blanket, forming a stain that looked like a landmass.

"Can this *Fleshpot* be outfitted for starhopping?" Baptizer asked.

"Very likely," I said. "And Jonnie himself comes cheap. All he wants is a chance to eat *The Lier-in-Wait.* That's what he *thinks* he wants."

"Tell me what happens when we get to Sabik," said Urilla.

"The piss siphon and I sample the plantations, one by one. Not an elegant strategy, not very efficient. I make just one claim for it: it will work."

Unanimity came quickly. We would not tell the police anything about the murder. Whoever was out to keep us from catching Hamadryad would clearly relish our becoming ensnarled in a web of red tape and *habeas corpus.* No one had seen us come. No one would see us go.

The Moloch House held one more *frisson*. As the anxiety caused by Atropos's murder reached my bladder, so that the organ took shape in my mind, I headed down the hall and into the bathroom. Starting toward the squatrocker, I passed near a sink in which brownish-black stains branched and re-branched like a river system. Above the sink was a mirror. Somebody had used the mirror for a writing tablet, his or her gloved hand for a pen, and Atropos's throat for an inkwell. Blood dribbled from thirty-three letters.

The letters made eight words. The words made one sentence:

AND GOTH SHALL REIGN FOR A MILLION YEARS.

PART TWO

6

Looking for Hamadryad

Thank God for psychic billiards. Or, to give credit where credit is due, thank William R. Wesgroot for psychic billiards. Had the good ship *Fleshpot* not come equipped with Dr. Wesgroot's remarkable invention, we would surely have gone as mad as Vorka victims during our long journey to the Sabik Hydrasteroid Belt.

While the game provided a margin of diversion sufficient to keep us from mutilating ourselves or engaging in regrettable sexual practices or talking to the walls or hearing the walls talk back, there was still plenty of boredom to go around. Boredom hovered about us like an unwanted relative. It haunted us like the specter in Zorcyst's *Tactics of the Wraith.*

Our copings were all in character.

Urilla, for example, began writing a draft of *Redemption of Things Past,* though it soon became obvious that her muse had deserted her somewhere between Zahrim's ionosphere and the gas planets. Many a time I entered our cabin to find crumpled spheres of paper littering the floor like the residue of a snowball fight and to hear Urilla say, "It's no good, Quinny! This trip is about as inspiring as *Carnage Pastorale!*"

Iggi and I used a team approach to boredom. We played chess, proved the existence of a Supreme Being, disproved the existence of a Supreme Being, invented a computer language consisting entirely of obscenities, and made an infinitely futile attempt to teach Basil the Cat to jump through a hoop.

As for Jonnie and Baptizer, when they weren't cheating each other at the psychic billiards table or drinking each other under it, they were incubibing. Even with rationing, their *vinum sanguinis* gave out a full month before we reached Sabik. Their dream-deprivation symptoms were severe. Pain, confusion, and blood-hunger clouded their eyes as they scurried around *Flesh-pot* like masochistic rats moving into a sinking ship.

Lilit's antidote for boredom was to draw a series of one-panel cartoons, all reflecting her chronic love for horror beans. A police cruiser approaches a hag-witch whose waftcar was evidently exceeding the speed limit, and the crone defends herself by saying, "I'm sorry, officer, but I have a child in the oven." Or a man, his mouth a mass of blood, lies writhing on the living room floor, flanked by a satiated-looking cat and an oblivious wife, who says, "What's the matter, dear, cat got your tongue?"

Lilit used Basil for her model.

"I'm concerned about those cartoons," I said to Urilla. "They're so morbid."

"Yes, but *Lilit's* not morbid, is she?"

"No."

"If she didn't *illustrate* her fantasies, she'd have to do something *else* with them."

"You're the psychobiologist."

"Give her more drawing paper, Quinny."

So I did. I gave her more drawing paper. I also gave her a cake. I made it myself.

The cake was a homely construction, the size and shape of

an electroderby. Its layers were awry, its candles were crooked, and its patchwork icing suggested a threadbare coat through which the wearer's skin could be glimpsed. The point here was not aesthetics, however; the point here was that Lilit was going to be fourteen, and one ought to do these things right.

I could tell that the notion of a birthday party embarrassed her, that she would just as soon we dropped the whole matter. Upon deliberation I decided to go through with it, birthday parties being something that a competent, responsible parent would arrange—a competent, responsible parent being something that I had not been feeling like lately. For all my misgivings, however, I refused to send her back to her mother. I refused to terminate the "lease." Despite her insults, despite her sweet-and-sour disposition, Lilit's presence was the main thing that made me happy in those days.

Everybody on board got an invitation, and everybody save Baptizer accepted. We fixed up the cocktail lounge with balloons and crepe paper, piled the merrily ribboned packages in the central crater, wheeled out the cake, and sang "Happy Birthday to You." Lilit failed to blow out all the candles in one puff, though I don't think she was trying very hard. Her score was ten out of fourteen. She got Jonnie, of all people, to help with the others.

Cautiously, as if they might be booby-trapped, Lilit unwrapped her presents. Her grin was tense with the obligatory happiness and mandatory gratitude of the situation.

Urilla gave Lilit a red silk scarf and a chronamulet—one of those technology-packed pendants that tell the time, the date, the temperature, and your fortune. Practical and pretty. A good choice. Lilit loosened her grin a notch.

Jonnie scraped the bottom of his cephapple barrel and came up with a mystery dream, *Wheat for the Reaper,* that he had not bothered to eat, knowing full well it would do nothing to relieve his craving for the *vinum sanguinis.* My own offering was a state-of-the-art vocalith machine that I had purchased back on Zahrim along with recordings by several singers whose popularity seemed intractable at the time. Not surprisingly, the strangest present came from Iggi, who, while the cake was being cut, announced that he wanted to share a riddle with Lilit. This turned out to be the famous conundrum that King Oedipus had successfully confronted several millennia ago. What walks on four legs in the morning, two at noon, and three in the evening? Lilit gave an answer of literal truth—planet Rabishu's celebrated Sphinx Beetle, denizen of a terrain whose solidity fluctuated with the passage of its sun and whose inhabitants were thus forced to predicate their mobility on varying configurations of limb. As my daughter contemplated and, finally, comprehended the classic solution—*Homo sapiens*—in all its metaphoric splendor, I could practically see her neurons grouping themselves into a new, fourteen-year-old level of cognitive organization.

Later, after the guests were gone, Lilit and I sat amid the joyous rubble, she toying with her vocalith machine, I batting the balloons around, both of us chatting. I was cheered and surprised not only by Lilit's willingness to talk, but also by the actual content of our rapport: the party itself, its buffoonish cake, its incongruous gifts. The vocalith machine was particularly popular, and my delight at her evident appreciation engendered in Lilit a corresponding delight that I in turn found highly satisfying. Our goodwill grew through endless reverberation.

"Iggi has been teaching me about natural selection." Lilit seemed not so much to occupy the crater as to flutter above it, lifted by her lighter-than-air bones. "He says there's a gene for whatever we do. A gene for fighting and one for talking and one for being unselfish. Does that mean everybody gave me those presents because they *had* to?"

"No, they wanted to."

"But if there's a gene for being unselfish—"

Flowering Judas, what was I doing neck-deep in the famous Biological Determinism Debate with a fourteen-year-old? I wished for a miracle—say, the entire faculty of Wendcraft

University materializing in the lounge, position papers in hand, or Jean-Jacques Rousseau himself strolling by, a presentation copy of *The Social Contract* under his arm. "Er . . . it seems to me that humans often end up doing things you wouldn't predict if all you had to go on was their genes. Things like writing poems and making phreneseeds and—"

"And giving birthday presents?"

"Yes. And giving birthday presents."

"So even *Jonnie* must like me."

Jonnie? I thought.

"I like *him*," Lilit continued. "Do you realize he *owns* this ship? He can *fly* it."

"Jonnie is . . . interesting." (Interesting. As all critics know, that is the most damning of faint praise.)

"Jonnie is *wonderful*."

"Well, well," I said, bent on changing the subject. "Fourteen. We should probably talk about that. Fourteen. We should really talk."

"Talk?"

"You know—fourteen. Talk. Menstruation."

"Menstruation?"

"Yes."

"What would you like to know about it?"

"Nothing. I mean, don't you have questions?" Looking up, I saw that the lounge's mirrored pillars were catching all this, so that nine different Quinjins were now making fools of themselves in front of nine different Lilits.

"I've been menstruating, as you put it, for three years now."

"Oh. Good. I mean, fine. I mean, I thought I should raise the issue."

"You sound like Mother. *Raise the issue*."

"I guess you miss Mother."

"The way I figure it, if you and she had never met, I wouldn't exist."

"Yes . . . or maybe you'd be somebody else," I said.

"So even with our . . . divorce"—she was stiffening again,

as if opening a new round of birthday presents—"even with that, I come out ahead."

"My divorce, not your divorce. It was between Talas and me."

"Yes, of *course* I miss her—only *she* would never have taken me to *Zero Gravity Werewolves* like you did—or the Barge of the Mad or a cephapple convention—or baked a cake—you're better than *she* is."

"Don't compare." To be perfectly honest, though, Lilit's remark pleased me. (You've done it, Quinjin! Respectful firmness pays off!) At least it pleased me until I saw a tear roll from her left eye.

"You're better, Father," she continued. "You're better," she sobbed.

And suddenly we were hugging, hugging with the wholly committed and unerotic passions of parent flesh against child flesh, hugging as I'd been wanting to hug her for four years, hugging with a conviction that said, me-to-her, *Yes, it's over for good, your mother will always be my ex-wife, but you'll never be my ex-daughter.*

"I'm not better, Lilit. I'm sorry. You don't need to say I'm better. I'm sorry. I'm not better. It's okay. *You're* better."

A shudder passed through Lilit's lighter-than-air bones. She sniffed the mucus back into her nose. A dollop stayed behind, drying, wrinkling her skin, telling me that someday even she would be old.

Exactly one year after we left Zahrim, the portal of Voodoo Vector 41 sidled onto the epic, oval viewport that dominated *Fleshpot*'s observation deck.

As befitting its occult function, the portal was weird. It looked to me like a sphincter muscle belonging to some huge, cosmologically desirable beast that ate chaos and excreted the Periodic Table of the Elements. At the center of a mandala made of jungjelly—that black, mysterious ooze laid down in certain geologic strata during the births of Terransector's more enigmatic planets—sat a hole exactly one kilometer in diameter. The hole would open, then close, then open, then close . . . Sneak your ship safely past this gateway, and the laws of starhopping would take over, hurtling you into the backyard of the Sabik system.

Getting on the intercom, Jonnie broadcast his opinion that we should go cocoon ourselves, and there was really no arguing the point. Failure to use a cocoon during a Voodoo Vector trip meant that you ended up looking like something the cat had declined to bring in.

Before the ninth century, interstellar spacecraft did not boast private cocoons. You put on your oxygen mask, shed your clothes, and joined your fellow passengers in a feet-first plunge into an immense vat of jungjelly.

Hugging Basil to my chest, I began a languid descent. Within minutes I was completely mired, totally blind, pleasantly warm, and, it would seem, as impervious to impingement as a tick in a mattress. I say "it would seem," because when the shock-wave came, bringing the annihilation of local time-space and leaving the Theory of Special Relativity in a shambles, the jelly was inevitably breached by strange particles, my body inevitably buffeted by supernatural winds. I needed all my strength to keep the terrified cat from clawing off his mask.

Vector 41 disgorged us.

I surfaced in time to see Lilit rising from the soup. She swam toward the edge of the vat. Lilit, my Lilit—innocent, unashamed, the thick, clinging jelly muting her fourteen years, turning her into the just-born child of a wise and fecund lake. The nereid gained the shore and vanished.

Baptizer, Urilla, and I had no difficulty agreeing that our base of operations should be Uggae, the one object in the Sabik Belt that was not a hydrasteroid but a genuine, inhabitable, oxygen-in-the-atmosphere, earth-on-the-surface, life-on-the-earth planet.

To keep our presence on this planet as unheralded as possible, we all moved into the Crazy Raven Inn, an antediluvian hotel situated a good hundred kilometers from the nearest population centers. Crumbling and unkempt, the Crazy Raven loomed above a lake of such dimensions that other planets would have been proud to call it a sea, a lake born of the union between a meteor crater and an underground stream, a lake named Rosamond. Money had obviously been no impediment to the Crazy Raven's construction, nor had taste. The dance floors were paved with gems; the Jolly Warlock Restaurant was a forest of basalt columns carved with concupiscent fauns; and in each of the eighty-two private suites, gilded, gloating wallpaper waged chromatic war on phosphorescent linen.

One look at the Crazy Raven's spaceport told you that the inn was in financial trouble. Other than *Fleshpot*, only a half-dozen ships, representing about twenty paying guests, were docked there. Stranded on an obscure, one-industry planet, the Crazy Raven seemed as purposeless as the circuitry on Iggi the Robot's face. Why, then, had the place been built? By tuning in some stray remarks at the Jolly Warlock's bar, I got a reasonably satisfactory answer. It seemed that, a few years earlier, a group of high-rolling entrepreneurs had decided to turn the Sabik Hydrasteroid Belt into a tourist trap. COME TO GIDIM-XUL, SEE HOW CEPHAPPLES ARE GROWN, SAMPLE THE MAJOR DREAMS OF TOMORROW. The idea died on the drawing board—which, unfortunately, is less than can be said for the Crazy Raven. The cornerstone was laid, the walls went up, and the inn began trapping not tourists but an unpredictable flux of recluses, refugees, exiles, expatriates, outlaws, outcasts, lunatics, hermits, and friendless faces with nowhere else to go.

And beyond the inn, beyond the lake: the City of Gidim-Xul.

Like any large and staggeringly profitable enterprise, the dreamweaver's art had certain inequities on its conscience. Gidim-Xul not only harbored these inequities but, through an accident of topography, actually seemed to satirize them, in the manner of a political cartoon. Sprawled at the feet of volcanic mountains were districts occupied by the city's working poor, the cephapple pickers, whose lives consisted of long, dreary hours commuting to the hydrasteroids and longer, drearier hours nurturing and harvesting dreams. Meanwhile, nestled in the sides of the mountains, overshadowing the pickers' houses, subordinating their psyches, were high-walled estates belonging to the Lords of the Industry, the planters. As luck and symbolism would have it, Gidim-Xul's third social stratum lived below both the picker districts and the planter mansions. The flotsams—for such was their self-explanatory name—had set up their shacks in great pits formed by the collapse of extinct volcanoes.

The flotsams were not unique to Gidim-Xul. Nearly every hydrasteroid belt in Terransector had lured its share of rootless wretches who came seeking work as pickers but instead found abjection, abasement, hopelessness, garbage, poverty, squalor, malnourishment, alcoholism, and the ash of bleak calderas. For those of us fighting to prevent another Vorka Massacre, however, the flotsams were neither parasites nor pariahs. Now that the search for Hamadryad had run afoul of a corpse, now that Atropos's murder was in the script, we had started placing strict quotas on the number of people we trusted. Of Gidim-Xul's three castes, only the flotsams would have more to gain by entering our employ than by stabbing us in our backs.

We began by loitering in the various saloons and bordellos that cluttered the flotsam neighborhoods, engaging the most likely barflies in card games. Seven Deadly Sins, dealer's choice. Our trip to the Walking Shadow Café is the one that has stayed with me—the one that, from the morass of trips, my memory has seized upon and turned into the quintessence. The flotsams we interviewed that night included a fifty-year-old retired prostitute named Abbie Veel; a laconic old kidnip addict whom everybody called Spike Hooter; and Moondial—just Moondial, folks—an adolescent boy whose face had been ravaged by pimples and dull razors.

The first big pot of the evening went to Baptizer. Spike Hooter's three Lechers and Abbie Veel's respective pairs of Sloths and Misers had succumbed to the pirate's four Gluttons. Raking in the chits, Baptizer asked, suddenly, "What's the most you've ever won in a night of Seven Deadly Sins?"

"Thirty veneers," said Spike Hooter.

"Sixty-five," bragged Abbie Veel.

"I know where you can get a hundred veneers for one cephalic apple," whispered Baptizer.

The three flotsams leaned forward, senses erect.

Reaching into his coat, the pirate pulled out a rolled map, unfurled it on the table. "So here's the belt—Uggae and her thousand farms." He placed his finger on a pentagram representing Gidim-Xul and began sliding it across an adjacent swarm of hydrasteroids. "Each dawn a convoy of space buses leaves the picker districts. The buses make a loop, dropping off work crews. They also drop off supplies."

"Crates filled with fertilizers and insecticides," I explained. Baptizer and I had our pitch down pat. "But sometimes one of those crates contains a stowaway. Understand? A *stowaway*."

"A stowaway," said Moondial lethargically. He was not one of your sharp-as-a-tack lads.

"So now you've smuggled yourself onto a plantation," said Baptizer, "and all you have to do is find a branch that's fruiting and pluck a sample bean."

"But stay awake," I said. "If you're caught in the act, the guards will assume you're a psychoparlor owner trying to reduce his costs."

"Noostree guards—a vile breed," said Baptizer, calling the kettle black. "Have you ever known one? They roam the gardens like hungry wolves, and their attention spans hold three words, no more: *shoot to kill*."

"They don't frighten me," said Moondial.

"That's not the end of it," I said. "Your helmet leaks—so you die of methane poisoning. Your magneclogs fail—so you zoom into the ionosphere. We mustn't forget the noostree's natural enemies. Venomous caterpillars. And wasps that would just as soon suck human blood as sap. We're painting a realistic picture because, if you're not a realist out there, you end up dead and you do us no good."

"*Piss* on those wasps," said Moondial.

Baptizer issued a black-toothed smile. "Statistics. Every flotsam we hire is assigned twenty farms. That's two thousand veneers if you meet your quotas. You won't find a better price for contraband dreams anywhere in the galaxy."

Abbie Veel told us that we were crazy.

Spike Hooter told us that he could make more money stealing cars.

Moondial told us that he would meet his quota before we knew what happened. "Twenty apples? Hell, I'll get you *fifty* by next month."

But such was not the boy's destiny. Rather, the boy's destiny was to botch his very first attempt to burgle a tree. A guard would shoot him in the back of the head—shoot him dead—while he was stealing a copy of a children's dream called *The Entirely Magical and Completely Wonderful Vegetable Patch.*

For the most part, however, our apple-smuggling ring worked like a cleverly designed and well-oiled engine. Day after day the dreams rolled in. The port of entry was the Crazy Raven's solarium, a fern-congested little room reminiscent of a noostree greenhouse. The odder the hour, the worse the weather, the more likely that a flotsam would appear with illicit fruit. Whoever was on duty—Urilla, Iggi, myself—took the apple, paid the thief, recorded the hydrasteroid number in the logbook, blotted out the corresponding farm on Baptizer's chart, and delivered the goods to a tester. These were golden days for Jonnie and Baptizer—a vacation, really, a dying-and-going-to-heaven. They stayed in bed around the clock, eating cephapples. Comedies and swashbucklers, I brought them. Spy thrillers and historical romances; murder mysteries and erotobeans; sometimes even an avant-garde effort bizarre enough to make their Sybaritic taste buds dance. They got to dream *Sea Changes* and *Falls the Shadow* and *Kron the Impaler* and *Man and Wife* and *The Worms Crawl Out* and *Hansel and Gretel Return to the Woods* and *Thuban Prime—Planet of Contrasts*.

But not *The Lier-in-Wait*.

Have you ever noticed that the things you most care about are also the things that give you the most trouble? Whether the object of your affection is an art, an idea, a pet, a parent, a mate, or a child, love always exacts its price. When not receiving booty, I spent my days at the Crazy Raven worrying about Lilit. In particular, I worried about her wanderlust, which I hoped was not a prelude to another kind of lust. Every afternoon she painted her teeth blue, left the inn grounds, and roamed Gidim-Xul in search of people her own age, boys especially. I could not blame her. For more than a year she had been carted around on a quest whose purpose was never entirely clear to her, and she had every right to break away. Unfortunately, the only sources of boys in Gidim-Xul were the pickers' hayseedy offspring and, worse, the ragamuffins of the flotsam neighborhoods. I toyed with the idea of enrolling Lilit in whatever passed on Uggae for a public education system, the better to keep track of her. I had tasted enough of the city, however, to assume—to *know*—that its high school was a hotbed of sin and mediocrity. In my mind I saw it all: the goonish students, the boorish teachers, the stultifying learningware, the badly lit hallways giving sanctuary to episodes of kidnip-chewing and impregnation.

I decided that Lilit would stick with Iggi's curriculum.

Enter Rudd Bruzbee, a lanky gamin nearly two years Lilit's senior. The pattern of dirt on his left cheek never varied. I thought it might be a skin graft. Were Rudd's parents pickers or flotsams? I never could remember, or care. In hanging around Lilit he could have only one goal.

"Worse things could happen to her," Urilla would insist

whenever I began speculating on Rudd's plans for Lilit's virginity. "Worse things happened to me when *I* was that age. She's not made of glass, you know. She can bounce—but she *can't* do without friends."

"Sure, sure," I would grump.

One morning Lilit and I actually discussed the matter, though not as successfully as the father and daughter had done in Hexclouter's instructional bean, *Coping with Your Adolescent.* We were engaged in a quotidian ritual, the best part of my day if not hers: breakfast on the inn's back veranda, an opulent, pier-supported affair jutting into Lake Rosamond. The sun was a bright stain on the gray clouds. Swift wedges of geese cut across the sky. Before us, the water stretched for several kilometers before disappearing into a fog so seemingly solid and permanent it should have been on the map.

"You see that lake out there?" said Lilit, using her fork as an index finger. A hunk of pancake dangled from the prongs. "Rudd and I sail on it. He built a houseboat."

"You're too young for . . . house."

"Don't worry, Father. We're not pumping in the bunk. I've still got my goddamned innocence."

"Oh," I said, smiling feebly and without volition.

"We're just friends. Not like Jonnie and me—I mean, not like it *should* be with Jonnie and me. But he just stays in his goddamned *room* all day."

My only response was "Jonnie, eh?" So—diagnosis confirmed. Lilit had a crush on my ridiculous friend. I knew I should accept this—Urilla and Hexclouter would want me to—but somehow I just couldn't.

"Tell me, how's the physics coming?" I asked. "Are you learning a lot from Iggi?"

"Physics," said Lilit, as if it were the name of an enemy. "Do you have to eat so *fast,* Father?"

"The so-called strong nuclear force is one of four basic interactions in the universe. Name the other three."

"Sex, hope, and gravity."

103

"If you can't take your studies seriously, little girl," I said with considerably more condescension than I had intended, "we can always put you in a *school*."

To which Lilit suddenly snapped, "I wish one of these days you would just leave me *alone*, Father, I really do."

"I *do* leave you alone." There was a bit too much firmness in my firm respectfulness. "More than most parents would. I leave you alone, and before I know it you're cruising around on some bacteria-ridden lake and"—my voice lurched toward a scream—"you go and get yourself infatuated with a blood-drinking—!"

"You know how much you understand about it, Father?" she screamed back. "*Tub of dung*, that's how much you understand about it!"

She flew out of her chair, rampaged across the veranda, and made a door-slamming departure. Two and a half pancakes festered in their syrup.

Painful and disturbing, our fight was also, I knew from Dr. Hexclouter, entirely typical, and besides instilling in me a mixture of anger, insecurity, sadness, self-pity, and guilt, it also had me recalling the best line from *Coping with Your Adolescent*: "It is easier for a grorg to pass through the eye of a needle than for the parent of a teenager to know peace of mind." Indeed, the following morning found Lilit and me sharing breakfast as if nothing had happened. We talked about physics and horror beans and the Crazy Raven and what Lilit wanted to be when she grew up. An artist, she said.

It was not yet time to open the wounds labeled HOUSEBOAT and JONNIE RONDO.

And the dreams kept rolling in.

Weeks passed, blurring into months. Baptizer and Jonnie tested a hundred apples, two hundred apples, three hundred, four hundred—and still more than half the belt remained unplundered.

The four hundred and fifty-first apple was brought by a

flotsam named Annie Stetch, a wizened woman who looked as if she spent her evenings stirring lizards' legs and owlets' wings into soups. "Hydrasteroid 888," Annie cackled as she pocketed her hundred veneers.

Routine, routine, boring, boring. I recorded the number in the log, erased the farm from the chart, and went upstairs. It was Baptizer's turn to test one. He yanked Annie's bean toward his mouth, punctured it with his incisors. A rivulet of juice disappeared into his beard.

"The taste is familiar," he said, "but is it the dream we want? What do you think, critic?"

"I wouldn't know."

Within the hour I knew. I was back in the solarium, buying fruit, when Boo Paesurely, proprietor of the Crazy Raven, rushed up making agitated noises and gestures. Boo was a pathologically shy young man who spoke only when spoken to and sometimes not even then; his agitation had been achieved with great effort. "Your friend," he said succinctly, cautiously, as if nearing his quota of words for the month. "That Baptizer Brown. He's out of control."

Together we left the solarium, and even before reaching the lobby I heard the telltale cries of "No key! No key!"

A circle had gathered. Jonnie, Lilit, Iggi, Urilla, and three drunks from the Jolly Warlock. In the center, Baptizer raged like an ambulant volcano. He staggered senselessly, knocking over chairs, crashing into urns filled with wild things from Lake Rosamond's swamps, turning the carpet into a decoupage of flowers, ferns, water, and shards. He was blind.

"No key!"

Whipping around suddenly, he steamed toward Lilit, who had the good, fourteen-year-old sense to get out of his way.

Then, to our collective dismay, we realized how the episode would end.

Baptizer spiraled toward the back veranda, and we all rushed out in time to see him hurtle belly-first into the balustrade. The impact sent his head pitching forward, his feet flying skyward. Flailing, falling, he bellowed his lotosbean catechism.

"My only god is Goth! My only—"

The splash seemed loud enough to drain Lake Rosamond. The spray sprinkled our faces.

"Goth!"

He did not drown. Once submerged, his body demonstrated a not unpredictable buoyancy, shooting to the surface and floating high.

Somehow Urilla and Jonnie got him to shore—tugboats towing a tanker.

I returned to the solarium. I consulted the log. I corroborated my recollection. Had Annie just come from Hydrasteroid 888? Yes, 888. We had finally flushed out our quarry. We had finally found the Unholy Grail.

Hamadryad was at bay.

7

Raid on a Dreamfarm

In a rare break with its usual starchy prose, the official handbook of the Terransector Navy notes that the sight of a vulcanbomber barreling out of the sky and landing is enough to make "plants wither from stress, animals die from shock, children faint from terror, and adults forget that they have ever been toilet-trained." When Boo Paesurely witnessed a vulcanbomber called *Dante* touching down at his inn's spaceport and *skreee*ing to a halt, he rushed into the Jolly Warlock emitting sounds that indeed suggested he would soon be requiring diapers.

Besides Urilla, Jonnie, and me, the restaurant's customers that afternoon included two bearded and seedy young men for whom the Crazy Raven was obviously a refuge from just deserts. Hearing the cries, everybody looked up—everybody except the bartender, who, over the years, had no doubt observed human behavior far stranger than Boo's. The seedy ones simply signaled each other through their respective beery fogs, probably something to the effect that they ought to go hide in their rooms. The rest of us followed Boo out of the Warlock, through the lobby, down a colonnade, onto the runway, and into the vicinity of an object that looked like a cross between a threshing machine and a pterodactyl.

For Urilla, Jonnie, and me, the vulcanbomber's arrival was considerably less surprising than it was for Boo. Five hours after Baptizer was fished out of the lake, he had stuffed himself into *Fleshpot*'s lifeboat and set off for Mulla-Xul, sister city to Gidim-Xul and "the illegal weapons capital of the galaxy." He had gone seeking illegal weapons and the personnel to operate them.

Every feature of *Dante*'s design—each fin and foil and turret and port—had evidently been included by virtue of its ability to frighten and depress the beholder. The vulcanbomber lay— no, *crouched*—on the runway barely five meters from *Fleshpot*'s docking bay, and in the valley between these two mountainous spacecraft I soon noticed Baptizer. His pressure suit gave his already bloated body the proportions of a grorg. His crash helmet had wings on it. Sealing the hatch, he swaggered toward us.

A lascivious wink for Urilla, then: "That Mulla-Xul, it's quite a town. Babylon with moving sidewalks. I could have traded the lifeboat for a goddamned *quark bomb* if I'd wanted." Baptizer gestured to the vulcanbomber as if he had given birth to it. "And *this* beauty is just our flagship. Tomorrow morning, when we reach 888, we'll be reinforced by twenty just like it."

"Flagship, eh?" snarled Boo with atypical extroversion. "Well, I don't want it *here*."

"Keep your nipples on, Paesurely. I'm merely picking up passengers. How about it, Dr. Aub? How about it, piss siphon? How about it, critic? You want to join the war?"

There were four simultaneous responses.

"Yes," said Urilla.

"No," said Jonnie.

"I'd rather eat *The Lier-in-Wait*," said I.

"What war?" said Boo Paesurely.

It might be assumed that my comparison between attacking Hamadryad and eating her fruit had put to rest any notion of my participating in the coming battle. But no. At dinner that night, Urilla kept bringing up the subject, mercilessly teasing my willingness to miss the adventure of a lifetime.

"I have to keep an eye on Lilit," I said.

Urilla asked how I expected to keep an eye on Lilit when she spent all day sailing around with Rudd Bruzbee. I snorted. Sensing a chink, Urilla battered away, piling on assertions to the effect that Iggi was entirely proficient at keeping an eye on Lilit, whereas *I* just made her nervous, then going in for the kill with insinuations that I was afraid to fight what she called "some silly bush."

Humiliation and anger welled up inside me, and I knew there was only one way out.

Dinner ended, Sabik went down, midnight came. A cool, thin drizzle bathed our faces as we stepped onto the runway and, with quite different degrees of enthusiasm, started toward the bomber; blurred by fog, the running lights winked at us, meshing with the stars and hydrasteroids over Gidim-Xul. Once on board, we watched Baptizer strip the ship for action. He tore out several banks of guns and instrumentation, declaring them irrelevant to a dreamfarm raid. Thus did he manage to fit his two passengers into a laser-cannon turret, a plastic bubble dripping from the bottom of the fuselage. The turret reeked of ancient sweat. Wads of cracked chewing gum hung on the seats. Urilla called the turret an airborne foxhole.

Baptizer fed the hydrasteroid's coordinates into a computer that had somehow survived his streamlining efforts, and minutes later *Dante* taxied down the runway and leaped into the star-pricked sky.

"We attack at dawn," the pirate said, a line I had last heard in *Uncharted Parsecs.* "The pickers and the guards won't have reported for work yet. It's my policy to kill innocent victims only when absolutely necessary." With Baptizer Brown, it was often impossible to tell when he was joking and when he was not. "Meanwhile," he added, "I suggest sleep."

He curled up in the cockpit, beneath a bright galaxy of compasses, altimeters, aileron switches, flap levers, and angle-of-attack indicators.

Nuzzling like puppies *in utero,* Urilla and I closed our eyes. Our pressure suits melted together. Our breathing synchronized. Within minutes my lover had slipped into dreams far more benign than those we were approaching.

The ride was smooth, soothing, but sleep was clearly the last condition in which I would be permitted to pass the night. My brain was far too preoccupied, not only with the physical discomfort of the airborne foxhole but also with the mental discomfort of knowing that tomorrow I might be murdered by a tree.

Dante hurtled beltward.

Given the option, I would at this point glue a hologram into each copy of these memoirs, for a hydrasteroid surmounted by a noostree is a spectacle not easily described. There is something gruesome, parasitic, carcinomatoid about the arrangement. The three adolescent farms that now appeared on *Dante*'s flatscreen monitor—each more than a hundred kilometers in circumference—reminded me of gigantic severed heads. To be precise, they were the heads of Gorgons, those mythological sisters of whom Medusa was the most famous. In this case, however, their scalps wriggled not with serpents but with branches—leafless, tentacular branches stirring the foggy climates of their host spheres.

Inside my body, it was morning. On Hydrasteroid 888, it was all times simultaneously. Kicking off the autopilot, Baptizer aimed the bomber toward an afternoon zone.

Urilla laid her palm on the screen, right beside the deathtree, and the contrast was striking indeed. Urilla's hand: five fingers, each delicate, ruly, clean. Selig's biotechnology: a million limbs, each knobby, twisted, polypous with fruit. I was mildly surprised that, monstrous as she was, Hamadryad ultimately looked no worse than her siblings. You can't judge a book by its cover.

We turned and headed for the sunlight, approaching, achieving, surpassing 888's spin. We descended, gravity tugging at our flesh.

The twenty mercenary vulcanbombers had arrived ahead of us. They buzzed around the hydrasteroid like ill-tempered dragonflies, harassing the northeast quadrisphere, giving off computerized screams. Hamadryad waved her Medusan locks.

Baptizer activated the transceiver and ordered his mercenaries to assume what he called "parquet formation." The bombers promptly lined up birds-on-a-fence fashion, then broke into four squadrons. Each squadron shot toward a different compass point, turned around, and hovered above 888. I was reminded of the kites that the corpses flew over the midnight graveyard in *The Necrophilia Waltz.*

Baptizer bellowed, "Attack!"—evidently one of his favorite words—followed by an equally zesty, "Flank speed!"

The bombers leaped forward, diving into the lowest ply of 888's misty-viscous atmosphere and excreting from their tails a green fluid that Baptizer called Lucifer's Drool. At the precise moment when the bombers crisscrossed, the descending streams of Drool burst into flames. Biblical violence: fire and brimstone.

The Drool lashed into the northeast quadrisphere, branding it with agonizing meridians and harrowing parallels. The branches writhed, spit sparks, tossed off bright orange comets. Overrunning their banks, the flaming rivers rushed toward each other, leaving in their wakes a charred and uninhabitable continent. Smoke billowed up, puffy and black, the cumulus clouds of hell. As our on-board sensecasters kicked in, we were rocked by the hydrocarbon-smell of Lucifer's Drool laced with the stench of burned xylem and boiled sap.

Having finished one successful strike, the mercenaries regrouped and did it all over again, slopping down death on the northwest quadrisphere, razing the whole terrain.

When they attempted to carry the battle into the south, however, Hamadryad was ready—was lying in wait—for them.

The tree curled in upon herself, twisting the pilots' orientation, beguiling them so they came in low. Too low. Before the Drool could be released, the tentacles—seductive, predatory serpents—sprang up and seized the bombers' fuselages. And I thought: Flowering Judas, what am I doing *here?* I could get *killed.* I tried to detach myself from the battle by pretending it was all a dreambean. *Vivid colors,* ran my mental notes. *Crisp pacing. Sledgehammer suspense.* Wait. Can suspense be like a sledgehammer? Oh hell, this won't work. It's real.

Goodness be praised: most of the ensnared bombers broke free.

Evil be damned: three did not; their missions were aborted in midair. Stronger than the bombers' thrusts—stronger, probably, than any biological force in the galaxy—the tentacles dismembered their prey, and a profusion of seats, instrument panels, Drool canisters, fuel tanks, cannons, spoilers, stabilizers, fins, flaps, ailerons, and engines tumbled into the sky.

Two of the pilots went down with their ships. Axe in hand, parachute blooming from his shoulders, the third pilot bailed out. A mistake. Had he stayed in his bomber, *Hephaestus* by name, death would have claimed him with compassionate speed. As it was, the hydrasteroid's winds sucked him into the branches. He chopped with his axe, swiftly, brutally, truly. Apples scattering, three severed limbs cartwheeled away. But now, as sap jetted from the throbbing stumps, a cluster of avenging limbs shot toward him. His bloody lips encircled a scream.

Baptizer told the autopilot to make *Dante* dive, and, while his intention was to bring us into the battle, the immediate effect was to fill the screen with a closeup of the entangled mercenary as the deathtree wrung him dry. The cockpit collected my groans, doubled their volume. While I witnessed this murder, my pity equaled my horror—yet both emotions disappeared abruptly when a new sensation arrived.

Oh God, oh Goth, let me be wrong.

I was not wrong. A force other than rocket-thrust now propelled our vulcanbomber.

Already I could hear sharp metallic crunchings, as if a grorg were chewing on a submarine. I felt faint. I was aware of a flurry of shapes and shadows, of red lights flashing, of emergency buzzers buzzing, of Urilla holding an axe and putting on a space helmet, of Baptizer barking orders. The next thing I knew, Urilla had gone and the pirate was hovering over me, head encased in a transplastic sphere. I was fairly certain that I was not dead. The noise of Hamadryad trying to tear *Dante* apart prevented anything remotely trivial from crossing my mind.

Baptizer snapped an oxygen tank onto my suit, shoved a regulator into my mouth, told me to breathe. He turned a valve—first on, then off. Springtime gushed into my lungs.

"If our fuselage gets punctured, you use this. The pressure change won't kill you, but the methane could. Understand, critic?"

"No," I replied, my tongue thrusting at the regulator. It fell out like a loose denture.

Baptizer treated this answer as if it had never existed. "There's a stick over there!" he shouted, pointing to an instrumentation rack located behind the pilot's seat. The words rattled around inside his space helmet. "Wait until I move my axe in a circle, then pull the stick like it will make you rich! The autopilot does the rest!"

"Where will you be?"

"Out kicking Hamadryad in the ass."

Studying the screen, I tried to grasp the exact nature of our predicament, but all I could see were the gray, glutinous whorls of 888's clouds. Then, suddenly, we zoomed into a more diaphanous region, and I gradually apprehended a fact so terrible I trembled and so baroque I laughed.

We were tethered to the tree. More than a dozen tentacles suckled our left airfoil. Yet we stayed in flight, spiraling crazily.

"Remember, critic," Baptizer called to me as he wedged himself into the airlock, "pull when I signal!"

I returned to the horror show on the screen. By dint of her magneclogs, Urilla stood upright on the trapped wing. Fiberfoil cords moored her to the fuselage. Cleaving fog, bark, and tissue with great sweeps of her axe, the Wonder Stepmother bled the tree of whatever strength it would have needed to haul the bomber out of the sky and dissect it. As *Dante* revolved, additional tentacles attacked, trying to gain purchase, but always they were cut down by the scything onslaught of the wing. Sap splattered everywhere, blotching Urilla's space helmet, drenching her pressure suit, trailing away in long green strings.

Now Baptizer joined the fight, and his gorilla strength soon completed most of the dismemberments that my lover had begun. As each limb was severed, the orphan half, a pulsing tangle of apples and arboreal muscle, stayed wrapped around the wing. Soon only one whole limb remained: warty, tenacious, vermicular.

Pivoting, Baptizer faced the portside camera, presuming to contact me with his eyes. He moved his axe in the agreed-upon circle. Flickering steel and gobs of sap arced across the screen.

I reached for the stick. My fingers curled around its bulbous handle.

Baptizer went for the final limb, found an open wound, applied his weapon. Again he chopped. And again. We were almost free. I was about to yank the stick when a particularly long and virile bough slithered up behind the pirate, shot forward, and coiled around his throat. Cephapple trees are normally plucked, but in this case Hamadryad did the plucking. She plucked Baptizer right off the wing. She plucked him like a ripe dream. Urilla saw the accident, ran to where Baptizer had been, but there was nothing she could do.

Still tethered, *Dante* kept moving in circles, so that every

114

few seconds, we flew past the plucked man. He flailed and kicked, but then, on the twelfth revolution, he merely dangled, executed, hanged unto death, his great simian tongue resting on his beard.

Turning her attention to the final limb, Urilla picked up the butchery where Baptizer had left it off. So frenzied was this climactic struggle, this orgiastic chaos of hacking blade and hemorrhaging bough, that my shock did not end even after onrushing billows of smoke threw everything into silhouette. Then, suddenly, like a rope used in a tug-of-war between Leviathan and Behemoth, the bough snapped apart in a shower of juice, dreambeans, xylem chips, and vegetative plasma.

The wing lurched free.

I pulled the stick.

Dante made a vertical ascent, retreating to safety, soon breaking completely with the hydrasteroid's pull. My weight slid from me like molten wax.

"Damn pirate!" Urilla exclaimed, tumbling out of the airlock.

Damn pirate. It was, somehow, the appropriate, the perfect, the *only* reaction one could have to the loss of a man like Baptizer. Neither of us felt much grief, of course, and pity was not a good word for our mood, either. What we really felt was a kind of bemused fatalism, a kind of "Oh yes, and then there's Death." Bad old Death. Death, who will employ without prejudice any of a hundred modes, from lingering and expected to—in Baptizer's case—quick and surprising.

We stood before the monitor like vulturine beneficiaries before a dying relative. Urilla stayed in her space helmet. She looked beautiful even under sap.

On the screen, the farm breathed its last, every quadrisphere a morass of smoke and flame. It seemed that Hydrasteroid 888 had become a small, planetless star.

Their job done, the mercenaries shot away from the fireball and headed for outer space.

"There's something wrong," I said. "That woman on the

Barge of the Mad, Marta Rem—she predicted that after the tree was killed, I would bear away a wondrous treasure. I have no treasure."

"What do you mean, 'no treasure'?" Urilla replied with disingenuous anger. "You have *me*, don't you?"

And so, after Urilla instructed the autopilot to take us back to Gidim-Xul, we used the airborne foxhole for what my daughter liked to call pumping in the bunk.

Because of the maimed wing, our touchdown at the Crazy Raven was the trajectile opposite of our takeoff from 888. Fuselage horizontal, retros gushing, *Dante* dropped straight out of the sky, settling onto the runway and rolling into the nearest bay. It all happened so quickly that Boo Paesurely didn't have time to become frightened or enraged. From my upside-down perch in the turret, I saw him advance a few meters into the spaceport, shield his eyes from the afternoon sun, scowl in our direction, and coordinate his arms into a definitive gesture of dismay.

We entered the lobby, two victorious warriors marching home. No crowds gathered, no throngs cheered. Lilit was probably on Lake Rosamond. Iggi was probably in the psychic billiards arcade. Jonnie was probably at one of the grubbier Gidim-Xul psychoparlors, ingesting an erotobean.

"I need a meal," said Urilla, starting for the Jolly Warlock.

"I need a drink," I said, following her. "Two drinks."

Once inside the Warlock, Urilla and I selected a table and launched into the ancient superstitious behavior of restaurant patrons, trying to exude whatever aura would catch the waiter's attention and convince him that we knew what we wanted. But the waiter just sat on the barstool, reading an electrozine printout.

Urilla was too pleased with herself to get angry at the waiter. "We did it, Quinny!" she warbled. "We're heroes, just like we said we'd be!"

"Yes," I replied quietly. I did not feel heroic. I felt nervous and exhausted and lucky to be alive.

I yawned. My eyelids crashed closed. And suddenly there he was. Baptizer. Baptizer the hanged man, screams whistling out of his black teeth, his deathdance playing over and over in my head like a loop of holofilm.

I cranked my eyes open. They settled on a large cylindrical object hanging above the bar. First came a fearsome spear-point, followed by a metal shank, followed by a small external pump, followed by a fiberglass pole. It occurred to me that, for all the many hours I had spent staring at the thing during my previous visits to the Warlock, I had never before bothered to realize that I did not know what the hell it was.

"A garden implement of some kind?" I asked, pointing. "A prop from a sword-and-sorcery play?"

"A grorg harpoon," Urilla replied in the voice she used when saying something indisputable. "Perhaps the very grorg harpoon that killed the beast in whom Baptizer staged his last dreambean party."

I was about to start a discussion of this piece of technology when a different piece of technology entered the place.

Iggi.

Because the robot had no stomach, his appearance here was puzzling. But the really odd phenomenon was his face. Lacking a full complement of muscles, robots of the genus *Pseudocortex* rarely wore unequivocal expressions. Yet, without saying a word, without making a gesture, Iggi broadcast a misery of the most abysmal degree.

"It's Lilit," he said.

Something detonated within me, accompanied by a knife-edge bleating of which I seemed to be the source. I was vaguely aware of Urilla saying, "She's hurt?"

"I think she ate a cephapple," Iggi replied. "I think she's in a trance."

I'm actually hearing this, I thought. It's really being said. There is nothing, no buffer, separating me from these words.

117

Between Urilla and me, only Urilla was capable of logic, sentences, questions. "She doesn't talk?"

"She doesn't talk—hardly. She just says the same thing over and over."

"What thing?" Urilla asked.

" 'My only god is Goth.' "

Urilla reached across the table, knocking over the salt and grabbing my shoulder. "She *couldn't* have eaten *The Lier-in-Wait*! We just incinerated the whole crop!"

"Yes," I gasped.

Then why was her only god Goth?

8

Murder by Art

We reached Lilit in what seemed like an indivisible instant, as if a voodoo vector linked the Jolly Warlock to the soundless, sunless beach where she lay. In truth, it must have taken us a good twenty minutes to leave the inn grounds, tramp through the woods, descend the cliff face, and arrive at one of the many lagoons that scalloped Lake Rosamond's eastern edge.

At first I did not see her. My awareness encompassed the lagoon, a vegetable soup of weeds and dark water. It encompassed Lilit's friend, Rudd Bruzbee—whimpering, twitching, stomping distraught figure-eights in the sand. And it encompassed Rudd's handbuilt houscboat, a hovel on a raft. The boat was moored to a tree stump. An antique internal-combustion engine clung to the transom.

Lilit was on the deck. Supine. Still. Suffused with the deathly serenity of the maiden floating down to Camelot in Pandriac's version of *The Lady of Shalott*. Dirt and fungus blotched the yellow threadworm parka she habitually wore when sailing with Rudd. Her eyes looked old, dim, rusted in place. Small wonder: their mental counterparts had recently seen a lifetime of bizarriana. She blinked in slow motion. Five seconds open, five closed, five open, five closed. Her lips twitched. Her thumbs trembled. But the worst symptom lay atop her head, where curls of a once-indisputable auburn had been bled and bleached into that tawdry bromide of fright, white hair.

"Lilit!"

Not surprisingly, my tottering cry failed to awaken her, and the kiss I placed on her forehead caused no fairy-tale resurrection. In moving toward her, however, my face was hit by short, rapid breaths. The breaths carried air but not words, no *help me*, no *Father*, no *Goth*. The air was good news: her brain would not starve. The aphasia was ominous: although the dream had ended, its effects had not. The Tree of Death possessed my daughter as surely as if one of its tentacles were wrapped around her neck.

I was about to double-check Lilit's respiration when Urilla guided me out of the way. Her versatile hands, so recently employed in fighting a noostree, now performed all those steps that this new crisis required: loosen clothes, take pulse, open airway, raise feet to channel blood toward brain. Urilla was the most clearheaded person I have ever known.

Hopping back onto the sand, I fidgeted uncontrollably, awaited the verdict. The peculiar thing was that, for all the morbidity and gloom crowding my brain, my thoughts centered on Hexclouter. Yes, Hexclouter, the endlessly glib Dr. Morris Hexclouter and his stupid *Coping with Your Adolescent* bean. All right, doctor. Let's see you handle *this* one. Let's see you cope with *my* adolescent. Let's see you cure a girl who's been shot with an arrow made of deathtree wood.

"I wish I could say it looked good, Quinny, but it doesn't. Lilit's no critic. She entered the apple in all innocence, unprepared. I suspect either frank neurological pathology or—no better—its mental equivalent." Suddenly Urilla changed shapes: scientist into friend. "Quinny, I'm so *sorry*."

It was, I realized, a triangular sorrow, embracing not only me and Lilit but also herself. Urilla's love for Lilit may not have been the frenzied, fretting, for-God's-sake-be-careful sort that was my special blood-parent franchise, but it was love all the same, no strings attached.

"This isn't my fault, is it?" moaned Iggi. "I keep thinking it's *my* fault."

Urilla caressed the robot's cheeks with a touch too subtle for his sensors. "You had no reason to suspect Lilit was playing near poison fruit," she said, voice splintering. "Hell, maybe *I'm* to blame. I took her to that goddamned *Necrophilia Waltz* show. She probably thought she could dream *anything*."

Rudd's fingers ensnared each other. "I *told* her not to do it. We were in our cave, and—"

"Your cave?"

"There's an island in that fog, a hidden island with a—like I was saying—with a cave. We always explore it, Lilit and me. And today, suddenly, there's a branch in the cave, all bristly with apples. One of them has a real gleam to it, an extra-ripe look. So Lilit says, 'I wonder what it could be?' And I say, 'Don't you dare!' and Lilit says, 'I'm going to eat it, you can't stop me!' "

I began dropping toward the sand, miscalculated, ended up kneeling in mud. The cold guck soaked through my pants, hit my skin. How hugely, unbelievably, it didn't matter.

"Let's get her out of here," said Urilla, transmuting back into a professional. "She needs warmth, tea, stimulation. I don't want her slipping into coma."

Coma. When you first hear the word *coma* in childhood, you instantly know it means something dreadful. *Homicide* could be a kind of polish. *Kidnapping* sounds almost comic. But *coma*.

"There's a hospital in Gidim-Xul," said Rudd. "They took out my appendix last year. A charity case, the doctor called it."

Why was Rudd talking about *that*? Couldn't things start making a *little* bit of sense?

"I told him to stuff my appendix up his—" Rudd's eyes were suddenly yoked in a stare that fell straight on Urilla. "She's going to be all right, isn't she?"

"Yes," Urilla replied. I scanned her face for conviction, found little. "But she won't go to any hospital, not if I can help it. They'll retain her in some ward, pump her full of some flashy new antipsychotic. Well, this isn't hebephrenia, it's not catatonia, and she's already *got* a drug in her."

"You're in charge," I muttered.

She smiled listlessly. A series of assured, efficient, typically Urilla procedures followed, with the result that my daughter now sat upright, propped against the cabin door, looking sick and somnambulistic but not particularly uncomfortable. "Lilit? Lilit? This is Urilla. We're taking you back to the inn."

What happened next jolted me to my feet, brought me to my daughter's side.

Laughter. Quite so—laughter, happy and vibrant, straight from Lilit's lips.

"It's Daddy!" I shouted. "You know—Father!"

The laughter kept going, overstaying its welcome, becoming at some undefined point a psychotic's cackle. "Her *father* is in a well," she gasped.

"Not anymore. I'm right here."

Her eyes immobilized me. "*You're* not anywhere. *You're* a dream. Don't try to trick her. She knows when she's dreaming. She knows whatever Lord Goth wants her to know. She knows—knows—*knows*—"

And then, as abruptly as it had arrived, the power of speech deserted her. Her skin acquired the texture of wet cheese, her eyes slammed shut, and I sensed she was not far from the coma of Urilla's worst fears.

Instantly the Wonder Stepmother went into action, monitoring Lilit's vital signs, confirming her light-reflex. Came the prognosis: we should not expect speech or mobility from Lilit for a long time.

The world seemed to spin around me, as if I were riding

the carousel I had created in the dreamweaving studio back at Wendcraft University. "This is all so confusing! How could Hamadryad be in two places at once?"

"Perhaps we've been misled." Urilla squeezed my hand until it hurt. "Perhaps we murdered *another* tree this morning."

An image rose up in my brain. *Dante*'s left wing. Severed tree limbs coiled around it. Cephapples studding the limbs. Cephapples by the dozen, each waiting to be turned into evidence of an unfathomable deception.

I felt lost to myself, lost and powerless and detached from my own actions. Jumping. I was out of the boat. Scrambling. I was atop the cliff. Running. I was on the grounds . . . near the spaceport . . . at the vulcanbomber. And then, with a mixture of curiosity and dread, I observed Quinjin the Critic performing the potentially suicidal act of plucking a cephapple, jamming it into his mouth, and bolting it down.

The bean carried me to a pristine suburban backyard. I did not want to be in a pristine suburban backyard. The bean turned me into a well-meaning chowderhead named Glitch. I did not want to be a well-meaning chowderhead named Glitch. The bean made me enact a series of efforts to construct a swimming pool, and after I had broken a lot of things and had other things spilled on me and fallen down many times, the whole benighted project climaxed with my drilling into a sewer pipe and showering half the neighborhood with sludge.

The dream ended.

I was still in the spaceport, lying beneath *Dante* and greeting with complete indifference the thought of my being run over by its landing gear. So—we had not eradicated *The Lier-in-Wait*. We had not even eradicated a horror bean of the sort incubibers used for their *vinum sanguinis*. We had, instead, eradicated a slapstick comedy, a slick, frivolous, obscenely insignificant slapstick comedy. I shall never forget the title, because it's the sort of fillip that shows how our existences are obviously being authored not by a solemn God Almighty but by a cosmic prankster with a merciless sense of symbolism. The crop we had killed by mistake was called *Fool's Paradise.*

Apart from my reaction to certain competently sentimental dreambeans, my adult life up until Lilit ate from the Tree of Death had included only two episodes of unrestrained weeping. Significantly, both involved her.

My divorce from Talas had caused the more recent of these episodes: tears wrung from my realization that Lilit would now be denied a central solace of my own childhood, namely, parents who habitually and joyfully and frequently *collaborated* in giving me pleasure. They bought me just the right sled for my ninth birthday, together.

And before the divorce: my very first experience with postadolescent weeping. By all the cringing clichés in the galaxy, there really are such things as tears of happiness! Lilit had been this ludicrous sack bulging from Talas's abdomen, and suddenly she was a newborn, shockingly complex baby, possessed of all those selective advantages, those thumbs and things, and aglow with an expression that seemed to say, "Where am I? The Milky Way? Fine! Let's get on with it!"

Now, as I watched over Lilit lying mindblasted in her bed at the Crazy Raven, my eyelids squeezed against each other, and the waters of old oceans again poured forth. These were not tears of mourning—superstitiously, I refused to cry tears of mourning, fearing they would somehow corroborate Lilit's insanity—but, rather, tears of an unutterable outrage. Outrage at Baptizer's apparent duplicity. Outrage at the devil-god to whom my daughter now prayed. Outrage at the Lier-in-Wait. Outrage at Clee Selig for inventing the cephapple. Outrage at Simon Kusk for discovering the Lotos Factor. Outrage at whoever would conceive a tree capable of striking down children.

Beyond noting my outrage, any honest account of my emotions at this point would have to include the word *guilt.* Rest assured that I shall not try to rationalize my myopia in bringing Lilit on the tree hunt. I shall not argue with those who call me a criminal for failing to see that any enterprise involving Baptizer Brown would eventually encompass doom. I shall merely note that, when my ego was hauled before the court of my conscience, when my dour internal prosecutor accused me of irresponsibility, when the judge sentenced me to live with myself for the rest of my life, I did not beg for mercy.

Kissing Lilit's juiceless hair, straightening her jaw, I perused the room. Nothing retained its intended neutrality; everything emanated corruption and decay. The bureau seemed in pain, the lamp malformed, the closet a breeding place for fungi, the rug covered with leprosy.

You shouldn't have criticized her blue teeth, I told myself.

Jonnie entered.

I did not want to see him, but he obviously wanted to see me. He had an agenda—hence the object slung over his shoulder, the grorg harpoon I had so recently contemplated in the Jolly Warlock.

"Urilla said you'd want me dead after hearing what I know about Hamadryad," he began. "She said you would ask me to fall on my sword."

Moving to the bed, he set the harpoon at Lilit's feet like an offering. Its weight grooved the mattress.

"The first thing you should understand," he said, "is that Baptizer promised to blow my head off—he kept showing me that tractorgun of his—if I ever told you where the real Hamadryad could be found. The second thing you should understand is that I would have told you anyway—let the bastard shoot me—if I had known anything evil was going to happen to your daughter. I would have come to you. Slipped you a letter. Something. Yes." He passed his hand above Lilit's trance-locked form.

Staring at the diseased rug, refusing to give him the comfort of my soft eyes, I told Jonnie to keep talking. "Baptizer's trigger finger is a bit stiff these days," I added in the tone I used when reading one of my more sarcastic reviews aloud. "You're in no danger."

The Nightcrawler blanched. "This mission you've set out on, Quinjin, it's not just a matter of tracking down some weird vegetable. There's a religion involved, and forces that won't bend to logic. What I know didn't hit me all at once. It's been a jigsaw puzzle made of jigsaw puzzles—I've had to put a lot of pieces together. But the voyage to this planet was long—*long*—and when the nights came, when Baptizer didn't get his blood-juice to drink, he turned to gin and kidnip, and eventually he was telling me things he didn't *mean* to be telling me. I'll put it simply. The Baptizer who went to that grorg-belly party was not the Baptizer who came back. The apple changed him. It turned him into some sort of religious fanatic. A Gothian, he called himself. He had finally seen God. I heard this a hundred times—God whose name is Goth. Yes, I know—he never let his conversion show, but it was there all the same, burning inside him, the flame of faith. And to protect Goth's tree, to keep the hiding place a secret—the underground continent, he called it—he was prepared to scheme and plan and betray and murder: all the skills he'd learned as a pirate. Yes—murder. That planter, of course. Atropos. A severed throat, as I heard it, followed by a message. *And Goth shall reign for a million years.* Dead men, you see, will not discuss the whereabouts of noostree plantations."

Moving toward the mirror over Lilit's dresser, Jonnie combed his red hair with his hand. "Next the plot calls for a wild-goose chase, so Baptizer starts hiring all those flotsams and sending them to look in all the wrong places. That was quite an act he put on for us in the lobby—pretending to have eaten *The Lier-in-Wait,* throwing himself into the lake. And then, at last, the grand finale, a vulcanbomber attack on a bogus crop."

"*Fool's Paradise,*" I said feebly. Stunned, shocked, flabber-gasted—I was all of these things and more.

"Clever title," said Jonnie. "But not as clever as Baptizer's idea of burning down the *Fool's Paradise* farm so you'd declare Hamadryad dead and abandon the hunt. The whole crazy charade would have worked, too—except that two little pieces of fate went against him. He didn't count on Lilit stumbling into Hamadryad's lair. And, of course, he didn't count on getting lynched by *Fool's Paradise*, did he now?" Jonnie issued a modest little *heh-heh-heh* that somehow managed to convey all of his vast, hard-earned hatred for Baptizer Brown.

It is difficult to describe my reaction to these revelations. I felt mouth-deep in a kind of tar—Baptizer's lies, black and thick—and I was sinking fast, swallowing hot gouts. *Atropos murdered by the same man who had led us to his corpse . . . Hamadryad thriving under our very feet . . . Baptizer a religious fanatic . . . a Gothian . . . a guardian of the death-tree!* (If the apple could warp a man like Baptizer so dramatically, what would it ultimately do to Lilit?) But then I saw Jonnie approach the bed again, saw him lift wisps of Lilit's hair and let them swim across his fingers, and I knew that beneath the tar, beyond the miasma, lay the possibility of action.

"An underground continent, did you say?"

"Apparently there's as much surface area as a hydrasteroid," Jonnie replied. "*More.* The right gases, too. Heat. Light. Moisture. Nutrients. Everything you need in a dreamfarm, plus invisibility. Believe me, if there'd been any hint that this girl was going to find the place, get into trouble, believe me, I would have told you everything. I'm not the child you think. I would have—"

"You already said that," I rasped. "You don't need to keep saying that."

Now Jonnie picked up the grorg harpoon, patted its backward-hooking barbs. "So the hunt goes on. Still in her adolescence, and already Hamadryad is . . . what did Baptizer keep calling her? The Grendel's Dam of noostrees! We must find Lilit's secret cave. Our vulcanbomber won't fit through the entrance, but that's all right; we can attack the bitch from the ground." He presented me with the weapon. "It's a matter of getting down into the continent, you see. We'll make our way to the trunk, dig away the earth, expose the taproot." My brain seemed wired to Jonnie's, telling him what to say. "And then, with the help of that needle, we'll feed Hamadryad enough belladonna-29 to drop a *herd* of grorgs."

So, once again, Marta Rem's prophecy had a chance to come true. What might it be, this treasure that I would bear away from Hamadryad's corpse? A medicine for Lilit's madness? Nothing less would be worth calling a treasure.

I kissed the weapon's cold metal shank. Lovely prickles rose along my neck. My heart changed modes—faster, stronger. A spectral power surged through me—the angry, conglomerated ghosts of all the creatures ever pierced by the barbs. Quickly the room began to heal itself. The bureau grew content, the lamp became normal, the rug was cured. In all of history, I thought, past, present, or future, no revenge will prove sweeter. Baptizer's campaign against Hamadryad may have been as false as a cephapple dream, but *my* hatred is real.

It is realer than real.

9

The Straw Boss

We were entombed by fog. It was one of those choking, melodramatic fogs that literal-minded weavers used to haul into a dream whenever it seemed to need more atmosphere. As Rudd Bruzbee's houseboat—an outright gift, so guilty did he feel over Lilit's accident—cut through the fog's soft contours and misty cowlicks, I found myself respecting and even admiring whoever had decided to conceal Hamadryad beneath planet Uggae. If the cave we sought was really the only entrance to the deathtree's lair, then her proprietors had indeed been justified in believing she would reach adulthood unmolested.

Leaning out of the deckhouse window, Iggi peered ahead and concentrated on the radar scopes behind his eyes. "A bit to starboard now!" he would tell Jonnie upon sensing a rock or a bird or a particularly palpable fog mass. "Straighten her out!" Meanwhile, I sat atop our piled-up gear—canteens, photorbs, sleepods, evaporridge, vitamins, ropes, shovels, vials of belladonna-29—and fretted about Urilla's absence. The motor sounded on the verge of death.

When I asked her to remain at the Crazy Raven and take care of Lilit, Urilla had, of course, protested extravagantly. She thirsted for Hamadryad's sap almost as much as I. But in the end, logic prevailed. With her background in psychobiology, she was a more qualified nurse, doctor, therapist, friend, and guardian angel than any of the rest of us.

At last we broke free of the fog, and Lilit's island appeared, a great craggy wart blemishing Rosamond's skin. Waves slapped the rocky shore. The dawn air smelled of aquatic flora and fauna. Iggi steered us into a cove, landed us on a swatch of beach.

Three hills peered above a green, wanton jungle. The farthest hill, Rudd had assured us, harbored the gateway to the underground continent. Progress, then. Enemy stronghold within view. I experienced a sudden calm, as if a severe nausea had abruptly lifted its thick, insistent thumb from my stomach. Prepare to render up your treasure, Hamadryad! I jumped onto the sand, charged forward. Prepare to yield my daughter's cure! Your executioner comes!

The sun rose.

Zliptt, zliptt, zliptt, sang Jonnie's sword as he slaughtered the underbrush that stood between us and the third hill. *Zliptt,* and a huge exotic flower was decapitated. *Zliptt,* and a great broad leaf took off like some organic kite. *Zliptt.*

Behind Jonnie walked Iggi, whose grease-and-steel muscles had enabled him to shoulder the majority of our provisions. The grorg harpoon seesawed on his pack like a yoke.

I brought up the rear, my pack rattling with a photorb, a canteen, and a belladonna vial, nothing more. For the moment my principal contribution to the expedition lay in my willingness to consult Lilit's chronamulet—her fourteenth-birthday present from Urilla—and announce the time whenever anyone asked. The chronamulet was slung around my neck, and as we trudged forward it rapped against my breastbone as if seeking entrance.

Zliptt, zliptt.

Rudd had mentioned the third hill's resemblance to a human face, but he had failed to prepare me for its expression. It was not my writer's imagination, not a mirage spawned by the hot sun, but hard topographic truth that made the hill smile: below brows that were bluffs, eyeballs that were boulders, and bristly nostrils that were birds' nests, stretched a great, grinning, crescent-shaped hole. I entered far more willingly than I had entered that other huge mouth—the grorg's—back on Zahrim. Swallowed, we walked forward.

Steering around stalagmites, ducking to avoid stalactites, I was put in mind of a plot gimmick beloved of weavers who specialized in science fiction. This was the famous homunculus device: a human being is shrunk to the size of a beetle, the better to perform some feat of surgery, espionage, or revenge. Just now I seemed to be inserted into a parody of this genre, cast as a miniaturized dentist crawling amid a patient's molars.

The cave constricted, became a tunnel. Its floor slanted fiercely, carrying us below the lake bed. Our descent was a battle against unwanted momentum. Planet Uggae's gravity and the tunnel's outcroppings repeatedly conspired to bark our shins. Brutish winds attacked. Gloom enclosed us like black cotton; we countered with photorbs. I could perhaps evoke the essential unpleasantness of this phase of our journey by printing the script of a Wexel McPoon avant-garde dream over and over in small type for the next fifty pages.

Until her corruption, of course, Lilit had faced these same hostilities with enthusiasm, brio, and a sharply honed sense of adventure. Where, I wondered, had she obtained such qualities? Not from me, certainly. And Talas's genes were all fussy little creatures who loved good weather. Obviously my daughter had unexpected potentialities, unguessed strengths, emergent properties. Or so I hoped.

As morning blurred toward noon, two good things happened. The tunnel floor leveled off. And Jonnie—Jonnie the incubiber who had decided to grow up, Jonnie who seemed to be maturing a whole month's worth for each passing minute, Jonnie with the sword in his hand—cried, "I see her!"

We ran.

Bumpy with dreams, the branch lolled out of the darkness like a grorg's tongue. It was fat and gray. I gauged the diameter to be at least one meter. The apples were as regularly spaced as a sow's nipples, so I had no difficulty telling where Lilit's attacker had once swung. The stem was black. I tore it away, threw it on the ground. Hamadryad shivered and lay still.

"Well, Jonnie," I said, pointing to a particularly red and juicy illusion, "here's your big chance. At long last you can eat *The Lier-in-Wait*."

"I have lost my appetite for Hamadryad," he replied wearily. Back to the chase.

The tunnel is narrowing: that was how I initially explained my claustrophobia. A context error. In fact, the branch was getting fatter. Moving against its taper, I began to worry that it would soon plug the tunnel completely, locking us in a cul-de-sac, marooning us many kilometers from the vulnerable taproot. The branch assumed the girth of a sequoia . . . of a giant bladderwood . . . of a sperm whale . . . of a grorg.

"Halt!"

When Jonnie cried out, Lilit's chronamulet was tolling the midday hour. *Clong,* it tolled. And *clong,* and *clong*—twelve times altogether, planet Uggae's period of rotation being so close to Earth's that hand-me-down calibrations were the rule.

Iggi and I drew alongside Jonnie and peered forward, whereupon the wisdom of his "Halt!" became clear.

The ground was gone. Before us stretched an oceanic pit. Arcing abruptly, Hamadryad's branch descended into a darkness our photorbs could not fathom.

My first reaction was a kind of retroactive terror for Lilit.

Only raw luck had prevented her and Rudd from pursuing their explorations to this point; in my mind I saw them neglecting to note the brink, falling, screaming toward certain death. My second reaction was to kick a loose stone into the pit and ask, "Now what? Are we stranded?"

Jonnie answered by scrambling up the monster's side. The numerous gnarls made superb footholds, and he gained the summit in less than a minute.

Now Iggi began climbing the branch.

And finally—after two false starts and several volumes of advice from my friends—I, too, stood atop Hamadryad.

Reaching out of the warm, rubbery bark, penetrating our boots, the deathtree's energies entered us. We could feel the heat of her sap, the surge and thump of her vessels, the electric buzz of her nerves. Turning our photorbs to maximum intensity, so that we did not dare look into their centers for fear of retinal burns, we started along Hamadryad in a single-file procession.

Life improved. With every step we took, the winds grew calmer, the air warmer. The darkness lost its depth, surrendering to our lamps. Tiny yellow birds cheeped sweetly. Best of all, the downward curve of the branch became gradual and even graceful: as long as the deathtree failed to sense our presence, we would not be cast into the abyss.

Six hours after our ascent of the branch, it revealed itself as a mere tributary in the general scheme of things, melding with a much larger limb. At the juncture lay a broad delta of bark, and it was here that we decided to bivouac. Although he did not number sleep among his psychobiological needs, Iggi agreed to pitch the tent. Within minutes the white cloth pyramid protruded from Hamadryad like a cocoon on a tree of more orthodox scope.

Jonnie and I slithered into our sleepods, closed our eyes. Silence pressed down on our camp. For the first time in months, my recurrent nightmare came. "You will never fathom my lotosbean, sleeper," said the Lier-in-Wait. "You will never free your daughter from my dream," insisted the remorseless mirage.

Why is the mind so cruel to itself?

The next several days were so uniform and devoid of surprise, they seemed stamped out by a machine. When Lilit's chronamulet said it was day, we journeyed down a limb. When the chronamulet said night, we camped. The deathtree's extremities continued to flow into each other. Every time we thought we were on a mainstream bough that would take us right to the trunk, it proved to be just another estuary. We feared that we were caught in a maze.

One fact, and one fact alone, maintained our *esprit de corps*. It was this: we were moving toward a light. Not a bright, religious light. At first simply an amber haze, a yesterday's dream of the sun. But the glow increased with each passing hour, convincing us that we had finally eluded the geographic tautologies of the continent. We rejoiced that Hamadryad's dark crown was forever behind us, packed our photorbs away, and continued.

There are places in the galaxy known as tropical paradises. Queen Hamadryad reigned over a tropical hell. On all sides, the deathtree's minor branches reached for a stone sky, an aspiration thwarted by great knobby vines. Flowers bloomed along the vines, flowers that were faces, faces mutilated by pain and defective genes. The vines undulated like cilia on a giant paramecium. True to her species, Hamadryad had no leaves, but her limbs did not want for chlorophyll. Moss cloaked them, green peltlike masses that I initially assumed were an extrinsic blight. I looked closer. The moss came from the limbs' own xylem, spilling through cracks in the bark and swaddling the lotosbeans as a living, intelligent nest might swaddle eggs.

Hamadryad: the one-tree jungle.

The bough on which we now walked was so vast that its true dimensions were accessible to my mind but not to my eye. It was an airstrip for space arks. It was a cylindrical world-let, complete with horizons. It was a great cosmic duct, the plumbing of the empyrean.

Explorers in a savage country, we tried to civilize it with names. On our left, sheer black cliffs rose behind the mesh of Hamadryad's twigs and vines, and before long we were blithely calling this feature Cronus Crags, as if some map had told us to. Eden Mire was our cynical name for the swampland that stretched to the right and passed beyond our vision in a blur of mud and underbrush. A river cut through Eden Mire: a wide, sinuous, bile-dark channel whose ingredients I could only guess at. Water? Sap? Leaking juice and dead-animal blood congealed into a *vinum sanguinis*? Harvested by their own weight, hundreds of lotosbeans floated on the surface, and we knew that only the name Lethe—the River of For-getfulness—would do.

We decreed a compass. By fiat, Cronus Crags lay to the north. In consequence the River Lethe ran west to east. As for south, that was the domain not only of Eden Mire but also of the light.

Even as I write these memoirs, I am not sure how large the flaming gasball was, or why it glowed, or what kept it in the air. I know only that we called it Gishbar, an ancient fire god. Hanging above us like a stopped comet, Gishbar turned Hamadryad's lair into a world of nocturnal sun.

That particular evening, nothing under the nocturnal sun seemed new. The chronamulet said 22:00:00, and our stiff muscles corroborated. Iggi pitched the tent. Jonnie dueled vines with his sword. The Lethe gurgled. So far, there was little to distinguish this night from the dozen that had gone before.

At some point in our trek down the great bough, Jonnie and I had discovered that sleeping in the moss was a pleasure comparable to aquacots and peltbass swimming pools. We had long since tossed our sleepods into the river. Locating a likely wad of the stuff on a lateral branch, I began rolling it into a ball, much as children roll snow to make snowmen. I did not get far. Embedded in the moss was a person.

Uncertain whether I had discovered friend, foe, or lotos-bean-gobbling lunatic, I summoned Jonnie and Iggi.

"So—I am found," said the man, pawing free like a chick fumbling out of an egg. His voice would have sounded considerably less strange coming from a puppet.

"*Who* have we found?" asked Jonnie.

"The straw boss," said the man. "I was asleep," he added.

"Sorry," said Iggi.

"You did me a favor. I was having a terrible dream. A *regular* terrible dream, I mean. Not—" He pointed to a nearby cluster of *Lier-in-Wait*s.

We nodded knowingly.

The straw boss pulled himself erect, but this did not come to much. He was short, lean, gibbonlike. His face looked stepped on, but was an otherwise pleasing assortment of gentle eyes, thin lips, delicate nostrils, and feathery brows. If he owned a razor or a sewing needle, he had long ago forgotten where he had put them, so scraggly was his beard and tattered his threadworm parka. Bits of moss sprouted from his hair, shoulders, palms, and knees.

"Are you looking for work?" squeaked the straw boss. "Forget it. I'd have gone home long ago, except in my case home is a runty little cottage with a leaking roof and a wife who never loses an argument, and furthermore the landlord hates my insides. So I've exiled myself. It's a better life here than I had above ground, much better. The river is full of food."

"No," I replied, leaping over the autobiography to retrieve his initial question. "We don't want work."

"If you're not flotsams, then what are you? Spies? Well, you go back to Gidim-Xul and you find Atropos, Number 2703 Primrose Lane. Say you heard it straight from Flick Long-slapper, because that's who you're hearing it straight from. Everything's going to hell, that's what you tell Atropos.

Hamadryad will grow up, but there's no one to harvest her. And if Atropos and his weaver friend don't like the situation, they can climb down here and pick the crop themselves!"

"Atropos is dead," I said.

Flick Longslapper invested huge stores of energy in squelching a smile. It was like watching somebody trying not to sneeze. Eventually he gave in, and his handsome teeth burst forth like burnished jewels. "Dead? Really? Dead? Well, well, well. Dead." Slowly the smile began shutting down, and his more customary suspicion-*cum*-bemusement returned. "If there's no more Atropos, then why are you—?"

Straight out, Jonnie said, "We've come to kill Hamadryad."

An entirely understandable blend of confusion and outrage spread across Flick's face. After all, the deathtree was this hermit's home, his world, and here we were casually proposing to destroy it—but then I told him the story of Lilit eating the apple, told it with all the feeling and righteousness in my vocabulary, told it with sobs.

"So it's *revenge* you're after" was Flick's first response.

"Revenge," I said, "and more. As long as Hamadryad lives, the whole galaxy is under her shadow. And more yet . . ." I told Flick of Marta Rem's claim that Hamadryad guarded a treasure. I confessed my hope that the treasure would be Lilit's cure.

"Give me a minute," said the straw boss.

The minute was lengthy. Syrup descended from a cold bottle. Snails crawled across paste.

The weight of moral choicemaking seemed to push little Flick even closer to the ground. "It's *right* what you're doing," he said at last. "This crop—good God, yes—a wicked thing, wicked. But if you're really intending to *kill* the beast, you'll have to know her powers of mind—know them as *I* do. You're going to *need* me, sirs."

Déjà vu. Baptizer Brown talking up his expertise so he could lead us astray.

There was a difference, though. Brown had frightened me

137

from the minute I met him. Flick, with his wispy physique and falsetto voice, could not have spooked a goose. Vulnerable, cautious, dwarfish, high-strung, ethereal Flick. But was he also honest? Should we trust him? No way to tell. As with my decision to eat *The Lier-in-Wait*, I would simply have to dive in and hope for the best.

All I said was "Welcome."

"You'll be glad of me," answered the straw boss. Reaching out, plucking a copy of *The Lier-in-Wait*, he passed it under our noses like a physician applying smelling salts. "There are bad doings down this river, sirs. Have you ever dreamt one of these?"

"Yes."

"Then please know that the real nightmare is still to come."

10

Bad Doings on the River Lethe

The River Lethe did not invite navigation. Its shallows were gummy and choked with dreams. Its depths wound between a Scylla of jagged rocks and a Charybdis of rapids. Its sandbars looked completely unprincipled. But when Flick pointed out that the currents would be with us, when he calculated that we might easily double our overland speed, I asked Iggi to start drawing up plans for a raft.

A catamaran would be feasible, he concluded. Get lots of reeds, he advised. Bundle them up, he instructed. Lash the bundles together with vines, he elaborated, and you've got yourself a hull.

So we did.

The same procedure gave us the second hull.

Next Iggi had us make a lateen sail from bark. We hung it on an A-frame mast supported by shrouds, forestays, and backstays of vegetable fiber. Decking, leeboards, sternpost, rudder, tiller: noostree wood served for all of these. With images of last month's fight against the false dreamfarm still vivid in our minds, we knew that plundering live branches for the needed planks would be sheer insanity. Fortunately, so many dead ones clogged the river that we did not have to risk Hamadryad's wrath. We fished them out, smoothed them down, fitted them into Iggi's design. Thus did our enemy make generous contributions to the campaign against her.

The deckhouse was a hut snuggled under the A-frame, its roof a checkerboard of bamboo mats. Our emergency skiff was a hollowed-out limb. And for aesthetics, a couple of wooden figureheads, one lashed to each bowsprit. Jonnie sculpted them with his sword. They looked like his android trollops.

When the raft was finished, we assaulted the portside hull with a transplastic canteen containing Lethe waters and coffee. We christened her the *Amaranth*. Amaranth: the flower that never fades. Our *Amaranth* drifted down the Lethe at fifteen kilometers per hour, a towline of braided moss leading from the sternpost to the skiff; the tiny boat cleaved to our wake like an imprinted duckling.

Bound for a violent and unwaning sun, we fell on dog days that lasted through their nights. Heat . . . heat . . . heat. Gishbar stuffed its fire down our throats, scraped its flame against our skins, lashed its glare across our eyes. The deckhouse proved the best defense, the shade of its interior compensating twice over for the inconvenience it caused when you wanted to go fore or aft. For additional relief, a swim in the Lethe served well. We had to keep our mouths closed, though. We had to be careful not to inoculate ourselves with *The Lier-in-Wait*.

I did not expect to appreciate Flick Longslapper. After all, how could there be any common ground between an art critic like myself and a man who had spent his life mewling at cephapple pickers and wondering whether there was enough fertilizer on *The Million Year Foreplay*? Imagine my comeuppance when Flick turned out to be as adept in the history and analysis of dreambeans as he was in their care and feeding.

Flowering Judas, he'd even identified *Known Quantities* as the masterstroke of the decade!

The *Amaranth* had been waterborne a whole week before I finally dared to ask Flick what he had meant by the "bad doings" that lay downriver. "Who does the bad doings?" I said. "Animals? Humans?"

"I suppose there's still something vaguely human about them," Flick replied in his puppet voice. He stood on the foredeck, sweat glistening on his bare chest like bits of embedded glass. "They used to be my pickers, only now they're addicted to the bean, and you have to look closely to believe they were ever the same species as you or I. We kept expecting Atropos, you see, and he kept not coming, and all that waiting unraveled our nerves. But the tree had to be tended around the clock, that's what Atropos demanded. Get caught sneaking back to Gidim-Xul for some gin or a bit of romance"—Flick opened his throat with the blade of his index finger—"*skleech*, you're out of a job. At first I thought Atropos had some sort of fortune tied up in the original seed, and he was bullying us because he feared for his investment. But then I realized that Atropos's *real* fear was what his partner would do to him if the tree proved unproductive."

"His partner," I echoed. "Hamadryad's weaver?"

A nod.

"Do you know who that is?" I asked.

"I've never had a hint, unless you call the . . . the . . . *anxiety* he obviously aroused in Atropos a hint. You can see the situation. A sick tree, a failed crop, and Atropos might as well start notifying his own next of kin." Flick's long left arm uncoiled, pointed to port and the great bough. "So here we are on the farm, and the yield is fantastic. What *happened* to the bastard, anyway?"

"A pirate named Baptizer Brown ate *The Lier-in Wait* and went insane. He took a knife to your planter."

"Yes, that's what Hamadryad will do to you, all right. Lucky for me I've never had the courage to try her. Can you imagine?

The pickers wanted me to join their cult! Even after it was plain to anybody with half an eye that once you get hooked on lotosbeans, your brain isn't worth the water that keeps it wet!"

"Just *one* is pretty potent," I said. "Ask me about it." My voice began crumbling. "Ask my daughter."

"Naturally I got the hell out of their village, and then I said to myself, 'Why bother to go home? Why not be a nomad and live off the fat of the farm?' Believe me, Mr. Quinjin, you've never had a proper meal until you've eaten a muckwasp or a wortfish that's been gorging on a noostree's sap. It's a certified Paradise here—as sure as God made little green apples!"

Ever eastward the Lethe flowed, bearing us toward our prey. Off the port, the great bough loomed along the shore, its walls of moss and nets of vine completely blocking Cronus Crags from view. On the opposite bank, Eden Mire seemed suddenly to fall under the goad of some vegetative lust. With each bend of the river, the swamp shed yet another inhibition, entering into orgies of proliferation and growth. The ferns became so plentiful, the flowers so fat, the brush so thick, the trees so tall, the creepers so ubiquitous that in a few days our starboard overlooked a jungle as epic as Hamadryad herself.

We were in an evolutionary showcase. On the water's surface, mats of algae drifted like ice floes. Suffused with warmth and evaporated water, the air upheld flocks of streamy-plumed birds, their churning wings granting us occasional respites from Gishbar. A colony of aquatic, omnivorous insects began to follow us, scavenging every scrap of food we tossed overboard. They sported their phylum's characteristic grotesqueries—eyes the shape of geodesic domes, feathery antennae that made my skin go bumpy when they fluttered, multinumerous legs joined at strange angles and moving in a disturbing cross-pattern—plus several surprises, including pincers that jutted from their wings like turbofan engines, and convoluted, blubbery exobrains that popped from their heads like great thinking hernias.

Then there was the slitherer. An eel, I suppose, but with a curiously mammalian head. Scum was its favorite food, and on finding a particularly delectable stratum it would swim forward with jaws agape, snagging green strands on its fangs. The eel hung around our raft for days, periodically rearing up like a cobra, fixing us with a mesmeric stare, and letting out a polyphonic hiss that left no doubt about who owned the river. All of this we took in stride. But when the eel flopped onto our emergency skiff and began sunning itself, Jonnie's temper shortened to a point. He grabbed his sword and put the slitherer out of its ecstasy. Slowly the beheaded body uncoiled, paying out into the water.

At least, I thought, it wasn't an albatross.

Thungara, thungara, thungara.

"What's that?" I asked, my eyes alighting on Flick. The sound continued, a crisp paradiddle.

Flick shushed me. Slamming his lips closed with a rigid finger, he showed this signal first to Iggi at the tiller, then to Jonnie, who was fishing off the roof of the deckhouse. More such pantomime brought the four of us together in the stern. We huddled as if cold, though with the exception of Iggi's our bodies were awash in sweat.

"Drums," said Flick efficiently, quietly. "Remember *Tropic of Passion*, sirs? The cannibal scene? Savage drums."

With each successive *thungara*, Iggi's grip on the tiller tightened.

"Is it a message?" I whispered angrily, as if Flick and not the lotosbeans were responsible for his pickers' descent into savagery. "They know we're here?"

"No message." Flick chose his words carefully, keeping them to a minimum. "A ceremony. Stay quiet, and we'll pass by."

Instantly Flick and Jonnie and I stiffened. Our breathing

143

dropped to subsistence level. We blinked only when our eyes threatened to dry up.

In the hour of *thungara*s that followed, the heart-stopping monotony was broken but once, and briefly. A thickly forested island appeared, splitting the Lethe as an axe splits a log. Southeast channel, northeast channel. The first was obviously infested with sharp rocks and white water. The second looked placid. Taking the tiller, Flick committed us to the way of logic.

As the channel sucked us along, its twin beyond the trees gurgled in counterpoint to the drums. *Gurgle, thungara, gurgle, thungara.*

The channels pursued their separate ways, the picker village grew distant, and the two noises faded simultaneously. Even now we did not dare resume the din of our respiration or the racket of our eyelids. Swerving first to the left, then to the right, the Lethe picked up speed.

The silence was ended not by a human action but by the abrupt and violent contact of our raft with the channel bottom. We were aground. Glued. I moaned in outrage. The last thing I wanted from this third-rate dreambean in which I found myself, this chapterplay attempt to sneak past an apple-crazed jungle cult, was another plot twist.

In an instant I was over the side, sloshing around, tallying the catastrophe. The water barely reached my ankles, and rose no higher as I moved thirty meters down the Lethe. Above my head, two enthused monkeys vaulted the river, leaping from the great bough to the top of a more conventional tree. I think they were in love. A parrot giggled and took flight.

Returning to the stuck raft, I walked up to Flick and delivered an accusation whose unfairness was clear to me even before I made it. "You led us down the wrong path! I thought you *knew* this place!"

"We'd have been pulverized!" he retorted. "Ground up like when the astrosquid eats the frigate in—"

"*Speeds of Light,*" I inserted. "Well, that *other* channel looked deep, and I want us to take it!"

"It might be deep, it might be shallow."

"There's a way to find out!"

Afloat, but barely, our skiff was now lodged against the sternpost. Running to it, I scrambled over the gunwale.

The towline was easily untied, the oar easily assembled by wedging blade into shaft. Then my troubles began. The channel flowed so swiftly that my progress was Sisyphean, with two meters lost for every three I gained. This was feeble comedy indeed, barely up to the standards set by *Fool's Paradise.*

Of those watching the show—Jonnie, Iggi, Flick—only Iggi thought to help me. He waded over to the skiff, muscled me out of the stern, leaped aboard, and snatched away the oar with a presumption I found irritating.

I ingested my pride.

Powered by its new, sentient engine, the skiff cruised into the onstreaming channel. The great bough flew by. Soon the *Amaranth* was out of view, and with it went the whine of Flick insisting that my venture was reckless, ill-considered, futile, foolish, contraindicated, and certain to end in disaster. (And I thought: So what? With the taproot so near, with the treasure so plausible, with my revenge so imminent, are not such actions the only conscionable kind?)

Onward we surged, our skiff against the Lethe, a scythe against wheat. In less than half an hour we had retraced the *Amaranth*'s wake as far as the fork. Odd—the picker drums, once so furious at this juncture, were now quiet. I found the nonsound sinister.

Using the oar as a rudder, Iggi sent us southeast. Turgid water came licking at our gunwales. The rapids coughed like a defective squatrocker.

Our entry into this channel was met by yet another attack of bad luck. Before we could determine their depth, the blanched currents reached out, grabbed us, bounced us up and down. Now a high tapering rock reared up, a shark's fin formed in stone. Iggi pulled hard on the oar. Turning sharply, avoiding shipwreck by mere centimeters, the skiff plunged into a whirlpool whose diameter equaled the length of our hull. The whirl-pool spun our boat—once, twice, three times—release!

We took off.

We flew.

We burrowed into the shore, tumbling onto a mound of sand as soft and inviting as any aquacot. By all other standards, however, this beach was the wrong place to be. As soon as I saw our captors, I knew that we had courted disaster well past consummation.

Postures erect, the twenty-odd pickers made of their bodies a stinking, fleshy dungeon in which Iggi and I were the only prisoners. They were a young bunch, evenly divided by gender. To a man, to a woman, they were hairy, dirt-flecked, and foul, possessed by an odor evocative of grorg stomachs and flatulent corpses. Armed with pruning hooks, chainsaws, twig shears, secateurs, weedcutters, insecticide harpoons, and other tools of their abandoned trade, they looked collectively like nothing so much as a suicide brigade about to join some hopeless and unholy war. Under Gishbar's persuasion the pickers had abandoned the habit of clothing, retaining only those few strips of cloth that the memory of shame demanded. Yet, while dress was out of fashion here, adornment was not. My frightened eyes traced helmets of spun moss, headdresses of parrot feathers, necklaces made from eel skulls, and tattoos formed by staining scar tissue with Hamadryad's sap.

"Don't try anything stupid, now!" Iggi roared at the pickers with stunning ferocity. "I'm programmed to turn violent when necessary!"

Sensing from this outburst that my companion was a creature to be reckoned with, the pickers fell upon him before he knew what happened. They bound his limbs with ropes, chains, and noostree vines. My own less impressive physique was accorded but a sinew. The pickers lashed my forearms into an X, then tied this arrangement to my chest, so that I looked ready for burial.

Mumbles, mispronunciations, thick accents, regionalized

vocabularies, and faulty grammar conspired to keep me from comprehending much when the pickers began jabbering among themselves. About all I could catch was, "I calleth them fallen angels, cast out by Goth." And, soon afterward, "No, they be spies for Atropos."

At the word *spies*, Iggi nearly burst his bonds with pride. "How right you are!" he said. "We're your planter's best agents!"

"And if you don't release us right now," I added, "you'll have a whole *army* of spies swooping down on you!"

One of the pickers responded to my threat by spitting on me. Another rammed the butt of his insecticide harpoon into my side, thus initiating what proved to be a five-kilometer walk through rancid mud, blistered ferns, vile insects, gruesome heat, warped trees, and decaying creepers. Near the end, I remarked to Iggi that the things I had been doing lately bore absolutely no resemblance to writing reviews for *Dreambeans Deciphered*.

Do dreambeans destroy free will? Many months earlier, pontificating at the Ganzir Cephapple Convention, I thought I knew the answer. Of course not. But now, seeing the pickers' village—a triangular stockade engulfed by jungle growth and protected by high wooden walls that culminated in points meant to impale—I was not so sure. Whatever say these people still had in their own actions, it was trivial compared with the power exerted by Hamadryad.

Apart from the pickers' living spaces—grass huts shaped like blueberry muffins—the entire village was an homage to *The Lier-in-Wait*. In one corner of the triangle, reeds from the river had been sculpted into a miniature replica of the hedge-maze. The second corner was jammed with obsidian renditions of the skull-headed statues. In the remaining corner I spied my old nemesis the goat, hewn from noostree wood.

All these exhibits I found slightly amusing. But the idol standing in the center of the village I found terrifying.

It was granite, humanoid, enormous—fifteen meters tall.

Its shadow spread across half the village. While I could say nothing definite about the personality of the deity whose likeness the idol embodied, its flared nostrils, tumescent eyes, bloated head, and blockish limbs broadcast malevolence, an emanation amplified by the terrible smell coming from the open mouth and also by the formidable stone slab resting approximately ten meters from the clawed feet.

An awareness infected me. The slab was an altar—a sacrificial altar. From each of its four corners drooped thongs whose only apparent purpose was to tether human limbs. Bas-relief images of skulls and beetles decorated the tapered sides and stubby legs. The surface was carved in a different way—in a Byzantine system of sewers and gutters guaranteeing that the effluvium of sacrifice would leave no stains.

Each of these observations I made under physical as well as mental duress. Not far from the maze model, six stockade poles had been pounded into the earth, and I was roped to one of these like a man about to be torched for practicing witchcraft. Witchcraft: the thought naturally conjured up the face of my favorite witch, Urilla, and after that came the faces of Jonnie and Flick. Before long, of course, my friends would realize that something was amiss, but the village was so secluded that their search-and-rescue missions were certain to be all search and no rescue.

The other poles were similarly occupied. One held Iggi, the others held pickers, two males, two females. I could not guess what terrible sin or satanic lottery had landed my co-prisoners in this predicament.

"Can you snap your bonds?" I asked Iggi shortly after we were brought into the village. It was not a premeditated question; it just came out. Obviously my subconscious was busily plotting prison-breaks even while my intellect went numb.

"Yes," he replied, and to prove the point he tore one of his arms loose and scratched his nose.

I said, "Why don't you escape?"

"Believe me, Quinjin, I've thought of that. Unfortunately, I am your slave." He slid his liberated arm beneath a loop of rope. "While you're alive, I am obliged to try keeping you that way."

"Here's my order. Go get Jonnie and Flick. Tell Jonnie to bring his sword."

"They'll kill you meanwhile," Iggi replied in his this-is-a-fact tone.

"I have a terrible suspicion you're *enjoying* this."

"What can I say? Being captured makes me feel like a spy, and feeling like a spy makes me happy. It's in my genes. It's part of my—"

The *thungara*s cut him off. The terrible *thungara*s we knew so well. In front of the wooden goat, a dozen percussionists slammed thigh-bone sticks into drums made from deathtree logs.

A rite was beginning.

After making two concentric circles around the idol, the pickers gave their bodies over to a complexly copulatory dance requiring a looseness of limb and a surplus of libido. The circles rotated in opposite directions. Arms lashed skyward, shimmying like anemones. Mouths opened in rutty cries followed by words that unsettled me even as they revealed the idol's identity.

"My only god is Goth!" the worshipers assured the statue. "My only god is Goth!" It was like some lurid adventure bean, of course—Pandriac's *The Last Aztec* came to mind, and so did Mewlmawker's *Mask of the Pagan*—but the moment went deeper than that, sucking me back to some remorseless, fear-saturated time before savages were noble, if ever they were, back to when much of the human mind was yet to be built, and reason was but a glint in God's eye. "My only god is Goth!"

I looked at Lilit's chronamulet, saw only glare. Twisting my head, I managed to block the endless sun long enough to learn that it was 23:17:04, the middle of the night.

A male picker was taken from his pole and affixed to the altar like a pelt. He stared directly at Goth, eyes aboil. His was a familiar fear. I had seen it two years earlier on the lotosbean goat, right before I eviscerated it.

A female picker approached the altar, her head encased in a wooden mask whose eyes were gibbous moons. Razor teeth guarded a vast mouth. The priestess—for priestess is what she must surely have been—held the tail of a monkey. One of her flock proffered a ceramic pot filled with noostree resins. Dipping the tail into the resins, she proceeded to use it as a paintbrush. Even from my poor vantage point, I could tell that the object she painted on the bound man's chest, directly over his heart, was a key.

The bound man began to whimper.

Now a second prisoner, a woman with hair to shame Rapunzel's, was released and dragged to the altar. Chunky, over-fed tendons bulged out of the half-dozen pickers who flanked and constrained Rapunzel's body. She was no freer than the spread-eagled man over whom she stood. She studied the painted key.

The masked priestess gave Rapunzel a saw-edged dagger whose grip was studded with jewels that looked like eyes. I knew that dagger. I had used its prototype when dreaming *The Lier-in-Wait*.

Somebody else gave Rapunzel a lotosbean.

"Eat God!" chanted the pickers. "Eat God! Eat God!"

Rapunzel ate God. Her kin began a vigil.

The dancers stood staring at Goth. Waiting.

The percussionists hovered over their drums. Waiting.

The victim trembled on the altar. Waiting.

Only the reluctant executioner seemed wholly alive. As *The Lier-in-Wait* invaded her, she moaned and shivered. Her rest-less dagger threw off little sparks of sun.

Trails of sweat crisscrossed my face. The air felt like glue.

At last came the time of lies, the season of deceit, the moment when a dreamer of *The Lier-in-Wait* finds himself impelled to sacrifice a goat in quest of the key that can save a loved one. I shall record the abomination with as little particularity as possible. I shall give it thirty words, not a syllable more . . . .

Rapunzel . . . pushing knife into victim's chest . . . sawing . . . circumscribing key . . . removing beating heart . . . tossing heart to priestess . . . priestess placing heart in idol's mouth . . . heart sliding down stone gullet . . . liquid echo . . . silence.

"No key!" cried Rapunzel. "No key! No key!"

I began to leak.

Sweat, vomit, urine, feces, and even blood . . . this last from a self-inflicted tongue wound. "Iggi!" I screamed. "Iggi! You've got to get me out of here! Iggi!"

"I hear you." Iggi spoke slowly, eyes fixed on the sleeping Rapunzel. She was now in the final throes of her nightmare. A litany of loyalty to Goth broke from her lips. The blood on her chest and hair shimmered like vinyl.

I looked at the dead man, the man without a middle. "Think of something!"

Rapunzel's behavior at this point merely added to my overall impression of a galaxy fallen into barbarity and madness. Awakening, seeing what she had done, the poor woman ran to the stockade gate, thrust it open, and broke for the jungle. When no one attempted to recapture her, I surmised that, by partaking of the Eucharist and parting with her mind, she had redeemed herself in the eyes of her tribe.

Iggi said, "I *intend* to think of something, Quinjin. Agents such as I, we're accustomed to tight spots."

"Flowering Judas, robot, this isn't a goddamned dream-bean!"

But that, of course, was not entirely true.

11

On the Luring of Roots

By Lilit's chronamulet it was 06:00:00. Dawn. Once again the village shook with the drums and dances and cries of sacrament, and once again the great god Goth was sated. I looked to my left: Iggi. I looked to my right: four empty poles. There could be no question about where the idol's next meal was coming from.

Considering the barbarity of their rites, our captors did not treat us badly. On one occasion a middle-aged woman approached and gave me water from a bowl that had once been a human cranium. On another, an adolescent male handed me a raw wortfish, which I quickly thrust into my recently emptied stomach. In both cases Iggi was also offered the refreshment, and in both cases he naturally refused. Despite his bogus coating of wires and such, the pickers seemed not to realize that my companion was an android, and they probably thought that his fast was an attempt to shame them.

About an hour after the second victim was removed from

the altar and heaved over the stockade wall, I was approached by a picker whose broad, winglike ears were, in this context, not even remotely funny and whose evident authority over the rest of the tribe prompted me to label him their chief. The chief asked whether I wanted to bathe. I said yes. When he failed to extend this courtesy to Iggi, I knew he was trying to punish the robot's seeming surliness. Iggi simply grinned.

I was taken beyond the gate, through the jungle, and down to the river, where I removed my clothes and washed off the stains left by my body's reaction to recent fanaticisms. A few meters away, a huge wad of moss lay on the sand, baking in the sun. Crabs wove their leggy way through the moss; my skin crawled. Presently I realized that I was staring at our skiff, astutely camouflaged by the pickers. Should I scream for help? The pruning hooks said no.

Now it might be supposed that my psychological state at this time was some indescribable amalgam of madness and terror. And it was. Yet superimposed on these feelings was an iron determination to prevail—not only over the lotos-eaters but over Hamadryad and over Lilit's illness and even over the weaver who had made the seed. And so it happened that when the pickers returned me to my pole and Iggi announced in a whisper that he had a plan for our salvation, my reaction was a firm, rousing, and optimistic "Good!"

"I'm supposed to be a spy," Iggi began.

My eyes turned skyward in silent sarcasm. "Oh," I sneered. "Is that so?"

But then Iggi revealed his plan, which hinged quite explicitly on his espionage heritage, and a very fine plan it was.

Ears flapping in a hot wind, the chief personally directed our removal from the poles and our short trip to the outdoor temple. Ten hands gripped my arms like organic manacles. The dancers began their libidinous ballet, kicking up dust that the wind carried right to my throat. I coughed. A new act had been added to the show, a chant, ear-punishing and profane, a screeching racial memory of what our Terran forebears had sung around the campfire to celebrate the invention of murder. The drums *thungara*ed.

Right away, things started going wrong. Iggi was handed the dagger, whereas our plan had called for me to do the sacrificing. Before I could be laid out, however, the robot broke free, dropped the dagger, and threw himself supine on the slab. It was a flawless performance from a master mimic, and he followed it with just the right words.

"No!" said the robot. "Take me! Willingly I lose my heart! Gleefully I nourish Goth!"

The pickers, impressed, nailed him down.

The priestess painted a key on his chest.

So total was the concentration with which I mentally practiced my role in the forthcoming playlet that I was not aware of being given the apple and the dagger. But there they were, *The Lier-in-Wait* in my left hand, the weapon in my right.

Now the dancing, the singing, the drumming all stopped, and a predictable, articulate roar—*Eat God! Eat God!*—enveloped me like a loop of surf. Opening my mouth, I inserted the bean, pretended to chew. *Eat God!* My teeth caressed the skin but did not puncture it—how careful I was! Then, a miscalculation, and the dream was breached. Vitriol trickling down my throat could not have felt worse than that nectar. Mercifully the leak healed itself, and the molecules that reached my brain brought no amnesia, no unwilling suspension of disbelief. Briefly I saw the Lier-in-Wait astride his goat, but it was all dim and ghostly and considerably less real than reality.

For twenty minutes I stood over Iggi, stood in the wind with an apple in my mouth. I realized that the accidental release of several drops was lucky, distracting me enough to keep me sane. And then it was time to act. My fingers probed the robot's painted key.

Iggi looked at me with lidless eyes. He had shut off his nerve endings, so I knew he was as insensate as bone. Nevertheless,

I hesitated to begin cutting, so convincing was the synthetic flesh that arched over his innards.

"Do it," said Iggi between clenched lips. "Do it or they'll kill you."

Tongue pinned by the apple, I could not reply.

Slitting the robot was more like opening a package than like performing a sacrifice. In the wake of the knife, a letter V spread across Iggi's chest. The sound was that of ice cracking underfoot. As the V widened, Iggi enacted a terrible scream, then presumed to faint. The pickers seemed persuaded. But I still had to move quickly, before the conspicuous absence of blood prompted them to charge the altar.

Iggi's organs made me think of those colorful cognitive-development toys that parents from intelligentsia backgrounds purchase in hopes of fattening their infants' brain cells. Feverishly I began my search. Disconnecting each organ was as simple as Iggi had promised; a quick tug, and pins popped out of receptacles. Where humans had a stomach, Iggi had a brown, corrugated cylinder that, if I remembered his lecture correctly, harbored mathematical abilities and a sense of fair play. I laid the stomach on the altar. The colon-equivalent was a coil of yellow spheres, each the locus of a different emotion. They were warm to the touch.

Most of the lotos-eaters were frowning now. Several went and got weapons.

"Can you see it?" Iggi muttered.

I peered into the cavity, and there it was, a blue cube no larger than a baby's fist. Magnetism riveted the cube to a five-sided pyramid occupying the domain of spleen. Freeing it was like getting a rock out of mud.

With a sharp puff I ejected *The Lier-in-Wait* from my mouth. It hit the dirt, rolled up to Goth's left foot, stopped. At this point I noticed that an insecticide harpoon and several pruning hooks were aimed at my stomach. Only the pickers' low-grade curiosity kept them from slaughtering me right then.

"Followers of Goth!" I shouted, displaying the cube as I

would a prop in a magic show. "Hear me! You believe you have captured mere men! False! False!"

The chief pricked his considerable ears. The rest of the village did likewise.

"Your folly was to capture us together! Apart, we are mortal! In tandem, our minds fuse and we are . . . *Varg!*" The meaningless syllable sounded even sillier than it had in rehearsal. "Varg, the Creator of Creators! Varg, the Slayer of Slayers! Varg, the Being from Whom All Godhead Pours!"

Iggi transmitted an instruction to the cube. It glowed. All around, eyeballs bulged and jaws descended.

"Behold the light of Varg!" I cried, rushing up to Goth's graven image. "Behold its truth! Behold its power over false gods!"

I hurled the cube into the idol's mouth. It rattled downward, hit the stomach.

Explosive devices of this type were standard equipment on all androids slated for espionage work. A reasonable organ, when you realize how easy it is to extract information from a captured robot spy. (No need for torture, just chisel out the memory chips and give them to the nearest computer for decoding.) Thus, after falling into unfriendly hands, a *Pseudocortex* with secrets in its cells was expected to blow itself to flinders at the first possible opportunity.

"Stoop down!" I cried. "Stoop down or the wrath of Varg will destroy you!"

An overwhelming majority of lotos-eaters saw that they had nothing to lose by obeying me. As they stooped, I dashed to the altar and crouched behind it in a manner that brought an unsought recollection of Broc Hornlaster hiding from the space pirates in *Uncharted Parsecs*.

"Now, Iggi!"

Iggi sent word to the bomb.

The sound of the explosion was oddly staccato and disconcertingly organic. Two undigested hearts shot into the sky. Great chunks of deposed deity cannonballed around the village, ripping through the palisade, mowing down the *Lier-in-Wait* exhibits, and felling the half-dozen pickers who had refused to stoop. When it was over, the only parts of Goth left standing were two abbreviated legs rising from the ground like tree stumps.

Slowly the sacred dust settled. The pickers got to their feet, and I noted with mixed emotions that, while bloody, the victims of the flying rubble were not seriously hurt. Everyone was entirely flabbergasted by the trick, and I sensed that a few were considering shouting "My only god is Varg!" But there was no time to enjoy our divinity. The robot needed getting together.

This part of the script was simple. I was to reinsert his organs and lash his chest closed with thongs. Iggi's sudden revelation that the tactic would not work constituted the worst moment of my life since Lilit ate the lotosbean.

"Never cut into a *Pseudocortex*'s chest," he said with a kind of frigid cheer. "You'll snap half his motor circuits. It's the truth, Quinjin. I can't walk."

"I'll carry you."

"Carry three hundred kilograms? Don't worry, I'll survive."

"No you won't—they'll *demolish* you! Without me around, they've no reason to stay afraid!"

All Iggi said was, "We should have written a better script."

"You bastard, you *knew* this would happen!"

"Yes. Altruism is in my genes—like spying."

"I can't just leave you here."

"Leave is exactly what you do, Quinjin—leave while they're still confused. You've got your little girl to save."

I wept. The robot could not weep, yet I knew that the yellow spheres on the altar were causing him to feel something besides preprogrammed altruism. Collecting his heavy, severed body in my arms, I hugged him hard.

"You're a hell of a spy, Iggi."

"Yes. Tell me I don't belong to anybody anymore."

"You don't belong to anybody anymore."

And then the robot said, "Give Lilit a kiss."

I had three exits to choose from. The idol's head and right hand had both knocked man-sized holes in the wall. One of his shoulders had opened the gate. I crossed the village by swaggering—my goal was the head-hole—and the pickers lurched out of my way like frightened children. Each face I passed was stiff with awe. Even the chief and the priestess deferred.

The instant I ducked through the hole, however, everyone broke into loud, irreverent chatter. Clearly I had seeded no religions here, founded no followings. Indeed, a sideways glance sent horrifying images smashing into my eyes. Pickers were gathered around the altar, finishing the bloodless dissection I had begun. Synthetic organs flew in all directions. Silently Iggi left this world and all others.

I ran. The jungle was full of stormy gestures. Wind-pressed, the leaves vibrated like piano keys under invisible fingers. Running, running. As I reached the riverbank the storm broke, a cool reconstitution of the Lethe's potent waters, a strange rain, at once cleansing and corrupt, a rain that, diluting the tears I shed for the best baby-sitter Lilit would ever have, promised to free the *Amaranth* and end my long search for death's fecund root.

In contrast with my escape from the village, my return to the raft was as simple and bland as *Fool's Paradise*. I uncovered the skiff, portaged it upriver, passed the rapids, got aboard, and steered toward the northeast fork. The currents did the rest. All this time the rain came down, deepening the Lethe. My wet clothes drooped from me like moss from Hamadryad.

Nearing the *Amaranth*, I made several simultaneous observations. First, the raft was already afloat, moored by a hawser angling into the river from a stern cleat. Second, Flick was either out searching for me or else asleep in the deckhouse. Third, coming back from the dead is a very lovable thing to do, because the moment Jonnie saw me—he was convinced I'd been skinned for drumheads—he swam over, hauled me out of the skiff, and kissed me on each cheek.

News. The *Amaranth* was ready to sail. Flick was indeed off looking for me. Briefly I chatted with my friend, reducing the ordeal to its barest bones—for Jonnie, as for me, Iggi had been an acquired taste, though in recent days the blood-drinker had come to regard the robot with genuine affection, and my description of Iggi's death brought a sadness I knew would linger—after which I walked my exhausted body into the deck-house and lay down.

Despite my half-conscious state, I recognized the sounds of Flick's arrival. From his tone I could tell that the straw boss was disgusted by my misadventure. Among his more coherent assertions: "I *knew* those rapids were a terrible idea!" And also: "I *predicted* it would end badly!" I could have fought back: "And I suppose you *also* knew a storm would come and rescue us!" But after you've lived with the lotos-eaters, mere verbal pointmaking starts to seem tiresome.

The noise of the rain against the deckhouse walls, until now a lush pitter-patter-pitter-patter, devolved into occasional, irregular thuds. Flick ordered the anchor weighed. I felt the Lethe take hold of us, and my knowledge that we were leaving the country of the mad pickers hastened my descent into a long and dreamless sleep.

The days came in, the days went out, and all we knew was sodden air, hot sun, and a river that seldom turned. Even Nature was bored. No insects scavenged our wake, no birds or monkeys protested our presence. Only Hamadryad's great bough, forever girding the portside jungle, assured us that our journey had purpose and direction.

Our capacity to annoy each other grew steadily greater. I had never before realized how loudly Flick ate, what rude articulation he brought to each click of tooth and clap of tongue. Flick, for his part, found it difficult to abide Jonnie's habit of juggling copies of *The Lier-in-Wait*. Meanwhile, my passion for rehashing recent escapades and my inability to stop moaning about Lilit kept everyone's opinion of me extremely low.

When all nerves aboard the *Amaranth* had been frayed naked, Flick went to the deckhouse and returned hugging his wire-lyre. A good idea—assuming he knew how to play it. One sour note, and his overwrought shipmates would no doubt heave him into the Lethe.

The melody was his own—sparse, slow, affecting. For lyrics he had appropriated five stanzas from "The Upas Tree," by a Terran poet whom Flick called Pushkin. I thought this a terrific name. If I ever got a different cat or a new robot or a second child, I would call it Pushkin.

In the niggard, sickly desert,
Where the earth is baked to stone,
Stands the upas, a stern sentry,
In the universe alone.

On a day of wrath did Nature,
Mother to those thirsty plains,
Bear it, saturate with poison,
Dead green leafage, roots and veins.

Through its bark the poison oozes,
Molten in noon's heat and rich,
Hardening as dusk advances
To a thick, transparent pitch.

Not a bird flies toward those branches.
Not a tiger nears; a black
Gust may briefly burst upon it:
Blight will follow in its track.

If a vagrant cloud should shower
The thick foliage where it stands,
From those boughs a rain of poison
Pours into the burning sands.

As soon as Flick finished, we had him sing it again.

Trunk. What a lovely sound—*trunk*—like the motor on Rudd Bruzbee's houseboat starting up—*trunk*—like a large, good-hearted dog jumping into an aquacot with you. The great wooden tower that was Hamadryad's trunk rose from the jungle and vanished into mist. Up and down its bark, limbs radiated toward every point of the compass, so that the bough we had been following seemed but a single spoke in some vast and mystic wheel. Where there is trunk, there is taproot. Our search was over.

No, not quite. As we approached the trunk, the river widened into a feature that Flick termed a "bayou lake," so expansive it included the trunk itself, and into this tract of silt and water and sap and guck Hamadryad's lower branches had dropped circle after concentric circle of adventitious roots.

"Flowering Judas!" I said, grasping the implications of this geography. "The taproot is underwater! Now what? I left my gills back in the goddamned Devonian Age!"

Flick's smile showed a majority of his teeth. "You think I would have brought you so far if the tree were impregnable? Don't worry, sirs. Hamadryad's weaver foresaw a time when Atropos or I would need to lure her brain."

"To *kill* her?" I asked, incredulous.

"To *cure* her. You never know when a noostree's going to take sick, Mr. Quinjin, and once you've got a really profitable one, you certainly don't want her dying or going crazy on you. Now Hamadryad, she's been healthy as a rock so far, but five years ago I worked in the belt, and it was more like being a doctor than anything else. We found about ten tumors in *Sea of Tranquility*'s brain. *Old Wives' Tales*—let's see, her root had a virus to interferonize. And without neurosurgery, *Pages from My Suicide* would never have gotten over her depression."

The closer we drifted to the adventitious roots, the more obvious it became that the *Amaranth* was too wide to fit through them. Jonnie suggested that we hack our way in with his sword, but then I reminded him of our disastrous encounter with *Fool's Paradise*. "Offend those roots, and they'll hang us by our necks until dead."

Flick went aft. Returning with the grorg harpoon, he began to load it with our belladonna-29.

"From now on," said the straw boss, "this expedition travels in the emergency skiff. I plan to enlist, and we're not worth anything without our pigsticker here, so that leaves room for one more. Somebody else had better join up, because—as the gin-soaked priest says in *Drowned Sorrows*—I'm not facing that beast alone."

"No," I said quietly. "You're facing her with me."

"I've been trying to imagine you luring Hamadryad," said Jonnie. "What do you use, flattery?"

Flick caressed the harpoon. "The weaver put a conjuration in her memory neurons."

"Sounds like sorcery," I said.

"Quite so," said Flick Longslapper: Straw Boss, Cephapple Expert, and Sorcerer.

12

The Treasure of the Tree

Bestriding the bayou like a million-legged crab, Hamadryad defied us to find her brain. All around, roots arced out of the water and, mingling above our heads, knitted themselves into a vaulted canopy through which no sunlight could pass. And so it was that our skiff moved through that rarest of phenomena in the deathtree's domain, darkness.

Lashed to the bow thwart, the grorg harpoon jutted headfirst over the water. A photorb swayed from the spearpoint. Flick and I faced each other, he in the stern, I in the bow, he standing, I seated, he busily poling us forward, I idly studying the root maze. My buttocks rested on the harpoon, its shaft elaborating my backbone into a barbed tail.

"I'm hungry," I said.

Flick gave the bayou an especially energetic poke. Hauling the oar aboard, he dropped to his knees and leaned over the gunwale. A family of silt-rooted flowers glided by. As he stalked his prey, his tongue emerged and pinned his upper lip to the corresponding gum. He struck. Success. The final flower was his.

"Eat this," he said, handing me the blossom. Its petals overlapped like scales on a snake, and its stamens did not look appetizing either. When I bit into the thing, however, I found myself consuming heady juices and delicious tissues. Poling again, Flick mirrored my smile in his own diminutive face.

"Good?" he asked.

"Great," I replied.

"You see why I love it here, Mr. Quinjin?"

"Yes. And when Hamadryad dies . . . ?"

"The whole garden dies."

"I'm sorry," I said. "I mean, I'm not sorry. I mean, I'm sorry for you. It won't be easy finding another Paradise."

Slices of sun broke through the canopy, covering the dwarf with nervous beetle-bright dots that scurried across his chest, arms, face, oar.

"I'll find another," he said.

We slithered on, our wake curling through the bayou like the thread unreeled by Theseus as he tracked his Minotaur. Braids of mist hovered above the water. With each turn, the smell of the marsh grew stronger, soon becoming indistinguishable from the sour, pungent, not altogether unpleasant odor that Pandriac managed to get into the laboratory scenes in *Idioms*, a bean about Isaac Newton's infatuation with alchemy.

Exactly three hours after our departure from the *Amaranth*, the roots thinned out, leaving us in a lagoon. The water was black, unimaginably black, entropy-black, a kind of molten ebony. Our photorb threw its rays as far as they would go, showing, close at hand, roots of burnished yellow . . . then auburn . . . then gray-brown . . . then no roots at all, but only the dome of night. Off the bow, more than a kilometer away, the great bellying wall of Hamadryad's trunk rose darkly from the water like a landfall.

A dire stillness. Unpumping hearts. Unligamented bone.

The lagoon was free of current, stripped of breeze. Flick gave a final stroke, and soon afterward we stopped, gripped by the tarry surface.

"The root is near," said the straw boss. "I can feel it."

Pressing one knee against the bow thwart, I untied the harpoon and picked it up, left hand on the pole, right hand on the shaft. A loaded grorg harpoon: twenty kilograms of alloysium filled with as many kilograms of liquid death. It was all I could do to avoid toppling into the lagoon.

I unscrewed the end of the pole, palmed the cap, tilted the shaft. A radio transmitter—the device by whose command the poison would be pumped—fell into my hand, clanking against the cap. I fastened the transmitter to my belt like a dagger.

We were ready for the Tree of Death.

"I've got to sing this at top volume," said Flick. "Remember *Scream Without End*, when the insane soprano shatters her husband's skull right inside his—?"

"I remember," I replied. "A terrible apple," I added.

Flick sang. He accorded the conjuration three times the energy he had used for Pushkin, each syllable rising high and whistling back to earth like a meteorite.

> *Soul of the seed, listen!*
> *Brain of the tree, come forth!*
> *Heart of the fruit, appear!*
>
> *Cease to be a sleeper in the earth!*
> *Cease to lie unwaking in the flesh of*
> *   this farm!*
>
> *You I summon!*
> *You I evoke!*
> *You I call in beholdable form to meet*
> *   your healer!*
> *Child of dreams, you are conjured!*

I glanced at the chronamulet. It was exactly, precisely midnight, a time that the device translated into an assertion of the most utter and redundant nullness, 00:00:00.

We waited.

At 00:10:05 the lagoon began to gurgle. Bubbles streamed to the surface, exploded into ever-growing rings. A large bird fluttered past, wings rustling like serge.

"Look!" yelled Flick, pointing to the agitated water. "She rises!"

Urilla later told me that at this instant—at 00:10:17—Lilit suddenly sat up in her bed at the Crazy Raven, tossed Basil off her stomach, and said excitedly, three times, "Goth's mother is coming!"

If you have ever been in a waftcar accident, you know that among the many simultaneous sensations one absorbs is the uncanny loudness of it all. So it was when we encountered Hamadryad's taproot in sudden vertical collision. As the beast came up under us, a *whack!* compounded of splintering skiff and reverberating xylem seemed to shatter my earbones. The noise startled me almost as much as the fact that we were flying through the air.

Flick's scream was a song.

Mine was a howl of animal terror.

I splashed down within two meters of the root itself, surfacing instantly. The harpoon—God and Varg and Physics be praised—was buoyant.

I kicked, twisting my body for rudder, and the harpoon and I spun ninety degrees. Initially all I saw was the staved-in skiff, the photorb bobbing near it like a fallen moon. Then I noticed Flick, whose flailings bore only a vague resemblance to the sidestroke he wanted so desperately to perform. Miraculously, he stayed up. Miraculously, he reached a cluster of roots, selected one of medium thickness, and hugged it.

"It's your fight now, Mr. Quinjin!" he called. "You're all alone!"

Alone.

Alone, I faced the Mother of Goth.

Certain vegetables are inherently, forever serious. No one laughs at beets or peas. Turnips, by contrast, are funny. So are carrots. When I say that the creature towering over me resembled a gigantic, upended carrot, however, I intend no humor. Faceless, facetless, the thing was of a hue that fused an unpleasant ochre with all the more fecal implications of brown. Death-white crevices cross-hatched its skin like amateurishly healed wounds, wrinkling the all-sided symmetry, accenting the heavenward taper. Silt, water, and bits of weed drizzled from the carcass, plopping into the lagoon with the sound of hail volleying against glass. Yet the most startling features of the taproot were the thousand-odd nodes that studded its body, thick phallic stalks culminating in organs of reception. Atop a third of the nodes lay a knurled form the size and complexity of a fist, and these I took for ears. Others supported bright green balls that seemed sensitive to light, while others—volcanolike structures crowned by famished beaks—enabled the ever-probing root to suck nourishment from planet Uggae.

Wobbling under its own weight, the root began to bend toward the lagoon. Spray warmed my cheeks as the thing broke the surface. The displaced water cloaked the lagoon in slumbrous black ruffles that quickly surged beyond the range of the photorb.

When the creature failed to sound, but instead floated horizontally like a great log bred to sustain hellfires, I knew that my chance had come.

Hamadryad used her nodes for sensing. I used them for climbing. The waterline had given the creature a semblance of conventional anatomy—a dorsal side in the air, a ventral side submerged—and so it was that slowly, clumsily, drippingly, I got on her back, dragging the harpoon behind me. The ear nodes recorded me, the eye nodes tracked me, the mouth nodes hungered for me with cartilaginous clackings.

Reaching my destination, I knelt as if in prayer, but there was nothing remotely sacramental about my intentions.

And suddenly I was Quinjin the Critic. I was analyzing when I should have been acting. What was I analyzing? My hesitation. Why was I hesitating? Because part of me was like the mad pickers and the late Baptizer Brown and anyone else who may have eaten *The Lier-in-Wait*. Part of me was a Gothian. Part of me knew that—despite my inability to recall the ending of the dream—the ultimate blasphemy would be to kill the mother of my only god.

Then I thought of Lilit. That was all it took.

For a target I chose the axis of the seven eyes and the seven beaks that surrounded my body. Intuition said this spot was vulnerable. The eyes leaned forward like poppies in the wind, the beaks stood ajar, and it was in this unnerving environment that I pressed every one of my muscles toward a great downward . . .

Thrust!

Whereupon, as Urilla would eventually tell me, Lilit let out a moan and immediately returned to her torpor.

The harpoon entered the root with the noise of a small but complex organism being stomped underfoot. Green resins spurted into my face, streamed down my cheeks in hot trickles. Blindly I reached toward my belt and threw the switch. As the poison burst into Hamadryad's ducts, her beaks yawned open, and the screams were whistles implanted in the throats of torture victims. As I wiped the sap from my own eyes, I saw that the tree's eyes were spinning atop their stalks, flinging out tears of pain as they went. Resolved that pity would not get the best of me, I yanked out the harpoon, struck the root again, and again, and again—and still it did not sound.

Now I buried the harpoon up to its pole, so that it jutted from the pooling wound like a buoy. Sap coursed into the crevices on the monster's flank, turning them into creeks. Hamadryad writhed, shook, and lay still.

It occurred to me that this was the worst review I had ever given a dreambean.

The screaming stopped. The beaks closed. But seconds later they began to part with a low, despairing *skreeeee*, as if they moved on overburdened hinges. Again the beaks emitted sounds, but instead of the anticipated death cries, I heard the articulate stutters of a being struggling to speak.

"Buh-buh-buh-buh-buh," said the stricken tree, marshaling about a third of her tongues into a low, asynchronous chorus.

"B-b-bells," said Goth's mother at last. Her voices were feeble but mellifluous hisses. "Bells."

"Bells?" I said.

"Bells," said the tree. "No bells?" she asked.

"None," I said.

"It's an illusion, then. I have many."

"An illusion," I repeated robotically. I was wonderstruck. "You talk!"

"Talk? Indeed! A fifth of my brain is linguistic cortex!"

Again I found myself at a loss for words other than those I had just heard. "A fifth of your brain," I muttered. "Linguistic cortex," I added.

"The problem," Hamadryad rasped, "is that, when I talk, no one answers. Hence, I hallucinate. Rooted here, day following day, one becomes . . . detached. Some people, I am sure, envy me. They suppose that, with so much time to kill, I have pried a truth or two out of the universe. They suppose me to be . . . enlightened."

"Are you?"

"Yes. It is boring. All these years, what do you suppose I have most wanted? A flute, that's what—and a hand to move the keys with. A real hand, I mean, not just a twig. Something with a thumb. A thumb is more important than the truth. Many a night I dream of thumbs. Am I dying, traveler?"

"Yes."

"Poison?"

"Belladonna-29."

"I thought as much. I tried to resist my creator's conjuration, but how could I? It's part of me. I knew we would come to this, me and my malignant apples. Do you suppose it's my apples I hear? Swinging on their branches, pealing their own death knell? But no, you've already told me, I'm hallucinating."

"My *daughter* ate one of your apples!" I yelled into Hamadryad's redundant ears.

She grunted. "You must loathe me. Just remember, I did not *ask* to have lotosbeans. If you understood me, you would know that I am more the all-for-love type. Will you honor a dying tree's last request? When I am gone, boil me down for pulp. Turn me into paper—into a book, a great book, a romantic book. There's enough paper in me for ten billion copies. Reincarnate me as a great romantic book, traveler—I have been *The Lier-in-Wait* too long."

I had indeed expected to "loathe" the tree. And yet I could not. Hamadryad, I realized, was not synonymous with her fruit. She was merely a vessel. A conduit. She was yet another victim of her creator.

"My *real* enemy is far from here," I said uncertainly.

"True, traveler. I wish I could help your daughter, but I—"

"Who *can* help her?" I looked Hamadryad in as many eyes as my stare could encompass.

"You must go to a distant star—to Ninnghizzida. On the planet Absu, beyond the city of Ushumgallum, lies a castle, Kharsog Keep. There my creator conducts his experiments, plans his depravities, instructs the students of the Lotos Institute."

"Ninnghizzida," I repeated softly. "But here I am stuck at the bottom of Uggae with your savage pickers all around."

"Climb my trunk," Hamadryad counseled. "Keep going. Straight up, no matter what. Higher, higher, all the way to my crown. You'll emerge near Mulla-Xul."

"You spoke of your creator's experiments," I said. "What is this Lotos Factor? How do your dreams achieve hyper-reality?"

"Such understandings are as forbidden to me as they are to you. Only my creator—"

"Your creator," I said slowly.

The root stared at me a hundredfold. "He gives his name as Baron Kharsog, but that is not who he is."

"Then who is he?"

"My creator is Simon Kusk," said the tree.

"Simon Kusk died before you were born," I protested. "Clee Selig bludgeoned him to death."

"My creator is Simon Kusk," the tree repeated.

"How can that be?"

"Bells," said every one of the mouths. "Inside my mind. Bells."

"Simon Kusk was—is—a bad man. And yet he can—?"

"Bells . . . Your daughter's hope lies at Kharsog Keep . . . Bells . . . That knowledge is the treasure I have to give you . . . Bells . . . Bells! Buh-buh-buh-buh—!"

A shudder spread beneath Hamadryad's hide like a huge mobile tumor. Her eyes flickered out. Her beaks snapped shut, sealed by indecipherable locks.

We were sinking now, the dead root and I. Lagoon water heated my knees, and I jumped off. A dozen swift strokes brought me to Flick.

"You were heroic," he said, meaning it. "You were Broc Hornlaster in *Uncharted Parsecs*. You were Prince Bizbac in *Castle Brimstone*."

"After we retrieve Jonnie," I said smoothly, surely, Hornlasterly, Bizbacly, "we're coming back here." I repeated Hamadryad's claim that we could escape by climbing her trunk.

"She *told* you this?"

"Yes. Hamadryad was . . . wise. And good. She rendered up her treasure. I feel . . . sorry for her."

"Good? Sorry?"

I turned.

Like a doomed frigate, the root's immeasurable hump disappeared beneath the black water. Bubbles rode the whirlpool. For a solid minute I stared at the vortex into which my enemy who was not my real enemy had dropped.

Simon Kusk!

PART THREE

13

Möbius Trips

I was in jungjelly when the truth came to me. *Fleshpot* had just skeeted through Voodoo Vector 4l, and I had decided to linger in the vat, comforting Basil while imagining myself a spermatozoan poised for its one-in-four-hundred-million shot at incarnation. And suddenly there it was, right in the middle of my thoughts, the truth.

Kusk had not been murdered—that was the truth. It was all a dream—a cephapple dream. Among the many practical applications of the Lotos Factor, it could provide one with that most impenetrable of disguises, that most perfect of alibis, death.

I was forced to wait a full standard month before discussing this truth with the person who would most appreciate it, Dr. Clee Selig. It took that long for *Fleshpot* to get within transceiving distance of Zahrim. As I paced around the communications deck, Selig's image shimmered inside the holovision tank; evidently the camera in his laboratory had a narrow field, for the tank accommodated nothing beyond his face, his torso, and a bottled brain sitting on one corner of his desk. The professor had lost much of his post-human quality. Once as straight as a noostree trunk, his backbone had begun to topple, carrying his shoulders down with it. Wrinkles were making belated appearances on his forehead. Hastily I informed him of our fortunes and misfortunes. Lilit mad. Baptizer hanged. Iggi wrecked. Hamadryad poisoned, her branches going stiff and dry, her apples becoming black shriveled grapes.

"You are Quinjin the Great," he said, voice crackling with joy, "Slayer of Noostrees."

"I am also Quinjin the Riddle Solver." I told him of the tree's startling claim that Kusk was still alive, and of my equally startling explanation.

The pleasure Selig had taken in Hamadryad's death was now eclipsed by a far more schizoid emotion, in which the relief of knowing that he was not really an assassin alternated with the pain of knowing that his hated protégé still lived. "It's quite clear to me now," he said. "I alone knew that Kusk was out to introduce a Lotos Factor into the medium. I alone was capable of directing suspicion his way. It was just as I told you—the viper fell upon me by night, knocked me unconscious. But evidently that was not the end of his diabolism. No, before I recovered he must have forced a custom-tailored lotosbean into me, a tale intended for my delectation alone. Maybe he got me to drink its juice, maybe he used a syringe. Either way, the dream enveloped me, and I fancied myself awakening in Kusk's hovel, then assaulting him with his spade, then destroying his seedling. Illusion after illusion, lie after lie." The professor laughed grudgingly. "To kill a man who threatens to expose your crime—that's a tangled web, best avoided. But to convince such a man that he's murdered you— why, it's foolproof! Far from going to the police, the potential informer becomes a fugitive himself!"

"So Kusk silenced you, leaving himself free to change his name and move to some backwater solar system." I stared at my left boot, uprooting it from the insistent suck of *Fleshpot*'s gravity. "To a *castle*, no less. The tree knew everything."

Now I looked at the holojected Selig, who was pulling on his holojected beard. "This time the viper won't trick us!" he said. "Give me the name of the planet, and we'll send the Terransector Navy swooping down like God took Gomorrah!"

"I can't let you do that." Quinjin the Great, Quinjin the Riddle Solver, Quinjin the Critic was also Quinjin the Father.

"Kusk is a wanted man!"

"And I'm a driven one. Before she died, Hamadryad told me that Kusk can help Lilit."

"*Help* her? His damn bean nearly *killed* her!"

I needed nothing more from Selig. I was finding him tedious. As I went to the control panel, my rigid mouth and brisk gait betrayed my intention.

"*What* castle?" Selig sputtered behind me. "*What* backwater system? Quinjin, you're shielding a criminal! You're an accessory after the—"

He never got to say *fact*. With a flick of my finger, I sent his image back to Wendcraft University.

I looked at Lilit's chronamulet. It was time for the low point of the day. It was time to visit my daughter.

Her cabin was only a few meters from the communications deck, but I still managed to consume fifteen minutes in procrastinating my way there. On the door she had hung one of her recent drawings—Goth her redeemer, Goth whose bloated-faced effigy I had exploded in the lotos-eaters' village. Herein dwells unreason, the drawing warned.

"She hears feet," said Lilit as, ignoring the warning, I entered. "Four feet on the goat in the maze, forty feet on the larva of Goth's sacred moth, four trillion feet on the followers of the true faith—but these are only *two* feet. A human, then."

Rising from her bunk, she floated toward the pantry like a

wraith in a horror bean. Her white hair resembled a dirty mass of hopelessly tangled fishing line. Veins entwined her eyeballs. She was a fourteen-year-old hag.

This time I did not even bother to insist that I was her father. Experience told me she would claim that her father lay in a well, chained to a rock.

So Lilit was talking again, and her mobility was normal. Initially I regarded these developments as signs of recovery. But in the last several weeks I had been forced to admit that they merely constituted a novel phase of her dementia.

Opening the pantry door, she grabbed a gross handful of chocolate gumbombs and stuffed them in her mouth like an artilleryman loading a cannon.

"I would like you to join us for supper," I said. "You're starving yourself, eating that rubbish all day."

"She does not dine with heretics, dream person. Goth forbids it."

"Goth, Goth," I muttered.

Everything was Goth. All during our return from Uggae, Lilit had kept claiming that she was pregnant by Goth. Rummaging through *Fleshpot*'s medical supplies, I had found the necessary kit, administered a blood test; she was not pregnant, by Goth or anyone else.

These non-conversations typically ended with Lilit walking over to the vocalith machine that I had given her and playing a vaguely obscene song to which she had formed a pathological attachment since our blastoff. This afternoon was no exception. The song was called "Sheath My Sword," performed by a former mental patient and known kidnip addict named Rodnie Quash.

> *Don't blame me if our love goes wrong*
> *Don't blame me if I wilt*
> *If you can make me moist and strong*
> *I'll take away your guilt*

I slipped out the door, leaving Rodnie Quash to anesthetize my daughter's intellect for the ten-thousandth time. It is a tribute to parental instinct that, during a hundred consecutive days of this behavior, I slapped her only once and wished her dead only twice.

Once past the Alpheratzan space buoy, we were free to change course and head for Voodoo Vector 72. We shot the metaphysical rapids, landed on the far side of the gateway. Ninnghizzida blazed through *Fleshpot's* viewports and glinted off its stabilizers. What was once merely a strange name had become the biggest star in the sky.

Thanks to *Parnwelter's Galactic Atlas*, I held no high expectations for planet Absu. Ninnghizzida's outermost captive had little to recommend it besides prodigal deposits of jungjelly ("O rare and wondrous ichor!" said Parnwelter, waxing something like poetic. "O buffer of starhops! O grease of voodoo vectors!") lying beneath a snow-covered tundra. Ushumgallum, the city toward which Hamadryad had pointed us, was apparently nothing more than a jungjelly-drilling town. (Every city north of Absu's equator was apparently nothing more than a jungjelly-drilling town.) As for "Kharsog Keep" and its "Lotos Institute," the *Atlas* did not admit that such a place existed.

Viewed from the air, Ushumgallum struck me as a hologram intended for placement in a pictorial dictionary under the entry QUAINT. There was no fear of ornament here, no obsession with straight lines, no commitment to the kind of dull, lucid geometry that characterized Nindukagga Square back in my hometown. The weather, which consisted almost entirely of snow, had much to do with Ushumgallum's quaintness. Every roof was peaked, the better to reduce the powdery accumulations. Every façade was alive with filigree and statuary, the better to defeat the planar sameness of the omnipresent drifts.

The city boasted a huge spaceport, an automated beehive of cargo ships arriving empty and taking off laden with unrefined jungjelly. But we searched in vain for a hotel. The best we could do was a midtown rooming house called Widow Flum's, a brooding three-story building presided over by a middle-aged and pathologically tidy woman whose imposing stature did much to corroborate her claim that she had given birth to twelve children in as many years.

"Six of them boys, six of them girls, and all of them jelly drillers," the widow informed us within a few minutes of our arrival. "Those jelly fields—*blechtk!*—pure crud. But my children, they've never tracked a speck of it in here, never once. They're as clean as that cat of yours, Mr. Quinjin. Last week my Alicia went over her quota by a hundred liters. Got a medal. I'm only telling you this because I see that *you're* a parent, too. Go ahead, brag about her."

We were seated in Widow Flum's front parlor, watching snowflakes bump against amber-tinted windows. The centerpiece of the room was a woodstove, and before speaking I tossed Basil off my lap, lowered my hands over the heat, and massaged the weather out of my finger bones.

"Lilit is sick," I said.

"She doesn't look sick," said Widow Flum.

"They think she's sick in her *head*," Lilit said. "They know nothing about it. They know nothing at all, not even the secret language of Goth." A droning came forth, hollow as the voice Marta Rem used when prophesying. "*Makesh kyrikush eshika morla kyrik kyrik*," said Lilit.

Urilla and I exchanged sad, pinched glances. *Oh hell*, ran our silent conversation, *another symptom*. Jonnie studied Lilit with annoyingly scientific curiosity. Widow Flum smiled.

The secret language stopped. "You'd be hurting, too," said Lilit, looking right at me, "if *your* father were chained to a rock."

"Once you begin to work in the jelly fields," said Widow Flum to my daughter, "you'll feel better."

The tolerance implicit in her remark pleased me. I sensed that as long as she tracked no unrefined jungjelly into the house, Lilit could be as psychotic as she liked.

"We didn't come to work in the fields," I said. "We just want to rest up for a few days, and then we'll be making our way to the Lotos Institute—you know, the Keep."

"The Keep?" The widow looked as if she were dreaming *Cacodaemon*.

"Kharsog Keep."

Her eyes zigzagged. She gulped down an enormous breath, released it as a sad whistle. "I'm no authority, sir, but I know that the Keep is a domain of evil. People go there and they don't come back."

People go there and they don't come back. This was the first of several bad lines from worse horror beans that the widow would use in repeating local rumors about Kharsog Keep. For example: *I'd stay away if I were you.* And even: *Folks say the castle is haunted.* When asked how we might locate the place, however, she gave a nonevasive answer in crisp, it's-your-funeral tones.

"Baron Kharsog has his own private maglev line. Go to the train station in Assalluxi Square, and they might sell you some tickets."

I acted on this lead almost immediately, leaving Jonnie and Urilla to check out our rooms and bring up our luggage. I simply had to know whether reaching Kharsog Keep was likely to be difficult or easy.

It was likely to be a pain in the anus. This I learned within minutes of entering Ushumgallum's large, tumbledown, predictably quaint train station. Brushing snow from my shoulders, I got in line at the least crowded of the five ticket windows. When my turn came, I saw that I would have to cope with a young man of such extraordinary thinness that his clothes seemed to be on a wire hanger.

"I'm going to Kharsog Keep," I said.

"Ha!" he replied.

"Will you sell me a ticket?"

"No."

"Oh?"

"You're in the wrong place."

"Which line do I use?"

"You don't use *any* line."

"Then what do I do?" I asked, making a fist but hesitating to brandish it.

"You *should* leave. But if you want to find one of Kharsog's servants, go downstairs. Room Seventeen or Twenty-seven or something. Or else it's Thirty-seven. There's a seven in it."

"Will the servant sell me a ticket?"

"Probably not."

I went downstairs.

Stepping out of the stairwell, I encountered a dusky, interminably long corridor reminiscent of troglobus stations and hospital basements. The right-hand wall was barren. The left-hand wall was breached every three meters by a door containing a frosted transplastic window and an arabic numeral.

I approached Room 17, tapped right on the 7.

"Come in."

I did. A small office. A desk. The man who had said "Come in" sat hunched over a computer terminal, and as I approached he looked at me with a shark's unblinking eyes. He was a giant: hair fat and unruly like a nest of caterpillars, lips that looked dead for lack of smiling, and the kind of unearned dignity that I associate with military personnel. On his tunic was stitched a circle containing one of those single-sided, figure-eight-shaped surfaces known as Möbius strips.

"I would like some tickets," I said.

"Are you an apprentice?" asked the ticket-seller.

"No."

"The semester is almost over, you know."

"I just said I wasn't an apprentice."

"You're not? Then what are you doing *here*?"

"I need to visit the castle."

"The new semester starts next month."

I brushed my shoulders, though the snow had long since melted. "Tell your master that my daughter is very sick. She ate a cankered cephapple. I have come a very long way, and I believe he can help her."

The ticket-seller scowled and typed something into the computer, banging the keys as if he wanted them to know pain. From where I stood, the characters that appeared on the screen were nothing but blurry twinkles.

"Now what?" I asked.

As his transmission evaporated, the ticket-seller settled into a cold, pernicious silence. He opened a desk drawer, took out a back issue of *Dreambeans Deciphered*. The Möbius strip on his chest expanded and contracted as he breathed.

I stood in the doorway for fifteen whole minutes, studying the room and raging mutely. The walls were covered with animadvertisements urging young men and women to learn dreamweaving at the Lotos Institute.

Twinkles popped onto the screen.

I coughed. After a moment of premeditated stalling, the ticket-seller glanced at the message.

"Baron Kharsog has reached a decision."

"Yes?"

"His decision is that you should come back in nine days."

The only psychoparlor in midtown Ushumgallum bore the telltale name Priapic. I was glad for the attractions here—erotobeans every one of them—not because they were any good but because they supplied Urilla with a lot more stimulation than she was getting from me. Ever since Lilit had eaten from Hamadryad, physical pleasure had become a blasphemy in my eyes, celibacy a basic need.

When not killing time at the Priapic, I trailed after Lilit as she made her mad rounds. Trailing after Lilit was a duty we all took most seriously in those days. We knew that for people in her condition, suicide was at best a preoccupation and at

183

worst an inevitability. Waking up with an idiot grin on her face, eating an unhealthy breakfast, hearing Rodnie Quash via vocalith, hearing Goth via hallucination, eating an unhealthy lunch, making a bunch of Goth drawings, staring into space while mumbling in her secret language, eating an unhealthy dinner: the order of my daughter's activities never varied, nor did their meaninglessness.

One cold and disconsolate night, Urilla remarked to me that it was Lilit's fifteenth birthday.

Of her three keepers, only Jonnie took a clinical interest in Lilit's behavior. Her symptoms fascinated him. He was forever trying to interpret them in terms of *The Lier-in-Wait*. "Was there a starvation scene in the dream?" That was the sort of thing he was always asking me. "Maybe she eats gumbombs because the Lier-in-Wait tried to starve her."

"I don't remember any starvation scene."

"*Think*, Quinjin. A starvation scene!"

"I really don't want to talk about this."

Day nine. Returning to the train station, Room 17, I learned from the ticket-seller that Baron Kharsog had no time to see me. A setback, but I was prepared.

"Tell your master that my daughter ate an apple called *The Lier-in-Wait*. Tell him that her only god is Goth."

By the time Kusk's response appeared, I had braved the ticket-seller's glare and sidled to within reading distance of the screen.

Come back in three days was the extent of Kusk's curiosity.

Planet Absu rotated thrice.

The verdict was waiting for me, shining forth in mocking green. Pointing to the screen, the ticket-seller cranked his lips into a sneer.

The case this man presents is of no interest to me, said Kusk. *He must go back where he came from.*

Desperation. It was time to tell lies. I saw no other choice. Before we parted company on Uggae, Flick had said to me,

"There's probably only one circumstance under which this Kusk is certain to grant you an audience. You must claim firsthand knowledge of his brain-child—you must pretend to be the straw boss on his dreamfarm. Go ahead—be me. Be Flick Longslapper. It's no bed of roses, I can assure you." And then the kindly dwarf had set off in search of his Paradise.

"Inform your master that my name is Flick Longslapper." Did the ticket-seller sense the reluctance in my voice, the fear? "I am the straw boss in charge of Hamadryad."

Kusk's answer: *Come back tomorrow.*

I had no more trumps to play, no more lies left in me, but somehow I knew this would not matter. The sun went down, went up, and the servant announced that Baron Kharsog would give me as many tickets as I required.

"I need four," I said.

"You have identification?"

To the degree that one can pull a small plastic rectangle from one's vest ostentatiously, I did so with Flick's passport. The ticket-seller snatched it, studied it, strained to appear unimpressed. I held my breath. Jonnie had deftly peeled away the holo of Flick—a typical skill of incubibers—and replaced it with a shot of me. If the seller noticed the deception, he did not admit it. Instead he opened the drawer in which he kept back issues of *Dreambeans Deciphered* and slowly removed four metal disks, each the size of a vocalith. As he laid them out on the desk, my stare traced the Möbius strip on his chest. Now I was moving along the outside, now the inside, now the outside, now the inside.

Outside.

Inside.

And never once a transition between the two worlds.

14

The Man with God's Face

The Jugglers of Bone. It sounded like an incubiber sect, but it was in fact the collective name of the eight travelers with whom we shared the maglev ride to the Lotos Institute. They were an itinerant acting troupe, bound for a command performance before Baron Kharsog and his students. With a mixture of curiosity and depression I wondered what sort of theatrics could possibly entertain the creator of *The Lier-in-Wait*. Did the Jugglers of Bone give birth on stage and then hang the babies from noostrees?

Universally youthful and aglow with health, our fellow passengers lost no time in informing us that good food was for them a sacrament. The more they went on about their diets, the more I recognized the sort of primitivists whose nutritional intake is so precise and pure you suspect that their bowels have not produced any waste products in years. The Jugglers of Bone talked too much and smiled too seldom. But for all this I found myself admiring them—admiring their earnestness, their energy, and especially admiring their director, Torin

Diffring, who merely had to give you the time of day to make you feel you were receiving an intense and loving kind of psychotherapy.

Kusk's train was a symmetrical creature. A computer-piloted observation coach at each end, a conventional coach in the middle. The coaches were as black—outside and inside—as the deathtree lagoon. Torin's Jugglers took over the first two, leaving the rear observation coach to my friends and me, a surfeit of privacy I greatly appreciated. Being around actors, any actors, made me nervous. I kept expecting to see my ex-wife in the troupe. ("Hello, Talas, good to see you again. Lilit? She's become quite an artist. Oh—and one more thing. She's insane.")

Our helltrain sped away from Ushumgallum on a soft cushion of repulsion. The guideway gushed beneath us like a steel cataract. Maglev travel: nirvana at five hundred kilometers per hour. The situation demanded a nap. I took one. My recurrent nightmare did not come. It had not come in months. A favorable omen, I thought.

I awoke. Lilit sat stuporously in the aisle, chattering to herself and churning out sketches of Goth: Goth in profile, Goth in three-quarter view, Goth in full-face surrounded by circular lightning bolts, Goth battling some demonic deity. A few seats away, Urilla was reading a back issue of *Dreambeans Deciphered*. Jonnie was pursuing a spirited conversation with Torin Diffring. Thin and muscular, Torin had a face that was clearly accustomed to looking in mirrors and liking what it saw.

Out on the tundra, jungjelly derricks rushed by, dark skyscraper-sized obelisks slicing into a snow-choked sky.

The incubiber called me over, motioned me to take a seat occupied by Basil. Snatching up the cat, I permitted him to extend his landing gear, then hurled him into the aisle.

"Guess what?" said Jonnie. "I'm going to be an actor."

"We were originally booked onto a night train," Torin explained, dividing his attention among me, his words, and his delivery, "but then a tragedy befell us." Only a person with Torin's superb diction could make "a tragedy befell us" sound like normal speech. "Paulie Wikanov—poor little waif, he just *had* to visit that wretched parlor in midtown Ushumgallum."

"The Priapic?" I asked.

"One and the same. Somehow he talked *all* of us into going— a piece of squatprod called *Money Where Your Mouth Is.*"

"I've eaten it."

"So we're about to leave the place, and Paulie starts complaining that something is stuck in his throat. And suddenly he's spouting a lot of dialogue from *Money Where Your Mouth Is.* The next thing we know, he's not breathing, and then he's on the floor of the lobby, and then he's rolling around, and then he's *dead.* The hospital found a half-dissolved piece of bean in his windpipe. From the lines he said before he choked, it must have been the chocolate pajamas scene."

"I remember the chocolate pajamas scene," I said evenly, staring out the window. Sleet battered the glass. In the distance, tall sharp mountains skewered dingy clouds.

Click, click: Torin was unfastening the clasps on his satchel. "My first impulse was to tear our little play apart, get rid of Paulie's character, but then I noticed that your Jonnie here bears a spooky resemblance to our fallen comrade. So I decided to hold a tryout."

"I did the Pushkin poem we used to sing down on the farm," said Jonnie. " 'From those boughs a rain of poison pours into the burning sands.' "

"He was very good," said Torin.

"I was very good," Jonnie agreed.

Rooting around in the satchel, Torin drew out an untitled manuscript bound in beefcock hide. "The rehearsal schedule won't get frantic until the final three days," he said, handing the script to Jonnie. "You'll probably have to cut a few classes then."

"I'm not an apprentice," said Jonnie, fondling the hilt of his sword.

"Oh? Then what brings you to the Institute?"

My friend tossed me a scowl that said, *You can answer that one.*

"We have been led to believe that Baron Kharsog possesses certain, er . . . therapeutic powers."

"Powers—yes," said Torin tonelessly. "Therapeutic? I'm not so sure. Kharsog pays handsomely for our services, so we let him call any tune he wishes. Otherwise I'd avoid him the way I would a critic."

My fur went erect. I was about to start defending my profession when Jonnie opened the script and read aloud. " 'The time of the play is all times simultaneously, for this legend lives outside of history.' "

"It's a new version of the old Thyestes myth," Torin explained.

"I associate Thyestes with the Terran Greeks," I said modestly. "I couldn't tell you the plot."

"Thyestes sins against Atreus. Adultery, you see, combined with a theft. So Atreus summons his chef—that's our Jonnie—and arranges for the head of Thyestes's favorite child to be baked into a pie, *which is then set before Thyestes to eat!*"

Torin delivered the final clause as if it were the punchline of a joke, and I actually believe he expected us to laugh or even applaud.

At last the director broke the dismayed silence. "There's only one performance, friend—learn your lines well."

Elaborating, Torin revealed that, every year, the Baron treated his apprentices to a banquet right before the midterm recess, with the Jugglers of Bone employed as after-dinner entertainment. "He claims that we give him inspiration for his cephapple scripts."

"Do you always put on *Thyestes*?" Jonnie inquired.

"No, but we never stray far from the genre. Some call it Grand Guignol. For others it is the Theater of Revenge. Baron Kharsog favors sensation."

I asked if they had ever done anything about a man chasing a goat through a maze. No, they hadn't.

For the next thirty minutes Torin alternately regaled and appalled us with accounts of midterm banquets past. The Jugglers' most memorable production—or, by Kharsog's criteria, their most inspiring production—was a retelling of *Oedipus Rex*. Near the end of this version, when the poor ruined king tried to blind himself, "eyeballs began shooting out of the actor's head, one after the other, pelting the audience." Torin was about to disclose how this memorable effect was accomplished when one of his ingenues—a fetching girl of Lilit-like beauty and porcelain skin—appeared to announce that our destination was near.

Jonnie and I followed the director into the forward observation coach. Several Jugglers were huddled in front of the viewbubble, jockeying for position. I jammed myself into the crowd, wriggled forward.

What I saw brought instant recollections of a certain noostree. Set amid the spindly mountains, Kharsog Keep reared up from the tundra like the trunk of the late Hamadryad, ascending into the clouds with a hubris not seen since the Tower of Babel. The cylindrical façade was cracked and cracked some more, so that the Keep had the appearance of a shattered vase reconstituted through a meticulous gluing together of pieces. Bright windows speckled the walls. Beyond, Ninnghizzida settled into the dark ranges.

I studied the approaching castle, trying to catch a glimpse of my enemy, my hope, but all I saw were lights and shadows and frenzied squalls of snow.

Kusk's private maglev line terminated inside a structure so hard and cavernous it seemed capable of generating echoes spontaneously. The size of the station struck me as particularly pompous when I realized that the whole thing accommodated but a single guideway. I would soon learn, however, that everything at Kharsog Keep was scaled to pomposity.

Bulky with luggage, we all left the train, clustering spontaneously into two groups, the cast of *Thyestes* and the fellowship of Lilit's salvation. It pleased me when Jonnie, hand on sword, allied himself with Lilit. Stone mosaics of nonfigurative pattern clacked beneath our feet. Tapestries depicting great moments from cephapple history swayed on the marble walls. The unmasking scene from *Tactics of the Wraith* was particularly well rendered.

Almost immediately we were greeted by a robot of the antique mechanical-man variety. His arms were perfect cylinders, his torso a sharply angled wedge of metal, his face a fierce cartoon of *Homo sapiens*. The robot moved on treads, as did the hopper that protruded from his rear like the horse half of a centaur.

"Your tickets, please." The Centaur's voice was full of static.

I pulled the four disks from my coat, fanning them out as I would a hand of Seven Deadly Sins. Instantly the Centaur snatched the tickets away and crumpled them into tiny wads of bronze.

"Place your luggage in the hopper," he said. "Including that sword," he continued, fixing on Jonnie.

I did not consider Basil a piece of luggage, so I decided to leave his carrycage on the platform. Otherwise we obeyed the order fully and quickly. The Centaur was not the sort of technology whose authority you questioned.

Zooming over to the Jugglers of Bone, the Centaur mangled their tickets, collected their luggage. He drove himself to a far wall and stopped beside a fountain where gold coins spouted from the mouth of a frog.

"She doesn't like it here," said Lilit. *"Morla kyrik eshika,"* she added.

"There's a man in this place who can help you," I replied.

"She doesn't want help."

Behind us, the black train began pulsing with silicon intelligence. It shunted its thoughts from its head to its tail and rushed off in the direction from which it had come.

My attention went to the south wall, to a triangular portal in which appeared an elderly person of indeterminate sex. I decided that he was a man and also a servant. His face recalled the shriveled but dignified necromancer in *Castle Brimstone*. Like the ticket-seller, he wore a Möbius strip on his tunic. The billowy gown was moored by a belt that, strangely, contained more than a hundred computer-terminal keys. A brass Möbius strip served as the buckle.

Without so much as a glance in our direction, the servant hobbled up to Torin. The two exchanged mumbles for several minutes.

Deigning at last to admit our existence, the servant approached and told me that his name was Prill and that mine must be Flick Longslapper. Lies again: I introduced Urilla as my wife, Jonnie as my son. Prill explained that our luggage would be returned to us "as soon as it was inspected" and that it would "not be necessary to dissect the cat."

He guided us toward the triangular portal. When he stepped across the threshold, I saw that he was standing on nothing but air. Beneath his feet, a dark elevator shaft plunged toward the center of planet Absu.

Noting my astonishment, Prill explained that his belt generated an antigravity field. It was safe for us to enter.

I closed my eyes, gulped twice, firmed my grip on Basil's carrycage, and stepped into the nothingness. The antigravity field was lumpy but firm. I felt as if I were walking on an aquacot. Urilla, Jonnie, and Lilit soon joined me.

Prill touched a key on his belt, and the magic carpet ascended, one, two, three, four . . . more than twenty levels.

Level Twenty-three.

My wayward stomach returned.

Disembarking into a naked antechamber, we followed Prill through a suite of rooms whose opulent furnishings and thick plushmuck carpets would thenceforth come to mind whenever I heard the words *luxury* and *class*. I felt more like a tourist of Kharsog Keep than like one of its guests.

Six bedrooms, each featuring a private bath and a tract of mattress so vast it was itself a kind of room, hemmed a central, circular hub. I loved that hub. It immediately replaced Clee Selig's library in my affections. There was a fireplace, fire in progress—a fire like none I have ever seen, a fire whose flames automatically shaped themselves into sculptural forms that cycled from a butterfly to a bird to a ram to a tiger and back again to a butterfly. There was a complimentary feast of ceph-apples, each in its own glass cube, the cubes stacked in a pyramid atop a bookcase and labeled with the titles of their respective dreams, a collection that included not only *The Toad of Night* but also two works I had been wanting to eat all my life, *The Last Time He Died* and *Illusion Travels by Spaceship*. There was a vending machine that dispensed everything from chocolate gumbombs to the most illegal varieties of psychedelic snuff. There was a reading chair that was both a sitting place and a seduction.

But the heart of the room was the mirror. It hung above the fireplace like a frozen elixir, encompassing in its fisheye stare the reading chair, the vending machine, and three bedroom doors. Gold and jewels flashed from an oval frame.

Before leaving, Prill assured us that, while Jonnie's sword naturally had to remain confiscated until our departure, the Centaur would bring up our luggage in one hour. The promise was kept, with five minutes to spare. As he turned to go, the Centaur announced that the snuff in the vending machine was really very good. How the hell would you know? I thought.

I missed Iggi.

Unpacking, Urilla and Jonnie and I became impressed by the integrity with which Prill had conducted his quest for hidden weapons and other treacheries. Everything was in its proper place, though he had not managed to erase all traces of his snoopings. I opened the electrobook printout in which I had intentionally inserted a white Lilit hair between pages 62 and 63. It was gone. Flipping to the endpapers, I noted with smugness a penciled note that said EX LIBRIS FLICK LONG-SLAPPER.

I snapped the book shut, studied the cover. Across the top were the words "*The Interpretation of Dreams* by Sigmund Freud." The reading chair showed me its come-hither softness. In the mirror I watched myself sit down. I started at the beginning.

"In the following pages," said Freud, "I shall demonstrate that there is a technique for interpreting dreams, and that, on the application of this technique, every dream reveals itself as a psychological structure, full of significance, that may be assigned to a specific place in the mental activities of the waking state."

It was midnight when the mirror first spoke to me.

On my lap *The Interpretation of Dreams*, open to Chapter Five, lay propped against Basil the Cat. Freud was reporting the dream of "an intelligent and cultivated young woman." As usual he detected nothing but sexual meanings, and as usual I wondered what Freud would make of a dream full of manifest vaginas and unequivocal penises; I like to think that the wise neurologist, who was not without humor, would have declared the penises to be symbols for asparagus. "This dream occurred at the beginning of the patient's psychoanalytic treatment," said Freud. "It was not until later that I learned she had been repeating in it the initial trauma from which her neurosis had arisen." I began to nod off. Freud went on without me. "I have since then come across the same behavior in other patients; having been exposed to a sexual assault in their childhood, they seek, as it were, to bring about a repetition of it in their dreams."

I was asleep. So was Jonnie, in his private bedroom. So was Urilla, in hers. And Lilit, in hers.

Two violet eyes shook me awake. I looked at the mirror, saw a light-limned face smiling from atop a light-limned torso.

"Hello," I said.

"I am Baron Kharsog," replied the image.

Simon Kusk fit none of the mental impressions I had inevitably formed of him over the past two years. I was expecting a kind of profane rhapsody on Clee Selig. I was expecting to see Selig's raw materials—his demiurgic frame, his soaring forehead—reworked into an archetype of evil. But no. The face I saw was small, puffy, and squat. Nothing grew on it. No lashes around the violet eyes, no brows above the thick lids, no hair or whiskers of any kind. I did not see it as a malefic face, a face given to observing sins of the flesh or to grinning over sins of the spirit, and despite the intervention of the holovision medium, a curious *joie de vivre* spilled down on me. All told, the face suggested nothing so much as a clean-shaven Saint Nicholas, the philanthropic elf king who annually deposited gifts beneath the nonsentient trees of those rare and dwindling societies that still observed Christmas Eve.

At first I assumed that the Kusk-Nicholas connection was a sufficient explanation for the bizarre and outrageous thing that happened next.

I was seized by a desire to worship the image. Yes, to genuflect before it, to kiss it, to show it every reverence that the Nicholas cult accorded its principal deity.

But then I saw something else in the face, a ghostly rapport of the sort that exists between a baby picture and the adult it predicts. The lotos-eaters' lack of artistic skill accounted for the discrepancy, but I could now see what they had been driving at.

The face in the mirror was the face on the great stone idol in the underground continent.

With this realization, my wish to worship the statue melted away, and my understanding of that wish became clear and certain. While the final moments of *The Lier-in-Wait* were still locked up in inaccessible psychic dungeons, it was a fair guess that they included an appearance by Simon Kusk in the role of Goth the Divine.

Basil growled at the mirror.

"Who nurtures my tree?" demanded Kusk. Hardly the voice of a god. It was weirdly childlike and rather sad. "Do I take it that Mr. Atropos has assumed your duties?"

Keep it simple, Quinjin, I warned myself. Be a truthful Longslapper, not a deceiving one. "I was hoping *you* might know where Mr. Atropos is, Baron Kharsog. I've not seen him in more than a year. He never returned from the Ganzir Cephapple Convention."

As Kusk became somber, his resemblance to the lotos-eaters' idol increased. "We must see if the police know anything. Ganzir, did you say? On Zahrim?"

"Yes. I appointed six people to run the plantation in my absence. Not pickers, I assure you—first-rank arborists. Their credentials await your inspection."

Kusk made a forget-it sort of gesture. "Tell me, Mr. Longslapper—how is my child?"

"Oh, she's a rare one, Baron. Thick fleshy branches, fruit like young breasts. Her bark doesn't have a single blemish. And *wise*—her taproot contains the finest brain I've ever seen in a noostree."

Briefly Kusk glistened with parental pride, then turned grim again. "Mr. Atropos's disappearance is very troubling."

"It certainly troubled *me*, sir."

"How did you determine where I was?"

"Hamadryad."

"Of course."

"Atropos is not the only person I'm worried about."

"I know," said Kusk.

I know: a small victory, but a treasured one. I had assumed that when I first raised the Lilit question, Kusk's response would be supercilious and oblique. But instead he had answered, *I know*.

"What could Atropos have been doing at that convention?"

That's simple; he was selling your *Lier-in-Wait*s behind your back. But what I said was, "Please . . . my daughter. Her mother is insane with worry." I realized that my vernacular use of the word *insane*, unplanned and poignant, could only help prove my sincerity. And indeed, Kusk now began to pursue the matter.

"How did it happen?"

"You know children—always curious." The scenes I painted for Kusk were quite congruent with the truth. Lilit sailing to the island . . . exploring the cave . . . discovering the branch . . . yielding to temptation, all the while unaware that this was "the very farm that kept her father away from home for months at a time."

"Will you see her?" I whimpered. "Will you?"

"Tomorrow morning Prill will lead your family to my private study. Meanwhile, I suggest that you eat one of the cephapples in your suite. It will give us some common ground. The title is *The Citadel of Pain*. Harmless, I assure you."

"I ate *The Citadel of Pain* a long time ago."

This was true. As a matter of fact, I had reviewed it for Francie Lem.

> *The Citadel of Pain* (A.G. 789). 96 minutes. Weaver:
> Balso DuPree. Lurid melodrama about Gorath, an
> insane dictator whose avocation is inventing torture
> devices. Don't take the children. Don't take the adults
> either.

"Then I wish you sweet dreams, Mr. Longslapper," said the Baron.

My dreams that night were not sweet. My dreams were of the Lier-in-Wait standing in a cul-de-sac, telling me that I had no hope of plumbing the lotosbean.

But at least I got some sleep.

15

History as Fruit

I grew up believing that a person who likes animals cannot be all bad, particularly when the animals in question are not themselves very likable. To judge from the animals whose company he kept, Simon Kusk was a very good man indeed.

After escorting Urilla, Lilit, and me to the forty-second level of Kharsog Keep, Prill ushered us into a private study that was also a kind of zoo. Although two of the walls were conventionally appointed with oak panels and rows of books, the others held glass habitats containing vertebrates of primal ugliness. There were more than a hundred different specimens. Initially I noticed a squat, tun-bellied creature reminiscent of the Toad of Night. Shortly afterward I spied a snapping turtle with a death's-head on its shell, an eel with teeth indistinguishable from sewing needles, and a rat whose body was tessellated with brown fur and bare pink skin. The vertebrates lived in a fixed hierarchy, mammals above reptiles above amphibians above fish, so that the total impression was of some astounding excavation in which a fossil from every epoch had been found occupying its appropriate evolutionary niche.

After warning us not to expect a long audience with his master—his master who was "so busy night and day struggling to bring forgotten wisdom and inner calm to the world"—Prill disappeared into an alcove containing a tall glass cylinder. The vulturelike sparrow inside the cylinder made nervous little helixes as it fluttered between floor and ceiling.

"Lord Goth is near," said Lilit. "She can feel him."

An accurate prophecy. Within seconds, Kusk was among us.

"Good morning, Mr. Longslapper—and family."

I recalled his lost-breeze voice from our vidiphone conversation of the previous evening.

He was an endomorphic man, smaller and chubbier than I had anticipated. His glossy fiberfoil robe sported two Möbius strips, one on each breast. The aquarium lights glared off his naked face and violet eyes. His skin looked water-soluble.

I should have been prepared for Lilit's behavior vis-à-vis Kusk. I should have seen foreshadows not only in the lotoseaters' sacraments but also in my own response when Kusk's face had appeared in the transceiver-mirror. The repeated prostrations, the moans suggestive of sexual climax, the kisses she planted on her redeemer's robe until I could see spittle stains— none of these observances should have taken me by surprise. But in those days epiphany was an unfamiliar phenomenon to me, and I was stunned. Stunned, afraid, and, in an odd way, embarrassed. Talas and I had raised Lilit in an environment of skepticism and reserve. We had taught her the sanctity of doubt. Yet here she was, a lapsed atheist quaking with faith.

"Lord Goth," she wheezed, "I am sinful, I am wicked"—it was vaguely comforting to hear Lilit speaking in the first person for a change, but I knew better than to see this as signaling a remission—"I am corrupt, I am depraved, I am vile, I am filthy, I am the Devil's own mistress."

"Go to your mother," said Kusk, studying the prone believer with the pleasure of a shopkeeper watching his first veneer cross the counter. Kusk, I could tell, wanted to collect my daughter. He wanted to tack her to his wall.

"*You* are my mother," Lilit replied.

Kusk's sluglike finger wriggled toward Urilla. "Go to that woman, stand by her side, and say nothing."

Lilit's compliance was instantaneous and unquestioning. Grasping my daughter's hand, Urilla forced a smile, then let her face slacken so abysmally it was as if her skull had dissolved. Good for you, Urilla. You are the original bereaved parent. We may bring this off yet.

On instructions from his master, Prill left the sparrow-vulture and grasped Lilit's free hand.

"Take these two back to their rooms," Kusk ordered. "I've seen enough."

"Now just a minute!" I shouted. "I think we deserve more than—"

"*More* is what I intend to give you," Kusk retorted. "Fifteen minutes from now I begin lecturing to my apprentices. Fully ten of those minutes belong to you, Mr. Longslapper. Use them wisely. I shall explain my diagnosis and then you can pass the facts on to Lilit's mother and brother."

Spontaneously I checked Lilit's chronamulet, which I had recalibrated to Absu's thirty-hour day. The message was 09:45:03.

When Prill, Urilla, and Lilit were gone, Kusk bade me sit down. The nearest available furniture was a couch not unlike the one I imagined Freud's patients using. It had flowers printed on it. For his own repose the Baron selected a jewel-studded, high-backed chair. The similarity to a throne was probably not accidental.

"The essential thing for you to understand, Mr. Longslapper, is that your daughter is not insane. She is the first of a new race. She has broken through to a higher plane of reality. In her you see *Homo sapiens superioris*."

I was wholly unprepared for this assessment. Lilit not insane?

"Please elaborate," I said, teeth locked like a ventriloquist's.

"Let me phrase it this way. Your daughter is insane only by the suffocating paradigms with which civilization indoctrinates us. The disease of our age is not insanity, my dear straw boss. The disease of our age is the straight line."

"I can't agree."

"That's because you have the disease." Kusk was the sort of prophet whose unctuousness came in a collapsible tube, and he now proceeded to squirt it all over me. "It's a tight box that reason and individuality stuff us into, and all its corners are ninety-degree angles, not a whit more or less. For the weed that lays waste our souls has its roots in the reductionist, bankrupt vision of the data-gatherers. Be honest with yourself—don't you want your daughter to achieve oneness with the Spirit of Absolute Being?"

"No, I want my daughter to know who I am."

"Tell me," he persisted, "how long has it been since you've had somebody to pray to? Don't pretend you've outgrown that sort of thing. Each of us needs a god. You, your wife, your son, your daughter. Have you ever been to Ganzir—to the Spiritual Nostalgia Room? People are *starved* for transcendence, they *lust* to cut through the sterile objectifications of the empiricists. A human mind can take just so much relativism, and then the craving for consecrated answers begins. Believe me, if we submitted your Lilit to a mental autopsy, we would find a consciousness cleansed of doubt. A consciousness at peace. Do you question my powers? You've lived on Hamadryad's farm—you've seen the light that rules it, felt the heat. I *made* that sun. Mine is a tree of certainty, Mr. Longslapper, and no wind in the cosmos can blow it over."

The shabby fact is that, for the moment at least, Kusk's arguments beguiled me. I was seduced. Hypnotized. Lilit enlightened, Kusk omnipotent, civilization a prison, selfhood a trap, reason a disease: I bought it all. I felt like a mortally ill patient coming to a doctor in hopes of a cure and instead being told that, while I was indeed doomed, death held certain heretofore unappreciated virtues.

"If peace is really what the apple gave Lilit"—I spoke slowly, cautiously, humoring myself with the thought—"then perhaps I've judged it too harshly. Still, wouldn't most people call her condition evil?"

"Evil—ah yes, evil. The great one-word cliché. Remind me to hold a seminar on evil. You say you've eaten *The Citadel of Pain*. What, exactly, do you make of Emperor Gorath?"

"I find Gorath to be . . . yes, evil."

"There! You see? We all walk around with such narrow models in our minds, such potboiler notions of what constitutes a villain. Gorath, if you'll remember, *tries* to be evil. A feeble characterization—I don't buy it. The *real* evil is caused by men and women who not only see themselves as moral but who impress other people as moral. Surely the Devil does bloody work—this we expect. But why are the saints' hands also red? A man makes a dream called *The Toad of Night*, the *sine qua non* of which is the primacy of conscience. So what happens? Suzie Freed eats the thing and gets inspired to kill her brother. You see how the human mind *really* works, my straw boss?"

At this point Prill came back into the study and again ensconced himself beside the sparrow-vulture.

Leaving Freud's couch, I stumbled toward Kusk's throne, exasperation pouring out of me. "Are you saying it's *my* fault that Lilit ate from Hamadryad? I was wrong to tend the tree, is that it?"

Kusk accompanied his reply with swift, delicate gestures, as if translating his own words into sign language. "I'm saying that your daughter is happier now than she's ever been. I'm saying that she will remain happy as long as she lives at the Lotos Institute. As for your own future: first, take comfort that there is a place for Lilit in the Church of Goth; second, realize that nothing can be done about her conversion; third, leave her with me and go back to the farm."

One, two, three. Kusk's commands left me trembling with bewilderment.

"You needn't fix your course now," he continued. "My words will not leave your brain. They will stay there, gathering sacramental energy, and in a matter of hours their truth will shine forth."

I glanced at the chronamulet. 09:51:08. I did not want a single one of the 235 seconds Kusk still owed me. The sooner I left this quag of confusion, this thicket of riddles, the better. At my request, Kusk told Prill to fly me back down to my suite. Before I left the study, the Baron wished me sweet dreams.

"This man is obviously a lunatic," said Urilla when she heard my report. "I'm sorry, Quinny, but Hamadryad must have lied to you. Kusk isn't the answer." She kept her voice low, aiming to elude whatever transceivers our host may have hidden in the walls. "There's a time to be hopeful and a time to choke down facts. And the essential fact is that we must take Lilit away from here."

She and I were in the hub, sitting on the floor before the fire-of-many-shapes. Jonnie lay athwart the reading chair, thumbing through his *Thyestes* script. Lilit was in her bedroom, devouring chocolate gumbombs while Rodnie Quash bleated away. Headphones mated her with the vocalith machine. I wondered how long it would be before she imagined herself pregnant by Mr. Quash.

My reply to Urilla was in a voice as calculatedly quiet as hers. "Obviously, you say? As I recall, you're the one who thought Baptizer Brown would *obviously* lead us straight to Hamadryad."

An ugly remark. To her credit, Urilla did not fight back. She merely walked over to the vending machine, obtained a bunch of non-psychoactive grapes, and began eating them. In her wisdom she understood my need to believe all that glup about Lilit being at peace. She realized that Kusk had told me, in essence, *It's out of your hands, you have no more parental obligations.*

Kusk had let me off the hook.

"And what do *you* think, Jonnie?" I whispered.

"I think . . ." Whatever Jonnie was planning to say, he detoured in midstream. "I think that Lilit is an exquisite person. A magic person." His voice could not have moved a bubble. "I also think," he said, facing his fears, "from what you've told us, that Kusk has figured out how to bottle slavery and sell it as enlightenment. I'm with Urilla. Let's remove Lilit from this place as soon as possible."

It was not what I wanted to hear.

When I said feebly, "Kusk believes that Lilit is happy," Jonnie and Urilla stared at me as if I were as insane as my daughter. I went into my bedroom and shut the door.

A few hours later, something happened to erase whatever sympathies I may have been feeling toward the Church of Goth.

Lilit entered. She approached the mattress on which I languished. Basil—the remnants of Basil—lay across her arms.

He had been emptied out. Eviscerated like the goat in *The Lier-in-Wait.* I did not need to hear Lilit's next words to know who the perpetrator was.

"She does whatever Goth commands," Lilit hissed. "You can see that now, can't you? *Kyrikush makesh morla morla!*"

A cat pelt is not at all like a cat.

Lilit set the bloody, gutted thing on the floor and left. At that instant I am sure that I hated her.

Nor was mine an inert hatred. It was, rather, a hatred that sent me running into Lilit's room. A hatred that made me thrust her aside. That made me smash her vocalith machine into tiny shards and stomp her Rodnie Quash recordings into a million slivers of mindlessness.

Silence.

And then, seeping everywhere, Lilit's sobs: anger, fear, and sorrow intermixed.

I kept my own sobs inside. All I could see, within and without, was my daughter on the Barge of the Mad, imprisoned in the violent ward, being visited by Talas and Urilla and Jonnie and me. She never recognized any of us, never once. Urilla was right. Hamadryad had lied. The tree's treasure was worthless. There could be no cure for Lilit at the Lotos Institute. Indeed, our sojourn here probably constituted the worst possible treatment, brine to the thirsty. I had to get her out.

And so I was back on the hook, dancing spasmodically, watching a shadow that was no longer connected to my body.

I girded myself for a night without sleep.

Came the conjuring hour, 00:00:00. I sat in the reading chair, in the company of Freud.

"It lies in the very nature of every censorship," said the father of psychoanalysis, "that of forbidden things the censorship allows those which are *untrue* to be said rather than those which are *true.*"

The events of the previous evening repeated themselves. First a violet stare wrested me from *The Interpretation of Dreams*. Then Kusk spoke. The closeup was so extreme that his eyes spanned the mirror and his jaw kept popping in and out of view.

"Tonight an important piece of news reached me," said Goth incarnate. "So important that it will change your life. Expect Prill after breakfast tomorrow."

"Will your news change Lilit's life, too?"

"What are you reading, Mr. Longslapper?"

Kusk, of course, did not care what I was reading. In ignoring my question he was punishing my directness.

"*The Interpretation of Dreams,*" I said. "By Sigmund Freud."

"Not much of it is true."

"My cat has been murdered," I said. "Lilit thought that sacrificing him would please you."

"It does not."

"Lilit loved that cat," I said.

"Lilit loves *me*," said Kusk.

I had assumed that our ascent would end, as before, on the forty-second level. Though numb from the previous night's insomnia, I nevertheless managed to grow apprehensive when the fiftieth level came and went in a flash. Not until we were well into the seventies did Prill begin to decelerate us. We made a complete stop at Level Eighty-five.

The hallway stretched past granite gryphons and tapestry renditions of the torture scenes from *The Citadel of Pain*. It ended in a white Lucite slab. When Prill and I approached the slab, it slid upward like a portcullis.

"Go in there," Prill commanded, and by the time I did, he was gone.

I found myself in the back of a room that combined the acoustics of a good lecture hall with the lurid intimacy of a surgical theater. The only person on the stage was Kusk. Behind him rose a plaster wall decorated with a fresco painting of a noostree. A real door had been cut into the trunk. The distance between myself and the Baron was terraced by velvet-upholstered seats, only a handful of which were occupied. I speculated that there was something psychologically lawful about the apprentices' dispersal, that they had unconsciously scattered themselves in a pattern guaranteeing maximum isolation from each other and, hence, minimum distraction from their master's words. They leaned toward the stage with taut, eager bodies, and I sensed that, for all Kusk's power to scrub brains and steal wills, his students still had minds of their own.

On the stage were two adjacent operating tables. An uprooted noostree seedling more than three meters long lay across both. Thrust into the trunk like acupuncture needles, plastic hoses delivered sap and anesthesia from a small, droning machine.

Kusk picked up a laser scalpel, pointed it toward his patient's taproot. "Some of you question why a dreamweaver needs to know a lot of dry-as-mummy-dust botany. Just remember, when you become a weaver you enter into psychic communion with another species." The Baron lectured with the careful fervor of a professional eulogist. "The more you know about noos-trees, the more successful is your art."

He activated the scalpel, turned the blue pungent beam on the root. As he made the incisions, xylem layers flopped away. Only a small amount of sap rushed out, accompanied by smoke from the burning tissue. The smoke collected into a kidney-shaped cloud; it seemed that the tree's soul was escaping. At length the brain appeared, looking from where I stood like a green and repeatedly perforated sausage. I simply had to accept Kusk's word for it that the thing had four distinct lobes. He named the lobes for his audience, pointed out their ana tomical interrelationships, described their functions. For the coup de grâce, he burrowed into a lobe and excised a malignant growth.

Applause.

"When next we meet," said Kusk, "it will not be in this amphitheater, it will be at the Midterm Banquet. I trust you can all attend. The Jugglers of Bone are to perform, and believe me, a novice weaver can't ask for better inspiration. Until then—I wish you sweet dreams."

A bell rang, and Kusk made a begone-evil-spirits sort of gesture.

Rising, the students channeled themselves into the center aisle. As they filed past me—five young men, six young women— I studied their faces for signs of why they had apprenticed themselves to Simon Kusk when hundreds of saner teachers were available. But apart from the Möbius strips on their tunics, the students struck me as a diverse and healthy group, interchangeable with those I had seen at Wendcraft Univer-sity, and I concluded that Kusk valued them more for their tuition payments than for their potential as good Gothians.

Descending through the tiers, I approached the podium, contemplated the naked brain. I pretended to understand what

207

I was seeing. One apprentice had stayed behind, an angelic young man with large eyes and a failed mustache. He was dutifully stitching up the root.

"I imagine my lecture was all *terra cognita* to you, my straw boss?" said Kusk.

"It's always salutary to review the basics," I said.

Kusk opened the door in the painted noostree's trunk. "Good! The man I seek cannot be arrogant!"

Before we left the amphitheater, Kusk instructed the apprentice, whose name was Creegmoor, to take the seedling to the recovery room.

Behind the painted tree stretched a phreneseed nursery reminiscent of the one back at Wendcraft. I followed the Baron down avenues lined with computer consoles and with stores of the purine and pyrimidine bases. Reaction chambers lay at the intersections, their rubber tubes poised to plop synthesized genes into petri dishes.

At first I thought that all the dishes were empty, but soon we were standing before a large and robust seed. The glass uterus lulled its occupant into a deep botanic sleep. Putting on a plastic glove, Kusk picked up the seed using his thumb and index finger like tongs.

"I believe this is our breakthrough," he said.

"A new edition of *The Lier-in-Wait?*"

"At the Lotos Institute we do not repeat ourselves, Mr. Longslapper. The convert who eats this dream will achieve a knowledge of good and evil that can only be termed encyclopedic. *Reap the Whirlwind*—that's the title—and it turns you into the only person who can save Terransector from thermonuclear annihilation. The ultimate responsibility, no? But the real question is, do you fail or succeed? Don't worry—I'm not one to spoil an ending."

"You have a critic's instincts."

"And you have a planter's. Am I right? If I gave you this seed, you would know what to do with it?"

"I could make it fruitful," I replied, sounding as if I believed myself.

"Of course, and there lies an injustice—no? The aristocrats get the glory, but it's you front-line workers who can actually keep a tree alive. Here's the crux of it—Atropos is dead. I want you to take his place."

"Dead?" (Good show, Quinjin. Your ex-wife couldn't have done better.)

"Last night I contacted the Ganzir police via neinstein wave, and they beamed me some highly unaesthetic pictures of a body found near the convention site almost two years ago. An unidentified body. I identified it for them."

Kusk supplied certain details that were not news to me.

"Is the murderer at large?"

"I don't know. I don't care. The point is, I've been studying the printouts on Atropos. True, there's very little in them about you, but he did venture three opinions. First, you love the dreambean medium. Second, while noostrees are not your main area of horticultural expertise, you have an unusual sympathy for the species. And, finally, you're honorable. In short, I am looking at one of the few people I can turn to in this crisis."

"Crisis?"

"A year from now my Hamadryad comes of age. Child to adult. She'll need someone by her side who understands her, someone who can make wise decisions. There are predator battles to be planned, fertilizer schedules to be worked out, pruning operations to be completed, inoculations to be given."

Funerals to be arranged, I thought. The fact that I had exterminated the entire *Lier-in-Wait* crop was the only thing that gave me pleasure anymore.

"And, of course, before we know it—the harvest. I realize that my offer is very sudden, Mr. Longslapper, and certainly there are dimensions to our relationship that make you an unlikely candidate. But tell me—was I right? Have you begun to appreciate Lilit's higher consciousness? Can you at last comprehend the hope and beauty and stability in this Church?"

It seemed a perfect time to make the speech I had memorized. At Kharsog Keep, I knew, fire must be fought with fire, Simon Kusk with lies.

"I've seen the serenity in Lilit's eyes," I said. "The rapture. She is the next step in our evolution. Your apples mark the path to transcendent knowledge and ultimate reality. I am grateful to you for making the universe so clear to Lilit."

I went on like that. A catechism of lies.

The Baron pushed the flab of his face into a smile. "I knew that the meaning of my tree would not elude you for long. How *wise* you have become."

Yes, I thought, Urilla called it right: the man is a lunatic.

"And yet," Kusk continued, "for all your wisdom, I doubt that you can grasp how much you'll profit from this job. Job? Did I call it a job? Oh, it's much more than that. Power and riches will be your daily bread! History will know you as the first Archbishop of the Church of Goth!"

The Baron turned toward the nearest computer console, its flat façade twinkling like a Christmas tree. He touched one of the lights and a panel zipped away, revealing a niche. In the niche I saw an electroderby.

"We are in a phreneseed nursery," said Kusk, "but it should be called a cathedral." He extracted the metal helmet with the gentleness he would have accorded a noostree's brain. "By the same reasoning, this is an electroderby, but it should be called a miter—that's how profoundly I have modified it! That's how high cephapple technology has risen at the Lotos Institute!"

The Prince of Lies crowned himself.

"So the choice is yours, sir," he said. "You can spend the rest of your life taking orders from a lot of pigfat planters, or you can stay here for a semester, learn more about dream gardening than anyone else in the galaxy, and help us move this mystic medium toward its destiny."

"I'd like to think it over," I said, employing the inflection that the young medical student had used for the same cliché in *Cut Cards with the Devil*. I spoke the truth. I did need to think it over, for it was still unclear to me whether agreeing to be Kusk's planter—his Archbishop—would work to my advantage or to my ruin.

"Follow me," said Kusk, returning the profane miter to its niche.

We entered the elevator shaft, and for the second time that morning, I was launched heavenward. We went to the end of the line, to Level One Hundred. I soon learned that Level One Hundred was not a level at all. It was the roof of the Keep.

A greenhouse sprawled before us, although the term "palace of glass" might better convey the ambitions behind its design. Above my head, mammoth panes of frosted transplastic rested on steel beams. The great star Ninnghizzida suffused the place with heat, light, and an aura of things primeval. Sniffing the air, feeling its hot, wet pull on my face, I fancied myself encased in a lung. The hair in my nostrils grew dank.

Kusk's little trees, none of them taller than four meters, were arranged in ranks and files. Simple arithmetic gave me their number. Seven times seven, plus two odd ones: fifty-one. They all looked newborn and vulnerable—only a third had begun fruiting—yet hardly innocent. They were teratoid, twisted, obscene.

Armed with a pruning hook, a decrepit gardener ambled through the orchard, seeking dead limbs. His body and gait were beetlelike, as if over the years he had come to identify with the pests on whom he waged war. Seeing Kusk, he went rigid with self-consciousness, and I knew he would not dare prune a twig while we remained in the greenhouse. The Möbius strip on the gardener's tunic was woven from fiberfoil; the threads sparkled in the morning sun.

"Your school is prolific," I said as we wandered among the latent farms.

"The Church of Goth requires many converts," Kusk explained. "Decades ago I tested a prototype—the Vorka Massacre, some blasphemers called the results. Many problems with that dream. It changed people's minds, yes, but it didn't bring them into the true faith. I never even bothered to transplant the sapling. Then, after years of research—Hamadryad! Breakthrough! Success! But, prolific as she is, she'll never provide us with enough fruit. Hence, the garden in which we walk."

"Did you script all of these?"

"Scripted them"—his nod was modest—"then burned the scripts. There's only one way to get knowledge from these fruits, and that's to eat. As for the actual seedmaking, I'm pleased to say that every tree here can be credited to a Lotos Institute graduate. Of course, these dreams won't *all* prove worthy of shipment to a hydrasteroid. They must pass certain tests of . . . conviction."

"Conviction," I repeated dully.

"We have any story, any plot, any dream you could want here," said Kusk. "Lies for all occasions. Coming up on your right, for example, the Lie of the Just War. The bean inserts you into one of the Terran Age wars of religion—into a blood-soaked siege called Magdeburg. Next, of course, we have the Lie of the Just Peace. And over on your left, the Lie of the Loving God, followed by the Lie of the Benevolent Dictator. Look to the right now: the Lie of the Greater Good, the Lie of the Lesser Evil, the Lie of the Innocent Child, the Lie of Holy Matrimony, the Lie of Free Will."

By now we were at the far end of the orchard, leaning against an open shed and looking, I am sure, more like two school chums waiting for a troglobus than like two middle-aged men plotting how to turn the human race into a cult. I speculated that the planks constituting the shed came from seedlings that had failed Kusk's tests of "conviction."

Kusk summoned his minion. "Horg!"

The gardener scuttled over. Presenting himself, he twitched with unease, periodically thrusting the pruning hook into the ground and pulling it out again.

"What do you know of the moon, Horg?"

"Tonight you'll be able to thread a needle in here, that's how bright it gets on the Twelfth of Lammas." The gardener's voice matched his body—thin and insectile. "But it won't be a *full* moon until tomorrow night."

"Tell me, Horg, do you believe that a noostree thrives best if planted during a full moon?"

"No, Baron Kharsog."

"Neither do I. Still, why go against the legends? Our *Reap the Whirlwind* seed is ready for planting. Put her in the ground at midnight tomorrow."

"Whatever you wish," said Horg, his obsequiousness bordering on mockery.

"Meet Flick Longslapper, the Institute's new planter." Kusk shot me a quizzical look. "You *are* the Institute's new planter, correct?"

"I haven't decided," I said.

Horg and I shook hands, and my palm touched sweat, dirt, and calluses.

After the gardener had returned to his deathtrees, I realized that the moment had come either to reject Kusk's offer or to accept it on one crucial condition.

"Very well, Baron Kharsog. I shall become your Archbishop—but first a question. You said that I am honorable. And I agree. But what about you? Are *you* a man to trust?"

Side by side we walked into the shade of the greenhouse's oldest tree, whom Kusk identified as *Pigs to the Market*. The limbs made random, creepy gestures, defiling the ground with the shadow of a beast that should never have been born. As a branch touched Kusk's head, he harvested one of its lotosbeans.

"History is fruit," said the Baron. "Prince Paris favors

Aphrodite with an apple of gold and the fate of Troy is sealed. Lord Newton sees a *Pyrus malus* fall, so wonder is banished from the galaxy. And let us not forget the Garden of Eden, where it is said that—"

"I don't want to know about history. I want to know about—"

"Of *course* you can trust me."

"Then you will grant Lilit and Urilla safe passage out of here. Yes, I am sure that my daughter loves your Church. But please. You must understand. Please. We *can't* give her up. Not yet. Not now. Not until she's . . . older."

For a long while Kusk said nothing, but merely polished the lotosbean with his sleeve. Suddenly he opened his robe, and I saw that his tunic was secured by elevator controls of the sort that Prill also wore. Unbuckling the belt, he draped it over my shoulder.

"Why this?" I asked.

"You'll need it to reach the train station tomorrow night. At Hour Twenty-nine an Ushumgallum shuttle leaves the castle to pick up provisions for the Midterm Banquet. You may place your wife and child on board. Accompany me to my study now, and I shall give you the necessary tickets. You look surprised, my Archbishop."

More likely I looked stupefied. "Quite surprised."

"Letting your daughter go is the only way I can prove to you that she belongs here. Once you apprehend her suffering, you will not know an easy conscience until she is back, restored to her holistic instincts, fused with the divine perfection. As a loving father, you will do what is best for her—this is certain."

I strapped on the belt. Was I suspicious? Of course. But then the hollow corpse of Basil the Cat flashed into my brain, and I resolved to put Lilit and Urilla on the train no matter what.

Kusk gestured toward his children. "So, what's the potential yield here, my Archbishop? Assume that half the orchard proves viable. How many apples do we reap?"

"If the hydrasteroids are rich, if the fungi stay away—ten billion."

"Ten billion." The words, I could tell, were honey on his tongue. "Good. And Goth appears in every one of them. The future is written, Your Grace. Before the century ends, the entire galaxy will be eating me!"

16

Audience Participation

The entire galaxy will be eating me! Try as I might, I could not exorcise Kusk's boast from my thoughts. Having seen the unholy grove, the orchard of deathtrees fruity with doom, I realized that countless innocent victims were now targeted for madness, Vorka Massacre after Vorka Massacre. *The entire galaxy will be eating me!* Not if Quinjin the Great could help it.

I spent the afternoon testing out my new wings. By evening, Kusk's elevator belt had me zooming up and down the shaft with the confidence and dexterity of the endlessly cycling sparrow-vulture I had seen in his study. And, like the sparrow-vulture, I soon discovered that perpetual motion is not the same thing as progress.

My probings of Kharsog Keep were as systematic as they were futile. I alighted on every floor in turn. Typically, my exploration ended abruptly in an antechamber where marble walls supported ponderous and impenetrable doors. The elevator belt was but a key to the familiar, a passport solely to the known. Level One, the maglev station. Level Twenty-three, our suite. Level Forty-two, Kusk's study. Level Eighty-five, the amphitheater and phreneseed nursery. Level One Hundred, the greenhouse.

To this list add Level Fifty-eight. Here the antechamber included no locks, no doors, but only the unadorned entrance to a stone corridor. A sign said BANQUET HALL.

Creeping down the damp, cylindrical, crudely lit passageway, I found myself recalling *Mr. Sparrow's Blasphemy*, an avant-garde cephapple in which you toured the large intestine of a sacred cow. Voices rattled off the stones. No mystery—rowdy feasts were probably a nightly event at the castle. I approached slowly, apprehensively, swallowing moist gray air. The voices grew louder, then fell away one by one, leaving only a basso profundo that I knew belonged to the director of the Jugglers of Bone.

Torin Diffring was yelling his tonsils out.

By now I was familiar with how reality was calibrated at Kharsog Keep. It seemed only normal that the banquet hall should be larger than a vulcanbomber hangar, that it should be illuminated by the sort of immense gasball that had incubated Hamadryad in the underground continent, that it should be heated by a shape-shift fire ablaze in a hearth the size of a grorg's mouth, that the nethermost doorway should be flanked by granite gryphons, that huge, wooden, jade-eyed ravens should be perched on the backs of the dining chairs, and that the table itself should be a polished marble slab of a weight and length sufficient to seal a dozen adjacent graves. The only true surprise was an object of relatively modest proportions. Not far from the table, a wooden platform supported three of Torin's actors, Jonnie among them. It was a stage of the most austere sort—no scrims, no footlights, no proscenium, no curtain. The only props were five wooden crates, each painted a different color, one of which held a large, crust-covered pie on its top surface. Such minimalism made sense, I felt, the Jugglers of Bone being practitioners of what is sometimes called pure theater, theater in the raw.

Torin stood on the table, pacing back and forth like a caged carnivore. He clutched a copy of his *Thyestes* script, as did each of the actors, a fact that explained the director's rage. Jonnie had not yet learned his lines. He was not yet "out of the book." Nor was his co-actor, an intense fellow with a chicken's scraggy neck and a beak-née-nose to match. Nor was his other co-actor, a svelte woman whose face alternated between plainness and sensuality with sly, Necker Cube shifts.

"You said you'd be out of the book by tonight," Torin fumed. "You *all* said that. Get out of the goddamned book or get out of the goddamned play!"

"Yes, love," said the Necker Cube Woman, half patronizing, half contrite.

"Don't melt," said the Chicken Man.

"Three days to the banquet!" said Torin. "That's 90 standard hours, 5400 standard minutes, 324,000 standard seconds, and fewer chronons than you think—tick, tick, tick!" He channeled all his frustrations into his left heel, which he hammered into the slab and then used as a pivot. His about-face brought me in range of his stabbing eyes. "Here!" he said. "*You* direct this thing!"

He pitched the script forward. It fluttered into my arms on paper wings.

"I just want to watch," I said.

Torin smiled, kept smiling, soon freeing himself of his anger. He turned and walked toward the stage, his boots clopping on marble. "Does anyone object if Mr. Longslapper observes our humble attempt to provide the Lotos Institute with some after-dinner entertainment?"

"Fine with me," said the Necker Woman.

"Let him stay," said the Chicken Man.

"Hello, Flick," said Jonnie.

Still holding the script, I pulled up a chair and its guardian raven, then sat down.

"Let's forget about the dialogue," said Torin to his cast. "For the rest of the evening we'll work on the *soul* of the play."

"Good idea," said the Chicken Man.

"Let us disappear into ourselves," said Torin, slipping his hands under his elevator-controls belt. "For Scene Sixteen to mean anything, the audience must feel your anguish over what Atreus made you do. Yes, you're merely servants, you were simply obeying, but your complicity in the crime is starting to eat you away. I want to *know* that guilt, not just hear it in the lines. I want guilt in your gestures. Your breaths. I want guilt to come slithering off that stage and infect the audience like a plague."

Thumbing through the script, I located Scene Sixteen. It consisted mainly of the servants recalling how their master, Atreus, had recently presented them not only with a corpse but also with instructions to bake its head into a pie. The corpse was, of course, that of the favorite child of Thyestes, Atreus's mortal enemy. Having followed Atreus's orders fully, the servants were now being attacked by their consciences; the scene climaxed with their mutual recognition that they lacked the courage to tell the police. Torin seemed to be making some point or other about self-delusion and apathy.

"Excuse me, love," said the Necker Woman, "but that's a load of squatprod and you know it. Kharsog didn't hire us so his apprentices can see what *guilt* looks like. He hired us to frighten the teeth right out of their skulls."

"A simple challenge, really," said the Chicken Man.

"Like getting laughs from a cow," said the Necker Woman.

The director sat on the edge of the slab and inflated his lips into a pout. "Yes, yes—but the word isn't *frighten*. It's *disturb*. Kharsog wants us to disturb the apprentices. You're right, though—the baked head simply won't do it. Everybody will say, 'Oh, that old chestnut.' It's a ludicrous idea anyway."

"Shakespeare used it," said the Chicken Man defensively, fearful that Torin was about to slash his part from the script. Suddenly Torin was on his feet, skipping merrily down the slab as if prefacing a cartwheel. "Ah-hah! Ah-hah! Genius time, folks! The show *has* to end this way!"

The Chicken Man's eyelids assumed a sardonic position. "You've never seen a Diffring brainstorm before, have you, Jonnie? Get out your umbrella."

In a single unbroken action, Torin jumped from the table to the stage and seized the pie. "The first step is to throw out *this* foolish thing!"

He hurled it discus fashion, sending it toward the gryphon-flanked door. Pie guts splattered everywhere.

"Terrific, Torin!" said the Necker Woman. "We'll finish off with a pie fight! That will just disturb them to *death!*"

Torin rubbed his hands together so intensely I could almost feel the heat. "Ready? It's the night of the Midterm Banquet! The apprentices file in, eat their fill—but the last course, dessert, never arrives. Okay? Our little play begins. Scene One, Scene Two, Scene Three . . . all the way up to Scene Sixteen. Now, in the *new* version of Scene Sixteen, the child's head isn't baked into one large pie! His *whole body* is baked into a lot of little ones! We'll have a spleen pie, a heart pie, a liver pie, a pancreas pie, a left-lung pie, a right-lung pie, a couple of kidneys—however many we need!"

Turning to Jonnie, the Necker Woman said, "No one ever accuses Torin Diffring of writing wishy-washy."

"Are you with me? Scene Seventeen: Thyestes sits down to eat his pie—the heart pie, let's say. At which point Jonnie here leaves the stage with the other desserts and gives one to everybody at the table. Get it? We'll be turning Kharsog and his disciples into Atreus's other dinner guests! We'll be putting them right in the middle of the goddamned scene! It's what you call audience participation!"

"It's what you call sick," said the Necker Woman. "I like it," she added.

"You'd *better* like it," demanded Torin. "We've not seen its kind since the flying eyeballs in our *Oedipus*! Pow! Pow! Of course, we'll just use *figs* or something in the pies. We won't dissect a child."

"Art is nothing but compromises, eh, Torin?" said the Chicken Man.

More stunts from the director: hopping from one wooden crate to another, broad-jumping back onto the table. He approached my side, took back his script, and crouched forward in a manner suggesting that I was about to receive a confidence. "If you dare tell Baron Kharsog about our little gimmick," he informed me smoothly, "we put *you* in the pies."

Torin probably thought this would get a laugh. It did not. Just then I was too obsessed—obsessed with the belief that there might in fact be a way to prevent a pandemic of Vorkas, obsessed with the possibility that in Torin's "little gimmick" lay a means of bringing down Kusk—to give anything a laugh.

When the rehearsal was over, I told Torin, in a voice too obviously straining to mask villainous thoughts, that Jonnie and I needed a few minutes alone. Afire with his audience-participation scheme, Torin offered no argument, but merely stated that they would wait for Jonnie by the elevator shaft.

"An opportunity like this will come only once in our combined lifetimes," I told Jonnie after the Jugglers had disappeared into the cylindrical corridor. My whisper was coarse and fearful. "Fourteen little fig pies, right?"

"Fourteen," he agreed, bewildered.

"Twelve benign ones for the apprentices, another benign one for Thyestes . . . and a poisoned one for Kusk. Can you arrange it, Jonnie?"

"Poisoned? You said poisoned? Hell, I'm no Kusk enthusiast, you know that, but—well, *poison* a person, and you'd better have a lot of reasons."

"The reasons are above us." I told Jonnie about the rooftop greenhouse and its fifty-one deathtrees. I explained how the orchard was an army poised to commit spiritual genocide, an arsenal pointed at the collective mind. "Don't try to argue me out of this, friend. I'm thinking of all those fathers whose daughters *haven't* yet eaten Kusk's fruit, and I'm doing what they would wish."

Jonnie's conversion happened with lotosbean speed and finality. "So Torin's minor melodrama has the potential to prevent a major tragedy," he mused. "I'll bake the pies myself, rig the Baron's, serve it to him when the appointed moment arrives—no chance of a mixup. How much toxicology do you know, Quinjin?"

"None."

Jonnie opened his script, searched out the obsolete versions of Scenes Sixteen and Seventeen. "Fifty-one trees, did you say? Then there must be poisons about. Pesticides. Herbicides."

"I'll get you some," I said. There followed one of those sudden plunging silences that are not intended but that happen anyway. The silence enabled us to hear the crackle of the shape-shift fire as it evolved from butterfly to bird to ram to tiger, and the echoing voices of Torin and the Necker Woman as they argued over a point of characterization.

"This is all rather insane," I said at last. "I hope you realize that. It's like something out of a goddamned dreambean."

"Right now only one fact keeps me from becoming Kusk's assassin."

"Only one?"

"Only this—Lilit is still in the castle. You must get her to Widow Flum's. If Kusk smells a conspiracy, he'll go after her, I know he will."

"You'd make a good father," I said, displaying the two maglev tickets Kusk had given me earlier that day.

"My affection for Lilit is not exactly the fatherly kind. It's something I've been meaning for us to talk about, Quinjin. When Kusk is out of the way, you and I are going to take this castle apart with a surgeon's kit—we're going to look behind

222

the tapestries, inside the vases, until we find some clue as to how he did that Lotos Factor, some hint of what the proper therapy might be. And should we fail, that won't be the end of our searching. No, we'll fly my *Fleshpot* from one end of Terransector to the other—we'll see doctors, consult psychiatrists, listen to quacks, try out shamans, hire researchers, bribe politicians. And if we find the antidote, if Lilit gets her 'I' back, it won't take her long to realize that weird Jonnie is doing everything he can to make her say, 'I love you.' "

"You *love* her?"

"I love her. You want me to draw you a dirty picture?"

"You're an incubiber," I said defiantly.

"I'll give it up."

"Okay, okay. It's fine, really. I'll even tell you something. She used to be really sweet on you. She used to talk about you all . . . the . . . time. She . . . used . . . to . . . say . . ." I realized that I was going to cry. "I can't think about this."

"Of course not."

Two tears now, and several sobs, none of them ashamed.

Jonnie ripped Scenes Sixteen and Seventeen out of his script. He crumpled each page with the aplomb of the Centaur destroying a maglev ticket. The fire crackled. The Jugglers of Bone bickered. Starting down the corridor, Jonnie dropped the obsolete scenes behind him, one at a time—Hansel leaving his trail of hope.

If the grorg has a seventh stomach, I thought upon entering the train station the next evening, it can't be drearier than this place. The only illumination came from the shuttle itself, which rested on its guideway like a twenty-eyed serpent. Beyond the vaulted ceiling, snowflakes were bucked by nocturnal winds.

My daughter's sleep was profound, the frozen sleep of the chronically enlightened, a fact essential to our mission. If awake, of course, she would have behaved just as Kusk so glibly predicted, claiming that we were kidnappers, screaming that we had no right to take her from God. She was draped across

Urilla's arms, carried the way the victims of the ape-monsters were carried in *Revenge of the Australopithecines*. The lights of the train made much ado over Lilit's white hair.

The Centaur, tireless sentry, buzzed over and submitted the tickets to a gaze that ranged across the entire electromagnetic spectrum. Convinced of their authenticity, he said haughtily, "Three passengers, but only two tickets."

"I'm not going," I explained. "I have further business here."

Out of either decorum or boredom, I don't know which, the Centaur went to the back wall of the station, allowing me privacy for my farewells. Unknown to the Centaur, he was also allowing me privacy for consulting Urilla in the matter of his master's murder.

And still I postponed the question, fearful that she would be so horrified by our aim or, perhaps worse, so contemptuous of our strategy that I would allow myself to be talked out of it. She was under the impression, carefully cultivated by me, that I was staying behind simply to catch Jonnie's performance in *Thyestes*. She knew nothing of Torin's audience-participation scene, nothing of the plan to have Kusk participate unto death.

"I'm sorry things didn't work out here," said Urilla. "From that first moment we saw her lying by Lake Rosamond, we both realized that she might never get well."

"Here's a bit of news," I said, ignoring her blasphemy. "Jonnie wants to marry her."

Urilla noted that Jonnie had better taste in love than he did in dreambeans. "So do you, come to think of it," she added.

Our kiss was short, awkward, punctuative. After that, I kissed Lilit's braids in the same manner.

Now it was here, the blessed point of no return. My duty was to embrace it without thinking, saying, "If you wanted to poison somebody, Urilla, what would you use?" The question came in a quavering voice that disclosed every single one of my doubts.

"Quinny, you're planning something ridiculous!"

"You have two choices. You can answer, or you can not answer."

"Yes, Kusk is a maniac, he did a terrible thing to Lilit, but assassinating him won't help, it's not your obligation."

"All right, I'll just *guess*."

"There are lots of poisons," she snapped. "Strychnine. And, of course, you are no stranger to belladonna-29."

"This time I'm limited to dreamfarming materials. Herbicides—"

"Forget those things. You must use a seed."

"A phreneseed?"

"Yes. They're indigestible, and they have a delayed reaction." Urilla the Psychobiologist. Urilla the Witch. "You can leave the scene of the crime before the crime occurs. But I still believe you're on a course that will make your stay with the lotos-eaters seem like a summer by the sea."

She started away. Divining her approach, the door of the central coach irised out, and she entered without breaking stride.

Before Urilla could lay Lilit down, the black train made a silent, skulking exit. I lingered on the platform, watching as the lanterns on the rear observation coach sped away like tracer bullets. The storm, the dark, the distance all claimed the train, and I turned my heart to the night's final task.

As I expected, Horg was punctual. The instant Lilit's chron-amulet flipped from 29:59:59 to 00:00:00, the gardener's spade pierced the greenhouse soil.

I was hiding behind the tree that Kusk had called *Pigs to the Market*. Glancing toward the transplastic membrane above my head, I saw that the storm was over. The light of the full moon flowed down, sheathing the apples in bronze.

Within minutes the womb was prepared. The gardener delivered the seed: the Institute's "breakthrough," as Kusk had put it, *Reap the Whirlwind*. Two scoops of fertilizer followed.

He sealed the hole, gathered up his things, and scurried to the wooden shed where Kusk and I had loitered on the previous day.

The shed could not have been organized more rationally. There was a compartment for herbicides, one for fungicides, one for pesticides, one for the pruning hook, one for the secateurs, and so on. Methodically, Horg deposited the spade and the fertilizer bag in their proper places. His sluggishness brought me to the verge of screams. It was like waiting for somebody to give birth.

At last Horg left the greenhouse. A long cloud glided across the moon.

Stealing out from behind *Pigs to the Market*, I went to the shed and seized the instrument of the fetal transplant I intended to perform. The loose soil yielded readily to my spade thrusts. Approaching the seed, I exercised the caution of a surgeon. At a depth of one meter, I abandoned the spade entirely and sifted through the dirt with my fingers.

The seed was compact, sticky, and warm. It sat on my palm like an obese snail.

I had thought of everything. From my vest pocket I produced a glass cube containing one of the complimentary dreambeans that had come with our suite—*The Citadel of Pain*, in fact. Prying back the lid, I removed the bean and replaced it with the unsprouted seed.

Another cloud came—another moon-scrim.

As an afterthought, I threw the *Citadel of Pain* apple into the hole and buried it.

I smiled.

It would be almost a week before the gardener realized that nothing was growing here.

And by then . . .

17

The Recombinant DNA
Eucharist

"*Pat-a-cake, pat-a-cake, baker's man,*" said Jonnie as he entered our suite and set the booby-trapped pie at my feet.

I freed myself from the reading chair's embrace, picked up the pie, hefted it. It was a compact concoction, no larger than the saucer from which Basil used to take his daily milk. The crust was brown and lumpy—the terrain of a continent I never wanted to visit. And beneath the surface, of course, a handful of figs and an unborn tree.

"There are thirteen more just like it back in the kitchen," Jonnie explained. "Well, not *exactly* like it, heh-heh. The stage manager will stick them in the oven during Scene Twelve so they'll be nice and hot for Scene Seventeen."

"I'll be honest, Jonnie. I'm having second thoughts—third thoughts. Something will go haywire, I know it. You'll give him the wrong pie."

"Highly improbable," he said, confidence running out of his pores. "You remember the rest of the rhyme, don't you? *Roll*

it and shape it and mark it with a B . . . Look at the crust."
A letter *B* was etched there. "*B* for what?" I asked, wishing
that Iggi could have been around for all this cloak-and-dagger
business.

"*B* for anything you like. *B* for Belial. Beast. Bastard."

"*And put it in the oven* . . . ," I said.

"*For baby and me,*" said Jonnie.

When my friend had gone, I realized that the banquet was
still forty hours in the future. Forty hours of anticipating the
forty ways in which our plot could fall apart. (What if Kusk
hated figs?) Forty hours in which I did not dare leave the suite
for fear of running into Kusk and inadvertently spilling the
whole thing. (Tell me, Baron, what are your preferences in
pie?)

How to pass the time? Further conversations with Jonnie?
Unlikely. With Zero Hour approaching, Torin had begun to
panic. He allowed his actors to leave the banquet hall only
when Prill insisted on practicing the place settings and running through the serving procedures. And even during these
intervals, Torin kept the cast together. He made them rehearse
in the elevator shaft.

I decided to spend my self-incarceration by going on a dream
binge. The stack of complimentary apples on the bookcase
grew steadily smaller. Wary of encountering a lotosbean, I
selected only those titles with which I was familiar. And so it
was that I ate *The Toad of Night*, becoming a sane adolescent
girl for the second time in my life. I ate *Known Quantities*,
becoming a sentient robot once again. On and on, bean after
bean, I ceded my reality to Selig's biotechnology.

My plan was to get through the banquet itself by becoming
the terminally ill marathon runner in *Twenty-six Miles to Go
Before I Sleep*. Upon returning to Quinjinhood, I would simply
pace around the suite until Jonnie showed up with the presumed good news. An hour before the event, however, Kusk's

face appeared in the mirror, and an unexpected invitation soon followed.

"Our Midterm Banquet will be less populated than I had supposed," he said. "There is a place for you at the table."

The question, of course, was whether Kusk's suspicions would be more aroused by a refusal to attend the banquet or by my inevitable fidgetings once I got there. I decided to risk the fidgetings.

"I warn you, Baron Kharsog, my appetite is practically illegal. You may run out of food."

"No danger of that, Your Grace. But first I insist that you join me for a pre-dinner drink. I shall break out the mead."

"The mead?" I asked.

"I used to raise bees here," he explained. "Until Horg accidentally murdered them all with his damned insecticides."

Despite Kusk's promise of mead, my arrival in his study was greeted by nothing beyond his usual non sequiturs and mystical slogans. This depressed me. Malty intoxication, I thought—any kind of intoxication—would certainly be the easiest state in which to endure the banquet.

"The Gothian knows total awareness," Kusk, enthroned, was saying. "The Gothian learns to recognize his pain, to love it, to master it. We all live continually in excruciating pain— did you realize that, Your Grace?—but each spasm is so short that we do not normally notice. So—was I right? Did your daughter refuse to board the shuttle?"

"To tell you the truth," I said, telling the truth, "she was asleep."

"Have no doubts, my Archbishop, Lilit is part of the body and blood of Goth now." Kusk's smug face made me think of a rooster with teeth.

Loathing the present topic, I endeavored to change it. "Your reason for inviting me—you said there was a reduction in the guest list?"

"A dramatic reduction," said Kusk. "Yesterday a contagion

broke out in the dormitory. All my apprentices are under quarantine."

Could Kusk be lying? Could bank presidents afford the best butter?

But—why this particular lie? What game was he playing?

"The fact is," my host continued, "you and I will be the only guests at the banquet."

My fear—large and private, its hard fingers squeezing my bowels—almost prompted me to ask, *And what of the play?* But no, I must not betray any unusual interest in that particular matter.

At this point I no longer cared whether asking for a drink would seem presumptuous. "You mentioned mead."

Rising, Kusk went to the bookshelves, where a pair of warty decanters, each filled with an amber liquid, lay between Madame Blavatsky's *Isis Unveiled* and George Steiner's *Occult Science.* Kusk removed the decanters, set one on the left arm of his throne, approached me with the other. The cap, I now learned, doubled as a glass. He poured me a drink, returned to his throne, poured himself a drink.

We talked. Or, rather, Kusk talked and I heard.

He talked of the "precognitive wisdom" his trees would be imparting to humankind.

He talked of his plans to flesh out the Church of Goth with the most impressive array of sacraments, sacrifices, libations, oblations, saints, sins, hymns, martyrs, relics, subgods, and holidays any religion had ever boasted.

He talked of how, once Hamadryad was harvested, he would next put me in charge of *Pigs to the Market* and *Basket Case.*

The mead was warm and faintly medicinal. I did not dislike it. Embarking on my second glassful, I realized that I was quite drunk.

"Your bees did not die in vain," I slurred. The room seemed squishy. I focused on Kusk's zoo—on a school of crimson spinnies pulsing through their aquarium like red blood cells.

For a few seconds I labored under the delusion that his pets were all outside their cages. Then, slowly, the worst of my intoxication passed.

"To the banquet!" Kusk was saying.

I thought: The corridor seems even darker than the last time I was here—is the mead dulling my vision? Only Kusk's hand on my shoulder kept me from wandering into the cylindrical wall. Prill stood at the end of the corridor, blocking our way so that he might make a good show of deferring as we passed.

As soon as we entered the banquet hall, the cause of the darkness became apparent. Someone had turned out the sun. The only light issued from the shape-shift fire, which blazed nervously in the hearth, and from the half-dozen candelabra on the table, each sculptured to resemble a noostree. The boughs clutched plump red candles. The flames' reflections played across the polished marble. Gold plates had been set along the perimeters of the table, six to a side, an arrangement that made the six candelabra seem like so many banquet guests. The utensils were patterned with Möbius strips.

A thirteenth gold plate lay on the near end of the table, where Prill indicated that I should sit, and a fourteenth plate lay on the far end, where Kusk now settled. He was so distant from me that we could have used the table for two simultaneous games of solitaire psychic billiards without mixing up the balls. His face looked bandaged by shadows.

Like the mead, the familiar presence of the stage did much to beat back my anxiety. The show, evidently, would go on.

"There will always be banquets," said my invisible host. "They are like dreambean orgies. If the present dish is not to your taste, perhaps the next one will please you. The medium is immortal."

I did not reply, but stared at my place setting. On the evidence of these items, the meal would hardly fulfill the expectations normally raised by the word *banquet*. There was a dinner knife but no butter knife, a main-course fork but no salad fork, a red wineglass but no champagne glass, a soup spoon but no dessert spoon. The lack of a dessert spoon comforted me, as this suggested pie for dessert and not ice cream or pudding. Dessert forks would have cinched the case, but, alas, there were none to be seen.

Prill disappeared through the gryphon-flanked door, returning shortly with a gold platter, its oval rim aswarm with engraved insects. The platter rested on an antigravity cushion. The merest prod from Prill's index finger was sufficient to move it forward.

Two soup bowls sat on the platter, steam ascending from them like a morning mist from Eden Mire. Kusk, naturally, received his soup first. After my own bowl was set before me, I lifted my spoon and froze, knowing better than to breach the surface before my host began eating. Then, too, it was not inconceivable that Lord Goth expected me to say a grace to him.

"At an Eternal Banquet," he boomed, "those who are invited do not always come." I could tell by the sounds that soup was rolling into his mouth. "On some nights we have many guests here. Tonight, of course, there is only you. Try your soup."

I did. It was a mercurial substance given to slithering off the spoon and escaping into the bowl. It smelled like cat food— a commodity I had been known to consume while waiting for payment to arrive from *Dreambeans Deciphered*—and tasted worse. I could manage no more than half a bowl.

When next Prill appeared, I was grateful to see two bottles of red wine flying before him. The wine, too, fell considerably short of a gourmet item, being simultaneously salty and sour, but it did wash away the foul aftertaste of the soup.

From the shadows Kusk said, "I assume that you find the stage puzzling. The answer is simple. Tonight we shall be entertained by some theatrics—by *Thyestes*, to be precise, the greatest revenge tragedy ever conceived. I can tell by your quizzical expression that the story is not familiar to you."

Between the present wine and the previous mead, I did not really know what sort of expression I was wearing. If Kusk said it was quizzical, then it was probably quizzical—though a sly grin would have been more appropriate to this unexpected confirmation that the Jugglers of Bone were waiting in the wings.

"The legend survives in several variations," Kusk continued. "Some say that Thyestes slept with Atreus's wife. Some say he skinned the golden fleece from Atreus's ram. Whatever the affront, the retaliation was creative and astonishing—crime elevated to an art. Atreus did Revenge honor. In a banquet hall not unlike this one, Atreus fed Thyestes his own favorite child!"

On that note, the entrée arrived. It was a substantial plank of meat, black with overcooking and resting on a foundation of onions and rice. My appetite was dead, a cumulative effect of the mead, the soup, the wine, and, of course, the apparent proximity of Kusk's downfall. The onions began to look like rheumy eyes, the rice like pustules.

Somehow I forced myself to eat. Once I had chopped past the char, the meat proved considerably more palatable than anything that had come before. Furthermore, the rice tasted remarkably like rice, and the onions had unquestionably been onions at one time.

"Thyestes's nightmare has an extraordinary denouement," said Kusk. "When he realizes what he has eaten, his reaction is not so much revulsion as frustration. Yes, frustration—Thyestes wishes that he had thought of this particular torture first! And what about Atreus? Does he experience even one jot of remorse? Wonder of wonders, he too is frustrated! Contemplating his crime, he finds that it missed being the masterpiece he intended. It should have climaxed with the child's head arriving on a platter!"

I could not see Kusk's smile, but I could hear his laugh. He said, "Naturally, one is tempted to dismiss both Atreus and Thyestes as psychopaths. And perhaps they were. But they were also princes—feared, loved, respected. If there is a moral to be gleaned from the myth, I cannot tell you what it is. Perhaps the moral is that most experiences have no moral. On a good day, existence is pointless."

I studied the nearest candelabrum. The little red waxballs accumulating in the drip pans seemed to me the eggs of some terrible, venomous worm.

When Prill made his fourth appearance, all of my former fears came with him. He was bringing dessert, two plum puddings lumping up from the platter like cerebral hemispheres. Each arrived with its own spoon. If Kusk ate his pudding, of course, he would have no appetite for pie, no hunger for figs and phreneseeds, no stomach for self-annihilation. Preoccupied with the performance itself, Torin had evidently neglected to tell Kusk's kitchen staff that the Jugglers of Bone would be supplying the desserts. Perhaps there was something I could say, something I could do, to prevent the Baron from plunging in his spoon.

"Most likely you believe that the play will begin shortly after dessert," he said. "A reasonable assumption—but entirely false! For you see, my dear guest, the play has already been performed!"

Kusk said it only once, but I kept hearing it over and over.

Already performed.

Already performed.

And then, in me: embryonic terror, incipient nausea.

And Kusk: "Can human lymph be incorporated undetected into soup? I say yes! Does human blood make the wine salty? Quite so! Might human flesh be seasoned and roasted until it cries beef? Again, true!"

And in me: the panic spreading to every extremity.

And Kusk: "Do you suppose yourself incapable of such an abomination? Thyestes had the same delusion."

The nausea brought me to the brink of vomiting; the terror drilled for and found tears.

Wax bled down the candle shafts.

"There remains the question of *who*? Ah, but you already know. Do you need your worst suspicions confirmed? All right, we shall have my servant return. But I warn you, at this banquet we do not make Atreus's mistake—we know how to commit the perfect revenge! Waiter—show my guest the one he loves best!"

Lilit is in Ushumgallum, I told myself. Ushumgallum! Ushumgallum! And yet, was there really any way to know that Kusk had not sent a squad of minions ahead of the train, had not ordered them to blow up the guideway, kidnap Lilit, and bring her back to the Keep?

Prill came through the door, past the gryphons, bearing the gold platter.

Why would Kusk do this to me? Me—his chosen Archbishop!

On the platter was a human head. By candlelight the features were indistinct. An aureole of blood encircled the base of the neck.

And suddenly the Baron was at my side, hovering like a fat wasp. "Yes, your sin is too dark to name. Your guilt could crush a sun. But then, just when hope seems gone forever, the one true god appears. See me—see *all* of me. My eyes are the candles on the Altar of Lost Knowledge. My teeth are the moonstruck pebbles that mark your path through the Vale of Chaos. My tongue is the pumice stone that scrubs the tarnish from your soul. My names are Kharsog and Pazuzu and Tiamet and Humwawa and Goth. Say that your only god is Goth, and your guilt will be taken away!"

Prill came nearer. The shape-shift fire caught the platter, splashing golden threads of light across my daughter's detached face.

I began, "My only god—"

But that is all I said.

18

Just Desserts

White, white, white, white, white, white: the six inside surfaces of my prison room were white. A white floor. A white ceiling. North wall, east wall, south wall, west wall: white.

The bed I occupied was likewise white. White sheets, blanket, pillowcase. White headboard.

I, too, was essentially white. I wore a white smock, beyond which article I was completely unattired. The elevator controls had been removed from my waist. My head lay in a puddle of my own sweat. The sweat felt white.

"I've never been here," I said aloud, to no one in particular. Inhaling, I found that the air was laden with an insistent, unpleasant cleanness.

"This is where they put you when you eat your father," said a male voice, chronologically young, yet cracked by trauma.

Until this instant I had not been aware of the second bed. Swiveling my head, I immediately recognized my roommate as Creegmoor, the apprentice who had cleaned up after Kusk's neurosurgery demonstration in the amphitheater. His eyes reminded me of Marta Rem's—hot, haunted, twitchy. His fingers, interlaced on his chest, quivered like dreaming worms.

"You suffer from delusions," I said firmly. "Kharsog was testing a special kind of dream on you. A lotosbean."

"He should be called Goth," said the apprentice. "Goth is the Baron's true name. My only god is Goth."

"Your only god is smoke."

By interpreting Creegmoor's symptoms this way, I was naturally trying to persuade myself that my own sin could be rationalized similarly. But the theory had far more going for it than my need to believe it. Did I not have, chief among my recent memories, a crisp mental image of waking up alone in Kusk's study and realizing instantly that I had not been to the banquet hall that night? Realizing, in fact, that I had never even risen from Kusk's Freudian couch? Did not an equal vividness inform my recollection of what followed? The Centaur entering the study. Tossing me into his gondola. Hauling me to the white room. Injecting me with a soporific. As for the Trojan Horse itself—the ruse by which the nightmare had invaded my brain—this was doubtless the mead. Surely a lotosbean could be dissolved in fermented honey as easily as in blood.

I did not need to submit Creegmoor to a synapscan to know that the dream had left him entirely insane. Out of simple decency I told the miserable cretin, over and over, that he had not eaten his father, but all he said was, "Goth will redeem me."

In his place, I too would probably have believed the dream. As a veteran of Hamadryad's fruit, however, I had learned not to take hyper-reality for truth. Unlike my roommate, I had eventually seen the disembodied head for what it was—an oblate and undifferentiated spheroid on which Kusk induced me to project "the one I loved best." Kusk could not sustain the illusion—not when his audience was Quinjin the Critic, Decipherer of Dreams, not when his audience was Quinjin the Great, Slayer of Noostrees.

Of course, it was inconceivable that I would experience a single pleasant moment until Lilit herself stood by my side. Yet I could find no reason to doubt that I had once again met the Lotos Factor and defeated it.

Beyond this conviction, my thoughts were in total disarray. Had there been a Midterm Banquet? Had the Jugglers of Bone put on their play? Had Jonnie served Kusk the poisoned pie?

Lodged in the wall, directly opposite the foot of my bed, was a two-meter-wide disk of the sort that normally protects great stores of gold. When it hissed open, Kusk entered. He did not bother to close the door behind him.

And I thought: So, Simon Kusk! You believe your Thyestes apple has turned me into a Gothian! Beware, viper! You are trifling with Quinjin the Great!

I pretended to be asleep.

"You may kiss this," said the Prince of Lies.

Spying from behind my half-lowered eyelids, I saw him lean over Creegmoor's bed. When Kusk extended his arm, the apprentice lunged for the sleeve and drew it greedily to his lips. He kissed it seven times.

"I am wicked, Lord Goth," moaned Creegmoor. "I am corrupt. I am—"

Kusk withdrew the sleeve. "Accept me, and you will be forgiven."

"My Lord—within these walls sleeps one who needs your forgiveness even more than I. That man over there—he calls my sin a phantasm. A lotosbean."

Kusk whipped around, sleeves flapping like black wings. His face sagged, as if he had recently undergone a dreambean orgy. His eyeballs were sunken, sallow, and rimmed in black.

"Blasphemer!" he screamed, coming toward me. "So, Quinjin, you dare to set yourself above the Lotos Factor!"

The headboard featured a red button. Pushing it, Kusk caused a wide metal slab to drop from the ceiling like a guillotine blade. The room was bisected. Creegmoor would hear no more blasphemies that day.

I said, "I'm Flick Longslapper."

Kusk refuted my claim by opening the drawer of the nightstand, taking out a book, and tossing it onto the bed. I recognized the volume immediately—*Oneiromances*, the one and only compendium of my apple reviews. There was an author hologram on the back cover.

"As soon as Mr. Diffring arrived at the Keep and told me his Jugglers would be doing a *Thyestes* variation," said the Baron, "I looked up the legend, studied it—whereupon I realized that it held the perfect premise for a lotosbean. And then—barely twelve hours after I had offered you an archdiocese—when fate bade me browse through my library—when I saw your picture and absorbed your treachery—*then* I knew I must rush the dream—your punishment—my revenge—into production. *Just Desserts*, that's what I call it. *Desserts* with two *s*'s."

"So the quarantine was a ploy to get us drinking together, eh, Kusk?"

By ignoring my thesis, Kusk proved it true.

He said, "Naturally I am eager to learn how a second-rate critic ends up conversant in such matters as the Lotos Factor and this castle's location and my former identity. I am equally eager to learn how his child ends up eating from my Hamadryad."

The laser scalpel that Kusk now pulled from his robe was phallic, silvered, and burnished to a grinning glow.

"But I shall be patient, Quinjin," he said. "Once I strap you to the operating table, once I start tweaking your cerebrum, the whole story will pour from your lips. True, you are not a noostree. Still, I can manage."

A blue beam leaped at me, pierced my ear, and burned

through the pillow. The pool beneath my head sizzled. My wounded lobe smarted.

I had never realized it was possible to hate anyone so much.

"I'll relieve your curiosity right now," I rasped. "Your troubles began when a copy of *The Lier-in-Wait* found its way to Wendcraft University—and from there to my stomach."

The pocks on Kusk's face darkened. "Prill was told to deliver it to Selig! Is there no end of betrayal in this universe?"

"Oh, Selig received the apple, all right. But he was afraid to eat it himself."

"I expected that. Still, there was always a chance of turning my oldest enemy into my first disciple. At the very least, I'm sure that I *scared* him."

"I saw his tears."

"Well, Quinjin, it would appear that I am looking at one of those rare individuals who are immune to lotosbeans. But where my trees could not convert you, my knife surely can. Once I have finished with your memory neurons, I shall stimulate those tissues where faith is born and ablate those where your unorthodoxy festers. I shall—"

My next action was one that I had never before performed in real life, though I had probably performed it in more than a hundred cephapple dreams. I made a fist and used it to smash a jaw. Kusk's jaw. *Uncharted Parsecs* and its swashbuckling hero, Broc Hornlaster, came immediately to mind.

Unprepared for such violence from a "second-rate critic," Kusk slumped to the floor, dazed.

In my best Broc Hornlaster style, I dove onto my enemy. He snarled. Seizing the laser scalpel, I yanked it hard, at which point the resemblance between myself and Hornlaster ended. Whereas Broc would have undoubtedly freed the thing from Kusk's grip, I couldn't make it budge.

My hand slid from Kusk's scalpel to his waist. My fingers probed the buckle of his elevator controls. Within seconds, the magic belt was mine.

Before I could pass through the thick doorway, Kusk was on his feet, aiming the scalpel at my turned back. The vector struck my left shoulder, a clean penetration, aft to fore. I welcomed the pain, pleasured in the sight of my good red blood. Pain. Blood. These things told that my cause was just. I would go to the greenhouse—that was my cause. I would get a pruning hook. I would search the castle. I would find Kusk. And then, when circumstances permitted, I would prune my enemy to death.

It was Kusk's neurosurgery threat that had set me on this path—his grade-B dreambean remark about strapping me to his operating table.

I have always hated bad dialogue.

The greenhouse. Muggy, coagulated air. A charnel stillness. Silently the branches grew, the roots nursed. The sun lay centered in the sky, but none of the fifty-one seedlings reached for its warmth. They were like corpses of trees, deathtrees rigid with death. Horg was nowhere to be seen. I moved through the grove with precise, predatory steps.

Beside Horg's shed, a newborn slept. It had fat, force-fed limbs and a crop numbering not more than twenty. This, surely, was the Tree of Just Desserts. If the Baron had his way, a billion unknowing psychoparlor patrons would eventually come to believe they had devoured their wives, husbands, parents, children, siblings, lovers, friends.

I seized a pruning hook. My good arm swished it through the air, rehearsing terrible violations of the body of Simon Kusk. The blade whistled.

Turning from the shed, I sighted down an avenue of deathtrees, seven on the left, seven on the right.

A shock.

At the end of the avenue Kusk waited, his laser scalpel aflame with midday sun. By Kusk's side stood Prill. Around

Prill's waist were the elevator controls that had enabled the Baron once again to seize the initiative.

Kusk took aim. This time, I knew, he would not settle for flesh wounds.

I ducked behind *Just Desserts.*

Kusk fired.

The vector zagged across the greenhouse, burrowing into a bough that jutted only a few centimeters above my head. Smoke poured from the black wound. As the limb hit the dirt, its dreams rolled in all directions.

But the dismemberment of *Just Desserts* was only the beginning of the chaos caused by Kusk's shot. Sap spurted from the stump, and then, soon afterward, flames.

The ragged fire curled around the next branch up. An easy conquest: the fire opened new fronts. The sap pop-popped. Now four limbs were ignited, now eight, now the whole crown. The little tree writhed redly, a child with her hair ablaze.

The confusion on Kusk's face was glorious to behold. He raised the scalpel, pondered the risk of starting a second fire, lowered the scalpel, raised it, lowered it. He shook and whimpered. He seemed ready to split in half, like the woman butchered by the mad magician in Reinwort's *The Illusionist.*

Inexorably the fire jumped to *Pigs to the Market.* Just as it had claimed branch after branch of *Just Desserts,* it now threatened to claim tree after tree of the unholy grove.

"Get help!" Powering Kusk's voice was his fatherly terror at seeing his children in mortal danger.

Prill ran to the elevator shaft and vanished.

The inferno roared like a hundred starving plasmidleopards. Firebrands rained down.

Although Kusk was approaching, death from smoke inhalation now seemed for me a more likely fate than death by scalpel cuts. I wept and gagged. My lungs screamed. The air attacked me, blasting me with heat, pushing the stink of scorched sap up my nose. Fifty-two lies burned brightly.

Tear-blinded, I ran, one hand outstretched, the other clutching the pruning hook. A wall reared up. The hot transplastic burned my palm, and this was followed by the similar pain of a laser beam splitting my cheek. Convulsed, I fell. Even the soil was hot.

Ear to dirt, I heard a peculiar sound. Not a mechanical sound. A voice, or, rather, a chorus—superhuman in its range, yet wholly human in its despair, a shrill mingling of rage, fear, grief, and physical torment. And suddenly I knew the source. The taproots. The poor, thinking, dying taproots, screaming under the earth.

As I rose, a taproot ripped its way to the surface, emerged amid a spray of loosened soil. The creature arced toward its blazing extremities, as if to extinguish them with its breath. Again the earth split open, again the dirt flew—and a second root burst out. Then another. Another. Another. Another. It was like watching the dead rise from their graves in a horror bean, but mainly it was like nothing I had ever seen or dreamt or hallucinated or imagined in my life.

Enshrouded by smoke, coughing volcanically, Kusk dropped to his knees.

I turned toward the wall, began chopping with the hook. Smoke tore at my eyes. Chop. A single fissure appeared. Chop. Then a spiderweb of cracks. Chop. Then a doorway framed in teeth.

A frantic jump, and the doomed orchard was behind me.

Exiting the inferno, I entered a nightmare.

The nightmare was *The Lier-in-Wait*, the dream that had started it all.

I was in a rearward sector of the hedge-maze. The thorny branches enveloped me. I tested a briar with the tip of my index finger. A pearl of blood appeared. The throbbings in my ear, cheek, palm, and shoulder masked the pain I would otherwise have felt.

This was no hallucination. No mirage. The hedge-maze was everything ever meant by the word *real*.

But what was it for? Why had Kusk cultivated such a thing on the roof of his castle?

And suddenly—I knew. At last I understood the Lotos Factor. Fully. Completely. I could have conducted a seminar on the subject at Wendcraft University.

When I first ran afoul of *The Lier-in-Wait* in Selig's laboratory, of course, the dream had been a cephapple. And before that, obviously, a seed. And before that, naturally, a collection of neural phenomena. And before that—a dreamweaver's chimera? A flight of fancy?

No. A reality.

A reality—an event every bit as tangible as a performance by the Jugglers of Bone, acted on a set every inch as palpable as the stage in the banquet hall. The weaver of *The Lier-in-Wait* had not been Kusk at all! No—only a naïve victim could have inspirited the seed with such pure, profound, and spontaneous dread. In my mind's eye, the technique stood revealed. I saw the Centaur waylaying an apprentice, strapping him into Kusk's "modified" electroderby ("modified," no doubt, so as to record the brain waves for later transmission to a phreneseed nursery), and dragging him to the threshold of this very set. I saw the apprentice start across the lawn. I saw the Lier-in-Wait approach him . . . hand him a dagger . . . tell him what he must search for in the goat, and why. I saw the apprentice dash through the labyrinth . . . slaughter the goat . . . watch helplessly as the keys became insects. Thus was the dream done to him. Thus was his mind turned into a phreneseed and planted in Kusk's greenhouse.

Smoke pursued me. Glancing at my pruning hook, I realized that I would not have to solve the maze through conventional trial and error. The dry, dead branches fell readily to my thrusts; like Sleeping Beauty's deliverer, I sliced my way forward, so transfiguring the maze that a brain-damaged rat could have solved it on the first attempt.

Within minutes I had cut a path to the central courtyard.

The four skull-headed statues stood in their usual positions, but their deterioration was severe. Fissures wrinkled their marble flesh. Weather stains blotched their limbs like birthmarks. As for the goat I had slain, there was nothing left of it but a skeleton. No, not a skeleton exactly. A framework, the matrix of a robot, its sheathing eroded by rain and snow. Of course— only a robot goat could have performed so reliably; only a robot goat could have tolerated all those keys in its horns. (The keys! Themselves robots! Programmed to transmute into beetles!) Bleached by sunlight, the framework lay on brown grass that had once been a piercing green. The bogus stomach, the fake lungs, the artificial viscera, the ersatz heart, the plastic kidneys—all had long since dissolved.

I swung my pruning hook, set my course for the maze entrance. Passing through the gateway, I hurried across the windswept lawn.

A naked and defunct android lay about five meters from the well. Limbs askew, it suggested a cast-off marionette. Its countenance was indistinct, its gender indeterminate, its age indefinite, its physique vague. In this manikin, I knew, the unwilling parent of Hamadryad had been made to see the one he loved best, so that all eaters of the fruit would subsequently project corresponding persons from their own lives.

A final truth enlightened me as I ran up to the android: *Just Desserts* had been tested on me and me alone. Creegmoor had not *eaten* that particular apple; he had *created* it. He had been the conduit of its script, the vessel of its enactment. Featureless, sexless, the climactic severed head was probably lying in some dismal corner of the banquet hall; once a crucial reality, it was now, like the android, merely a plastic prop from a closed-down play, thrown aside to rot.

While the existence of the android was easily explained, its condition was not. Blood—or a facsimile of blood—speckled the flesh from head to toe. Deep, serrated wounds striated the torso. Why had—?

A laser discharge whizzed past my left temple. I turned,

and my eyes confirmed what my heart feared: Kusk had escaped the holocaust.

I made a rash, Broc Hornlaster sort of gesture, hurling the pruning hook at Kusk. It missed, struck the dead lawn, stayed upright.

My enemy advanced two steps.

Instinctively I raised my hands in front of my face: ramparts of straw, flood-dikes of sand.

It was at this low point in my fortunes that a question I had asked myself in the white room—had Jonnie served Kusk the poisoned pie?—suddenly surged through me. And I became Quinjin the Great again. I refused defeat. I embraced hope. I elected to fight back. Not with a weapon—I had none—but with fifty-six words that had been ringing in my ears ever since the real Flick Longslapper had sung them back in the underground continent.

"Soul of the seed, listen!" I shouted from behind my hands. *"Brain of the tree, come forth! Heart of the fruit, appear! Cease to be a sleeper in the earth! Cease to lie unwaking in the flesh of this farm!"*

A taproot conjuration was obviously not among those things Kusk expected me to say. His jaw went limp. The scalpel descended a few blessed centimeters.

"You I summon! You I evoke! You I call in beholdable form to meet your healer!"

Kusk screamed.

"Child of dreams, you are conjured!"

His scream, however, did not bespeak belligerence. It bespoke terrible confusion and worse pain. It was like the screams of the burned-alive deathtrees. And suddenly the scalpel was falling impotently to the ground, and suddenly Kusk was wandering around as if intoxicated.

He had begun to germinate.

A branch popped out of his left shoulder, tearing through his tunic and robe, migrating sunward. He made several awkward grabs, eventually seizing the young shoot and snapping it off.

From his right buttock a root emerged, giving him a lizard's tail. I could smell his blood. Now a second branch appeared, piercing his left breast, forking and reforking into a cluster of twigs. A ripping noise—ripping cloth, ripping skin. And now a second root, sprung from the soil of his right kidney. For an instant it seemed that Kusk was giving birth to the tree, that he was having it through some grisly variation on cesarean section.

Kusk stopped screaming. Evidently a twig had destroyed his brain's pain center.

"Why, Lord Goth," I whispered as he staggered up to me. "I believe you've been eating pie."

"This is extraordinary," he said as two branches came out of his side and grew twigs.

"I agree," I replied.

It amazed me that he was still alive. I sensed that the seedling energized him even as it ruined him. His branches ran red. Blood drops showered down like petals.

Again he spoke. *"Reap the Whirlwind?"*

"Yes."

"I can tell."

He continued sprouting all the way to the well. I heard him say "Extraordinary" once more. The twig in his nose gave him a nasal voice.

There was no splash when Kusk tumbled in. The well had gone dry.

I ran forward, lowered my gaze, beheld the sort of bizarre tableau one does not normally see outside the influence of the *vinum sanguinis*. The Tree of the Reaped Whirlwind lay atop the rock, feeding on Kusk. And at the base of the rock, chained as the android had been chained in *The Lier-in-Wait*, was a goat skeleton. A goat skeleton? The same skeleton I had just seen in the center of the maze? Perhaps. But who had moved it here? When? Why? Were there *two* goats in the dream? I could remember only one.

Kusk's branches shivered. His arms and legs twitched. His brainy taproot underwent a kind of epileptic seizure. A macabre tranquility played across his face.

"Here's the curtain line, Kusk!" I screamed down at him. "Your Hamadryad is dead! I slew her myself! And still Lilit is not avenged!"

Kusk looked eager to reply, but all that came out of his mouth was a staccato gurgling. His many appendages stiffened, and he died open-eyed.

In a matter of minutes, the corpse was completely consumed. Only the deathtree remained. Crucified from within, Kusk had become one with his dream.

19

My Original Sin

"This won't be easy," said Urilla. "You must stop being a critic for a while. You must abandon control and jump into the buried parts of yourself—the rooty material, if you will. For starters, try to relax."

I complied as best I could, stretching belly-down along Kusk's Freudian couch in a cat-move that brought me sad memories of Basil.

We were about to embark on an experiment. In recent hours I had become convinced that, as a result of actually standing and walking and running on the set of *The Lier-in-Wait*, my frozen memories were beginning to thaw. Most especially, the goat in the well—that mysterious second skeleton—had made me feel that I was not far from knowing the lotosbean's true ending. With a bit of prodding from a person gifted in matters psychological—a person like Urilla—the final moments would, I believed, come back to me.

Urilla clicked on a vocalith machine and eased into Kusk's

throne. She seemed at home there, as if it were she who had deposed Goth, and not Jonnie and I. Her presumption did not offend me. I still loved her, and apparently she still loved me. At least that was among the first things she had said when I vidiphoned her at Widow Flum's to insist that she and Lilit return posthaste to the castle.

The study was ours now—the whole damned Keep was ours. Kusk's empire had fallen without a fight. The Centaur, as it happened, owed his free will to a computer embedded in his neck, and after we pushed the appropriate keys, this potential antagonist became docile and obliging. As for Horg, he was naturally distressed to see a year's worth of gardening reduced to cinders and rubble, yet he needed only the mildest goading before saying things like, "I never trusted Baron Kharsog," and, "An evilness lived in those seeds." In the case of the apprentices, it took nothing beyond the sight of poor mad Creegmoor to make them realize that graduating from the Lotos Institute meant having your brain take root in the profane grove. (And your final fate? Prill offered a gleeful description. You were coated with silicon chips and sold to the jungjelly fields as a menial-class robot.)

Once aware of our takeover, Prill started claiming that the Ushumgallum police would soon arrest us for premeditated murder. I countered by reminding Prill of his complicity in the Baron's far more enterprising designs. The threats stopped. Before leaving the Keep, Prill went to the trouble of cremating Kusk's remains—or, rather, of cremating the seedling that was the best available analog of Kusk's remains. Standing on the castle battlements, the old servant sowed the winds with death-tree ashes. He took the next shuttle back to town. I was glad to be rid of him. I hated him for performing in *Just Desserts*.

Flipping over on my side, I dug my fingernails absently under the little buttons that held the upholstery in place. Enduring a cannibalism nightmare, surviving a lunatic's scalpel, seeing the orchard burn down, cracking the Lotos Factor, witnessing Kusk's destruction—the last three days had been ridiculously eventful. It felt good to be lying here, simply lying, accomplishing nothing.

But Urilla would not allow it. We had work to do, she knew. We had a dream to decipher. Drumming on the lid of the vocalith machine, she said, "Talk whenever you want."

My eyes were attracted to the reptile level of Kusk's menagerie, to the snapping turtle with the death's-head on its shell. "The minute I saw the second goat," I said, "all I could think was, 'Flowering Judas, *that* wasn't in *The Lier-in-Wait!*' "

Urilla nodded. "I heard the vocalith you made for Selig. You reported only one goat. The one with the keys in its horns. You believed that the climax of the bean—the event intended to drive the dreamer crazy—was the keys turning into beetles and escaping."

"That's what I *wanted* the climax to be. That's what I *remembered* as the climax. But my brain lied to me."

"Repression," said Urilla.

"Repression," I agreed. I studied her beguiling face, her irrefutable breasts. Even with a beard, she would not have looked much like Freud.

"Let's start with the goat's horns cracking open, the keys tumbling out. You found twenty-four keys, right? They scurried across the grass in the central courtyard."

"Scurry, scurry."

"And then they took to the air?" asked Urilla.

"Yes," I replied.

"All of them?"

"Yes."

"Every last one?"

"Correct."

"Really? Think, Quinny. No. *Feel*. Not just words. *Feelings*."

I felt. I disappeared into myself, as Torin Diffring had told his actors to do during the *Thyestes* rehearsal. Slowly, slowly,

I stopped being Quinjin the Critic, started becoming Quinjin the Dreamer. I was part of the lotosbean now, remembering.

Yes—there it was. A solitary beetle, lying dead in the impossibly green grass.

"One insect stayed behind," I confessed to Urilla. "It turned back into a key."

"You picked up the key," said Urilla, prompting.

"I went through the maze."

"You got to the entrance?"

"Yes."

"And then you ran across the lawn?"

"Yes. There were goat guts on my fingers. I reached the well, and . . . and . . . and . . ."

"God in heaven—she had drowned?"

I rubbed my bandaged hand against my bandaged cheek. My wounds were painless but itchy. I would have preferred pain. "True!" I said hastily. "She had drowned! That is, the android onto which I was projecting her had drowned, and then—"

"And then the dream ended?"

"Yes. It was finally over."

"So when did the second goat appear?" my analyst asked pointedly.

Aphasia possessed me. In my mind, a tribal lotos-eater painted a key on my lips, then another cut out my tongue. I felt that I would never speak again.

"Quinny, you're still lying to yourself."

"Perhaps," I croaked.

"Lilit *wasn't* drowned."

"Perhaps."

"She *wasn't*."

"No?"

"Go back to the well, Quinny. Look in. Is Lilit chained up?"

I went back to the well. I looked in. "She's gone."

"Is the well empty?"

"No. The rock is still there. I see blood swirling around it. And chained to the rock . . . taking Lilit's place . . . the damned goat."

"The goat you *just slaughtered?*"

"Yes. It seems that way. It *feels* that way. The goat has been magically restored! As if I never touched it!"

"The logic of dreams," said Urilla.

"The logic of dreams," I concurred. (And how had Kusk created the illusion? Ah—*that's* where the second goat came into play! While the captive apprentice was chasing the first goat through the maze, a stagehand—Prill or the Centaur or even Kusk himself—must have climbed down into the well with the animal's doppelgänger, unchained the human android, and made the switch.)

"So *The Lier-in-Wait* ended with your seeing a resurrected goat?" Urilla asked.

Another oceanic silence. My eyes dropped to the next level down. Amphibians. Toads of Night. "I turned around. The Lier-in-Wait came out of the maze." Each word was a briar in my throat. "He had something draped across his arms. Something ripped and bloody . . . all manner of blood, unbelievable wounds . . . a corpse. A human—"

"No wonder you—"

"Repression," I said. My teeth were chattering now. Kusk's study was warm, and my teeth were chattering. "It was as if, somehow, when I was in the maze, killing the goat . . . it was as if I had made a . . . terrible . . . *mistake.*"

Urilla rose from her throne. "What mistake?" she asked. "Name it," she commanded.

My sweat plastered me to the couch. It saturated my bandages. "It was as if I had used the dagger on . . . as if that stomach I had just cut out . . . those kidneys . . . liver . . . brain . . . heart . . . they belonged to . . . the corpse was . . . my victim was . . ."

"Only a dream."

"My victim was Lilit!" I screamed, thrusting my head forward. "I butchered my own daughter!"

And then I collapsed on the couch.

The silence that followed might have been a minute long, it might have been an hour long. At Kharsog Keep, time had been shorn of its fraudulent Newtonian absoluteness. All disguises were gone, all masks peeled away, all shells husked off, all veils rent.

At last my vibrations stopped, my breathing became regular. I realized that Urilla was standing over me, staunching my sweaty forehead with a handkerchief. She said my name three times in soft, pitying tones.

"Save your pity for Lilit," I muttered. "She doesn't realize the Lier-in-Wait was carrying an android. She thinks she killed *me*."

"*Part* of her thinks she killed you." Urilla was simultaneously lecturing me and having a revelation. "But her conscious mind screens out the entire event. That's why she keeps saying her father is in a well. Repression again. A repression far deeper than yours was, Quinny—knowledge pounded down into the sub-subconscious."

Walking over to Kusk's bookshelves, Urilla studied his collection, saw that his tastes ran the phantasmagoric gamut from alchemy to Zoroastrianism. Soon she noticed the volume that had nearly been my undoing, my own *Oneiromances*. She plucked it, glanced at the incriminating author hologram.

She said, "There's one thing left to tell, right? The 'My only god is Goth' business."

I was staring at Kusk's fishes. I could see the whole dream now. Everything. "The Lier-in-Wait tossed Lilit's corpse aside."

"He tossed an *android* aside," Urilla reminded me.

"He approached. He flipped back his hood and—"

"It was Kusk?"

"Yes. Kusk, calling himself Goth."

Here I digressed, giving Urilla a full account of my experiences with the *Thyestes* lotosbean. Entering the banquet hall. Eating the strange courses. Hearing that *Thyestes* had already been performed. Seeing the severed head. Being comforted—if that is the word—by Goth.

"*The Lier-in-Wait* used the same ending," I explained. "Goth promised to purge my guilt if I would follow him—if I would call him my only god. Hell, I'll wager that *every* tree in the orchard ended that way."

"So guilt was to be the cornerstone of Kusk's Church," Urilla mused. "You eat an apple, you become convinced you've committed some monstrous evil, you need a religion to cleanse you."

I launched into a passable impersonation of Kusk/Goth. " 'Your sin is too dark to name. Your guilt could crush a sun.' "

Urilla returned *Oneiromances* to its place, ran her finger along the spine of Blavatsky's *The Secret Doctrine*. "So where does this leave us? Normally a session so revealing would promise new health and happiness for the patient. But in your case there's still Lilit, locked in her nightmare, trapped by her guilt."

"Nightmare," I repeated. "Guilt. So—how to get her out?"

I unplastered myself from the couch.

When an idea grows in me, it takes over my body. My head and trunk and limbs were now becoming a wonderful notion. "I assume you have read *The Interpretation of Dreams*," I said quickly.

"Freud is obsolete."

"Not quite." In my voice I heard excitement and hope, edged with desperation. "He speaks of traumas. Traumas produce symptoms. And dreams. The subconscious becomes a stage for reenacting the repressed material over and over in a kind of code. But with a lotosbean it's the other way around—a dream produces a trauma. So what Lilit needs is an antitrauma, right? Not talk, not analysis. An antitrauma." My brain tingled.

"I believe that Goth can be destroyed by another of his kind. I believe that Goth's dominion extends across the real world only. But in the lotos world, he is vulnerable. *That's* my interpretation of *The Lier-in-Wait*. I'm a better critic than you know, Urilla."

"A good critic, yes. But a therapist?"

"A therapist. Hamadryad *didn't* lie to me—the cure *was* at Kharsog Keep, in its phreneseed nursery, in its noostree greenhouse." I was talking at twice normal speed, breaking the words at odd places. "Remember the Barge of the Mad? Marta Rem? She saw a great work growing in me. She said that at the ripe moment I would bring it forth. I'm going to make a tree, Urilla. The tree of *The Sleep Teacher*. But I can't produce it without you. First, of course, we'll need a script. Yes—*The Sleep Teacher*."

"A healing tree," Urilla mused, and for the first time I sensed her skepticism toward my interpretation giving way to faith.

"You and I, Urilla—the great new dreamweaving team, just as we always wanted! The hell with *Redemption of Things Past*! The hell with Sallie Sequenzia! *This* is our big collaboration!"

"Quinny, you're finally getting parenthood right."

And then we began making love on Freud's couch.

Urilla's praise sustained me when, a few hours after we had finished a first draft of *The Sleep Teacher*, I went to visit my daughter and found her even more abusive than usual.

Her symptoms were fully on view. The bedroom walls held a dozen drawings of Goth engaged in a yet-to-be-named sexual practice with a nubile woman who I feared might be Lilit. Whenever I tried speaking to her, she shut me out by thrusting the vocalith headphones—the one component of her fourteenth-birthday present I had not destroyed—over her ears. Whenever she tried speaking to me, it was through great wads of chocolate.

"What are *you* doing here, dream person?" she demanded

the instant I opened her door. She was sprawled on her mattress like a lotos-eater on a sacrificial altar. "Did you come to *kidnap* her again?"

Because of her blocked ears, she didn't get to hear me say, "The other night I had a terrible dream. I was at a banquet and—"

"Take her to Goth again! Take her!" She spoke by spitting. Some of the saliva hit my face.

If she could have read lips, she would have known that I said, "Goth is dead, you little shit!"

"Get away from her! *Eshika kyrikush makesh!*"

"There *is* such a thing as reality!" I said. "I love you," I added, and fumbled out of the room.

It was all up to the Sleep Teacher now.

20

The Sleep Teacher

Dreams have been called rehearsals for life. Then what do you call a rehearsal for a dream? Whatever its name, that was what the *Sleep Teacher* company was about to undertake—a rehearsal for a dream. Urilla, Jonnie, myself—the dream had been brilliantly cast. Milling around outside the hedge-maze, we hugged ourselves against the cold and waited for our director to show. Winds rushed across the lawn, raising tides in the grass. Clouds of breath puffed from our mouths. We appeared to be suffering from internal combustion.

Everything was in readiness.

We knew our lines.

The lawn had been restored to its former greenness, despite the brutal climate that prevailed atop Kharsog Keep. Horg was a world-class gardener.

The well had been replenished. Once again, blood swirled and gurgled around the prison-rock and its chains: two kiloliters, to be precise, with another kiloliter on tap.

Only the sky was wrong. Years earlier, when *The Lier-in-Wait* was played out on this very spot, the heavens had been infested with storm clouds and painted a deathly gray. Now they looked clear and blue. Nothing to do about that.

The artificial blood was just one of the many strange commodities we had uncovered on breaking into the Keep's forbidden levels. Lotosbean props, lotosbean costumes, and lotosbean sets filled the treasure rooms. Entering them, we felt ourselves to be violating the most secret sanctums of Kusk's imagination. One room contained nothing but androids fashioned as mythological beasts. Another contained nothing but weapons, including Jonnie's sword. Another: operating tables and medical supplies. Another: torture instruments. Another: heads.

"Where the hell is that *Torin?*" Jonnie suddenly yelled, unsheathing his sword. "If he doesn't appear in five minutes, *I'm* going to direct this thing."

For Lilit's new dream, nothing but the best. Torin Diffring, fresh from his triumphant production of *Thyestes*. (At the moment in the play where Atreus told his dinner guests the truth about the pies they had just consumed, no fewer than five of Kusk's apprentices had screamed out loud.) Ridiculous, clever Torin Diffring. Immediately on hearing the story of Lilit's corruption, Torin had agreed to lend his talents to her cure. "I mustn't rest on my laurels," he had said. "This *Sleep Teacher* will keep me in shape."

Now, as if cued by Jonnie's outburst, Torin strutted onto the lawn, a *Sleep Teacher* script parked under his arm. Horg followed, carrying a coil of rope, an electroderby, and a metal pail. A terrible smell shot from the pail.

The director lined us up like army recruits.

"You each have plenty to do in this show," he began, "so let's not waste time discussing subtext and motivation and that sort of squatprod. Perform your actions carefully, purposefully, and the emotions will follow."

He locked brows with Jonnie. "You've got the hardest job, Rondo—or at least you've got the most to say." He waved the script in Jonnie's face. "Except for one or two lines, this stuff is carefully written. Treat it like famous words."

Urilla and I exchanged self-satisfied grins. Torin's approval felt better than a Growers' Association Award.

The director's next stop was me. "Now Quinjin, by contrast, has the easiest job. At least I assume that you will not find it difficult playing yourself."

"Chocolate cake."

Arriving at Urilla, Torin said, "As for you, my dear, I'm sure your inclination is to empty your intellect and just let the events unfold. But that won't work. After all, you know what's going to happen, your name is on the script. Just remember that you are Lilit. Try to see the world as Lilit saw it before she ate the apple. Ever dream *The Toad of Night*? That's the kind of feeling I'm after. When your attention drifts, fasten it on to some adolescent obsession—love, or sex, or—"

"I thought *Jonnie* had the hard job," said Urilla anxiously.

"Listen, my dear, I could have put one of my own ingenues in this part. But I wanted somebody who knows Lilit. Knows her, *loves* her. Be receptive, that's the key. Not mindless, receptive. You must see everything, hear everything, feel, taste, smell, *believe*."

"I'm not an actor, I'm a psychobiologist."

"No difference," Torin said. "Run-through!" he shouted. "Places, everybody!"

Horg presented Jonnie with the coil of rope. The incubiber hung the rope on the hilt of his sword. Entering the maze, he disappeared into its clutches.

When Horg brought the foul-smelling pail to Urilla, she thrust her hands inside. She pulled them out, and a pungent jelly rolled from her fingers. Reaching into his coat, Horg produced the famous key from *The Lier-in-Wait*, gave it to her.

Urilla passed under the briary arch, made a right turn, stopped.

Horg had no props for me. Walking to the well, I inhaled fully, closed my eyes, clutched myself, and jumped. The blood—warm, deep, and impregnated with an odor like singed lilacs—closed over my head. My buoyant lungs brought me up. Sputtering, I swam to the prison-rock, heaved myself aboard. Blood cascaded from my shirt and trousers. The chains made idiot music as I scraped them across the granite. Carefully I manacled myself into a sitting position—manacles on my ankles, manacles on my wrists. The cold iron bit me.

"Curtain rising!" called Torin.

Though trapped in the well, I knew exactly what was happening. I could have recited the stage directions from *The Sleep Teacher* without missing a comma.

Horg turned on the pump. The blood in the well began to rise.

Urilla rushed down the thorny corridor. She squeezed the vital key, just as Lilit had done in *The Lier-in-Wait*. She wrung goat guts off her hands, just as Lilit had done in *The Lier-in-Wait*. She left the maze and ran across the lawn toward the well, just as Lilit had done in *The Lier-in-Wait*.

Now our variations began. When Urilla/Lilit looked into the well, she saw no resurrected goats, only her helpless father. I played the part methodically. Chattering from terror and cold, I tugged on my chains. Flesh fought iron with convincing futility. I picked up the padlock, feigned several attempts to smash it apart on the rock.

"Lilit!" I cried. "Darling, rescue me!"

The blood kept rising.

Key in hand, Urilla/Lilit leaped into the well, flutter-kicked her way through the blood. Clambering onto the rock, she stabbed the padlock, gave a quick twist. The inner workings groaned. The clasp popped open. I was free.

Standing together, we hugged and hugged and hugged.

At this point I found myself fighting the sexual arousal that Urilla's closeness naturally inspired. I succeeded. I was not about to purge Lilit of *The Lier-in-Wait* only to give her an incest trauma.

Urilla/Lilit said one of her two lines. "Father!"

"My brave daughter," I replied. "No longer a child." Urilla had written that. At the time I liked it, though now it seems a bit much.

The blood lapped at our shins.

Every dreambean needs an action climax. From the bottom of the well a monster emerged, the most impressive prop in Kusk's entire collection. (The instant we had come across the thing, we knew we must work it into the script somehow.) It was loathsome. Its immediate ancestors included the octopus, the lobster, the scorpion, the grorg, and such diseases as cancer and bubonic plague. It had horns. It had fangs. It had scales. It had tusks. It had four eyes. Horg could control it by means of a radio transmitter.

Rearing up on its back flippers, swishing its spiked tail, the monster slithered toward Urilla/Lilit and me. It bellowed. Fire leaped out like the jet of a blowtorch. When the monster closed its mouth, Urilla/Lilit counterattacked. She brought her palms together, interlocking her fingers into the kind of gesture one can use either for praying or for bludgeoning. Raising her fused hands high, she brought them down sharply—chop!—on the monster's snout. Again—chop! Again. After the third blow, the monster sank into the red depths, never to darken anyone's dreams again.

A voice called out, "Lilit, my friend—you've won!"

We looked toward the top of the well, where Jonnie waited like "the paragon of all the handsome princes in all the fairy tales ever written" (so said the script). He yanked the rope from his shirt, grasped one end, threw the coil toward the inundated rock. The rope payed out smoothly. Urilla/Lilit caught it in midair and—*beau geste*—handed it to me.

Jonnie pushed his sword into the earth, burying it to the counterguard. He secured the rope to the grip using "an elegant, sculpturesque knot."

Hand over hand, I hauled myself out of the well, Urilla/Lilit right behind. The three of us huddled briefly on the lawn, watching the breath spout from our mouths, the smiles beam from our faces, the blood plop from our clothes.

Jonnie guided Urilla/Lilit to the maze entrance. Pinned by thorns, a black cloak—booty from one of the costume rooms— lay stretched across a section of hedge. Plucking the cloak away, Jonnie threw it contemptuously onto the grass.

"The Lier-in-Wait is gone now," he said. "He was a shadow-thing, feeding on guilt and delusion. When you saved your father, you starved your enemy. The spell broke. I saw it all. The Lier turned into a stinking glop of lava, flowed out of his cloak, and seeped into the earth."

I'll admit that "a stinking glop of lava" isn't exactly what you call natural dialogue, but, after all, this was a dreambean.

Jonnie laid an affectionate hand on Urilla/Lilit's shoulder. "You've done a lot of growing up today, Lilit—so much growing up that I must seem like a little boy to you. But if you decide to see me as a friend—or something more—that would be exquisite. Because I care about you. Lots of people do."

"Lots of people," Urilla/Lilit repeated—her other line.

Jonnie said, "This has all been a dream, of course. Even I'm a dream. Does the dream have a name? Some call it *The Sleep Teacher*. I have entered your dream to teach you the truth. And the truth is not only that you are worthy of love, but that I love you."

Pure therapy talk. Urilla and I felt it was necessary. There is no better medicine, and we knew Jonnie would deliver each word with conviction. (Ah, what Freud could have done with this medium!)

The Sleep Teacher ad-libbed two more "I love you"s, and then he initiated a right-on-the-lips kiss. The two of them embraced so tightly that the blood on Urilla's breast became printed all over Jonnie's shirt; unlike me, Jonnie had no obligation to keep his sexuality at bay, and I'm sure he indulged in all the *ménage à trois* fantasies that the situation suggested.

I did not enjoy this part of the script. It was necessary, of course. As Lilit's rite of passage, the dream had to lead her toward the truths of adult sexuality. But does any father actually want his daughter to get that old? I realized that if—God forbid—Lilit ever ate *The Lier-in-Wait* again, it would not be me she hallucinated when invited to behold the one she loved best.

The great kiss continued.

"Curtain!" called Torin.

Horg turned off the pump and applauded.

Once again our director lined us up. To Urilla he said, "Your performance—how did it feel to you?"

"I got my lines right."

"Don't cheat yourself, dear. Every moment was right—except possibly the swimming. Make it more awkward next time."

If Urilla hadn't been soaked with artificial blood, I'm sure she would have hugged him.

His reaction to Jonnie: "And you, Mr. Sleep Teacher, you've obviously been studying with a master—someone equal to Torin Diffring, I daresay."

"It shows, doesn't it?"

Torin was considerably less enthusiastic about the Father. "You're holding back, Quinjin. Remember, you're being delivered from death's door—by your own daughter, no less. Let's pull out a few stops."

I told Torin that I was saving my energy for the actual weaving. Then I added, "Doesn't that kiss at the end go on too long?"

"No." He consulted his script. "But this line here—'Darling, rescue me'—is awfully bald."

"It's supposed to be."

"Leave it in?"

"Leave it in."

"All right, everybody!" he called. "Now we do it for real!"

The cul-de-sacs of the maze became our dressing rooms.

Hastily I traded my bloody street clothes for the brown leotard that the android had worn in *The Lier-in-Wait*.

Jonnie strode out of the maze sporting his gaudiest incubibing costume, jewel-encrusted cape and all.

When Urilla emerged, I saw that she wore a threadworm parka of the sort that Lilit had favored in the days before her conversion.

Now came a coronation, Horg putting the modified electroderby on Urilla. My throat thickened, and the machinery of tears started up—all these good people, working together, trying so hard. Ninnghizzida struck the derby. Urilla acquired a halo. I approached, tapped her metal skull.

"Give it all you've got," I said.

"I'm going to dream my goddamned head off," she replied.

We were artists in those days.

Two hours later we assembled in Kusk's phreneseed nursery. The computers whirred. The gene synthesizers gurgled. We stood shoulder-to-shoulder around a petri dish. Our collaboration napped peacefully. Its husk was fat and rosy. Already a root poked out like a beak from an egg.

I gave the seed a rave review. I called it brilliant.

"It's got your ears, Quinny," said Urilla.

"Let's plant the bugger," said Jonnie.

When Horg found me, I was in Kusk's study, dismantling the various animal habitats and crating them up for shipment to the Ushumgallum Zoological Gardens. His entrance was so noisy and sudden that I nearly dropped the eel's aquarium. Looking up, I noticed on Horg's tunic a figure-eight made of threadworm bits, remnants of his decision to tear off the Möbius strip and throw it away.

"The crop's here!" he yelled. "We've got apples!"

I raced him to the elevator shaft, won.

By now I was accustomed to the blasted terrain of the greenhouse. I had been coming here once every four hours or so, impatient to see the Tree of Life emerge from the dark earth and, later—when the creature had indeed taken root—equally impatient to see some sign that she was fecund. A sea of ash flowed through the orchard, its surface broken by charred stumps. The stumps looked like tombstones, markers on the graves of the galaxy's most anonymous and forsaken failures; Kusk's seedlings had commemorated their own deaths. Our lifetree rose incongruously amid the blackened mounds, defying the carnage, a jewel set in rust.

As I started forward, two vivid and diverse odors sought me out. I smelled burnt wood; this was familiar, expected. And I smelled a wondrous sweetness, the fragrance of everything in creation that was just then young and vital and casting eager eyes on the future.

The noostrees had always been a strange species. Myths had accumulated around them from the moment Selig announced their invention. *Every millionth tree is sacred,* ran one myth. *And if that millionth tree chooses to bless humanity, it will bring forth flowers whose very scents can vanquish pain and heal unhappiness.*

Our tree was in bloom. I saw red blossoms, orange blossoms, yellow blossoms, the entire long-wavelength end of the visible spectrum, petals as soft and gentle as a lynx's ears, leaves of organic velvet. The blossoms arrayed the tree completely, obscuring all branches, turning it into an enormous bouquet. Awestruck, I paused, breathed, savored.

Costumed as the Lier-in-Wait, Jonnie stood under the boughs. When I joined him, he reached toward a cluster of blossoms, drew them aside as he might a curtain concealing a tiny fairy realm. The lotosbean I saw was ripe and plump, a perfect sphere of gold. Ninnghizzida shone on its tempting skin.

Jonnie plucked the antitrauma, concealed it in the breast pocket of his cloak. "I've sent for Lilit," he said, hoisting up his hood. "We mustn't waste time."

Horg and I hid behind the tool shed, a hot place. The gardener had dutifully repaired my assault on the greenhouse wall, and no quenching breezes drifted in from the tundra. As we waited, a bit of verse came to mind, a Terran Age couplet that I found simultaneously dreadful and moving.

Poems are made by fools like me
But only God can make a tree

Jonnie paced nervously beneath the seedling, pausing occasionally to sniff a blossom or to rub the apple at his breast.

And suddenly Urilla and Lilit were in the elevator shaft, the Wonder Stepmother and the Mad Stepdaughter rising toward ` what I prayed would be the end of the tale. Lilit saw the tree. Under the blossoms, her god beckoned. One instant she was racing across the greenhouse, the next she was standing before him, the next she was throwing herself onto the ashes.

"My Lord Goth," she whined. "I am so depraved."

Jonnie retreated, backing against the trunk. His left arm shot from his robe like a Bough of the Reaped Whirlwind erupting from Simon Kusk. In his hand he held the first fruit of the first crop of *The Sleep Teacher*. He pinched the stem between his thumb and index finger. The golden dream rocked briefly, lay still.

"Eat this," he commanded, clipping each syllable.

Lilit took the apple, pressed it against her mouth. Her hesitation was visible, protracted. "Why?" she asked.

I feared that if Jonnie said much more, Lilit would spot the voice of an imposter.

"It will teach you." Just four words. Good for you, Jonnie.

Lilit suckled the dream. Her teeth entered it. Juices rolled from her lips. Despite the puffiness induced by the chocolate gumbombs, her body looked frail. I did not see her as a woman, or even as an adolescent, but rather as a lost little girl—friendless, afraid, and a long way from home.

And then, before my eyes, Lilit ate of the tree.

21

Amaranth Out

I shall not bore you with a full rehash of Giles Torquist's Pangalactic Senate Subcommittee Hearings on Murder by Art. The whole thing was pretty dull. If you didn't see my testimony on your holovision set, you read about it in the electrozines.

The Society for Unconditionally Purging Entertainment by Restoring Ethics and Godly Order had been waiting for such a windfall. They had been lying in wait for it. Before my testimony was completed, their legions had swelled tenfold, and their coffers were too heavy to lift. So when SUPEREGO's pet senator, that Lucretia Traft person, introduced legislation aimed at closing down the psychoparlors, no one doubted that it would soon be lobbied into law.

Unmitigated evil—that was what Clee Selig had called Simon Kusk's ambitions. I wouldn't go quite that far. The Church of Goth might have made many of my race happy. One must never underestimate the human appetite for self-deception, our innate need to have revelation spare us the burden of thought. Let us call the Church of Goth a mitigated evil. Mitigated evil makes strange bedfellows. In the old days, the days before Hamadryad, I was forever attacking SUPER-EGO and all those who confuse censorship with public hygiene. And yet, every time a senator at the Torquist hearings asked me how I felt about the Traft Amendment, which a sister subcommittee had just been convened to study, images of Kusk's converts—Lilit, Creegmoor, Baptizer Brown, the lotos-eaters—flooded my brain, and I stated my hope that the measure would pass. SUPEREGO might have had the wrong reasons, but in the final ironic analysis they were doing the right thing.

The Lotos Factor was just too simple, too accessible. A few modifications in an electroderby, a few thousand veneers to rent a phreneseed nursery, and any monomaniac could promote himself to the rank of God. Even my enemies—the parlor owners and others rendered jobless by my testimony—see that.

I am not a primitivist. Over and over, I told the senators that I find technical ingenuity wonderful, miraculous, thrilling, essential, aesthetic, erotic, fun. But when a machine turns against you, when it makes you tell lies, you have to be grown up enough, and awake enough, to get rid of it. "We got rid of fission power," I said to Senator Krippenkeg. "We got rid of quark bombs. And now we must get rid of noostrees."

So the species is extinct. The farms lie fallow. The studios decay. The parlors are dust. The hotels no longer host cephapple conventions. The anonymous company that forged the Growers' Association Awards has retooled to produce those statuettes people get for winning the Ganzir Marathon. Sybarites no longer sneak into grorgs to have dreambean orgies.

I understand that most of the planters and pickers eventually found jobs in conventional farming. That cabbage you had for dinner may have been grown by a man who once spent his mornings knocking caterpillars off *The Toad of Night*. And the dreamweavers? The practical ones, the ones with a survival instinct, found other ways to turn their inner visions outward, becoming painters, sculptors, architects, choreographers, fashion designers, and holovision directors. The impractical ones have simply passed into obscurity, withering away like the unpicked harvests of the hydrasteroids. I must not leave the incubibers out of this epilogue. Some of them, of course, have opened new frontiers in self-abuse and sin, including, I believe, such recent *haute despair* phenomena as suicide clubs, grave-robbing societies, and kill-it-yourself restaurants. Many of them, however, have made unexpected about-faces. Did you know that the primary patron of the Shadu Symphony Orchestra is a former blood-drinker? So is the fund-raising coordinator of the Verthandi Clinic. My friend Jonnie Rondo spends his free time zooming around in *Fleshpot*, dispensing vaccines and other biomedical amenities to those one-horse planets where experiments in agrarian utopianism have recently devolved into Stone Age brutishness.

As you might well imagine, my most vivid memory of the Torquist hearings came when Senator Woojek asked me whether my support for the Traft Amendment was not simply an irrational reaction to what *The Lier-in-Wait* did to my child. I immediately sized up Woojek as a pimp for the dreamweaving magnates. Indeed, it turned out that the Growers' Association had been smuggling him more than five thousand veneers a day.

With both my eyes I looked Woojek in both of his.

"It could have happened to *anyone's* child," I said. "If the noostrees stay with us, it will eventually happen to *all* our children. Irrationality, Senator, has never been more reasonable."

From that moment on, everyone knew the industry would fall.

The Tree of Life's first apple did not restore Lilit, but it did make her amenable to taking additional treatments. Jonnie,

Urilla, or I needed to say nothing more beguiling than "They're good for you," and Lilit would eat.

Before going off to seek employment in the jungjelly fields, Horg and the Centaur helped us transplant the seedling to Jonnie's space yacht. The peltbass swimming pool made a perfect garden. *The Sleep Teacher* was the first noostree ever to be nourished hydroponically.

Seven apples: that was the total Lilit had taken by the time *Fleshpot* reached the homeward side of Voodoo Vector 72. Seven Sleep Teachers versus one Lier-in-Wait. Seven anti-traumas sketched on the palimpsests of her brain.

An hour after eating the eighth apple, Lilit called me Father, and lights went on in my soul. The breakthrough occurred in her cabin. Pictures of Goth threatened us from all sides. I was trying to persuade her to join us for lunch, and suddenly she said, "Father, I feel strange. I just woke up, only I haven't been asleep."

"We hope you can eat with us."

"Tell me the menu."

"Stewed tomatoes—stewed by me."

"That's okay—I could eat *anything*," she said. "I could eat a grorg."

Subsequently there were mild relapses, occasional Goth portraits emerging on her drawing pad, but nothing so insidious that I feared she had lost her "I," misplaced her "me," again.

After the ninth apple, Lilit overcame her addiction to chocolate gumbombs. "These things are really terrible," she said. "They're making me look like a hot-water bottle."

After the tenth apple, the color began returning to Lilit's hair.

After the eleventh apple, Lilit and Jonnie started going in for public displays of what, in my *Altars of the Heart* review, I had called ritualized fornication. They kissed at meals, hugged on walks, fondled during psychic billiards tournaments.

After the twelfth apple, Lilit brought me one of her drawings. The subject was the Lier-in-Wait's labyrinth. Except that the courtyard statues wore normal heads, not skulls. A horse champed the green grass. It stood in the exact place where the goat had died. It was the largest, healthiest, best-drawn horse I had ever seen. Even Quinjin the Critic liked it.

I showed the picture to Urilla, who said, "Obviously she's cured."

Obviously.

And yet I didn't really believe it until I was back on Zahrim, attending my own birthday party. I was forty-five that day. Jonnie gave me a copy of *Known Quantities* that he had squirreled away in *Fleshpot*'s deep freeze. Clee Selig gave me a Lucaizai sculpture that looked like an angry fruit salad. Urilla gave me a seduction.

And Lilit gave me a kitten.

"I owe you this," she said.

The kitten was female, but I named it Pushkin anyway.

This is a story with several happy endings. Its heroes are all doing well. They have not lived happily ever after, but neither are they slaves to panaceas, gods, neuroses, or kidnip. They have lived copingly ever after.

I wish I could still review dreams, of course, and at least once a day my head has to inform my heart that murdering Simon Kusk was no sin. But I am not dissatisfied. My three-volume history of the medium, *The Dreams We Shared*, garnered respectable sales and notices I might have written myself. Then, too, I've got my dear Urilla, whose libido has yet to hear the news that it is sixty-five. Someday we may marry—though, as Urilla says, "Marriage is for when you want children." Long ago, Urilla and I decided against children. One great work, one big collaboration, was enough for us.

The reader may not know that my Urilla Aub is the same Urilla Aub responsible for a popular book called *Kernels of Thought*. Not surprisingly, with the extinction of the noostree, Urilla resumed her original career in psychobiology. *Kernels of Thought* teaches you how to keep what she calls "unpleasant notions" from invading your mind spontaneously. A useful technique. The book is selling so well that I may never have to buy another beach chair in my life. But if hard times do come, I suppose we can always accept a handout from our son-in-law.

"Too young for marriage," Urilla kept saying, but Jonnie and Lilit went ahead and did it anyway. Before long, both of them were dating other people—in adolescent marriage, "dating other people" is a more knowing judgment than "committing bilateral adultery"—and I breathed several sighs of relief that there hadn't been a baby in the meantime. After two years on the greener sides of the fence, however, they returned to each other's folds, and now there *is* a baby, and I'm delighted. It's a girl, Darcy Quinjin Rondo. She has Jonnie's dramatic hair, Lilit's bubbly cheeks, Talas's clanging voice, and my modest ears. Amid the soiled diapers and the spit-up milk, I smell a winner. The only time I see Talas is at our granddaughter's birthday parties, which are always gala affairs held aboard *Fleshpot*. Talas and I are unspeakably civil to each other. We adore Darcy Quinjin Rondo.

Clee Selig is dead now, a heart attack, but I would still call his a happy ending. Before the Reaper we are all wheat. You probably know that he responded to the passing of the dreambean by inventing the Olfactory, those little crystalline spheres that enable you to fill your house with the smells of your childhood. He left the Milky Way wealthy, free of pain, and pumped full of nostalgia for his boyhood dogs and swimming holes.

Then there's Hamadryad. Perhaps you recall that the tree's dying request was to be turned into a book. I have never forgotten that wish, and recently I have set about arranging for it to come true. If all has gone well, you are currently holding a piece of Hamadryad, a *memento mori*, in your hands.

But the happiest fate of all belongs to Flick, clever little Flick, Flick who finally found his Paradise. He found it right here in Shadu City. Ten years ago, our Chamber of Commerce resolved to build a downtown park—a network of duck ponds and greenery displacing dozens of streets that nobody misses except when the troglobus system breaks down. As this metropolitan Eden was nearing completion, the Chamber advertised for an arborist. Flick got the job. He is responsible for two acres of woodlands, five hedge-mazes, eight separate rose gardens, three hundred flowering shrubs, and more than a thousand trees. His olives win prizes. He hangs the ribbons from the branches, like silken fruit.

It's not easy to produce a book when you're my age. Your body no longer does everything you tell it to do. But I manage. Just this moment, for example, I am enjoying a late, warm, fragrant afternoon on the roof of my apartment building. A kitten is hopping around on my thoughtwriter—not Pushkin, but Pushkin's grandson—inserting letters randomly into the text. I can see the Tree of Life, her apples sparkling like gold goblets. The landlord let me put a garden up here. He was very understanding. There are petals all over the place.

Lilit does not need her Sleep Teacher much anymore. She takes one apple per month, just to be safe. She is the last dreamer, consuming the last noostree. Once a week, Flick comes over after work. He fertilizes the tree, prunes it, douses it with the chemicals that keep it a dwarf. He administers his growth-stunting formula from an ordinary watering can. The watering can is battered and red. He calls it the Fountain of Youth.

As I write these final words, the star Alpheratz descends, throwing the garden into silhouette. I am thinking about sleep. Watering can at the ready, Flick putters near the tree. Bees hover amid the blossoms, pollinating passionately.

Flick tilts his watering can.

Now the bees pause, as if to honor the elixir as it falls onto the soil, sparkles in the sun, and begins its journey to the roots.